A DREAM BORN FROM TYRANNY

Athas, world of the dark sun. Ruled for thousands of years by power-mad sorcerer-kings, the cities of Athas have become vile centers of slavery and corruption. Only heroes of the greatest strength and bravest heart can stand against the might of these overlords. The Prism Pentad is a tale of such heroes. . . .

Rikus—the man-dwarf gladiator whose ragtag legion is all that stands between the city of Tyr and a mighty army sent by a rival sorcerer-king to destroy the free city.

Neeva—the beautiful and deadly veteran of Tyr's slave arena, torn between her love for Rikus and her growing realization that the hero may be leading his legion to its doom.

Caelum—the noble dwarven cleric from the lost city of Kemalok, able to call upon the dark sun itself for the power to destroy those who stand against him . . . including the man-dwarf Rikus.

———————————

PRISM PENTAD

Troy Denning

Book One
The Verdant Passage
October 1991

Book Two
The Crimson Legion
April 1992

Book Three
The Amber Enchantress
October 1992

Book Four
The Obsidian Oracle
Spring 1993

Book Five
The Cerulean Storm
Fall 1993

The Crimson Legion
TROY DENNING

THE CRIMSON LEGION

Random House and its affiliate companies have worldwide distribution rights in the book trade for English language products of TSR, Inc.

Distributed to the book and hobby trade in the United Kingdom by TSR Ltd.

Distributed to the toy and hobby trade by regional distributors.

Cover art by Brom.

DARK SUN and the TSR logo are trademarks owned by TSR, Inc.

First Printing: April 1992
Printed in the United States of America
Library of Congress Catalog Card Number: 91-66505

9 8 7 6 5 4 3 2 1

ISBN: 1-56076-260-8

TSR, Inc.
P.O. Box 756
Lake Geneva, WI 53147
U.S.A.

TSR, Ltd.
120 Church End, Cherry Hinton
Cambridge CB1 3LB
United Kingdom

Dedication:

To my parents, for always believing in me.

Acknowledgements:

Many people contributed to the writing of this book and the creation of this series. I would like to thank you all. Without the efforts of the following people, especially, Athas might never have seen the light of the crimson sun: Mary Kirchoff and Tim Brown, who shaped the world as much as anyone; Brom, who gave us the look and the feel; Jim Lowder, for his inspiration and patience; Lloyd Holden of the AKF Martial Arts Academy in Janesville, WI, for contributing his expertise to the fight scenes; Andria Hayday, for support and encouragement; and Jim Ward, for enthusiasm, support, and much more.

THE TYR VALLEY REGION

0   5   10   15

Miles

MOUNTAINS

FOOTHILLS

SANDY WASTE

BOULDER FIELD

STONEY BARRENS

FOREST

SCRUBLAND

FOREST RIDGE

RINGING MOUNTAINS

TYR

Lake of Golden Dreams

The Crater of Bones

Ogo

Makla

The Smoking Crown

Oasis

URIK

Citadel   Oasis

Kes'trekel Nest

Kled

THE TABL

SAND   WASTES

Silver Spring

Ambush Site

ALLUVIAL

PROLOGUE

Concentrate.

A white globe appeared in the black grotto that was the mind of King Tithian I, casting a brilliant light over the warped spires and gloomy depths of the cave's snarled terrain. Sable-winged bats and ebon-feathered birds—dark thoughts given form by his mind—fluttered away into murky nooks and alcoves, angrily screeching and chirping.

"I've done it!" Tithian reported.

You've done nothing until you project it, came the answer, echoing inside the king's mind.

Tithian opened his eyes. Before him sat the disembodied heads who were tutoring him in the elusive art of the Way. One was sallow-skinned and sunken-featured, with cracked lips that looked like shriveled leather. The other was grotesquely bloated, with puffy cheeks and eyes swollen to narrow, dark slits. Both wore their coarse hair in long topknots, and the bottom of their necks had been sewn shut with thick black thread.

"Where?" Tithian asked.

Over the arena, answered Sacha, the bloated head.

1

"Yes. It's time your subjects learned to fear you," agreed Wyan, now speaking aloud.

Being careful to keep the ball glowing inside his mind, Tithian looked toward the stadium. From his pedestal atop the roof of the Golden Tower, he could see the largest part of the vast arena, which lay between the tower and the crumbling bricks of the previous king's ziggurat. Instead of gladiators, the immense fighting pit now swarmed with craftsmen and free-farmers bartering a wide variety of goods —thornberries, sweet lizard meats, ceramic vessels, and knives and spoons of carved bone. They had all covered their wares with tattered cloaks and shabby blankets, for a hot driving wind was scouring the field with sand and dust.

At the sight of the bazaar, the king could not help recalling how the marketplace had come to exist. At the suggestion of his boyhood friend Agis of Asticles, Tithian had written an edict converting the stadium to a public market. When he had sent it to the Council of Advisors for approval, Agis and his fellow councilors had removed mention of the levy the king wished to impose for selling goods in the stadium. Without advising Tithian of what it had done, the council had then issued the edict across the entire city. By the time the king had seen a copy of the edict "he" had issued, the field had been filled with cheering citizens.

Agitated by the memory, Tithian's dark thoughts took to their wings and fluttered about his mind. He pinched his eyes closed, desperately trying to brighten the light and force the errant beasts back to their nests. It was a losing battle, for angry thoughts teemed out of their black holes in countless numbers. They swarmed the light, shrieking and screeching in frenzied hatred. Tithian fought back, summoning as much energy as he could. A stream of warmth rose from deep within his body and flowed into the glowing ball.

A brilliant glow erupted from the king's eyelids and a

deafening clap of thunder blasted the Golden Tower, shaking it from the foundations to the merlons. The boom reverberated through Tithian's chest like a drum and set his ears to ringing.

"Did I do that?" he gasped, opening his eyes again.

Sacha rolled his eyes. "We're having a storm."

The king looked up and saw that the day had grown as dark as his mood. A black haze of wind-borne silt hung over the city, reducing the crimson disk of the sun to a pink shadow of itself. The billowing mass of darkness reminded Tithian of the rainstorm he had seen ten years ago, but he knew better than to hope a downpour would quench the thirst of his city today. The thunderclouds overhead were filled with dust, not water.

"You couldn't get a spark from striking steel, much less create a lightning bolt," added Wyan. "Your meditations are pathetic."

Tithian closed his eyes again. The ball of light inside his mind had disappeared entirely. All that remained in that black grotto was a whirl of dark thoughts.

"Don't bother trying again," said Sacha.

"You're about to receive a messenger," explained Wyan.

"When you hear his report, your pitiful mind will neglect the ball of light anyway," finished Sacha, his snarl revealing a set of broken yellow teeth.

Knowing that the malicious heads would not reveal the messenger's news even if he asked, Tithian unfolded his aching legs and slipped his gaunt body, clothed only in a breechcloth, off the pedestal. Regretting the laziness that had kept him from mastering the Way of the Unseen as a youth, the king asked, "Am I really so hopeless?"

"Completely," answered Wyan.

"Absolutely," added Sacha.

The king grabbed his two confidants by their topknots and walked toward the edge of the roof.

"What are you doing?" demanded Wyan.

"If I have no hope of mastering the Way, then I'll never become a sorcerer-king," Tithian growled. "That means I have no need of you two!" He heaved the two heads off the tower roof.

Instead of falling into the gauzy moss-trees at the base of the palace, the heads simply hung in the air, a dozen feet from the roof. Tithian's jaw fell slack, for he had never seen Sacha or Wyan levitate. Still, he suspected that he should have known they would not be destroyed so easily. The pair could not have survived a thousand years by being as helpless as they seemed.

"Quite amusing," said Wyan, baring his gray teeth at Tithian.

"Kalak would have gotten an axe and hacked us to pieces," added Sacha. "You're not brutal enough."

"That can be remedied," Tithian warned.

"I doubt it," Wyan returned. "You're a coward at heart."

Before Tithian could rebut Wyan, Sacha added, "You've ruled Tyr for six months, and the Golden Tower's treasury is emptier than when you killed Kalak!"

Tithian could not deny Sacha's charge. Instead, he spun away and looked toward the city's bustling Merchant District. Now that the iron mine had been reopened, Tyr was once again doing a booming mercantile business, but the Council of Advisors was using every coin of the caravan levy to fund the pauper farms surrounding the city. Of course, that was Agis's doing—as were all of the programs diverting the treasures that should have been filling the king's vault.

Reading the king's thoughts, Wyan suggested, "Assassinate him."

Despite his past relationship with Agis, it was not friendship that made Tithian hesitate. "That would only make things worse," he growled. "Rikus, Neeva, and Sadira would take Agis's place in an instant. A self-righteous noble is bad enough, but slaves . . ." Letting his sentence trail off, the king turned back to the heads and saw that they were drifting toward the roof.

"Kill all four," said Wyan.

"You can't believe things are that simple," Tithian growled. "Half of Tyr saw Rikus wound Kalak, and it's common knowledge that Agis and the others finished the task. If I execute them, the city will rise against me."

"I have the names of several minstrels adept with poisons," offered Wyan, his sunken eyes burning with a murderous light. "Kalak often used them to good effect."

"All four dying of mysterious illnesses? How stupid do you assume the citizens of Tyr to be?" Tithian snorted. "I'll find another way."

Tithian's chamberlain climbed onto the roof, putting an end to the debate. She was a blond woman of statuesque proportions, with icy blue eyes and a humorless mouth. Like most of Tithian's bureaucracy, she had been recruited from the ranks of the templars who had previously served Kalak.

Behind the chamberlain came a haggard young man wearing dusty riding leathers. Though he was covered with grime, Tithian could see that his clothes were well-made and his hair neatly trimmed. He had a patrician nose and a proud jawline that was slack with amazement at the sight of the floating heads.

"I present Taiy of Ramburt, second son to Lord Ramburt," said the chamberlain, raising a brow at the floating heads.

"How dare you come before us in such rags," Sacha snarled. "And did your father not teach you to bow before your king?"

"Kill him!" spat Wyan.

The color drained from Taiy's face. "I beg your forbearance, Honored King," the youth said, bowing.

"You have it—for now," Tithian replied, amused by the

youth's anxiety. "Let us hope your news justifies my patience."

Swallowing hard, Taiy stood upright. "Honored King, I have just returned from hunting in the Dragon's Bowl."

"That's near Urik, is it not?" Tithian asked, scowling.

"Which is the point of my visit," Taiy answered. "As my party was returning to the road, we saw a great cloud of dust approaching from the horizon. When I investigated, I found an army, complete with siege engines, a war argosy, halfling scouts, and five hundred half-giants. They were marching under the banner of the lion that walks like a man."

"King Hamanu's crest!" hissed Wyan.

"He's coveted our iron mines for five centuries," added Sacha, sneering at Tithian. "How will you defend the city? You've an empty treasure vault and no army."

Tithian cursed, barely keeping himself from lashing out at the young noble who had brought him this disastrous news. He would not have bothered to restrain himself, except that his subjects credited him with Agis's endless stream of reforms, and Tithian wanted to cultivate his reputation as a noble ruler.

Instead, Tithian bit his lips and stared out over the city. At last, a wicked smile crossed his lips. He still had no idea of how to stop Hamanu's army, but he had hit upon a way to remove the problem of Agis and the three slaves without resorting to Wyan's minstrels.

Tithian dismissed Taiy with a wave of his hand, simultaneously addressing his chamberlain. "Summon the freed slaves Rikus, Neeva, and Sadira, as well as Agis of Asticles." The king felt a pang of regret as he spoke his old friend's name, but he shrugged off the feeling and continued with the business at hand. "Tell them the safety of Tyr hangs upon their swift arrival in my audience chamber."

ONE

Ambush

Rikus looked down the steep slope to where his warriors waited in the shadow of the sandstone bluff. The two thousand Tyrians stood in a quiet column, their thoughts fixed on the coming battle. There were humans, half-elves, dwarves, half-giants, tareks, and other races, most of them gladiators who had fought in Tyr's arena until being freed by King Tithian's First Edict. In their hands, they carried double-bladed axes, sabers of serrated bone, fork-headed lances, double-ended spears, and a variety of deadly arms as infinite as man's desire to murder.

Rikus was certain they would make a fine legion.

He stood and waved his arm over his head to signal the attack. His warriors roared their battle cries, then charged forward in a single screaming mass.

"What are you doing?" demanded Agis, stepping to Rikus's side. The noble was robust for a man of his class, with a strong build and square, handsome features. He had long black hair, probing brown eyes, and a straight, patrician nose. "We need a plan!"

"I have a plan," Rikus answered simply.

He looked to the base of the hill. There, in the sandy valley, stood a single rank of Urikite half-giants, all wearing red tunics that bore the crest of Hamanu's yellow lion. They cradled huge battle-axes with obsidian blades, and their only pieces of armor were bone bucklers strapped to their enormous forearms.

"Attack!" Rikus shouted.

With that, he rushed over the crest of the hill. Discovering that the sandstone slope was too steep to descend gracefully, Rikus fell to his back and continued his drop in a controlled slide.

Had he been a full human, he might have reconsidered his method of descent, for only a hemp breechcloth protected his bronzed skin from the grating surface of the sandstone. But Rikus gave the scouring little thought. He was a mul, a human-dwarf crossbreed created to live and die as a gladiatorial slave, and he was as inured to pain as he was to death. From his dwarven father he had inherited a heavy-boned face of rugged features, pointed ears set close to the head, and a powerful physique that seemed nothing but knotted sinew and thick bone. His human mother had bestowed upon him a proud straight nose, a balance of limb and body that made him handsome by the standards of either race, and a supple, six-foot frame as agile as that of an elven rope dancer.

Rikus had descended only a few feet before Neeva, his long-time fighting partner, slid into place at his side. Although a full human, she was protected from the abrasive stone by the lizard-scale cloak she wore to protect her fair skin from the sun. In her hands the big blond held a steel battle-axe nearly as large as those carried by the half-giants below. Most women could not have lifted the weapon, but Neeva was almost as heavily muscled as Rikus and, as a freed gladiator, more than capable of swinging the mighty blade. Despite her powerful build, she retained a distinctly feminine figure, full red lips, and eyes as green as emeralds.

"Our legion is outsized five times over!" she exclaimed.

Rikus knew that she referred not to the hundreds of half-giants directly below, but to the thousands of Urikite regulars in the valley beyond. The long column of soldiers was already past the point of the Tyrian attack and was continuing onward at a steady pace, relying on the half-giants to protect their rear. Following close behind the regulars came dozens of siege engines, carried on the backs of massive war-lizards called driks. The rear of the long file was brought up by the lumbering mass of an argosy, a mammoth fortress-wagon full of weapons, supplies, and water.

Her eyes fixed on the long procession, Neeva demanded, "What can you be thinking?"

"One Tyrian gladiator is worth five Urikite soldiers," Rikus responded, fixing his gaze on the half-giants below. The huge soldiers were cradling their battle-axes and glaring defiantly toward the side of the bluff, where the Tyrian mob now approached in a tumult of wild screams. "Besides, this is the king's doing, not mine. Tithian's the one who would give me only two-thousand warriors."

"He didn't tell you to get them killed in a reckless charge," Neeva countered.

"It isn't reckless," Rikus answered.

The pair ran out of time to debate the issue, reaching the bottom of the slope just as the first wave of gladiators spilled into the sandy valley. Rikus and Neeva had come down near the flank of the enemy line, only a few dozen paces from several glowering half-giants. The towering Urikites held steady, waiting for the mul and his partner to move into striking range.

Rikus looked toward the pair of half-giants anchoring the end of the enemy line. In contrast to most of their kind, they were stoutly built, with a powerful shape to their torsos. Their hair had been shaved away from their thick-boned foreheads, and their drooping jaws showed no sign of the customarily flabby chin of the race. They were even somewhat taller than most half-giants, standing at least twice as high as the mul.

"Those are our two," Rikus said, raising his weapons. He carried a pair of cahulaks, which resembled two flat-bladed grappling hooks connected at the base by a rope. "Come on."

Before Neeva could object, he took off at a sprint, angling away to force the half-giants to leave their formation. At first, Rikus did not think they would fall for his ploy, but an officer finally barked, "Cut them off!"

A tremendous clatter sounded from the center of the enemy line as the first wave of Tyrians reached it. A few half-giants bellowed in pain and collapsed to the hot sand, but most used their small bucklers to deflect the gladiators' assaults. In unison, the Urikites hefted their black-bladed axes, and Tyr's first wave of attackers disappeared in a spray of blood.

Rikus felt a knot of anxiety forming in his stomach, but the hiss of heavy feet shuffling through deep sand drew his attention back to his own foes. The two half-giants he had lured away from the line were almost upon him and Neeva.

"Break right!" Rikus called, naming a trick he and Neeva had often employed when they fought together in Tyr's arena.

Instantly, Neeva slid several steps to her right, then sprinted forward to place herself on the flank of the half-giant approaching her. Rikus followed, moving toward the same half-giant and whirling a cahulak at his side. The Urikites attacked, trying to keep Rikus and Neeva from double-teaming either of them.

The mul threw a cahulak toward the half-giant attacking Neeva, intentionally overshooting. The weapon sailed over the shaft of the battle-axe and swung back toward Rikus as it reached the end of its rope. The mul caught the cahulak and ducked, entangling the half-giant's axe.

With flawless timing, Neeva leveled her steel axe at the other half-giant, who had been moving to attack the mul from behind. Rikus heard the sound of shattering stone. Black shards of obsidian rained down on the raw skin of his back, and the Urikite's headless axe handle banged harmlessly into his shoulder. Neeva leaped over Rikus's back, drawing her axe back for another stroke, and a loud scream announced that her blade had found its target.

As Neeva's half-giant collapsed into a bellowing heap, Rikus got to his feet and jerked the other's axe from his hands. The Urikite's mouth fell open, and he tried to retreat. Rikus followed, burying the tip of a cahulak deep into the tall soldier's thigh. In retaliation, the half-giant swung a huge fist. Rikus ducked, at the same time pulling his enemy off his feet. The Urikite had barely dropped to the scalding sand before the mul smashed his other cahulak into the half-giant's head.

When Rikus tried to remove his weapon from the half-giant's skull, he found that it was stuck in place. A quick glance around told him that he was in no immediate danger, so he began to twist the blade back and forth to free it.

As the mul worked, a warm glow of satisfaction spread over him. The feeling was not due to any joy he felt over the Urikite's death, but to the skill with which he and his fighting partner had worked together. Rikus and Neeva had not fought together since their days as a matched pair in Tyr's gladiatorial arena, and the mul missed the intimacy of those battles. When they were fighting, they moved and thought as one person, sharing thoughts and emotions deeper than even their passions while making love.

Neeva stepped to the mul's side and wiped her gory axe blade on the half-giant's red tunic. By the ardent smile on her full lips, Rikus could tell that her thoughts were the same as his. "We haven't lost our touch," she said. "That's nice to know."

"You couldn't think we would?" Rikus asked, finally freeing his weapon from his opponent's head. "No matter what, we'll always have our touch."

A triumphant roar sounded from the center of the Urikite line. Rikus looked toward the commotion and saw that the second wave of his warriors had fared as well as he and Neeva. The enemy formation was in complete disarray, with Tyrians swarming the half-giants from all sides. The greatest part of the legion, however, was pouring through the shattered line and rushing toward the center of valley.

There, the driks and their siege engines had already moved ahead, but the argosy was just now pulling even with the point of attack. The moving fortress stood three stories tall, and at each corner rose a small tower manned by guards with crossbows. A plethora of arrow loops dotted its sides, and its great doors were shut fast. The massive wagon was drawn by a team of four mekillots, giant reptiles with mound-shaped bodies and rocky shells. To Rikus, the beasts looked more like mobile buttes of solid stone than living creatures.

Motioning for Neeva to follow, Rikus rushed toward the knot of Tyrian warriors chasing the argosy. After circumventing the last of the battle with the half-giants, they joined the mass of jubilant gladiators and worked their way to the front of the crowd.

There, they found Agis trying to keep the mob under control, his forehead creased with irritation. As Rikus approached, the nobleman clenched his teeth and looked away as if trying to master his temper.

At Agis's side stood Sadira, her long amber hair bound in a loose tail, draped over a shoulder to reveal one elegantly pointed ear. In her hands, the winsome half-elf held a wooden cane with a pommel of black obsidian.

An uncomfortable chill ran down Rikus's spine at the sight of her weapon. It was one of two magic artifacts that had been loaned to him and his three companions for the purpose of killing Kalak, the thousand-year-old sorcerer-king who had ruled Tyr before Tithian. Rikus had sent his artifact, the Heartwood Spear, back to its owner shortly after they succeeded in assassinating Kalak. Sadira, however, had ignored the advice of her friends and elected to keep the cane. The mul secretly feared they would all pay dearly for the half-elf's decision.

"The battle's going well enough so far," Sadira observed. She glanced at Agis and lifted a peaked eyebrow at the noble's uncustomary display of anger, then asked Rikus. "Now what?"

"Let's smash the argosy," Rikus answered, fixing his gaze on the huge wagon.

"And what of the rest of our legion?" Agis demanded, finally breaking his silence. "Even you can't think it will take two-thousand soldiers to destroy a single argosy."

Rikus glanced around. The half-giants had been completely overrun, and the rest of the Tyrian legion was moving forward to continue the attack. "We're in a fight," he answered simply. "Our gladiators know what to do."

"We're not all gladiators," Sadira reminded him. "What about the templars and Jaseela's retainers?"

"It would be better if they stayed out of the way," Rikus answered, grinning. "We don't want them to get hurt."

"You're being too sure of yourself, Rikus," Neeva said. "This is a battle, not a grand melee. Agis might be right about making a plan."

"I have a plan," Rikus answered. He started toward the argosy, bringing the conversation to an end.

It took the companions only a few moments to catch the slow-moving wagon. Several hundred warriors followed them, but the largest part of the Tyrian mob acted on its own initiative to rush after the driks and the siege machines. Agis and Sadira seemed surprised at how neatly the mob had divided itself, but Rikus was not. When it came to fighting, he trusted the instincts of his gladiators more than he trusted complicated plans and orders.

Rikus circled around to the rear of the argosy, hoping to decrease its firepower by approaching from the narrowest wall. Despite his caution, the mul could see that gaining entrance to the wagon would be no easy thing. The side was lined with at least three dozen arrow loops, the black tips of crossbow bolts protruding from each slit. From the corner towers, the guards were shouting a constant stream of warnings down into the wagon.

The mul saw the tips of several fingers poke out of the lowest slit on the wagon, then heard a woman's voice call upon King Hamanu for the magic to cast a spell.

Over his shoulder, Rikus cried, "Get down!"

The mul grabbed Sadira and threw her to the ground, dropping on top of her as a tremendous crash boomed out of the argosy. A fan-shaped sheet of crackling red light flashed across the sand. Behind Rikus erupted a tumult of screams, which abated as suddenly as they started. The mul looked over his shoulder to see the headless bodies of dozens of gladiators crumple to the ground.

Neeva reached out from Rikus's side and slapped the back of his bald head. "Fighting partners are supposed to protect each other, not their mistresses," she said. Though her tone was light, her green eyes showed how hurt she was that it had been Sadira and not her the mul had defended.

"I knew you'd be able to take care of yourself," Rikus explained.

The muffled clacks of dozens of crossbows sounded from inside the wagon. A wave of black streaks flashed from the loops, then dozens of gladiators screamed in pain.

Rikus regarded the argosy with renewed respect. He was

beginning to see why the fortress wagons were a favored mode of caravan travel. Any tribe of raiders could catch one, but stopping it might well prove to be impossible.

After the bolts had passed, Neeva gestured at Sadira's hand, which was the only part of the winsome half-elf showing from beneath the mul's massive body. "You'd better get off before she suffocates."

As soon as Rikus rose to his knees, Sadira turned her pale eyes on him and frowned. "How do you expect me to cast spells from underneath you?"

Before Rikus could apologize, Sadira pointed the cane at the argosy. "*Nok!*" she cried. A purple light glimmered deep within the weapon's pommel.

Rikus cringed, hoping that what happened next would not frighten his own superstitious gladiators as much as it injured the Urikites. Normal magic drew spell energy from the life force of plants, but Sadira's cane extracted its power from a different source.

Sadira called, "*Dawnfire!*"

Rikus experienced an eerie tingle in his stomach, then started to grow queasy. Behind him, gladiators gasped and cried out in alarm as they, too, felt the cane drawing its energy from their life spirits.

The sick feeling stopped an instant later, and a ball of scarlet flame streaked to the argosy. The roiling sphere spread out like a fog, engulfing the rear quarter of the wagon in ruby-red fire. The Urikites in the towers plunged from their stations, screaming in agony, and in half-a-dozen places the back wall burned away like parchment.

Despite the sorceress's devastating attack, the mekillots continued to pull the argosy forward, oblivious to what was happening behind them.

"Into the wagon!" Rikus cried, resuming his charge—and hoping that his gladiators were not too distracted by Sadira's magic to follow.

Hundreds of battle cries informed him they were not, and soon he was leading a mass of screaming men and women after the smoking argosy. A few muffled clacks sounded from inside the wagon, but Sadira's attack had taken its toll. Less than half-a-dozen black bolts shot from the arrow loops, and only one found its mark.

Rikus charged over the scalded body of a woman dressed in the yellow cassock of Hamanu's templars, then caught up to the argosy. Without breaking stride, he whirled a cahulak and tossed it into one of the smoking holes overhead. After tugging the rope to set the blades, the mul swung up and onto the lowest deck of the wagon's rear firing platform.

The horrid stench of burning flesh filled his nostrils. Fighting the urge to gag, Rikus looked around and saw that the deck had been reduced to a shambles. Scorched bodies and smashed weapons lay scattered everywhere. Flames licked at the rear wall in a dozen places, searing even the mul's bronzed skin and filling his lungs with caustic fumes. Through the smoke, Rikus could see a doorway leading deeper into the argosy. To either side of this doorway, a ladder ascended through a manway in the ceiling.

Facing the rear of the wagon again, Rikus kneeled and gave Neeva a helping hand up. As she climbed onto the deck, she peered past his legs and said, "Two behind you." Her voice was as calm as if she had been spotting birds leaving their roosts at dawn.

The mul spun on his heels, swinging a cahulak at the full length of its rope. Through the haze, he saw two soot-covered Urikites pointing their crossbows at him. Rikus dodged to one side, and the soldiers triggered their weapons. A pair of bolts sizzled past his head, thumping into the wood at the back of the wagon. At the same time, the cahulak took the first guard in the knee, its blade sinking deep into the joint. The mul tugged the rope, pulling the man off his feet.

The second soldier reached for the obsidian short sword

hanging at his side. Rikus sprang at this one, planting his foot squarely on the lion embroidered on the Urikite's red tunic. The man dropped to the floor clutching his chest.

As Rikus finished off the two soldiers he had disabled, Neeva reached down to help Agis into the wagon. Once the nobleman was inside, he helped Sadira up, and behind her came a steady stream of gladiators. Soon the platform was crowded with Tyrian warriors, all coughing and gasping from the thick smoke. The mul directed a few up the ladders to eliminate any survivors on the higher decks, then motioned for his friends and the others to follow him through the back doorway.

After descending half-a-dozen steps, they found themselves in a corridor where the smoke was not so thick. On the walls hung a series of nets. Each held a glass ball that swung in time to the rhythmical sway of the wagon, casting a flickering green light over the floor.

The hall ran a dozen yards to both the right and left, then turned toward the front of the wagon. The mul motioned for the first squad of gladiators to follow him and his companions into the narrow hall. "Tell those behind you to go the other way," he ordered.

They started down the corridor at a cautious jog. Upon rounding the first corner, Rikus came face-to-face with ten Urikites carrying leather fire-blankets. The mul cut down the first three before they could reach for their weapons, but not before they screamed an alarm. The rest fell into a deep slumber as one of Sadira's spells dropped a blue cloud of magical powder over their heads.

"Easier than I thought," Rikus observed. "Maybe we'll take this argosy back to Tyr as a battle prize."

Agis shook his head, saying, "Your victory declaration is hasty. The battle just grew more challenging."

The mul faced forward to see a hulking thri-kreen stomping toward him. The huge insect-man stood so tall that his short antennae brushed the ceiling, and as he moved forward his yellow carapace knocked the glowing balls from both walls. He held weapons in three of his four arms—a whip, an obsidian short sword, and a gythka, a short pole-arm with blades of crystal rock at both ends.

"Sadira?" Neeva asked hopefully.

"I can't do anything without killing us, too," the sorceress answered.

"Give me some room," Rikus said.

"I'll aid you with the Way," Agis said, motioning the rest of the group back around the corner.

"I'd appreciate that." Rikus gave the noble a nervous grin, then added, "Not that I need help."

Despite his brave words, the mul shared his companions' concern. As menacing as the thri-kreen's four arms and weapons were, the beast's mouth posed the real danger. In his days as gladiator, he had fought many mantis-warriors, and he knew that if he allowed the thing to so much as nip him with a mandible, the beast's saliva would paralyze him.

The thri-kreen waded through the blue cloud of Sadira's sleep spell without suffering the slightest hint of drowsiness. The mul set his cahulaks to whirling in an interweaving pattern, then calmly awaited his foe's approach.

With little hesitation, the mantis-warrior jabbed the tip of his gythka at Rikus, also lashing out with his whip. With one cahulak, the mul knocked the gythka aside and allowed the thri-kreen's whip to wrap itself around his other cahulak. Rikus stepped forward, moving into striking range for his weapons. The thri-kreen leveled a short sword at Rikus's throat, and the mul ducked in time to keep the beast from lopping his head off. Before Rikus could recover, the thri-kreen's clacking mandibles descended toward his neck.

Rikus dropped to his back and kicked upward with his heel, catching the mantis-warrior square in the thorax. The blow would have smashed a man's chest, but it hardly even rocked the thri-kreen. After a momentary pause, the chattering mandibles continued their descent, dripping saliva over the mul's face. His heart pounding in fear, Rikus swung both cahulaks at his foe's bulging eyes.

The mul's reach fell short and the bone blades smashed into the thing's snout, barely scratching the beast's chitinous armor. Nevertheless, the attack gave the thri-kreen pause, and he retracted his head, moving his vulnerable eyes out of Rikus's range. The mul hammered his cahulaks at the carapace on his foe's chest, driving the huge insect off him.

"Don't kill him, Rikus!" Agis called.

"Why not?" Rikus demanded, standing.

"He's not entirely hostile," the noble responded. "If I can help him, he'll help us."

Rikus regarded the thri-kreen cautiously, waiting for Agis to make good on his promise. The mantis-warrior seemed confused for a moment, then glared over the mul's shoulder and rushed forward with his attention fixed on Agis. Realizing that the noble's mental contact had done little more than distract the creature, Rikus took advantage of the moment to dart forward and slip to the thri-kreen's side, where the mantis-warrior would have trouble reaching him with both weapons and mouth.

Seeing Rikus slip into this dangerous position, the mantis-warrior stopped his charge and used two arms to smash the mul into the wall. The blows drove the breath from Rikus's lungs, filling his torso with a dull, crushing ache. The thri-kreen dropped his whip and lashed out with the claws of a three-fingered hand. The mul barely saved his eye by turning his head away, but the thri-kreen opened a jagged gash down his cheek.

Rikus struck at the beast's head, releasing the cahulak so he would have the range to reach his target. This time, it was the thri-kreen's turn to duck, and the weapon passed over the back of the thing's neck. As it reached the end of its rope, the cahulak circled around and reappeared on the close side of the mantis-warrior's head. The mul caught the shaft and tugged with all his might, pulling himself onto the thing's back. He started to call for help, but never got the chance.

The thri-kreen stood upright and smashed him into the ceiling. The mul's cry ended with a stifled groan. Rikus tried to cry out again, then gave up and settled for merely retaining his hold. The mantis-warrior smashed the mul's aching back again and again into the ceiling.

Taking advantage of the close combat, Neeva slipped around the corner with battle-axe hefted. Agis grabbed her by the shoulder, preventing her from moving forward.

Rikus yelled, "What do you think you're—"

The mul hit the ceiling again and his question came to an abrupt halt. Already, his spine felt like it had been cracked in a dozen places and his arms burned with numb weariness.

Agis stepped past Neeva, his hands held out before him and his brown eyes fixed on the thri-kreen's. All at once, the mantis-warrior stopped smashing Rikus against the ceiling. The beast stared at Agis for a moment, then he dropped his weapons and lay down on the floor. The nobleman continued forward, silently nodding to the mantis-warrior.

"Why'd you stop Neeva?" Rikus demanded, his breath coming in short gasps. "You could have gotten me killed!"

As the mul slipped his cahulak rope off the thri-kreen's neck, Agis laid a restraining hand on the weapons. "But I didn't," he answered, still staring at the mantis-warrior. "The thri-kreen is a slave. Now that I've freed his mind from his master's grip, he'll help us."

Rikus looked doubtful and pulled his cahulaks free of the noble's grasp.

"C-Comrade," chattered the mantis-warrior, speaking in the Urikite language. "Help you."

Because he had been born and raised in the slave pits of a

Urikite noble, Rikus understood the mantis-warrior's words. Nevertheless, he remained suspicious.

"No one arms a thri-kreen slave," he said. "Especially one that fights this well."

"The argosy pilot's been using the Way to control his mind," Agis explained, gently moving the mul's weapons away from the thri-kreen. "K'kriq didn't want to attack us."

"Kill d-driver, kill Ph-Phatim," the thri-kreen stammered. "Help you."

When Rikus still did not agree, Agis said, "I was inside his mind. I'll vouch for him."

Rikus reluctantly stepped away from the mantis-warrior. "Okay, fall into line," he said. In Urikite, he added, "But you do what I say, and no weapons."

The thri-kreen opened his six-mandibles in a star-shaped gesture that could have been a smile. "N-No regret," he answered, also in Urikite.

The mul faced forward without replying. Normally, he would not have accepted a former enemy into his group, but Agis was a true master of the Way. If he said the thri-kreen could be trusted, Rikus believed him.

The mul led them toward the front of the wagon. As they moved, thick smoke began to roll down the corridor from the rear of the argosy. Within a few moments, they could hardly see the glow balls swinging in their nets, and chunks of burning wood began to drop from the ceiling.

Soon, the small group reached the front cargo hold. The exterior doors had been opened to vent the smoke, and, through the thickening fumes, Rikus saw a dozen Urikites standing guard. After passing a whispered warning to those behind him, the mul charged out of the smoke-filled corridor and hacked down the first guard from behind. Neeva leaped past him with her battle-axe flying, taking down two more. K'kriq rushed past her and, unarmed, killed five more in flurry of flashing claws and snapping mandibles. The four survivors jumped from the argosy before Agis or Sadira struck a blow.

Rikus cast a nervous glance at the five men K'kriq had stricken down, then peered out of the open cargo door. In the sands to the side and just ahead of the argosy, he saw the waddling driks and their drivers trying to escape his legion. The war-lizards were not faring well. Their low-centered bodies and heavy shells were not suited to speed. The beasts' sluggishness was compounded by their loads, for the siege engines they carried were made from sun-bleached mekillot bones, as large as trees and twice as heavy.

Already, a dozen driks lay toppled, flapping their heads and roaring helplessly, unable to continue their escape on hamstrung legs. Another dozen beasts had dug into the sand and were trying to defend themselves from the Tyrian warriors.

The mul was shocked to see that there were no Urikite regulars in view. While it was true that the main body of soldiers had been far ahead of the attack, Rikus found it strange they had not returned to join the fight.

K'kriq touched the mul's shoulder with a bloody claw, then pointed forward. "Kill Phatim, s-stop Urikites," the thri-kreen said. "No water, no food, no siege missiles."

Rikus raised a brow, then said, "Lead the way."

Agis caught the thri-kreen by a sticklike arm. "No," he said. "We'll have to find the driver ourselves."

The mantis-warrior insisted, "M-Me kill Phatim."

The noble shook his head. "If the pilot sees you, he'll take over your mind. Stay here and help our warriors destroy the supplies—in case we can't stop the wagon."

K'kriq snapped his six mandibles open and closed angrily, then turned and began hacking at the interior cargo door.

Rikus assigned the gladiators to help K'kriq, then led his three companions forward. Although the narrow corridor remained smoke-filled, it was not nearly so murky as the section aft of the cargo door. By the light of the swaying glow balls, the mul could see that, here and there, fumes were seeping through the planks in the ceiling.

The hallway turned toward the center of the wagon, and they came to a pair of bronze-gilded doors, one on each side of the corridor. Both were secured with heavy iron latches.

Rikus motioned at the door on the right. "Neeva, you check that one."

The woman nodded, then smashed the door open with a single blow of her axe. She stepped into the dark room beyond, Sadira following close behind.

Rikus kicked the other door open, then charged into the room beyond. He found himself standing before a ladder leading up to a small deck overhead. Thick whorls of smoke clouded the air.

"The pilot's deck," Agis noted, coughing and rubbing his eyes.

The mul grabbed the ladder and climbed. As he moved higher, a streamer of smoke descended and entwined itself around his neck. Rikus thought nothing of it until the tendril rubbed across his skin like a coarse rope, then abruptly tightened. Instantly, the rush of blood filled the mul's ears. His eyes felt like they would pop from his head, and he could no longer draw air down his throat.

The mul jumped off the ladder and landed at Agis's feet. Falling to his knees, he dropped his cahulaks and clutched at the tendril. His fingers sank through it like air.

"Rikus!" Agis cried.

The noble's voice seemed distant and faint. Rikus's vision went black.

To his surprise, the mul did not pass out. Instead, his consciousness turned inward, to the terrain of his own mind. He saw himself kneeling on a featureless plain of mud, the great tentacle of some horrid beast extruding from the wet earth, wrapping itself around his throat. It was trying to pull him into the soggy ground, to suffocate him in the muds of oblivion.

Rikus's stomach tightened with fear. He realized he was being attacked mind-to-mind, and that knowledge only frightened him more. The mul was a master of physical combat, but when it came to the Way, he was not even a novice.

Rikus fought back by trying to imagine himself hauling the tentacle from the mud. No matter how hard he pulled, the beast was too strong for him. It bent his torso back, kinking his spine until he feared it would snap.

The mul grabbed the tentacle and pulled with as much strength as his oxygen-starved body could muster. He slowly managed to turn himself over and braced one arm against the muddy ground. He used the other to dig, hoping to the dredge the slimy creature from its burrow. Though he excavated a hole several feet deep, he found nothing but an endless tendril that continued to pull him downward. Rikus bit the thing. It's blood burned his mouth like acid.

Then the mul grew aware of great, sloshing footsteps approaching from behind. He twisted around to meet the new horror his attacker had sent to destroy him. If there had been breath in his lungs, he would have sighed in relief. Standing before him was a familiar figure, save that it now towered overhead in the massive form of a full-giant.

"Agis?" Rikus gurgled.

The giant nodded. "What have we here?" he boomed, stooping over to grasp the tentacle.

Agis the giant pulled the tendril from the ground effortlessly, freeing the mul's throat. The writhing thing was nothing but a long gray tentacle. As Rikus watched, both ends flattened out and a set of eyes appeared on the top side. Below each pair of eyes, a long slit opened into a broad mouth filled with wicked fangs.

"The Serpent of Lubar!" Rikus gasped. The beast resembled the crest of the noble who had bred the mul, the family in whose cruel pits the young mul had been trained in the arts of killing.

As Rikus stared at the living crest of his first owner, the snake's heads both turned toward Agis and struck simultaneously. The noble's giant arms stretched outward, preventing the fangs from reaching him. The snake lengthened its body, and the arms stretched farther. An extra set of long-clawed hands suddenly grew from the giant's rib cage, then seized the snake behind each of its heads. Moving with lightning speed, the sharp claws tore great gashes along the length of the snake's body, reducing it to a bloody mess of shredded scales and minced flesh.

Agis threw the snake into the mud, then watched it wither into a desiccated husk. "Why didn't you defend yourself?" he asked, glancing at Rikus.

"I have no training in the Way," Rikus answered, stung by the giant's chiding tone.

"You don't need any to form a basic defense," the giant countered. "It's instinctual—or should be. Everyone has some ability with the Way. Your mistake was emphasizing strength over form. The Way is more subtle than that."

Agis changed from a giant into a leather-winged bird with a sharp, hooked beak. "Next time, use your imagination." With that, he launched himself into the air and flew away.

Rikus opened his eyes and saw that he was back in the argosy, lying at the base of the ladder. The nobleman sat beside him, breathing in shallow gasps.

"Agis!" the mul gasped. "Are you hurt?"

The noble smiled and shook his head. "Tired," he whispered. "Go on, before the pilot recovers."

After glancing into the corridor to make sure Agis was in no imminent danger, Rikus left the noble to rest and climbed the ladder. Near the ceiling, the pilot's deck was filled with a thick smoke that had seeped through the planks separating it from the rest of the argosy. By dropping to his hands and knees, however, the mul could crawl forward without scorching his lungs on the caustic fumes.

Rikus found the pilot's deck to be a spacious platform with a large panel of thick glass overlooking the dune-sized shells of the lumbering mekillots. Before this window sat a well-padded chair, no doubt where the pilot, a master of the Way especially trained to dominate the creatures, would sit.

The mul advanced on the pilot's chair, laying his cahulaks aside. Despite his fear of the mindbender, he had to take the man alive if he wanted to halt the argosy. From what he had heard about mekillots, if the stupid beasts were suddenly freed of their mental reins, they would be just as likely to continue trudging forward as to stop.

A long black blade flashed toward Rikus's eyes, a man-shaped blur dropping out of the smoke behind it. The mul crossed his wrists and thrust them over his head, catching the attacker's arm between the backs of his hands. Before the mindbender could withdraw his dagger, Rikus turned his palms over and grabbed his attacker's arm, then slammed his victim to the floor.

"If I even suspect you of meddling with my thoughts, I'll finish the job, Phatim," Rikus threatened, snatching the obsidian dagger and pressing its tip to the man's throat.

The pilot's gray eyes widened at the sound of his own name spoken in his own language. The gaunt man nodded his head of unkempt hair to show he understood, then looked down his hooked nose at the dagger pressed to his throat.

"If you want to live, stop the mekillots," Rikus said. "But I warn you—"

"I'm too tired to betray you with the Way," the pilot said.

Phatim closed his eyes and concentrated for a moment. The argosy lurched to a violent stop. Rikus flew over the mindbender's prone body and slammed into the back of the chair.

The pilot was on him in an instant, using one hand to pin the mul's dagger arm to the floor and, with the other, drawing a shorter knife from his boot. Rikus barely managed to slip his head out of the way as Phatim's steel blade sliced down at him.

"Die, slave!" Phatim hissed, spraying Rikus's face with warm spittle.

"*Freed* slave," Rikus replied.

The mul brought his knee up, striking Phatim in the back of the thigh. The blow propelled the pilot forward and knocked him off-balance. At the same time, Rikus ripped his arm free and thrust the dagger under Phatim's ribs. The pilot cried out, then abruptly fell silent as the tip of the long blade found his heart. Hot, red blood ran down Rikus's fingers, and Phatim collapsed.

Rikus pushed the pilot's lifeless body off him, shaking his head at the man's foolishness. The mul had hoped to question the mindbender about his choice of the Serpent of Lubar as an attack form.

Phatim's death did little to dampen Rikus's joy at stopping the argosy, however. Without the fortress-wagon and the drik-mounted siege engines, the Urikites would find it much more difficult, perhaps even impossible, to capture Tyr. The mul even dared to hope that he had just brought the war to an early end.

After a quick inspection to make sure there were no more surprises lurking on the smoky pilot's deck, Rikus returned to the ladder to make sure Agis was well. On the floor below, he saw both Neeva and Sadira standing with the noble. In her hands, Neeva held a green cloth.

Rikus collected his cahulaks and started down the ladder. "What did you find in the other room?" he asked.

"The commander's wardroom," answered Sadira.

Rikus jumped the rest of the way to the floor. "Did you kill him?" the mul asked eagerly.

"The general wasn't there," Neeva said, tossing the cloth to the mul. "We found this hanging over his bed."

Rikus unfurled the pennant. It was emblazoned with the red emblem of a two-headed snake, the mouths at each end of its body gaping open to reveal a mouthful of curved fangs.

"The Serpent of Lubar," Rikus hissed, his mood changing from victorious to murderous.

TWO

The Black Wall

The scalding wind had died away, leaving the fumes from the burning argosy to rise skyward in arrow-straight trails. Rikus stood in the shade of the fortress-wagon, drinking from one of the water casks his warriors had thrown from its cargo hold. Also gathered around the keg were Neeva, Sadira, Agis, and the commanders of the legion's three different contingents: the templar Styan, the noblewoman Jaseela, and a freed half-giant gladiator named Gaanon. The thrikreen K'kriq waited patiently at the mul's back, showing no interest in the water or the company.

The rest of the legion stood nearby, clustered in a hundred small assemblies of fifteen to twenty warriors. At the center of each group rested a keg of Urikite water, upon which the Tyrians were gorging themselves. Soon Rikus would give the order to drain the casks into the barren Athasian sands, and it was only natural for them to use as much of the precious liquid as they could.

"Are you mad, Rikus?" Agis snapped, throwing his wooden dipper back into the open water barrel. He waved an arm at the dead half-giants, crippled driks, and disassembled

29

siege engines littering the valley's red sands. "It's one thing to burn an argosy or kill a few driks, and quite another to assault a trained legion of Urikite regulars."

Rikus looked westward, toward the sandy hill over which the enemy's army had disappeared a short time earlier. So far, none of the observers he had sent after the Urikites had returned, and he took their absence to mean the column was continuing toward Tyr. The mul was as distressed as he was surprised that his enemy had not stopped to fight. To him, their willingness to abandon their siege engines and the argosy suggested that they were confident they could sack Tyr without these things.

"Our attack comes from the rear," Rikus said, his eyes narrowed in determination. "That gives us an advantage."

"Being outnumbered five-to-one is no advantage!" Agis exclaimed. The three company commanders lowered their gazes to the packed sand of the road, wanting no part of an argument between Agis and Rikus.

Lowering his voice, Agis continued, "This has less to do with protecting Tyr than taking your petty vengeance on Family Lubar."

"A slave's vengeance is never petty," said Neeva. "You'd know that if your back had ever felt the lash."

Before the argument could continue, K'kriq pointed two chitinous arms at the sky. "Who that?" he demanded.

Rikus looked upward and gasped. There, hanging far up in the blistering pink sky, was the cloudlike head of King Tithian. It looked to be made of misty green light, though its vaporous nature did not prevent the king's sharp features and hawkish nose from appearing anything less than distinct.

As Rikus's companions turned to see what he was looking at, Tyrian warriors began to cry out in delighted astonishment. As they watched, the head dropped like a meteor, until it hung less than a hundred feet overhead and blocked out so much of the sky that the day faded to the purple hues of dusk. The entire legion broke into a rousing cheer that the mul knew would not soon end. Like the rest of Tyr, most gladiators credited the crafty king with freeing them. They had no knowledge of Agis's role in forcing Tithian to issue his famous First Edict.

"Tithian! What's he doing here?" demanded Neeva, yelling to make herself heard above the tumult.

"How did he get here?" asked Rikus. "I thought he didn't know magic!"

"He doesn't," Sadira answered. She gestured at the apparition and uttered an incantation. A moment later, she added, "And that doesn't feel like normal sorcery to me."

"It isn't the Way, either," said Agis, rubbing his temples. "I can sense the presence of Tithian's thoughts, but their power is boosted far beyond anything he's capable of."

Agis and Sadira studied each other with troubled expressions, while Rikus and Neeva nervously awaited their conclusion. Finally, Agis dared to speak the possibility that troubled the four. "It could be dragon magic."

"Dragon magic? What's that?" asked Jaseela. The silky-haired woman's words were slurred, for, in a battle preceding Kalak's overthrow, a half-giant had hit her in the head. Now, one hazel eye drooped low over a smashed cheekbone, her nose wound down her face like a snake's tail, and her full lips were twisted into a lop-sided frown that dipped so low it touched the broken line of her jaw.

"Dragon magic is sorcery and the Way used together," Sadira explained.

"Tithian can't do that—can he?" gasped Neeva.

The king spoke, preventing an answer. "Soldiers of Tyr, I have been watching," said Tithian. His voice echoed over the battlefield like a peal of thunder, instantly silencing the warriors. "Well have you executed my plan!"

"*His* plan!" Rikus snorted. His remark was lost in the

cheer that rose again from his legion's ranks.

"You have struck a great blow for Tyr," Tithian continued. "When you return you shall find your reward."

This time, even the king's voice could not be heard over the din of the screaming warriors.

A few moments later, the king's thin lips began to move again, and the legion fell quickly silent. "Our enemies are foolish to return," Tithian boomed, his beady eyes turning toward the hill. "You shall drive the Urikites before you like elves before the Dragon."

An alarmed murmur rustled through the legion's ranks as the warriors looked west. To Rikus's astonishment, he saw that a high wall of absolute darkness now ran across the crest of the small hill. He had no way of telling what lay behind it, but he immediately guessed that the Urikites had returned to salvage what they could of their siege engines and the argosy.

Before the mul could give the order to drain the water casks, Tithian continued his speech. "Kill the Urikites, and remember what awaits you in Tyr!" the king cried, his radiant form dissipating into translucent wisps of yellow steam. "With the strategy I have given to Rikus, Tyr cannot lose!"

All eyes turned toward the mul.

"He didn't tell me anything," the mul said, speaking quietly, so only those standing next to him could hear.

"Of course not," Agis said, his brown eyes glimmering with anger. "He's trying to get us killed."

"The king would not do such a thing!" objected Styan. The templar was a weary-looking man with sunken eyes and unbound gray hair that hung down to his shoulders. Like the rest of his company, he wore a black cassock that identified him as a member of the king's bureaucracy. "To suggest he would is treason!"

As Styan spoke, Rikus noticed him slip a small crystal of green olivine into the pocket of his black cassock. Instantly, the mul knew how the king had learned of their initial triumph so quickly. He had once seen another of Tithian's spies use such a magical crystal to communicate with his master.

"Styan, did the king tell *you* his strategy?" Rikus asked.

"No. How would he do that?" Like most templars, Styan was a practiced fraud. The only sign he gave that he was hiding the truth was to remove his hand from his pocket.

"If that's true, Agis must be right about our king's intentions," Rikus said. He glanced to the west and saw that the wall of darkness descending the hill at the pace of a slow march.

"I also think Agis is right," agreed Jaseela, one of the few citizens of Tyr who instinctively sensed the truth about the king. "Without Agis and you three to counter his influence, Tithian will find it easy to force his self-serving edicts through the Council of Advisors."

Rikus looked to Agis, Sadira, and Neeva. "You three leave the battle and go back to keep Tithian in line."

"What are you going to do?" asked Neeva.

"Finish the Urikites—and kill their commander," Rikus answered, glancing at the hill. The wall of darkness had descended more than halfway and was now less than a quarter mile away from his legion. "I'll catch you after the fight."

Agis's jaw dropped. "I can't believe you're saying this," the noble gasped. "How can you expect to win the battle now?"

"Because I have to," Rikus snapped. "Even if I could convince the gladiators to run, the Urikites would only chase us down. By fighting, at least we'll buy you the time you need to reach the city."

"We will win," declared Gaanon. The half-giant was sunburned, with a flattened nose and a gap-toothed mouth. Like many half-giants, he was a consummate mimic who tried to adopt the habits and appearance of those he admired. At present, he had shaved all the hair from his body and, like

Rikus, wore only a hemp breechcloth. "To lose is to die," Gaanon said, repeating a favorite gladiatorial saying.

"I'll stay, too," Neeva said.

"So will I and my retainers," added Jaseela.

The mul looked to Styan. To his surprise, the templar gave a reluctant nod. "The king's orders were explicit," said the old man. "We're to stay with the legion."

"What did *you* do to anger our wonderful king?" Jaseela asked, raising the brow over her undamaged eye.

"Your jokes are not amusing," sneered Styan.

Next, Rikus turned to K'kriq and explained the situation in Urikite, suggesting that the mantis-warrior accompany Agis and Sadira back to Tyr.

"No!" the thri-kreen cried. "Stay with hunting pack. Drive wagon for you, smash black wall."

"You can pilot the argosy?" Rikus asked.

"Phatim make K'kriq steer when he sleep," the thri-kreen explained. "Start, stop, turn."

"Then you stay," he said, warmly slapping the thri-kreen's hard carapace. The mul checked on the advancing wall of darkness and saw that it had reached the bottom of the hill, only two hundred yards away. He ordered Gaanon and the gladiators to throw the Urikite water on the burning argosy, then turned to Agis and Sadira. "You two had better go now."

"Fight well," Agis said, holding his hands palm up in a formal gesture of farewell. "I will be hoping that Hamanu's soldiers do not."

"It won't matter," Rikus answered, returning the noble's gesture by clasping both upturned hands. "They'll fall."

"We can only hope," Sadira said. She stepped to the mul's other side and squeezed his arm. "Do what you must, love, but be careful." She glanced at Neeva, then added, "I want both you and Neeva back alive."

"We'll be fine," Rikus replied. He took her head between

his hands and gave her a lingering kiss. "You and Agis are the ones who should be careful. After all, we're only outnumbered. You two are facing Tithian."

With that, Agis and Sadira trotted away from the battle. Rikus turned to Styan and Jaseela, assigning the templar to take his company to the left flank of the wall of darkness and Jaseela to take hers to the right.

When he issued no further instructions, Styan asked, "And what do you wish us to do there?"

"Fight," Rikus answered, scowling. "What do you think?"

"Your battle plan doesn't seem very complete," ventured Jaseela. "Are we to push the flanks in on themselves, slip past to attack from the rear, hold our positions, or what?"

"How can I tell you that? I don't know what will happen anymore than you do," Rikus answered, motioning for them to return to their companies. "You'll know what to do."

After Jaseela and Styan left, Rikus ordered the gladiators to fall in behind the argosy, then turned toward the wagon himself. The muffled hissing and sputtering of dying fires sounded from inside the wagon, and huge billows of white steam poured from every opening. Gaanon's helpers were hefting the huge water casks into the cargo door. Inside, the vapor was so thick that Rikus could barely make out the half-giant's form as he grabbed a keg and disappeared deeper into the wagon.

From what Rikus could see, the back of the wagon had been burned down to its frame of mekillot bones. Forward of the cargo door, the argosy was still more or less intact, with gray fumes rising from the upper levels and steam from the lower. Clearly, the wagon would never carry supplies again, but it might serve to bull through a line of Urikites—assuming that was what the Tyrians found on the other side of the dark wall.

"Smash those casks and take up your weapons," Rikus

yelled, sweeping his arm at the large number of water barrels that had not yet been hoisted into the wagon. "The argosy will hold together long enough for what we need."

As the warriors obeyed, he led Neeva and K'kriq into the steaming wagon. They stumbled forward, coughing and choking, finding their way toward the pilot's deck by green halos of light shining from the glass balls on the walls. Although Gaanon had already put out most of the flames in this part of the wagon, the walls and floors were still flecked with the orange embers of smoldering fires. The heat in the corridors was thick and oppressive, scalding Rikus's bare skin and searing his nose and lips with each cautious breath.

Paying the heat no attention, K'kriq led the way up to the pilot's deck. As they climbed the ladder, Rikus heard the hiss of evaporating liquid and saw Gaanon throwing water from a large barrel as though it were a mere bucket. The half-giant's efforts were to little avail, for the fire had already burned through the back wall in numerous places, with yellow flames shooting between the planks in many more. Fortunately, the air on the deck was now clear, for any smoke drifting into the room was sucked back through the holes in the rear wall.

"That's enough, Gaanon," Rikus called. "Get your club."

The half-giant breathed a sigh of relief and smashed the water barrel, still half-filled, against the burning wall. Gaanon disappeared in the resulting cloud of steam, but his heavy footsteps let the mul know that the huge gladiator was moving toward the ladder.

Rikus followed K'kriq to the pilot's chair. After pausing long enough to stomp on Phatim's half-charred body, the thri-kreen stood motionless and stared out over the mountainous shells of the mekillots. Fifty yards beyond the great reptiles was the Urikites' curtain of blackness.

After the thri-kreen had concentrated for a moment, all four mekillots raised their shell-covered heads and started to lumber forward. The argosy lurched once, then settled into its familiar, swaying rhythm. The distance between the wagon and the Urikite wall closed quickly.

When the black curtain showed no sign of adjusting to the advancing argosy, Rikus asked, "What's wrong with them? They can't just let us punch through their formation."

"Maybe they can't see us through the black wall," suggested Neeva. "For all we know, there might not be anyone on the other side."

A brilliant flash of silver erupted from the wall, and Rikus decided she was wrong.

"Magic!" the mul cried.

K'kriq spun around, using two of his hands to grab each gladiator and pull them into the shelter of his carapace. In the same instant, the tintinnabulation of shattering glass crashed over the deck, drowning out even the thunder of the magical bolt that had demolished the window. Shards scraped along one of the mul's shoulders that had been left exposed, opening several long but shallow lacerations in his tough hide. Neeva escaped without injury.

When the attack passed, Rikus stepped away from K'kriq. The mantis-warrior stood ankle deep in broken glass, but there was not even a scratch on his tough carapace.

A pair of smoking red balls shot from the dark wall. Instead of streaking toward the pilot's deck, however, the flaming spheres sizzled straight at the lead mekillots. All four reptiles stopped in their tracks, retracting their heads as the crimson spheres hit. Great rivers of flame washed over their shells, then the earth rumbled and the argosy lurched to a stop as the great beasts dropped to the ground.

The mekillots lay motionless as wisps of fire danced over their shells, but the mighty beasts did not seem to be either panicked or in pain. A moment later, after the flames had faded to smoke, they returned to their feet and jerked the argosy into motion again. This time, they trundled forward more rapidly, in the mekillots' equivalent of a charge. Without looking away from the animals, K'kriq pointed a single arm toward the back of the deck.

"Go," he said. "Bad place for soft-skins."

"What about you?" Rikus asked, taking Neeva and moving toward the back of the deck.

In answer, the thri-kreen dropped to the floor and pulled his limbs beneath his carapace, leaving only his compound eyes visible.

Neeva started down the ladder without another word. Behind her, Rikus took the time to glance out the front of the deck. The lead mekillots had reached the curtain of darkness. The tips of their noses had no sooner disappeared into black barrier than the mul heard the sizzle and sputter of more fireballs.

Screaming, he threw himself into the pit, knocking Neeva off the ladder as he dropped past her. The gladiators crashed headlong into Gaanon's massive form, and all three tumbled to the floor in a heap. A loud whoosh sounded over their heads. Long tongues of crimson flame shot down the wall, licking at their legs and their backs, stopping just shy of the floor itself.

When Rikus spun over, he saw nothing but a blazing inferno overhead. There were flames of every color: red, yellow, white, blue, and, he thought, even black. He could not see the wall or ceiling, only raging fire.

Despite the holocaust, the argosy continued to trundle forward.

Rikus and his companions collected their weapons and rose. Not seeing how the thri-kreen could have survived such a firestorm, the mul touched his hand to his forehead, then held it toward where he imagined K'kriq's charred remains would be lying. "You fought like the Dragon," he said, giving the mantis-warrior the gladiator's greatest farewell salute.

With that, the mul led the way back toward the cargo door. They reached it just as the argosy itself was passing from the Tyrian side of the dark wall to that of the Urikites. From this side, the barrier was not opaque. Rather, it had the translucent quality of a sheet of thinly cut obsidian, and the Tyrian gladiators were visible on the other side as dim, charging shapes.

Rikus saw immediately that his use of the fortress-wagon had upset his opponent's carefully laid battle plans. The Urikite regulars had been spread out in long ranks behind the black wall, and most of them were now wildly rushing toward the wagon. Already, hundreds were gathered near the argosy to await the Tyrian gladiators. With some of their spears pointed toward the wagon and some toward the gladiators following it, the soldiers were in a disorganized mess that Rikus knew his gladiators would quickly decimate.

Rikus could see that the Urikites were a little more organized at the far side of the valley. A fair-sized company was marching toward Jaseela's flank. He could only assume that, on the other side of the wagon, a similar company of Urikites was rushing toward Styan's templars.

A series of brilliant flashes flared from near the front of the wagon, followed immediately by several deafening cracks. The smell of burning wood and charred bone filled Rikus's nostrils, then the argosy ground to quick halt. When he peered around the edge of the door, the mul saw a small group of yellow-robed templars standing near the front of the wagon. Their smoking fingers were pointed at the thick shaft that connected the mekillots to the wagon.

At the rear of the argosy, the first of the gladiators emerged from the darkness, screaming their battle cries and charging into the disorganized Urikites.

"Let's fight!" the mul yelled, raising his cahulaks.

Rikus leaped from the smoky wagon into the bright crimson light. He had no sooner landed than a pair of Urikite soldiers jabbed their speartips at him, simultaneously raising their shields to protect their faces. Rikus swung a cahulak, cutting their weapons off at the heads.

Before the mul could move forward to finish them, Gaanon's joyful warcry boomed over his shoulder. The half-giant slipped past the mul and leveled his mighty war-club at the spearless Urikites, smashing their bucklers as if they were glass. The blow knocked the pair back into the crowd and sent a half-dozen men sprawling. Neeva followed Gaanon's attack, smashing bones and rending flesh on both the fore- and back-swings of her axe.

It was all Rikus could do to keep his companions from wading into the midst of the Urikite mob. "Wait!" he called, hitting their shoulders with the shafts of his cahulaks. "Leave them to the others. Come with me."

Rikus moved toward the front of the wagon, where Hamanu's yellow-robed templars continued to attack the mekillots with bolts of energy and balls of fire. Though no longer attached to the argosy, the reptiles remained in their harnesses and were turning back toward the Urikite lines.

To the mul's amazement, the shape of a thri-kreen was hunched down on the centershaft between the rear mekillots. His carapace was black with soot, and one of his four arms seemed to be hanging limply at his side, but the mantis-warrior apparently remained in command of the reptiles.

The templars were so intent on stopping K'kriq that they did not even notice Rikus and his two companions coming up behind them. The mul killed four with a quick series of strikes. In the few seconds it took him, Neeva and Gaanon finished the other five.

When the magical barrage fell silent, K'kriq peered up from between his mekillots. He raised a clawed hand in Rikus's direction, calling, "The hunt is good!"

The thri-kreen's mekillots snapped and stomped into the

soldiers massed near the argosy, ripping a wide swath of destruction through the middle of the throng. Aided by the enemy's confusion and fear, the Tyrian gladiators tore into their foes like a cyclone into a faro field. Within moments, the coppery smell of blood filled Rikus's nose and the shrieks of dying Urikites rang in his ears.

"What now?" asked Gaanon.

Before answering, Rikus took a moment to study K'kriq's progress. The thri-kreen turned his mekillots straight into the long file of Urikites rushing toward the battle, followed closely by hundreds of gladiators. The maneuver brought the enemy's charge to an abrupt halt and sent those leading it scrambling for their lives. The soldiers that did not fall to the mighty reptiles' snapping jaws were quickly killed by Rikus's warriors.

"It looks like K'kriq has this part of the fight well in hand," the mul said, turning his gaze toward the terrain behind the battle. "Let's find the commander."

"This is no time to think of vengeance," objected Neeva.

"Sure it is," Rikus countered. He spotted a small group of figures upon the shoulder of a small sand dune that had spilled down from rocky bluffs of the valley wall. Several messengers were running from them toward the growing rout in front of K'kriq's mekillots. "At the most, we can kill only a few thousand Urikites. The rest will flee, regroup, and probably attack Tyr later. But if we slay their commander today, we'll finish the battle for good."

With that, Rikus returned to the rear of the wagon and gathered a small force of gladiators from the long line still pouring through the wall of darkness. He sent the rest to the other side of the argosy to reinforce the warriors who did not have the benefit of K'kriq's mekillots, then started toward the sand dune with his company.

They reached the base of the dune at a run, sweating heavily. Rikus charged straight up the steep side, stopping to rest only when they were within a few dozen yards of the top. At the crest waited a small line of Urikites, their spears pointed down at the gladiators. They peered over the top of their shields as they nervously awaited the Tyrian attack.

Rikus ordered his followers to spread out, deciding to let the Urikites contemplate their fate and give his warriors a few moments to rest. He took the opportunity to look over his shoulder and saw that the battle was going better than he had dared to hope. Jaseela had turned her flank back toward the main attack. The sands between her company and the argosy were red with Urikite blood and littered with more than two thousand Urikite soldiers. Many thousands more were fleeing the field in a long stream, pursued closely by howling knots of Tyrian gladiators.

On the far side of the argosy, the scene was not so lopsided. Even with the extra reinforcements Rikus had sent their way, the Tyrians were badly outnumbered and barely holding their own in the vicious combat. Styan and his templars were doing little to help the situation, merely harassing the Urikite flank with half-hearted forays that were easily turned back.

Nevertheless, the mul was not worried. Having routed half the enemy legion, K'kriq was moving toward the troubled spot as fast as his lumbering beasts could carry him. Yet as Rikus watched, the thri-kreen suddenly guided the mekillots into a knot of gladiators. The reptiles began crushing and biting not Urikite soldiers, but Tyrian warriors.

"He betrayed us!" cried Gaanon, taking a step back down the dune.

Rikus caught the half-giant's arm. "That makes no sense. Why would he have bothered to help us in the first place?" asked the mul. He studied the thri-kreen's distant form more carefully, and was barely able to see that K'kriq's head was turned toward the crest of the dune.

The mul looked to the top of the dune again, and quickly

found what he was searching for. In the middle of the enemy line, standing between a pair of burly bodyguards, was a small bald man of feeble build and delicate features. His pale lips were pinched tight in concentration, and his gray eyes were fixed on K'kriq's form. Over the bronze breastplate that covered his gaunt chest, the sickly-looking man wore a green cloak bearing the two-headed Serpent of Lubar.

"Maetan!" Rikus hissed.

"What?" asked Neeva.

"Maetan of Family Lubar," the mul explained, pointing at the little man. Rikus had last seen Maetan over thirty years ago, when Lord Lubar had brought his sickly son to see the family gladiator pits, but the mul had no trouble recognizing the pointed chin and thin nose that had distinguished the boy's face even then. "His father was a master of the Way. My guess is that he is, too."

"He's taken control of K'kriq's mind," Neeva surmised.

Rikus nodded, then waved his gladiators forward, hoping to disrupt the mindbender's concentration and free the thri-kreen again. "Attack!"

A Urikite officer barked a sharp command, and a dark cloud of spears descended from the ridge above. Rikus ducked. Neeva did the same, using her axe handle to deflect a low flying shaft. Like dozens of others, Gaanon was not so quick. One of the javelins struck him in the leg, causing the half-giant to bellow out in pain.

Cursing the effectiveness with which his enemy had stalled the charge, Rikus looked over his shoulder in Gaanon's direction. The half-giant lay on the steep slope, clutching a spear that had lodged itself in his thigh.

"I'll be fine," Gaanon said, plucking the weapon from his leg. "Just give me a moment."

"Stay here," Rikus said, taking the spear from him. "You'll only get hurt."

He spun around and threw the weapon at Maetan. A

bodyguard pushed the mindbender to the ground, putting himself in front of the spear. The Urikite grunted loudly, then dropped off the dune crest and slipped down the slope in a limp heap.

Maetan glared at Rikus for an instant, then returned to his feet and stepped back from the crest until only his gray eyes showed over the top. The mul glanced at K'kriq long enough to see that the thri-kreen and his mekillots remained under the mindbender's control. Growling in anger, the mul raised his cahulaks and resumed his charge. This time, with no more spears to throw, the Urikites could only draw their obsidian short swords and await the onslaught.

When he reached the summit, Rikus pulled away from the flashing tip of a low blade strike. He countered by swinging a cahulak at the Urikite's legs, slicing the veins behind the knee. As the screaming soldier grabbed for his savaged leg, Rikus pulled the man off the crest and sent him tumbling down the sandy slope.

Seeing the disadvantage of this location, the Urikite officer shouted another command and the entire line took two steps backward. Followed by Neeva and the rest of the gladiators, Rikus scrambled over the crest of the dune, being careful to keep one hand free to protect himself. The Tyrians had no sooner crawled onto the ridge than the enemy officer ordered his men forward again, thinking to push the gladiators off the dune.

His strategy might have worked against normal fighters, but gladiators were accustomed to fighting from disadvantaged positions. As the soldiers stepped forward, the Tyrians cut them down in many different ways. Rikus blocked his attacker's swing with a cahulak, then hooked the other one behind the man's back and used the Urikite's own momentum to send him flying off the crest. Neeva swung her big axe and chopped her opponent off at the ankles before he could strike. Other gladiators rolled at the enemy's feet, protecting themselves with a whirl of flashing blades. Still others leaped up with amazing speed, then beat the astonished soldiers back with sheer strength. When the initial clash ended, half the Urikite company lay bleeding in the sand, and only a handful of Tyrian soldiers had been pushed off the dune.

The survivors backed slowly away, their fear showing in their faces. The gladiators stood with predatory grins on their faces, allowing the Urikites' fear to work against them. Rikus used the momentary lull to search for Maetan's diminutive form and, following the resentful gazes of several enemy soldiers, found the mindbender running down the gentle side of the dune.

The mul glanced over his shoulder and saw that K'kriq's mekillots were turning back toward the argosy. Looking back to the line of frightened Urikites standing ahead, the mul yelled, "Kill them!"

As the gladiators moved forward, the Urikites began dropping their shields and running after their fleeing commander. In their panic, they opened a surprisingly large gap between themselves and the shocked gladiators, who were not accustomed to seeing their opponents flee in terror. The officer frantically chased after the line, cursing their cowardice and cutting his own men down from behind. After the initial surprise of the rout wore off, the Tyrians joined the chase with a chorus of thrilled howls.

Maetan paused near the base of the dune and looked up at the mass of soldiers trailing behind him. The mindbender's shadow began to lengthen, spreading across the sands like a dark stain of ink across a parchment. It retained the basic shape of a man, but not the proportions. Its limbs were long and ropy, with a serpentine body that seemed more appropriate to a lizard than a man. When it reached a length of four or five times Maetan's height, a pair of sapphire eyes began to shine from the head. A long azure gash appeared where the mouth should be, and wisps of ebony gas drifted skyward from this slit.

A gap opened between the shadow's feet and those of Maetan. The shadow beast rolled onto its stomach, then its body began to thicken and it moved into a kneeling position. When it had assumed a full, three-dimensional form, it rose to its feet. The thing stood as tall as a full giant, towering over the men below it like the great trees of the halfling forest.

The Urikites stopped their retreat, frightened murmurs of "Umbra!" rising from their disorganized ranks.

Neeva grabbed Rikus by the shoulder and stopped him. "Wait!" she cried. "You can't do this alone."

The mul slowed enough to look around and see that Umbra's appearance had stopped his gladiators as well. The warriors were standing motionless on the slope, their jaws slack with astonishment and their eyes locked on the huge shadow beast. Rikus would have hesitated to say that they were frightened, but they were certainly spellbound.

Umbra pointed a finger at the routed Urikites, then, in a throbbing voice so deep it seemed bottomless, he said, "Fight! Stand and fight, or I swear I'll take you with me when I return to the Black!"

As if to emphasize the threat, the thing strode halfway up the dune in two steps, then reached down and closed his sinuous fingers around the torsos of two Urikites. Their chests and midsections disappeared in darkness. In vain, they cried for mercy as Umbra's shadow crept down to their feet and up over their heads. Within an instant, their forms had simply melted into the creature's black shape.

"Now, form your lines!" Umbra cried. He pointed toward the Tyrians. "For the defense of Lubar and the glory of Urik, die like heroes!"

The Urikites turned around and dressed their lines, pointing their black swords toward the Tyrians.

"For the freedom of Tyr!" Rikus yelled, charging.

Neeva followed close behind, screaming, "For Tyr!" An instant later, a hundred voices were crying the same thing.

Rikus reached the enemy before they had completely reformed their wall, tearing into it in a maelstrom of whirling cahulaks and kicking feet. Almost before he realized it, he had ripped the swords from a pair of Urikites' hands and felled two more with crippling kicks to the knees. To Rikus's right, Neeva hacked a defender nearly in two, then killed another with the backswing as she pulled her axe from the body of the first.

No sooner had Rikus and Neeva cleared their opponents away than a tremendous crash reverberated across the sandy dune as the rest of the gladiators hit the enemy line. The clatter of bone and obsidian weapons filled the air, followed by a growing chorus of pained cries. A handful of enemy soldiers threw down their weapons and turned to flee. Umbra prevented the rout from spreading by snatching the cowards and absorbing them into his shadow.

Rikus caught sight of a black blade streaking toward his ribs. He blocked with the shaft of a cahulak, then raked his other weapon across the soldier's throat. The man dropped his sword and turned away, grasping at the bleeding wound below his chin.

The mul spun around to attack the person who had slammed into his back, then stopped when he realized that she was one of his own gladiators, a red-haired half-elf named Drewet who had earned her fame in the arena by killing a full giant single-handedly. At the other end of her two-pronged lance hung a gasping Urikite, but beyond her were nothing but more Tyrians.

The mul faced the other direction and saw that, on the other side of Neeva, Tyr's gladiators were beating the last of the Urikites into the sand. At the bottom of the dune, Maetan had not moved. He stood alone, watching the battle with no indication of concern.

Rikus was about to start down the slope when a rustle of astonished cries rose from the Tyrian ranks; Umbra had opened his blue mouth and was facing the battlefield. A wispy stream of blackness shot from between the thing's lips and poured over the gladiators like a thick, sticky mist. As the billowing mass spread over the slope, Umbra shrunk as if he were spewing his own body over the dune. Horrified screeches and anguished screams rose from whoever the black haze touched.

"Run!" Rikus yelled. He grabbed Neeva's wrist and sprinted forward, angling toward the bottom of the dune and away from the spreading vapor.

As fast as they ran, it was no use. The black fog caught them only a few steps later, lapping at their legs like the waters of an oasis pond. Instantly, an icy wave of pain shot through Rikus's feet and up into his thighs. The closest thing he had ever felt to it were frigid rains in the high mountains, but this pain was a hundred times worse. The rain had been uncomfortable and made him shiver, but the darkness stung his skin and numbed his flesh to the bone. His joints stiffened and would not move, reducing his legs to dead, aching weights.

Rikus felt himself falling, and Neeva cried out at his side. He shoved her forward with all his strength, sending her sprawling half-a-dozen steps ahead of himself. An instant later, the mul landed face-first in the sand.

The blackness did not overtake the rest of his body. He lay sprawled on the dune, groaning loudly as his mind struggled to make sense of the contradicting sensations of scalding sand beneath his torso and the icy numbness in his legs. Rikus looked over his shoulder and saw that Umbra was gone, or rather had spread his entire body over the gentle slope. The mul lay at the edge of the shadowy form, his legs lost in the blackness behind him. In addition to himself and

Neeva, Drewet and perhaps six more gladiators had escaped the frigid cloud, some of them by narrower margins than the mul. Most of the company had been engulfed.

Neeva limped back to Rikus, then kneeled at his head and asked, "Are you hurt?"

"I can't feel my legs," Rikus answered. As he spoke, a terrible thought occurred to him. "Pull me out, please!" Rikus peered over his shoulder at the darkness beneath his thighs. "My legs must be gone!"

"Calm yourself," Neeva said, gripping the mul under the arms. "Everything's going to be fine."

She pulled him from the shadow. His legs were as white as ivory, but at least they remained attached. The mul put a hand to his thigh. It was colder than anything he had ever felt, and there was no sensation in the leg.

"What's wrong with them?" the mul cried, wondering if the heat would ever return to his frozen flesh.

As he spoke, Umbra's black shadow shrank to the size of a normal man. Where the shadow beast had lain, the sand was clean and sparkling. There was not a single corpse, stray weapon, or even a puddle of blood to suggest that there had ever been a battle on the dune.

The shadow slipped down the slope and assumed his rightful place at Maetan's feet. The Urikite commander hardly seemed to notice, studying the site with an air of distaste. Finally, a small sandspout rose around his body, hiding the mindbender from the mul's sight.

Rikus pushed off the ground and drew his numb legs up beneath him, then tried to run down the slope. His knees remained stiff as stones, pitching him face-first into the burning dune.

Maetan's sandspout rose high off the ground, then drifted out into the valley and hung over the heads of a throng of Urikite soldiers that was being pursued by a mob of blood-thirsty gladiators. For a few moments, Rikus feared that

Maetan was awaiting an opportunity to launch some devastating mental attack, but at last the whirlwind traced a semicircle in the air and shot up the valley.

Neeva helped Rikus to his feet. "I hate to admit it, but I'm a little surprised," she said, slipping his bulky arm over her shoulders. "We won."

"Not yet," Rikus said, watching the sandspout fade from view. "Not until we have Maetan."

THREE

Village in the Sand

The thirsty Tyrians stood beneath an arch of golden sandstone, taking what shelter they could from the white-hot sky. Their eyes were fixed far below, on the slowly spinning sails of a small windmill. With each rotation, the mill pumped a few gallons of cool, clear water from a deep well and dumped it into a covered cistern.

Unfortunately, the cistern stood in the middle of a small village. The plaza surrounding it was basically round in shape, with a jagged edge of curving salients that resembled tongues of flame. The circle was paved with cobblestones of crimson sandstone, and the whole thing reminded Rikus too much of the scorching ball of fire hanging in the center of the midday sky.

The huts enclosing the plaza also resembled the sun, with rounded red flagstone walls. The buildings stood only about five feet high, and none were covered by any semblance of a roof. From his position on the hillside, Rikus could look directly down into their interiors and see the stone tables, benches, and beds with which they were furnished. Of course, on Athas there was little need to protect one's belongings from rain, but the mul thought it foolish that the residents left themselves and their belongings exposed to the brutal sun all day long.

The huts, standing in a series of concentric rings, were enclosed by a single low wall of red brick. At the moment, the wall was manned by eight hundred Urikite troops. Two hundred more stood at the edges of the plaza, their spears pointed inward toward a frightened mass of men and women huddling together in the circle.

The prisoners were all short, standing only about chest high to their guards, and with squat, angular builds that made even Rikus look undermuscled by comparison. Their bodies were completely hairless and sun-darkened to deep mahogany, save for a patch of orange skin covering the ridge of thick bone along the top of their heads.

Towering above the dwarves, in the center of the circle next to the cistern, stood Maetan of Family Lubar and four large bodyguards. Though the distance separating them was great enough that Rikus could not make out the Urikite's expression, the mul could see that the mindbender was sipping water from a wooden dipper and staring up at the arch where he and his companions stood.

The mul shifted his gaze from his enemy to the terrain surrounding the dwarven town. On the side closest to Rikus, slabs of orange-streaked sandstone, speckled with purple spikeball and silvery fans of goldentip, rose at steep angles to become the foothills of the Ringing Mountains. The other side of the village was dominated by a barren mound of copper-colored sand.

Thirsty Tyrian warriors covered the dune and the sandstone slabs, sitting in plain sight and staring down at the cistern with yearning eyes. In the olive-tinged hours just after dawn, Rikus's legion had taken up positions surrounding the village and had been awaiting the order to attack ever since. But with the Urikites waiting for his troops to make the first move, Rikus was in no hurry to give the order.

"If we attack, Maetan kills the dwarves," the mul growled, shaking his head and facing the five people with him. "If we don't, we die of thirst."

The Tyrian army had run out of water two days ago, after five days of tracking Maetan and fighting a running battle to keep him from regathering the Urikite army. Thanks to his mul blood, Rikus was not suffering too badly from the lack of water. The same was true of K'kriq, who only drank once every ten or twelve days in the best of times.

Unfortunately, the rest of their companions were not so hardy. Neeva's full lips were cracked and bleeding, her green eyes sunken and gray, and her skin peeling away in red flakes. Jaseela's black hair had become stiff as straw and the tip of her swollen tongue protruded from the drooping side of her mouth. Styan's throat was so constricted that he could hardly gasp when he tried to speak.

Gaanon was the worst off, though. Because of his great size, he required more water than most warriors, and thirst was taking its toll on him faster than anyone else. His throat was so swollen that it choked off his breath if he didn't consciously hold it open. Simply taking a few steps strained his big body so severely that he had to lie motionless in order to calm his pounding heart. To make matters worse, the wound in the half-giant's thigh had festered, and now a steady dribble of yellow pus ran from the puncture. Rikus had no doubt that Gaanon would die if he did not have water soon.

"I don't know what to do," the mul admitted.

"There is only one thing we can do," Styan whispered. Still dressed in his black cassock, he was the only one of the group wearing anything more than a breechcloth, halter, and a light cape. He claimed the heavy cloak trapped a layer of moisture next to his skin, but Rikus had his doubts.

"Yes," Jaseela agreed. "We must leave."

"Are you mad?" Styan croaked.

"I won't be responsible for the death of an entire village," the noblewoman countered, waving her hand toward the crowded plaza below.

"They're only dwarves," objected Styan. "And crazier than most, judging from their village."

Rikus raised his hand to silence them. Their comments had provided no help, for he was already well aware of the situation: either his legion died, or the dwarves did. "What do you think?" he asked Neeva.

She did not hesitate. "This is our fight, not that of the dwarves. We can't sacrifice them to save ourselves."

"We're also saving Tyr," Styan added.

"You care less about Tyr than you do about the dwarves," Jaseela hissed.

"That's enough." Rikus stepped between them. "I know what we have to do."

"What?" gasped the templar. From his hostile inflection, Rikus knew that Styan would not be happy with any answer that did not mean water.

Rikus faced the village again, where Maetan was wasting water by pouring it over the heads of his captives. "We'll capture the cistern—without letting Maetan kill anyone."

"It's well to say such things," Styan said, "but as a practical matter—"

"We'll try!" Rikus snapped, keeping his gaze fixed on Maetan. Though he did not say so aloud, he feared that Maetan would wipe out the dwarven village even if his legion left. At the very least, the hungry Urikites would loot the dwarves to the point of starvation.

"How?" It was Jaseela's soft voice that asked the question.

The mul had no answer. Not for the first time that day, his thoughts turned to Sadira and Agis, but he quickly tried to put them out of his mind. By now, they were halfway back to Tyr. No matter how much he lamented the absence of the half-elf's sorcery or the noble's mastery of the Way, he and his legion had to solve this problem on their own.

For what seemed an eternity, Rikus simply stood and watched Maetan dump water on the dwarves. Finally, a plan occurred to the mul. "We're going to surrender," he said, facing his companions.

"What?" they asked together.

Rikus nodded. "It's the only way to put ourselves between the Urikites and dwarves before the fight starts."

"This is beyond belief!" Styan said, his strained voice cracking with anger.

"Without weapons, we'll be at a severe disadvantage," Jaseela said. "We'll lose a lot of warriors."

"Not if we lead with gladiators," Rikus offered. "In the pits, before you learn to fight with weapons, you learn to fight without them." He glanced at Neeva and asked, "What do you think?"

The big woman remained quiet for several moments. Finally, she asked, "Are you doing this because you're afraid we won't catch Maetan again?"

"If Maetan was all I'm after, we would have attacked by now," Rikus snapped. Neeva's question hurt more than it should have, and he realized there was some truth to what she implied. Still, he thought he was making the right decision. "Besides, this is the only way I see to give both us and the dwarves a chance to survive."

When Neeva offered no further argument, Styan said, "The templars won't have any part of it."

"That's your choice," Rikus said. "If you think this is a bad idea, I won't ask you to send your company along."

"We're ready to fight, but for Tyr—not any dwarven village," he sneered. The templar reached into his pocket and withdrew the small crystal of green olivine that would allow him to contact Tithian. "And I don't think the king will want us to sacrifice our warriors for a bunch of dwarves, either. I warrant we'll have a new commander in a matter of—"

Rikus clasped the templar's hand. "This isn't the king's decision," he said, prying the stone from Styan's fingers. "You have only two choices. Join us and help, or wait here and hope we succeed."

Styan stared at Rikus, then jerked his hand out of the mul's grasp. "I'll wait."

Paying the templar no further attention, Rikus slipped the stone into his leather belt pouch, then gave Neeva and Jaseela instructions to be passed along to the others. Rikus laid his cahulaks aside, then moved to leave.

K'kriq stepped to his side and started down the sandstone slope with him. Rikus stopped and shook his head, "I have to go alone, K'kriq," he said. Though the thri-kreen was quickly learning Tyrian, Rikus spoke in Urikite. He did not want any misunderstandings.

The thri-kreen shook his bubble-eyed head and laid a restraining claw on the mul's shoulder. "Pack mates."

Rikus removed the claw. "Yes, but don't come until the fight starts," he said, starting down the hill again.

K'kriq ignored his order and followed. The mul stopped and frowned at the thri-kreen. As much as he valued the mantis-warrior's combat prowess, the mul remembered how easily Maetan had taken control of K'kriq's mind in the last battle. He did not want to risk the same thing happening before the fight was in full swing.

Deciding to put his order in terms that K'kriq seemed to understand, Rikus pointed at Gaanon. "If I'm a pack mate, so is Gaanon," he said. "Stay here and protect him."

The thri-kreen looked from the mul to the half-giant. "Protect?" His mandibles hung open in confusion.

"Guard, like your young," the mul explained.

"Gaanon no hatchling!" K'kriq returned, cocking his

head at Rikus. Nevertheless, the thri-kreen turned away and went to the half-giant's side, shaking his head as though the mul were crazy.

Breathing a sigh of relief, Rikus descended the sandstone slope alone. As he approached the village gate, which did not stand even as tall as he did, he raised his hands above his head to show that he was unarmed. The mul could have reached the top of the village wall without leaving his feet, and caught the railing atop the gatehouse with a good leap.

When Rikus had reached a comfortable speaking distance, a Urikite officer showed his bearded face above the wall. "That's far enough," he called, using a heavily accented version of the common trade dialect. "What do you want?"

"I've come to surrender my legion to Maetan of Urik," Rikus answered. He did his best to look both remorseful and angry.

"Maetan has no use for your legion—except as slaves," the officer returned, his dark eyes narrowed suspiciously.

"Better slaves than corpses," Rikus answered. Though he did not mean them, the words stuck in his throat anyway. "We've been out of water for days."

"There's plenty in here," the officer answered. He grinned wickedly and studied the mul for a moment, then motioned for the gate to be opened.

Rikus stepped through, allowing himself to be seized by the officer and several soldiers. They bound his hands and slipped a choking-loop around his neck, then led him toward the windmill and cistern at the center of the village. They passed a dozen rows of the round huts. As he peered down into them, Rikus could not help noticing that they were all arranged in a similar manner. To one side of the doorway was a round table surrounded by a trio of curved benches. On the other side of the door stood a simple cabinet holding a variety of tools and weapons. The beds, stone platforms covered with several layers of assorted hides, were located opposite the door. The only variations between individual buildings came in the number of beds and how neatly the residents kept their homes.

When they reached the plaza, Rikus's escorts pushed him roughly through the ring of guards, then used the tips of their spears to prod him toward Maetan. As Rikus passed, the dwarven prisoners stepped aside and studied him with dark eyes that betrayed both respect and puzzlement. A few commented to each other in their own guttural language, but were quickly silenced by sharp blows from the mul's escorts.

In the center of the plaza, Maetan of Urik waited beside the stone cistern, still holding the dipper in his hand. His cloak was so covered with dirt and grime that it was more brown than green, and even the Serpent of Lubar had faded from red to pastel orange. The mindbender's thin lips were chapped and cracked, and his delicate complexion seemed more pallid and sallow than Rikus remembered from the battle.

As the soldiers pushed Rikus to their commander's side, the Urikite's four bodyguards stepped forward to surround the prisoner. The brawny humans all wore leather corselets and carried steel swords. Rikus raised an eyebrow at the sight of so many gleaming blades, for each was worth the price of a dozen champion gladiators. On Athas, metal was more precious than water and as scarce as rain.

After staring into the eyes of Rikus's escort for a few moments, Maetan waved the officer away. "How do you know my name, boy?" the mindbender demanded, addressing Rikus in the fashion of a master to a slave.

Rikus was surprised by the question, for his escort had not made a verbal report to their commander. Realizing Maetan must have questioned the officer using the Way, Rikus reminded himself to guard his own thoughts carefully, then answered the question. "We've met before, many years ago."

"Is that so?" asked Maetan, his cold gray eyes fixed on Rikus's face.

"You were ten. Your father brought you to see his gladiatorial pits," the mul said, remembering the meeting as clearly as if it had been the day before.

Until he had seen Maetan for the first time, Rikus thought that all boys learned to be gladiators, working up through the ranks until they became trainers and perhaps even lords themselves. When Lord Lubar had brought his sickly son to the pits, however, Rikus had taken one look at the boy's silken robes and finally understood the difference between slaves and masters.

Maetan studied the mul for a time, then said, "Ah, Rikus. It has been a long time. Father had high hopes for you, but, as I recall, you barely survived your first three matches."

"I did better in Tyr," the mul answered bitterly.

"And now you wish to return to Family Lubar," Maetan observed. "As a slave?"

"That's right," the mul said, swallowing his anger. "Unless we get water, my warriors will die by sunset tomorrow."

Maetan's gaze swept along the line of gladiators ringing the village. "Why not come and take it?" he asked. "I've been asking myself for hours why you haven't attacked. We couldn't stop you."

"You know why," Rikus answered, glancing at the dwarves.

The Urikite turned his white lips up in the semblance of a smile. "Of course, the hostages," he smirked.

"Giving up won't save Kled, Tyrian," cackled the voice of an old dwarf, using the language of Tyr.

Maetan's head snapped in the direction of the speaker, an aged dwarf with jowls so loose they sagged from his chin like a beard. "Did I give that man permission to speak?"

A bodyguard pushed through the crowd toward the dwarf. As the Urikite grabbed him, the old dwarf made no effort to resist or escape. Instead, he said, "See? Nothing good comes—"

The Urikite's pommel fell across the back of the speaker's skull. The old dwarf collapsed to the ground, striking his head on the hard flagstones with a sickening thud. Indignant cries of astonishment and anger rustled through the crowd. One defiant dwarf stepped toward the guard, his fists tightly clenched and his rust-red eyes fixed on the bodyguard's face. Aside from the color of his eyes, the dwarf was unusual in that he stood nearly five feet tall and had a crimson sun tattooed on his forehead. His build did not make him resemble a boulder quite so much as his fellows.

"Be quiet, or I'll have his head removed completely," Maetan snapped, using the smooth-flowing syllables of the trade tongue.

The dwarf stopped his advance, though the anger and hatred did not drain from his eyes. At the same time, a resentful murmur rustled through the throng as the dwarfs who understood the Urikite's words translated the threat for their fellows. The plaza slowly fell silent.

After pausing to sneer at the red-eyed dwarf, Maetan returned his attention to Rikus. "So, Tyr's legion will surrender on behalf of the dwarves of Kled?"

"Yes," Rikus said. "This isn't their fight. We have no wish to see them harmed."

"You'll understand if I'm reluctant to believe you," Maetan said.

"It should surprise no one that the freed men of Tyr place a higher value on justice than a nobleman of Urik," Rikus countered. One of the bodyguards tightened the choking loop around the mul's neck; Maetan himself showed no reaction to the insult. Rikus continued, "If we intended to attack, we would have done it by now." He was forced to gasp by the rope constricting his throat.

"I'm sure you intend to tell me what I stand to gain by

accepting your surrender. Why shouldn't I just stay here and let your legion die of thirst?" The mindbender motioned for the guard to ease the tension on the mul's throat.

"Two things," Rikus said, swallowing hard. "First, you'd do well to return home with two thousand slaves. That's all you're going to bring back from Tyr."

Maetan's thin lips twitched in anger, but he gave no other indication of his feelings. "And the second?"

Rikus pointed his chin toward his warriors surrounding the village. "Even a Tyrian's concern for justice goes only so far."

Maetan shocked Rikus with a quick answer. "I accept." The mindbender pointed at the tall dwarf with the rust-colored eyes and motioned for him to come forward. As the defiant-looking man obeyed, Maetan said, "Caelum speaks Tyrian. He'll relay your words to the gladiators."

The dwarf's mouth fell open. "How did you—"

"That's not for you to know," a bodyguard snapped, pushing the dwarf toward Rikus.

"The courage of you and your men is admirable, but not very wise," Caelum said, looking into the mul's eyes. His jawbone, chin, and cheeks were well-defined and pronounced, but not as massive as those of most dwarves. There was even a certain symmetry and grace of proportion between his nose and the rest of his face, with uncharacteristic laugh lines around the corners of his mouth and eyes. "If you do this, there's nothing to stop the Urikites from killing us all."

"The choice is ours," Rikus said, deliberately avoiding the dwarf's red eyes. If Maetan was capable of reading Caelum's mind, the mul did not want to plant any suggestion of what he had planned. Instead, he pointed to the sandstone arch on the hillside above. "Just deliver the message to the people up there."

Once the dwarf was out of sight, Maetan sneered at Rikus. "Your men will be sold into slavery as you asked," he said. "You, however, shall die a slow and bitter death for the pleasure of King Hamanu."

Confident that he would have his revenge later, Rikus remained silent while Caelum climbed up to the arch. The mul found Maetan's quick acceptance of their surrender unsettling. He had expected the Urikite to react more suspiciously, pondering the proposal for a few moments. His immediate agreement suggested that the mindbender was already well aware of the dangers of accepting the Tyrian surrender. Still, Rikus did not consider calling off his plan. Whether Maetan had anticipated it or not, it was still the only way to save both his legion and the dwarven village.

A few minutes after Caelum's departure, the first Tyrians marched into the village. Unlike Rikus, they remained unbound, for tying them would have taken more rope than could be found in all of Kled. As the plaza began to grow more crowded, Maetan moved himself and Rikus to the far side, then ordered the dwarves to return to their homes and stay inside under penalty of death.

Soon the square was packed shoulder-to-shoulder with unarmed Tyrians, all clamoring for water and struggling to reach the cistern at its center—as the mul's generals had instructed them to do. The Urikites previously standing guard at Kled's wall now ringed the square, their shields and spears pointed toward Rikus's warriors.

As the last Tyrians were escorted into the plaza, Jaseela and Neeva were brought to Rikus's side, along with Caelum. Only the templars and K'kriq, gathered in a small group beneath the arch, remained outside the village.

Ignoring their absence for the moment, Maetan peered at Neeva from between two burly bodyguards. "An excellent girl," he said, catching Rikus's gaze with his pearly gray eyes. "Did she also come from my father's pens? Or doesn't your mul-brain allow you to remember that much?"

As the mindbender asked the question, a hated memory flashed into Rikus's mind. In a dark corner of the Lubar pits, a young mul, his body already knotted with muscles and covered with scars, stood alone before a man-sized block of white pumice carved into the semblance of a gladiator.

"Hit it," growled a familiar voice.

The boy, Rikus at ten years, looked over his shoulder. Neeva stood at his back, a six-stranded whip in her hand. He started to ask her what she was doing in his memory, at a time where she did not belong, but, before his eyes, she changed from an attractive woman to a fat, sweating swine of a trainer.

Rikus shook his head, trying to free himself of the memory. Once before, a mindbender had slipped into his head by hiding behind a memory. Thanks to Neeva's inappropriate appearance, the mul had no doubt that Maetan was using a similar attack against him now.

The trainer cuffed the side of young Rikus's head, snarling, "Do as you're told, boy."

Rikus tried to ignore the trainer and focus his thoughts on the present, but the memory had a life of its own. The gladiator found himself, as a young mul, facing the punching dummy and tapping it with his fist. The rough surface grated the soft skin of his hand, opening a line of tiny cuts across his knuckles.

The six-strands of the trainer's whip snapped across Rikus's bare back, opening a line of cuts that burned like viper bites. The boy clenched his teeth and did not cry out. He had already learned that to show pain was to invite more of it.

"Harder!" the trainer spat. "I swear I'll strip the hide off your scrawny little bones."

Rikus punched the statue again, this time with as much force as he could. The blow tore the skin off his knuckles and sent a sharp pain shooting from his hand clear to his elbow.

"Again!" the trainer sneered. His whip cracked and ripped another strip of flesh off the boy's back.

The young mul hit the dummy again, this time imagining it was the trainer that he was attacking. He struck again and again, throwing his weight behind each blow. Soon he had reduced his hands to unfeeling masses of raw meat and painted the pumice statue red with his blood.

Rikus's awareness of the present returned, and Maetan looked away. Unfortunately, the mindbender's probing remained strong enough that the mul could not shut out the painful images inside his mind.

Maetan looked to Neeva and Jaseela, then motioned to the arch where Styan and his black-robed men waited. "Aren't your templars thirsty?"

"They refuse to come down until they see how you treat us," Jaseela offered.

"Everyone else is here," Neeva added, glancing at Rikus.

The mul knew what his fighting partner was hinting at: the Tyrians were ready to attack. Rikus opened his mouth to give the order, but Maetan's head snapped around and the mindbender fixed his gray eyes on those of the mul.

Inside Rikus's mind, the fat trainer clamped a pudgy, begrimed hand over the young mul's mouth. Rikus grasped at the arm and tried to pull it away, but he was still young and far from a match for the older man's bearish strength. The trainer opened his lips to speak, revealing a mouthful of rotten and broken teeth.

"Forget about the plan," the trainer said. "We're really surrendering."

To Rikus's surprise, he heard himself repeating the words. Neeva scowled in anger, and Jaseela's jaw dropped open.

"What?" they demanded.

Caelum looked from the mul to the two women, rubbing a hand over the bony crest of thickened skull atop his head.

Hoping to alert the two women to his plight, Rikus tried to shake his head—and found himself unable to move. In his mind, the fat trainer's powerful hand was locked over the boy's chin, keeping it held firmly in place.

Rikus decided to switch tactics. Remembering how, during the battle to capture the argosy, Agis had rescued him from Phatim's mental attack, the mul substituted his own image for the one Maetan had introduced into his mind. Instead of a young boy, he saw himself as a mature gladiator, stronger than the trainer and hardened by hundreds of fights.

He felt a queasy feeling in his stomach as a surge of energy rose from deep within himself, changing the young mul in his thoughts from a boy to a man. This new Rikus slapped a hand over the grimy fingers covering his mouth, then used the heel of his other hand to drive his captor's elbow into the air. Keeping the trainer's pudgy hand clamped over his lips, the mul ducked under the entangling arm, then snapped it at the elbow by pushing down with one hand and pulling up with the other.

As soon as the trainer's hand left his mouth, Rikus screamed, "Now, Neeva!" The words sounded both in Rikus's mind and in the dwarven village.

Neeva raised her brow and Jaseela shook her head in confusion. Caelum peered at the mul as if he had gone sun-mad, then slowly shifted his gaze to Maetan. The mindbender was wincing as though his own arm had been broken.

Hoping to spur his companions into action, Rikus kicked at Maetan's guards, gasping, "He's taken over my—"

The mul's attack and his explanation came to an abrupt end as Maetan recovered from the shock of Rikus's mental counterattack. Inside the mul's mind, the trainer whirled around, changing from a man to a vulgar, hairy spider. The immense, bulbous thing lashed out with two clawed legs, forcing Rikus to retreat, then snapped at him with two pincers dripping brown venom.

Rikus dodged to the side, trying to change himself into an equally large scorpion. The effort was too much for him. A spurt of energy rose from deep within his stomach, then abruptly faded away. The mul felt queasy and weak, his legs trembling with exhaustion and his heart pounding at his ribs like a smith's hammer. He barely managed to keep his feet as the spider attacked again.

In the plaza, Neeva and Jaseela realized what was happening. Neeva dislocated the knee of the nearest bodyguard with a lightning-fast kick, ripping his steel sword from his hands. She drew the blade across the rope that bound Rikus's hands, cutting him free, then turned and sliced a second guard open in one fluid motion. Jaseela grabbed this man's blade and raised it to the sky, crying, "Now, warriors of Tyr!"

A great shout rose from her retainers and the gladiators. The plaza broke into a clamor of thuds, cracks, and pained cries as the Tyrians moved to strip the weapons from their captors' hands.

Seeing this, Caelum raised a hand toward the sun and uttered a series of words in a strange, rasping language that vaguely resembled the sound of a crackling fire. His bronze arm turned blazing crimson. He pointed at Rikus's head, saying, "This will protect you, Tyrian."

Rosy light streamed from the dwarf's fingers and gathered around the mul's head in a scintillating sphere. Inside Rikus's mind, a fiery wall sprang up between him and the spider, just as the horrid thing leaped at him. The beast disappeared into the flames, screeching in anger.

Instantly, Rikus's mind was free of the mindbender's attack, his attention returning to the plaza and the present.

The mul's legs felt as heavy as iron, his breath came in deep gasps, and his arms ached with fatigue—but he was free to act.

Looking past Maetan's two surviving bodyguards, Rikus grinned at the mindbender. "Now it's my turn," he said, stepping forward.

The Urikite's face, already betraying the pain he had suffered from the fire inside Rikus's mind, went pale. "Kill him!" Maetan ordered, stepping back. "The dwarf, too!"

Rikus dodged the clumsy lunge of Maetan's first guard, twisting away as the sword thrust past his body. He grabbed the man's arm with both hands, holding it steady as he brought a knee up to break the bone. The mul caught the sword as it dropped to the ground. Then he spun around and smashed the pommel into the next Urikite's jaw. The soldier collapsed into an unconscious heap.

Realizing he had left his back exposed, Rikus glanced over his shoulder and saw the last bodyguard stepping toward him with a raised sword. Without bothering to face his attacker, the mul leveled a vicious thrust kick at the soldier. The heel of his foot drove square into the man's ribs. The Urikite stumbled backward, gasping for breath and holding his side.

"Should have broken him in two," Rikus said, realizing for the first time how much energy he had expended in his mental battle against Maetan.

The mul stepped toward the gasping Urikite, who raised his sword into a defiant guarding position. Snorting in derision, Rikus feinted an attack, then slashed the bodyguard's hand off at the wrist. With his free hand, the mul grabbed the back of the soldier's head and pulled downward, smashing it into his knee. There was a loud crack. Blood sprayed over the mul's leg, and the lifeless Urikite fell to the ground with a cracked forehead.

Rikus looked around and saw that he was no longer in dan-

ger. On all sides of the plaza, the Urikites were already retreating down the narrow lanes between the dwarven huts,
pressed hard by the Tyrian warriors who had stolen their
spears and obsidian short swords. Every moment or two
came a pained scream from deep within the warren of stone
huts, attesting to the fact that the dwarves were taking
vengeance on their former captors.

Rikus returned his attention to the immediate vicinity,
searching for Maetan. He spotted the hated mindbender
twenty yards away, at the end of the one of the sun plaza's
curving salients. He stood between two huts, his gray eyes
fixed on the mul.

When Rikus stepped toward the mindbender, Maetan's
bitter voice echoed inside his head. *Don't be a fool, boy.* As
he spoke, the Urikite's frail-looking body grew translucent
before Rikus's eyes. *I will find you when I'm ready to end our
fight.*

With that, Maetan faded entirely from sight. Rikus started
to yell for a search party, then decided against it. Remembering how the mindbender had ridden a whirlwind away from
their first battle, the mul realized that the Urikite would not
have shown himself without being sure of his escape. It
would take more than cornering a part of the Urikite legion
to kill Lord Lubar.

Caelum came to the mul's side. "Only in the words of our
storytellers have I heard of men who fight like you, Tyrian,"
he said. He held his hands toward Rikus, palm up in the
sign of friendship. "I am named Caelum."

"I'm Rikus," the mul said, putting his sword beneath his
arm so he could return the dwarf's greeting. "Without your
help, I'd be dead. I owe you a life."

"And we owe you many," the dwarf replied, gesturing toward the plaza.

Now that the battle had moved away from the circle,
Rikus could see that their quick victory had not come with-

out a price. Nearly two hundred gladiators, and more than a few of Jaseela's retainers, lay bleeding and groaning around the perimeter of the plaza. Already, the dwarven men and women who lived closest to the square were bringing bandages and satchels of soothing herbs to help the wounded.

As they studied the scene in the plaza, Neeva, who was standing a dozen yards away, screamed, "Look out!"

She snatched a spear from a dead Urikite and threw it in Caelum's direction. The weapon streaked to the ground about a yard behind the dwarf, striking something soft and fleshy. A man's voice cried out in pain, then an obsidian dagger clattered to the ground at the dwarf's heels.

Rikus peered over Caelum's shoulder and saw that his fighting partner had killed the bodyguard that had been knocked unconscious earlier. Apparently, the Urikite had been preparing to attack the dwarf from behind.

Caelum looked from the dying soldier to Neeva, his mouth opened in astonishment. "I've been saved by a queen!"

"Not quite," Rikus chuckled, motioning Neeva over.

She had no sooner joined them than Caelum seized her hands and fell to his knees. "You saved my life," he said, kissing her palms. "Now I give it to you."

"You can have it back," Neeva said, regarding the dwarf with an expression as amused as it was leery. She disentangled her hands, adding, "You'd do the same for me."

"For you, I would do that and much more," Caelum replied, still not rising. "You must accept my gift. I could not live if I did not repay you—"

"Maybe there's a way for you to do that," Rikus said, taking the dwarf by the arm and pulling him to his feet. "The mindbender who attacked me used his art to disappear. Can you find him for me?"

Tearing his red eyes away from Neeva, the dwarf shook his

head regretfully. "I can offer some protection from the Way, but my powers are those of sun. They are of little help in seeking out a mindbender who wishes to remain hidden—though I wish matters were otherwise. For what he did to our village, the Urikite must be punished."

"He will be," Rikus promised. "He'll pay for what he did to Kled, and for much, much more."

Tower of Buryn

Rikus's eyes were fixed on the hand of Caelum, which was glowing fiery red and smoking from the fingertips. It shone so brightly that it was translucent, save for the dark network of thick bones buried beneath the flesh.

"Hold him tightly," the dwarf said. "For its magic, the sun demands payment in pain."

Rikus pulled Gaanon into his lap, slipping his hands beneath his friend's massive arms and locking his thighs around the half-giant's thick waist. "You're sure this will work?" asked the mul.

Caelum glanced at the disk of flame hanging in the olive-tinged sky. "Each morning, do you also doubt that the sun will burn itself free of the Sea of Silt?"

"No, but this is—"

"May I proceed?" Caelum interrupted, using his free hand to point at his glowing palm. "This is quite as painful for me as it will be for your friend."

At the other end of Gaanon's long body, Neeva gripped an ankle under each of her muscular arms. "I'm ready."

Rikus nodded to Caelum, and the dwarf plunged two

smoking fingers into the half-giant's ulcerating wound. Tongues of light shot outward from the wound like the strands of a spiderweb. Gaanon's leg grew as translucent as Caelum's hand, his veins showing through his skin like thick cord.

The gladiator's eyes popped open. A thunderous bellow roared from his lips and echoed off the huts of Kled. He instinctively tried to sit up, and it took all of Rikus's abundant strength to hold him down. At the half-giant's ankles, Neeva repeatedly bounced on the flagstones as she struggled to keep his legs relatively motionless.

Gaanon pulled against Rikus's arms, trying to reach down and knock the dwarf away from his wound. The mul held him, but only barely. Keeping a wary eye on the screaming half-giant, Caelum continued to hold his fingers in the wound. Slowly, the color faded from his hand and the flesh once again grew opaque. When all the fire had left his fingers, the dwarf withdrew them and stuffed a wad of cloth into the freshly scorched puncture.

The half-giant's leg continued to glow, and Rikus fancied that he could even see tiny flames flickering along the sinews and veins. Gaanon stopped screaming and laid his head back in Rikus's arms. A moment later, he closed his eyes and fell to breathing in the heavy rhythms of deep slumber.

"It's safe to release him now," Caelum said. He secured the plug in the half-giant's thigh by wrapping a bandage around the leg, then glanced at Neeva. "You're very strong. Because you held him so well, my work was much easier than it could have been."

Neeva wrinkled her brow and did not reply, unsure of how to accept the compliment.

"What now?" Rikus asked, laying the half-giant's head on the ground. "Do we pour water down his throat?"

"Too soon," said Lyanius, shaking a crooked finger in Rikus's direction. The old dwarf, who wore a bloody bandage around his head, was the one who had spoken out to warn Rikus against surrendering. Lyanius was also Caelum's father and the village *uhrnomus*, a term that seemed to mean "grandfather" at some times but also, in a context of grave respect, "founder."

Lyanius took Rikus by the arm and guided the mul to his feet. "You will wait for a day before he awakens."

"A day?" Rikus gasped. "That's too much time."

K'kriq, who had been assigned leadership of the scouts, had already sent a runner to report that the survivors of the morning's combat were moving toward a large group of stragglers from the first battle. There was no sign that Maetan was with the Urikite army, but now that the legion had filled its waterskins, Rikus wanted to resume their pursuit as soon as possible.

"The sun will do its work in its own time," Caelum said. "I am sorry, but there is nothing I can do to hurry your friend's recovery."

"Cast another spell on him," the mul demanded. "Even if it takes you a few hours to look it up in your spellbook and memorize it again—"

"I am no sorcerer," the dwarf snapped, the corners of his mouth turned indignantly downward. "I am a cleric of the sun."

"What's the difference?" asked Neeva, placing herself between Rikus and the dwarf.

Caelum's expression softened when he spoke to her. "Sorcerers steal their magic from plants," he explained. "Mine is a gift of the sun. Using it takes nothing from any living thing."

"So why doesn't everybody use sun magic?" asked Jaseela, stepping to Neeva's side and peering at the blazing ball in the sky. "There's plenty of it, and everyone would benefit from magic that doesn't ruin the soil."

"Clerical magic is not something one takes, it is a gift

bestowed on those who commune with the elements," lectured Lyanius. The old dwarf waved his liver-spotted hand at the village. "Out of all these people who dwell beneath the sun, only Caelum has been favored with the fire-eyes."

"So your son can't do us any good," Rikus said, biting his lip in frustration.

"You mean more good than he already has," Neeva corrected, covering for the mul's inadvertent rudeness.

Caelum shook his head and looked at the ground. "I'm sorry. Of course, if you wish to leave the half-giant with the others . . ."

The dwarves had offered to take care of Tyr's wounded, but the mul was not anxious to leave a powerful fighter like Gaanon behind.

"We could use a rest," Jaseela said, pointing her chin toward the plaza. "The past few days may not have seemed a hardship to you, but it's been a true test of endurance for those of us who aren't muls."

Rikus looked over the rest of his legion. Most of his warriors were gathered around the cistern, wearily filling their waterskins or hiding beneath their cloaks in a vain effort to shield themselves from the sun.

The mul nodded. "You're right, Jaseela. Pass the word."

"Good," said Lyanius. "My people will pack supplies for your legion." The ancient dwarf motioned for Rikus to follow. "You will come with me."

"To where?" Rikus asked. "What for?"

Lyanius gave him a sour-faced scowl that made it clear the *uhrnomus* did not enjoy being questioned. After Rikus had averted his gaze, the old leader summoned a dwarven girl with a round face and twinkling eyes, then gave her a long series of instructions in the guttural language of his village. Rikus took the opportunity to call Styan over. The templar had been keeping his distance ever since the mul had summoned him and his men down from the arch.

"The dwarves are giving us supplies," Rikus said, laying his heavy arm across the templar's shoulders. "You and your men will carry them. If any of you opens a sack without my permission, I'll have all your heads."

"But—"

"If you don't like it, return to Tyr," Rikus snapped.

"You know I can't," Styan said, narrowing his ash-colored eyes. "I am to stay with the legion and report."

"Then follow my commands," Rikus replied. He fingered the pouch into which he had slipped the templar's crystal. "And the only reports Tithian receives will be those I send."

Styan gnashed his teeth, then asked, "Am I dismissed?"

In answer, Rikus removed his arm from the man's shoulder and looked away.

As the templar left, Lyanius took Rikus by the arm once more. "This way," he said, pulling the mul toward the far side of the village. "You come too, Caelum."

As the tall dwarf started after his father, he asked, "Are we going to Kemalok, *Urhnomus*?"

Lyanius nodded slowly, giving rise to astonished, though approving, murmurs from the throng of young dwarves that seemed to hang about him at all times.

"We must ask Neeva, as well," Caelum said, his voice as firm as his father's. "She saved my life, and fought as well against the Urikites as Rikus."

Lyanius fixed his sharp eyes on his son, scowling at his impudence. When the younger dwarf did not flinch under the harsh stare, the old dwarf sighed and said, "If it makes you happy, I will allow it."

Beaming, Caelum gestured to Neeva, then fell into step behind Rikus and his father. The old dwarf proceeded at a stately pace to the village wall, just below the great sand dune. There, a pair of dwarves stood guard. They were armed with steel battle-axes and stood to either side of a bronze-gilded door decorated with a bas-relief of a huge, serpent-headed bird. The beast's wings were outspread, its claws were splayed, and its snakelike head was poised to strike. The door itself stood slightly ajar, and Rikus could see that it opened into a deep tunnel that led beneath the dune.

"Why is this door open?" Lyanius demanded, addressing the two guards.

The young dwarves looked at each other uncomfortably, then one answered, "It was open when we returned to our posts after the battle."

Caelum frowned in concern. "How could the Urikites—"

The old dwarf raised a hand to cut off his son's question, then stared into the serpent-bird's eyes for several moments. Finally, he reported, "The door opened of its own accord."

"How often does it do that?" Rikus asked, concerned.

"Now and then," Lyanius answered, giving the mul a cryptic smile. "But I am not worried. Two Urikites did creep through after the door opened, but they will quickly regret their mistake."

"Why's that?" asked Neeva.

The old dwarf looked away without answering, then said, "Leave your weapons with the guards."

With that, the old dwarf looked up at the bird sculpture and gave a short, squawking whistle. The door creaked fully open, its hinges screeching so loudly that Rikus suspected the sound could be heard on the far side of Kled.

Somewhat reluctantly, Rikus and Neeva left their blades with the guards and followed Lyanius. The mul did not like being without his weapons, but it was clear the *urhnomus* would tolerate no arguments.

Inside the tunnel, Lyanius retrieved a pair of torches from the floor. Caelum lit them by simply passing his hand over the tops.

Lyanius eyed Neeva sourly, then said, "Three of us have no need of these." He was referring to the fact that, like elves, dwarves and muls were gifted with the ability to sense ambient heat when no other light source was present. "But because you're along at my son's request, young woman," he said, flashing her an unexpected smile, "we will use these anyway."

After handing one of the brands to his son, Lyanius led the way down a cool tunnel. To keep the sand from cascading in and burying the excavation, the passageway was lined with wide strips of animal hide, gray and cracked with age. This lining was supported by wooden beams, the ends of which rested on stone pillars. The narrow corridor was so low that Rikus and Neeva had to crawl to pass through it.

Just when Rikus was about to ask how much farther they had to go, the tunnel opened up into a small chamber. The path led to a small stone walkway that looked as though it had once been a bridge. Beside this causeway lay more than a dozen weapons of various materials. Several of them looked to be quite ancient, judging by the rot of their wooden handles or the yellowed brittleness of their bone blades.

Two of the weapons, however, were quite new. A pair of obsidian short swords lay to one side of the bridge, the white fingers of a man's lifeless hand still gripping the hilt of each weapon. The remainder of the bodies were not visible, having slowly sunk into the powdery sand that now filled the moat beneath the bridge. Still, Rikus had no doubt that the swordsmen wore the red tunic of Hamanu's soldiers, for the shape of their weapons was identical to those carried by the rest of the Urikite legion.

A deep, full-bellied laugh escaped Lyanius's lips and echoed off the still walls of the sandy cavern. "Heed the words of the ancients, or such will be your end," he said, leading the way across the bridge.

On the other end of the bridge, the small group stopped beneath the arched gateway of a magnificent stone wall. In-

scribed into the spandrel were several strange runes that
Rikus took to be the letters of a written language.

"Beyond this gate, place your trust in the strength of your
friendship, not the temper of your blade," translated
Lyanius, a crooked smile on his ancient lips.

The old dwarf led them to a gateway, where, a few feet
above Rikus's head, hung a portcullis of rusty-red iron. It
was supported by thick chains that disappeared through a
set of openings into the gatehouses that flanked the pathway.
The walls of these buildings were constructed of white marble, so finely cut and carefully fit together that even a sliver
of torchlight could not have slipped between them.

"Welcome to Kemalok, lost city of the dwarven kings,"
Lyanius said, waving his guests through the gate.

"I've never seen so much iron in one place," Neeva said,
running her gaze from the portcullis to the chains. "What
king could afford this?"

"What you see here is nothing compared to the wonders
of the keep," bragged Caelum. "Follow me."

The dwarf stepped beneath the portcullis. When Neeva
and Rikus tried to follow, a chest-high figure stepped from
around the gatehouse corner and blocked their path. It
wore a complete suit of black plate mail, trimmed at every
joint in silver and gold. In its hands the figure held a battle-
axe with a serrated blade of steel flecked with scintillating
lights, and its helm was capped by a jewel-studded crown
of gleaming white metal, the like of which Rikus had never
before seen.

As magnificent as the figure's armor was, it was the
thing's eyes that arrested Rikus's attention. The orbs were
all that was visible of a face swaddled in green bandages, and
they burned with a glow as yellow as the afternoon sky.

"Don't move!" commanded Caelum.

Rikus obeyed, as did Neeva. The mul had no idea what
the thing was, but he knew he did not wish to anger it.

"Rkard, last of the great dwarven kings," explained Lyanius, stepping back to them. He brushed past the mummified king as casually as he moved past his own son. "He means you no harm. Show him that you bear no weapons."

Rikus and Neeva did as Lyanius asked. When they faced forward again, Rkard stepped aside. As soon as the two gladiators passed, the ancient king again blocked the gate.

"Strange," mumbled Lyanius.

"Maybe there are more Urikites around," Rikus suggested, peering into the darkness on the other side of the moat.

"Don't be daft," the old dwarf snapped, pointing at the two obsidian swords stuck in the moat. The hands previously wrapped around the hilts had vanished completely. "Two Urikites came in, and two have died."

With that, Lyanius led the rest of the way through the gate. On the other side, a confusing warren of tunnels branched off in a dozen directions, leading down what had once been the grand avenues and hidden alleys of a sizable metropolis. The greatest part of Kemalok still lay buried under mounds of sand, but enough of it showed for Rikus to see that most of the buildings were constructed of granite block. The five-foot doors and narrow, chest-high windows left no doubt that this had, indeed, been a dwarven city.

Caelum guided them down the widest tunnel, while Lyanius explained, "I found Kemalok two hundred years ago."

"How?" Neeva asked.

"I happened upon a short section of parapet the wind had uncovered," Lyanius answered, a faintly amused smile on his wrinkled lips. "I knew instantly I had found a dwarven city from the time of the ancients. The merlons were too short for you people, and the stonecraft was far beyond anything the paltry masons of our age can achieve."

The old dwarf went on to describe the next century and a half of excavations, working alone at first, and eventually coming to be the leader of an entire village focused upon the eventual reestablishment of Kemalok. Rikus paid him only cursory attention. Instead, the mul listened for footfalls behind them and glanced over his shoulder every few steps. The fact that the door guarding this secret city had "opened of its own accord" set his nerves on edge, and he did not place much faith in Lyanius's body count.

Eventually they came to another bridge leading to a gate. This time, the bridge was made of wooden planks, now half-rotten and patched here and there with the wide, flat ribs of a mekillot. Caelum pushed open an immense set of iron doors, then led them through a short tunnel lined by chest-high arrow loops. On the other side, Lyanius's dwarves had dug a series of vaults, revealing the outer bailey of a great castle.

As they passed through this area, Rikus peered into the windows of what had been the shops and homes of the castle's smiths, tanners, fletchers, armorers, and a dozen other craftsmen. Their tools, made mostly from steel and iron, still hung in the racks where they had been neatly stored thousands of years ago. Rikus could not help gaping at the vast treasury of metal.

They passed through another gate and into the inner bailey. In the center of this courtyard, a square keep of white marble rose high overhead, the roof lost in the sand overhead. At each corner of the keep stood a round tower, its arrow loops commanding much of the courtyard below.

"This is the Tower of Buryn, home to dwarven kings for three thousand years." Lyanius proudly opened the doors.

"Three thousand years?" gasped Neeva. "How do you know?"

The old dwarf frowned at her as if she were a child. "I know," he answered, motioning her and Rikus inside.

On each side of the entrance foyer sat a pair of stone benches, one sized for the short legs of the dwarves and one for the longer legs of humans. In the corners stood full suits of dwarven plate, the shaft of a double-bladed battle-axe gripped in the armor's gauntlets. Both the armor and the weapons were made of polished steel, gleaming as brilliantly as the day they had been forged.

Remembering the greeting they had received at the city gates, Rikus cautiously studied the fantastic armor. Fortunately, behind the helms' visors he saw neither gleaming eyes nor anything but dark emptiness. Nevertheless, the mul did notice that the suits were too small for a dwarf. While they were about the right height, they were far from broad enough for the massive shoulders and bulging limbs typical of the dwarven race.

Noticing the mul's careful study of the armor, Lyanius said, "Our ancestors were not as robust as we are today." The old dwarf's cheeks reddened and he looked away. "They even had some hair," he added testily.

Neeva raised an eyebrow, and Rikus bit his lips to keep from showing his own aversion. Muls and dwarves generally prided themselves on their clean skin and scalps. The idea of having their bodies covered by a matted growth of sweaty hair was considered repulsive by most members of both races.

Caelum walked into the next open area, a huge hallway running the perimeter of the keep. The floor was arranged in a pattern of polished black and white squares. At even spaces along the walls, tall white columns supported the vaulted ceiling above. Between each set of arches was a mural painted directly onto the wall.

Neeva stepped over to the nearest and inspected it closely. "You don't exaggerate, do you Lyanius?" she asked. "When you said hair, I didn't imagine anything like this!"

Rikus joined her. The painting before Neeva portrayed a dwarf dressed in a full suit of golden plate armor, a huge war-club cradled in his arms. From beneath his golden crown cascaded a huge mop of unruly hair that hung well past his shoulders. That was not the worst of it, either. His face was lost beneath a thick beard that started just below his eyes and tumbled in a tangled mass clear down to his belly.

"Come along!" ordered Lyanius. "I didn't bring you here to mock my ancestors."

He hustled them down the hall, Caelum following close behind. As they passed the other murals, the mul saw that they, too, portrayed grossly bearded dwarves. The painting usually depicted dwarves standing in the somber halls of dimly lit keeps or in the dark chambers of some vast cave.

When he reached the last mural in the line, Rikus stopped. He had no doubt that the picture depicted the guardian of the city, King Rkard. Like the figure that had met them at the city gate, the dwarf in the painting had golden-yellow eyes and wore black plate mail trimmed in silver and gold. His helm was crowned by a jewel-studded crown of strange white metal. In his hands, the picture king even held a battle-axe identical to the one carried by the gate-guardian. The weapon's serrated blade was flecked by tiny sparkles of light.

As interesting as the king's picture was, it was the background that fascinated the mul. Behind Rkard, the ground sloped down a gentle hill blanketed by the green stalks and red blossoms of some broad-leafed plant Rikus did not recognize. At the bottom of this slope, a wide ribbon of blue water meandered through a series of lush meadows. In those fields grew food crops of every imaginable color and shape. In the far background of the painting, the river finally disappeared into a forest of billowing trees ranging in color from amber to russet to maroon. Behind this timberland rose a mountain range, its peaks and high slopes covered strangely with white.

"Rkard is the king who led our ancestors into the world," explained Lyanius.

"What world?" Rikus gasped, his eyes still fixed on the painting.

"This one, of course," Caelum answered, also studying the painting. "Don't let the mural mislead you. The artist must have been given to a certain amount of embellishment. Perhaps that green land is his idea of paradise—or maybe the afterworld."

"Not so," said Lyanius, his tone strangely morose. "Dwarven artists painted only what they saw."

"What do you mean?" asked Neeva, wrinkling her brow at the mural. "Who has ever seen anything like this? It is even more magnificent than the halfling forest!"

Lyanius looked away. "Come on," he grunted. "This is not what I brought you to see."

The dwarf led the way around the corner and down the corridor until they reached a bronze-gilded door with the bas-relief head of a bearded dwarf. The sculpture's blue eyes, made of painted glass, followed the movements of Lyanius and his guests as they approached.

Rikus and Neeva glanced at each other, uneasy at the sight of an animate sculpture.

Stopping in front of the door, Lyanius spoke to the head at length, using a strange language of short, clipped syllables. When he finished, the unblinking eyes studied Rikus and Neeva for several moments, looking them up and down. Finally the head's metal lips began to move, and it replied to Lyanius's query in the same staccato tongue. The door swung open.

As the door moved, Rikus heard the faintest scuffle in the hallway behind them. "Did anyone else hear that?" he asked.

Lyanius frowned. "I'm certain it was just the echo of the door opening."

Nevertheless, the old dwarf passed his torch to Rikus. Motioning for the others to stay behind, Lyanius shuffled down

the corridor into the murky blackness, where his dwarven vision would not be nullified by the light of the torches.

"Shouldn't we go with him?" Rikus asked.

"Not if you value your life," answered Caelum. "My father is quite touchy about taking care of himself."

They waited for what seemed an eternity before Lyanius
stepped silently out of the shadows. "There's nothing
there," he said irritably. "Probably just a wrab."

"Wrab?" asked Neeva.

"A tiny, flying serpent," explained Caelum.

"Filthy blood drinkers," added Lyanius, stepping through
the door he had opened earlier. "Normally, they're as quiet
as death, but every now and then they bump into something."

Frowning, Rikus peered back down the corridor. When he
saw nothing to contradict what the old dwarf had said, he
followed the others into a small room. It was lit by a flaxen
glow of ambient light that issued from no apparent source,
yet filled the chamber like a haze. In the center of the room,
an open book hovered in midair, as though it were resting on
a table that Rikus could not see.

"I wanted you to know that when you saved Kled, you
saved more than a village," said Lyanius, motioning at the
book proudly.

Its binding was of gold-trimmed leather, and the long
columns of angular characters on its parchment pages
glowed with a green light of their own. In the margins,
brightly painted pictures of horned beasts moved before
Rikus's eyes, grazing or leaping as though they still roamed
the glens in which the artist had first seen them.

Despite the magical pictures in the book, Rikus was more
interested in what he could not see. Passing his hand first
under, then over the tome, he asked, "What holds it up?"

"What holds it up?" snapped Lyanius. "I show you the
Book of the Kemalok Kings, and you ask about the mechanics

of a simple enchantment?"

"I've never had much interest in books. There's little time to learn reading in the slave pens," the mul said, self-consciously shifting his attention back to the volume.

"Neither can I—at least not this book," answered Lyanius, calming. "It was written in the language of our ancestors. I have learned to translate only a little of it, enough to know that this volume tells the history of Kemalok."

"That's—ah—interesting," Rikus said, glancing at Neeva to see if she understood why Lyanius placed so much import on bringing them here.

"I think Rikus will find the Great Hall more to his interest, *Urhnomus*," Caelum said, noticing Rikus's puzzled expression. "What matters is not that our friends understand the importance of what they did, but that they kept the *Book of Kings* out of Urikite hands."

Caelum's words calmed the old dwarf. "You're very wise for someone yet under a hundred," he said, nodding proudly.

After they left the little room, the bas-relief head spoke briefly to Lyanius, then the door closed of its own accord. The old dwarf led his friends farther down the corridor and turned another corner. This time, they stopped before a pair of massive wooden doors so infested with dry rot that Rikus was surprised they still hung on their hinges.

Despite the deterioration of the doors, the strange animals carved into each one remained handsome and distinct. The snarling beasts resembled bears, save that, instead of the articulated shells armoring the creatures Rikus had fought, these were covered with nothing more protective than a thick mat of long fur. The mul wondered if the carvings depicted some gentler breed that the ancient dwarves had kept as pets.

As Lyanius stepped toward the great doors, they swung open, revealing a magnificent chamber so large that the

torches could not light it from one side to the other. Still, as
the four wandered around the perimeter, the mul saw that it
had once been a great feast hall. From the walls hung dozens
of steel weapons of all sizes and sorts, interspersed with huge
murals vibrant in color and stroke. These paintings depicted
either scenes of romance between a handsome dwarven noble and his beautiful lady-love, or valiant struggles in which
lone dwarven knights vanquished giants, four-headed ser-
pents, and dozens of red-eyed man-beasts.

Lyanius led the way to the front of the room, then asked
Rikus to stand before the great banquet table located there.
The mul cast a dubious glance in Neeva's direction, but did
as the old dwarf wished. Lyanius handed his torch to his son
and disappeared into the darkness.

For several moments, the aged dwarf rummaged around
the perimeter of the room, banging shields and axes about.
Finally he returned to the trio with a black belt slung over
his shoulder and a steel sword in his arms. He laid the belt
on the table, then faced Rikus with the long sword and
slapped the mul's left arm with the flat of the blade.

"In the name and presence of the one hundred and fifty
kings of the ancient dwarven race, I acknowledge your bravery and skill in driving the Urikite invaders from the gates of
Kemalok," Lyanius said, giving Rikus a stern smile and
slapping the mul's other arm. "I name you a Knight of the
Dwarven Kings, and present you with this weapon of magic, the Scourge of Rkard."

As the old dwarf held the weapon out to him, Rikus's jaw
dropped open. "Won't carrying a weapon in Kemalok anger
Rkard?" he gasped. "Especially when it's his?"

"This isn't Rkard's weapon," Lyanius answered, the corners of his mouth turning down. "It's the blade that inflicted his last wound, the one that killed him. As for Kemalok's
law—guests are forbidden to carry weapons, but you are no
longer a guest. You are a knight of the city."

As soon as Rikus's hand touched the weapon's hilt, his mind began to whirl in confusion. Suddenly he could hear his companions' hearts pounding in his ears like the drums of a Gulgian war party, and their breathing sounded to him like a dust typhoon storming its way across the Sea of Silt. From behind Rikus came the harsh grate of huge claws scratching across stone. The mul instinctively leaped to his feet and spun around, only to discover the sound had been caused by a black beetle scurrying across the floor several yards away.

No sooner had he relaxed from this strange sound than he heard the throb of wrab wings beating the air outside the great hall. Shoving past Neeva and Caelum, he rushed to the chamber doors and pushed them shut. The creak of their hinges rang in his ears and ran down his spine like a lightning bolt. The deafening crack of the clicking latch nearly knocked him from his feet. An instant later, the wrab alighted on the outside of the door with a deep rumble. A series of terrific rasps echoed through the wood as it searched for a crack. Rikus shook his head and stumbled back from the doors, raising the Scourge of Rkard to defend himself.

As the gleaming blade came into view, the mul's confused mind slowly began to make sense of the situation. The sword was magic, he realized. With it, he could hear any nearby sound as though it were made by a giant right next to his ear.

"Rikus, what's wrong?"

Neeva's concerned voice boomed through his head like a thunderclap, scattering the thoughts he had just managed to collect. The sharp pain that shot through his ear made him cry out. At last Rikus dropped the sword, then fell to his knees.

"What's the matter with him?" Neeva demanded. Her words still pained the mul's ears, though they no longer seemed as loud as they had a moment ago.

"Rikus, pick up the sword again," ordered Lyanius. "I should have warned you about what to expect and told you how to control the magic."

When Rikus did not reach for the sword, the old dwarf shuffled toward him.

"I don't think I want that sword," Rikus said, glancing fearfully at the blade.

Lyanius stopped next to him. "Pick up the sword," the dwarf whispered. "Concentrate on one sound, and the others will fade. You will find that it is a useful thing to have."

Reluctantly Rikus obeyed, focusing his thoughts on the old dwarf's breathing. To his surprise, all of the other sounds faded to mere background noise. He remained aware of them, but they no longer reverberated through his head or hurt his ears. Unfortunately, the old dwarf's breathing still sounded like the roar of the Dragon to him.

"Now, while concentrating on the sound you picked, speak in a normal tone of voice," Lyanius said.

Keeping his attention fixed on the old dwarf's breathing, Rikus answered, "Fine. What now?"

The rush of air into and out of the old dwarf's lungs faded to the volume of his own voice, and Rikus found he could think again.

"Now come with me," Lyanius said.

Rikus stood and followed the dwarf back to the banquet table. "Does the sword do anything else?"

"I don't know," Lyanius answered. "I've seen it mentioned in the *Book of Kings*, but I can't read enough of the entry to know all the weapon's possible powers."

As Lyanius spoke, Rikus adjusted his magically augmented hearing by concentrating on the dwarf's words. "Thank you for the blade. This is a great honor."

"We're not done yet," said the old dwarf, taking the black belt off the table.

Lyanius held the belt out to Rikus, its stiff leather crackling like pebbles falling on cobblestones. The thing was so wide it was almost a girdle. The buckle was hidden by a field of red flames, with the skull of a fierce half-man in the center.

"This is the Belt of Rank," Lyanius said, strapping the belt around the mul's waist.

Rikus stepped away, asking, "What does it do?"

His question brought a chuckle to the old dwarf's lips. "There is no need to worry," Lyanius said. "Its magic is not as intrusive as that of the Scourge of Rkard. For three thousand years, this belt was passed from one dwarven general to the next, a symbol of authority over all the armies of the dwarves."

"Why are you giving it to me?" Rikus asked, allowing the old dwarf to fasten it about his waist.

"Because you are the only knight worthy of it."

"In fact, you're the only knight," Caelum added. "There is no one else to wear it."

Rikus was about to thank the old dwarf again when he heard an alarmed cry echo from the other side of the closed doors. Though he could not understand the words, he recognized the voice as that of the glass-eyed sculpture on the door where the *Book of Kings* was stored.

"The book!" he exclaimed, turning toward the doors.

"What about it?" gasped Caelum.

"The door just screamed," he shouted, motioning for Lyanius to follow him.

Before he could explain further, the mul heard Maetan's bitter voice cry out in surprise. A loud boom followed the mindbender's yell.

When Rikus reached the doors to the hall, they opened of their own accord. The wrab that had been clinging to them took flight and swooped down on the mul, but he swatted the nasty little beast from the air before it came close to striking him.

Rikus turned down the corridor and heard the door
scream again. There was another explosion, the sound
ringing in the corridor and making everyone's ears ache.
The mul took off at a sprint, trusting to his companions to
follow.

After the violent explosion, the keep fell ominously silent.
To the mul, it seemed to take forever to retrace their steps.
The corridor was much longer than he remembered, and his
frustration was compounded by mistakenly turning into several alcoves that looked similar to the one where the book
was safeguarded.

Finally he reached the correct alcove, and this time he had
no doubt that he had found the right one. In front of it lay
the inert figure of King Rkard, the heft of his great axe
snapped in two and his black armor dented and scorched
from an explosion. Rikus reluctantly peered into the helm
and saw that the green cloth swaddling the king's face had
been burned away. Now only a charred skull, half-covered
by taut leathery skin, peered out from beneath the visor.

As the mul studied Rkard's face, a yellow light began to
glimmer deep within the corpse's eye sockets. Not wishing
to be the first thing that the king saw when he returned to
awareness, Rikus moved away and turned toward the chamber where the book was stored.

The bronze-gilded door hung off its hinges, twisted and
mangled as though a giant had kicked it open. The bas-
relief's glass eyes had been ripped from the face and now lay
shattered on the stone floor.

Lyanius came up behind Rikus, then rushed into the room
and let out an anguished scream. "It's gone!"

"What happened?" Caelum asked. "Who could have
done this?"

"Maetan," Rikus answered, looking down the long corridor.

Neeva rushed up behind them, her torch casting a flickering circle of yellow light over the small group. She did not need to ask what had happened.

Lyanius hurried out of the room and grabbed Rikus's hand. "You must find him! That book is the history of my people!"

As the old dwarf spoke, King Rkard's corpse rose to his feet and looked around as if searching for something, paying no attention to Rikus or his companions.

The mul stepped away from the others. "Quiet. I'll use the sword to track Maetan."

For several moments, the mul gripped the hilt of his new sword, listening to the sounds of the ancient dwarven city. He could hear the nervous breathing of his companions, the occasional squeak of metal as Rkard changed positions, even the soft hiss of the torches they had left behind in the great hall—but he did not detect the faintest hint of Maetan's presence.

"He's gone," Rikus said at last.

Lyanius groaned and buried his face in his hands. "How?"

"The Way," Neeva answered.

Rikus rested the sword tip-down on the sand-strewn floor, a look of grim determination on his face. "I'll recover the book," he said. "Even if I have to chase Lord Lubar all the way to Urik."

"I'll come with you," Caelum said forcefully. "And so will many of the village's young dwarves. There are many who would make this quest their focus."

Rikus nodded. "Your help will be welcome."

Lyanius's eyes lit up. As if to prove his newfound champion was not simply a cruel illusion left by the thief of his priceless book, the old dwarf reached out and touched the mul's arm. "Can you do it?"

"Think before you answer, Rikus," Neeva said. "Don't promise something you can't deliver."

In answer, Rikus placed a hand on the Belt of Rank, then started toward the exit. "We start for Urik in an hour."

"You haven't earned that belt yet, my love."

Though Neeva whispered the words beneath her breath, to Rikus they boomed as loudly as the magical explosions Maetan had used to defeat Rkard and capture the *Book of the Kemalok Kings*.

FIVE

Wrog's Ring

"Keep a watch, and I will search out someone to be my spy," said Maetan, tucking his frail body between a pair of wind-scoured boulders.

"I do not relish being invoked for such mundane tasks," objected Umbra. In the flaxen light of Athas's twin moons, the shadow giant was hardly distinguishable from the more natural darkness surrounding him.

"Until I avenge my honor against Rikus and his Tyrians, no task is mundane!" snapped Maetan. "Do as I command —or does the Black no longer value my family's obsidian?"

A wisp of ebon-colored gas rose from Umbra's down-turned mouth. "Your stone has value, but someday you will overestimate its worth," he snarled, peering up at the pale moons. "A shadow needs light to give it shape and substance. It pains me to serve you in such conditions."

"If I do not present these slaves to King Hamanu in shackles, my family name will be shamed," Maetan said. "Do you think I care about your pain?"

"No more than I care about your honor," Umbra replied, creeping away to do as Maetan ordered. His dark form fused with the other shadows mottling the hillside.

Maetan turned his attention to the sandy gulch below. There, surrounded by a tight picket of drowsy sentries, the Tyrian legion was camped.

The gladiators rested at the mouth of the gully, scattered in a disarrayed jumble wherever they could find a soft place. A short distance up the draw, the retainers of some noble lay clustered in cordial groups of ten or twelve warriors, many of which were still conversing in polite tones. Close to them, the dwarves of Kled slept in regimented circles, each dwarf lying flat on his back within an arm's reach of the next one.

Farthest up the gulch slumbered the templars, their cassocks tightly fastened against the frigid desert night. They had arranged themselves in a pyramid, those most favored lying closest to the leader, and those least favored spread along the bottom edge. Maetan did not understand why the Tyrians had sent along the bureaucrats. With Kalak dead, the templars had no sorcerer-king to grant them spells, and they would be no more useful in battle than average tradesmen.

"It matters little," the mindbender told himself. "When the time comes, they will die with the rest."

With that, he gathered a fistful of sand, then held it over the outstretched palm of the other hand. Slowly, Maetan let the grains slip from between his fingers. At the same time, he used the Way to summon a stream of mystic energy from deep within himself, and he gently breathed this life force into the sand as it dropped from one hand to the other.

When he finished, a naked, finger-length figure stood in the palm of his hand. She whipped her barbed tail back and forth, blinking her soft green eyes and giving her tiny wings a languid stretch.

Maetan lifted his hand toward the Tyrian camp. "Go, my darling, and look into their nightmares. Find one who will betray his fellows, one who yearns for wealth beyond his grasp, perhaps, or one who fears his master."

The homunculus smiled, showing a pair of needlelike fangs, then flapped her wings and rose into the air.

"When you have succeeded," Maetan said, "return to me and I will make him ours."

*   *   *   *   *

Etched into the cliffside, far above Rikus's head, was the image of a kes'trekel. The giant raptor's barbed tongue coiled from its hooked beak, and it held its claws splayed open. The creature's ragged wings were spread wide to catch the wind, and at the elbows of these wings were small, three-fingered hands. In one hand it held a bone scythe, and in the other it carried a furled whip of bone and cord.

"How'd they get up there to carve that?" Rikus asked, his eyes searching the cliffside.

"Why would they bother?" returned Neeva, looking away from the rock-etching. "Kes'trekels are hardly a subject for art. They're nothing but overgrown carrion-eaters."

"Kes'trekels may be death-followers, but they're also as vicious as halflings, as cunning as elves, and some are as large as half-giants," Caelum said, still craning his neck to study the depiction. "I'd take this engraving as a warning."

Along with Styan, who remained stolidly silent, the three stood in a barren canyon flanked by towering cliffs of hard, yellow quartzite. The gorge was so deep and narrow that just a sliver of the olive-tinged sky showed overhead. Only the sweltering heat and a blush of crimson light on the canyon's rim indicated that the morning sun already hung high in the sky.

Above the kes'trekel, someone had chiseled a huge hollow into the cliffside. A warren of mudbrick compartments had been constructed inside this alcove. From the outside, Rikus could see little of the burrow except a wall several stories high, plastered with lime-paste and speckled with square windows. At the base of this wall, a part of the warren overhung the valley. In the center of this section was a large circular opening.

"I'd say that's where our warriors disappeared to," Rikus said, motioning at the overhang.

Neeva looked around the canyon. "I don't see anywhere else they might have gone," she agreed. "You think both K'kriq and the scouts you sent after him are up there?"

"That's my guess," the mul said.

At dusk the night before, the legion had made camp in a sandy gulch at the mouth of a narrow canyon. Since thri-kreen have no need of sleep, Rikus had sent K'kriq ahead to scout the next day's route. The mantis-warrior had not returned by first light, so the mul had sent five gladiators to look for him. When that group had not come back either, Rikus had entered the canyon to investigate for himself. He had brought Neeva and Caelum along in case he ran into trouble. Surprisingly, Styan had asked to accompany them.

After two miles of slow travel, the cliff-huts were the only unusual thing the group had seen in the valley.

"How will we reach the doorway?" Caelum asked, eyeing the sheer cliff beneath the opening.

"Why would we want to?" Styan demanded, speaking for the first time. He glared openly at Rikus. "It's enough that you ignore Caelum's advice and cross these badlands, but to risk *our* lives for a thri-kreen and a few warriors—"

"They'd do it for us," the mul answered gruffly. "As for crossing the hills, it's the only way to reach the oasis ahead of Maetan."

K'kriq had seen Maetan traveling with a large group of Urikite soldiers. They were moving around a tongue of rocky badlands that jutted several miles into the sand wastes. From what the thri-kreen had reported, the mind-bender's company was traveling toward a brackish pool of water where a handful of Urik's infamous halfling rangers had stopped to rest. Determined to reach the oasis ahead of his enemy, Rikus had led his legion into the winding canyons and contorted ridges of the badland foothills.

Before the legion could continue its journey, however, Rikus had to find out what had happened to K'kriq and the other scouts. He dropped a hand to the sword hanging from his new belt. As the mul's fingers closed around the Scourge's hilt, a dozen discordant sounds crashed over his mind in a deafening tumult. His ears were filled with the thunder of beating hearts and the roar of the morning breeze. From distant caves came the rumble of chirping crickets, and the piercing drone of his warriors' impatient conversations echoed up from the canyon mouth.

Rikus felt sick and dizzy at the torrent of noise. He wanted nothing quite so much as to shut it away, but he forced himself to hang onto the sword and search out the sounds coming from the warren. Finally, he managed to distinguish a stream of wispy voices gushing from the hole above. Concentrating on those sounds, the mul asked quietly, "Who are you? What have you done with my scouts?"

Of course, the voices did not answer, but the other sounds faded to the point that he could concentrate on what was being said inside the warren. Rikus quickly discerned that there were well over a dozen men and women watching him from above, most asking concerned questions of someone named Wrog. In the background, he could hear a faint clacking noise that sounded like K'kriq gnashing his mandibles.

Taking his hand from his sword hilt, Rikus called, "Wrog! Return my scouts and I'll leave in peace."

They waited a few moments for a response. When none came, Neeva asked, "Who's Wrog?"

Rikus shrugged. "A name. I thought—"

A terrified scream interrupted him. He looked up and saw a man, arms flailing wildly, drop from the opening overhead. In anger, Rikus reached for the Scourge of Rkard. Instantly, he heard many voices roaring in laughter.

The falling man plummeted toward the mul for what seemed like an hour. A half-giant's height from the rocky ground, his terrified scream ended with a pained shout as his descent stopped. For several moments, the man hung motionless and silent in midair. To the amazement of the mul and his companions, there was no sign of a rope, or any other line, between the faller and the hole from which he had come. The unfortunate fellow simply dangled a few yards off the ground with no visible means of support.

Recognizing the gladiator, Rikus exclaimed, "Laban!"

"Are you injured?" asked Neeva.

"I'm more frightened than hurt," came the shaky reply.

As Laban spoke, he began to descend more slowly. The half-elf's normally robust complexion was the color of salt, his peaked eyebrows were arched much more than normal, and his bloodshot eyes bulged halfway from their sockets. Otherwise, Laban seemed remarkably composed and well for a man who had just fallen several hundred feet.

When the gladiator descended to within reach, Neeva took him by the shoulders and helped him to his feet. "Wrog sent me down to invite you to the nest," he said. He pointed at the dark circle in the bottom of the warren. "Stand under the door, and he'll bring you up."

"What sort of people are these, Laban?" Rikus asked, moving into position.

"They call themselves the Kes'trekels," the half-elf answered. "They're a slave tribe."

"Good," Rikus said. "It won't be hard to work things out."

"Don't be too sure," Laban said. He gestured at the mul's sword. "He said no weapons."

Rikus frowned, then unsheathed his sword and held it out to Neeva. "You know what to expect from the Scourge?" he asked.

She cast a wary eye at the blade, but nodded. "I was there when Lyanius gave it to you."

As soon as her hand touched the hilt, Neeva's eyes rolled back in her head. "Quiet!" she screamed, dropping to her knees.

At the same time, Rikus began to rise at a steady rate. "Listen to my voice," Rikus said. "You'll be able to hear what I say up there."

In answer, Neeva screamed.

As he ascended, Rikus continued speaking to Neeva, giving her advice on how to control the sword's powers. At first, she dropped the weapon and covered her ears. A moment later, she picked it up again and held onto it.

"That's better," Rikus said. "If you're able to control the blade, at least a little, and can hear me, step toward Laban."

Neeva continued to glare at the mul, but did as asked. Breathing a sigh of relief, Rikus looked toward the warren, studying it and its surroundings. The nest was much higher off the ground than he had realized. His companions, now far below, seemed no larger than his thumbs, and their forms were shrinking at a steady pace. By the time he neared the warren's entrance, he knew why the slave tribe had chosen this place for their aerie. It was the highest accessible spot in the gorge. Long sections of canyon floor were visible in both directions. Even without a formal watch, the Kes'trekel tribe would have a good chance of seeing intruders from the windows of their homes.

More importantly, the nest afforded a view of both ends of the canyon. At the mouth of the gorge, a dark blotch of tiny figures—the Tyrian legion—waited in a field of orange and brown rocks. In the other direction, the ravine cut through the badland ridges like a great sword gash, running more or less in a straight line to the yellow dunes of the sand wastes beyond. It was exactly the shortcut the mul needed to beat Maetan to the next oasis.

Rikus reached the nest entrance and a dark shadow fell over his shoulders. As he drifted up past the floor, the mul was temporarily blinded as his eyes adjusted to the dim light. The clammy room stank of sweat and unbathed bodies, though the tangy scent of fresh silverbush helped mask the stench.

"Do I know you?" growled a throaty voice. The mul took it to be Wrog's.

Rikus looked up and saw the hulking form of a huge half-man silhouetted against the scarlet light of a window. The shadowy figure stood easily two heads taller than the mul, with a body both more massive and more heavily muscled. Wrog held one hand over Rikus's head. The glint of gold on one finger suggested that an enchanted ring provided the magic that had levitated him into the room.

"I'm Rikus," the mul said. By the whispers of recognition rustling through the group, he guessed that at least some of the escaped slaves in the large chamber knew him from his days in the arena at Tyr.

Wrog glanced around the room. "It appears I should be impressed." After a short pause, he added, "I'm not."

As his eyes grew accustomed to the dimness, the mul saw that Wrog was a lask, one of the new races periodically born in the deep desert. His leathery hide, mottled orange and gray, would serve as excellent camouflage in the rocky barrens that covered much of Athas. The hands that hung at the end of the half-man's gangling arms had only three fingers and a thumb, all of which ended in sharp claws. Wrog's head was flat and squarish, with a crest of golden points rising from a mass of wrinkled skin. His large, orange-rimmed eyes were set above a thick, boxlike muzzle, from which protruded a pair of sturdy golden fangs, slightly curved inward like an insect's pincers. In Rikus's days as a gladiator, the lask might have been an interesting challenge.

Now, however, the mul was interested only in winning Wrog's friendship. Rikus stepped to the wooden floor. Glancing around the chamber, he saw nearly thirty escaped slaves of all races. Many had ghastly scars on their hands and legs, no doubt earned in the obsidian quarries of Urik.

Scattered in a dozen places around the room were archers armed with long, double-curved bows. They all held obsidian-tipped arrows nocked on their bowstrings, and peered down at Neeva and her companions through small openings in the floor.

In one corner lay K'kriq. The thri-kreen was tightly wrapped in a net of red, thorn-covered cords. Rikus was surprised to see that his friend had actually shredded part of the mesh, for the mul had often used similar snares in the arena and knew them to be all but unbreakable and uncuttable. The strands were made from the tendrils of an elven rope, a contorted mass of cactus that lashed out with its needle-covered tentacles to entwine careless animals and draw their life-giving fluids from their bodies.

Although K'kriq's arms and legs were pinned to his sides, four men surrounded him, their obsidian-tipped spears ready to thrust at the slightest movement. Nearby kneeled the rest of the Tyrian scouts, their hands bound and their mouths gagged with tanned snakeskins. Although a few had suffered minor cuts and bruises, it appeared their captors had not mistreated them severely.

After inspecting the room, Rikus looked back to Wrog. "You didn't hurt my warriors, so there's no need for trouble between us. Use your magic to let us down safely and we'll be on our way."

Wrog lifted his upper lip in what could have been a sneer or a smile. "I can't do that," he said. "You and your warriors can stay here with us, or leave on your own." He peered through the hole in the floor meaningfully. "The choice is yours."

The mul narrowed his eyes. "There's no reason to start a fight with us. We're from Tyr, the Free City. All we intend to do is march through your canyon and catch Maetan of Urik on the far side."

"What for?" asked a crusty old dwarf. He had a horrible red scar running across both of his forearms.

"To kill him," Rikus answered. "Lord Lubar led an army against Tyr, and now he'll pay with his life."

Many of those in the room uttered approving comments, which did not surprise the mul. In addition to its gladiatorial pits, Family Lubar owned the largest quarrying concession in Urik. No doubt, many slaves in the large chamber had been raised in the grimy Lubar pens.

"I say we let them go," said the old dwarf. "We've all heard about the rebellion in Tyr. The Kes'trekels have nothing to fear from a legion of theirs."

Several of those marked by grisly quarry scars voiced their agreement, but many others shouted them down. Wrog looked at the contentious group with one eye narrowed. After studying them for a moment, he turned back to the mul.

"When it comes to Maetan of Family Lubar, I don't think you'll be the one who does the killing, Rikus," Wrog said, spitting the mul's name out disdainfully. "To send a scout up our canyon was smart. It saved your legion from being ambushed. Dispatching a second group to meet the same fate as the thri-kreen wasn't so smart. But coming yourself, that was stupid—even for a mul."

"We value each of our warriors, as well we might," Rikus countered hotly. "We've already defeated a Urikite legion five times our size." The mul did not add that they could defeat a slave tribe just as easily, though his glare carried the unspoken threat.

Wrog's orange-rimmed eyes showed more anger than concern. "You would find the Kes'trekels a more cunning enemy," the lask replied. "If you value the lives of your warriors as dearly as you claim, you have but one choice: join our tribe. Try to do anything else, and I will destroy your legion as you say you destroyed the Urikites."

Only the knowledge that starting a fight could result in the quick deaths of K'kriq and his other four scouts kept the mul from lashing out at Wrog. Despite his growing anger, Rikus realized that fighting was not the best way to solve this problem. Even if he managed to escape the nest with K'kriq and the four gladiators, he would lose too many warriors trying to fight through the slave tribe's narrow canyon. He had to find a better way.

"If it comes to a fight between your tribe and my legion, both of us will lose more warriors than we like," the mul said, swallowing his pride. Deciding to take a bold risk, he continued, "Instead, we should fight together."

"Why should we risk our lives for Tyr?" Wrog demanded, his voice haughty and disdainful.

"For a home in the Free City," the mul answered, looking around the chamber. "If you fight with us, you'll receive land and protection from slave-takers."

Before any of his followers could voice their opinions, Wrog spat out an answer. "Land will do us no good. We are not farm slaves," he sneered. "As for slave-takers, we have less reason to fear them here than we would in your city. So far, Urik's legions have not found our nest. They can find your city readily enough."

"You have nothing to offer us," said a young, red-haired man. The area around his eyes was covered by a pair of star-shaped tattoos.

"Iron," said K'kriq. The thri-kreen's guards tapped his shell with their speartips, but the mantis-warrior paid them no attention. "Slave tribes like iron."

Rikus smiled. "K'kriq is right," he said. "Tyr can pay you in iron."

Even Wrog could not ignore this offer. "How much?"

"One pound per week, for every hundred warriors who join us," Rikus answered.

"I'm with you," said the man with the tattooed eyes.

"Me, too," said a female mul. Her face was only slightly less rugged than Rikus's, and when she grinned she showed a mouthful of teeth filed to needle-sharp points. "I could use a good axe-blade."

As several others also announced their intentions to join the Tyrians, Wrog studied Rikus with a suspicious air. Finally he said, "We accept your offer, but only if you prove your readiness to pay such a high price."

"You have my promise," Rikus said.

"You can't make an axe out of a promise," growled the female mul.

The man with the tattooed eyes also withdrew his offer, as did the others who had pledged their support.

Angered by the sudden change of mood, Rikus scowled. "If anyone doubts that my word is good—"

"Show us the iron," Wrog interrupted, his upper lip raised in his peculiar imitation of a smile. "Then we will not doubt your promise."

"No legion carries raw iron with it," the mul snapped.

"What of your weapons?" asked Wrog.

"My warriors' blades are not mine to pledge," Rikus answered. "Besides, we have only a few steel weapons."

There were more than a few sighs of disappointment, but no one suggested taking the mul at his word. Wrog smirked at Rikus, then pointed at the nest's exit. "That leaves your original decision. Stay or jump."

Or fight, Rikus added silently. He did not like the third option any better than the first two. Even for him, it would be difficult to destroy so many opponents before the escaped slaves killed K'kriq and the four gladiators. Not even Neeva and her companions would survive long enough to flee, for the mul did not doubt that Wrog would order his archers to fire as soon as a fight broke out.

Realizing that he had nothing left to lose, Rikus decided to chance a desperate gamble. "If the king of Tyr promises to pay the iron I offered, will you join my legion?"

"How can he do that?" Wrog demanded. "Is he with you?"

"He's in Tyr," Rikus answered. "Will you agree?"

Wrog started to shake his head, but the man with the painted eyes interrupted him. "The caravan slaves say this Tithian is a king of the enslaved. They say he freed them from their noble masters, and that he lets them drink from his wells for free. If such a man promises, I'll fight."

One by one, the man's fellows echoed his sentiments, and at last Wrog nodded his square head.

The mul reached into his belt pouch and withdrew the olivine he had taken from Styan. "With this crystal, you'll hear and see King Tithian," he explained.

Wrog narrowed his flaxen eyes. "I know better than to trust a sorcerer," he said. "You could be tricking me."

"I'm no sorcerer," Rikus snapped. He pointed at the lask's ring. "You have your ring, I have my gem."

When Wrog did not object to this line of reasoning, Rikus held the olivine out at arm's length and stared into it. A moment later, Tithian's face appeared inside the green depths of the gem. The king was wearing the golden diadem he had taken from Kalak, and there was scowl of displeasure on his heavy lips. From the angle of the king's narrow stare, it appeared that he was staring down at someone who was either kneeling or lying at his feet.

Rikus did not hesitate to interrupt him. "Mighty King."

Tithian's liver-colored eyes looked up and his mouth fell open in shock. "Rikus!" he hissed. "You're alive!"

"Of course," the mul responded.

Before he could continue, Tithian continued, "What of

Agis and the others?"

"Haven't you heard from them?" Rikus asked. According to his estimates, the pair should have reached Tyr several days past. "After we smashed the Urikite legion, Neeva and I went to chase the enemy commander. Agis and Sadira went back. . . ."

The mul let the sentence trail off, realizing that Agis and Sadira might have elected to keep their return secret.

Unfortunately, Rikus's slip was not lost on Tithian. "If they have returned to the city, it is unfortunate they did not elect to announce their arrival. I would have liked to prepare a proper reception," the king said, an angry glint in his eye. "Now, tell me what you want."

The mul explained the arrangement he was trying to work out with the Kes'trekel slave tribe. Although he knew better than to think Tithian would help him personally, Rikus hoped the king would realize that killing Maetan would make Tyr—and therefore himself—more secure.

When the mul finished his explanation, Tithian ran a thin finger along his hawkish nose. "I'd like to do as you ask, but how do you expect me to pay for your iron?" Although the mul could hear the words clearly, anyone not holding the gem could neither see Tithian's face nor hear his words. "The city's iron is already pledged to various merchant houses, and I can hardly afford to buy it back. You know that the Council of Advisors has rejected all edicts designed to replenish the royal treasury."

Under his breath, Rikus cursed the king as a blackmailer and a thief. Nevertheless, when he spoke, his tone was respectful and courteous. The slave tribe could hear his end of the conversation and he didn't want to alarm them. "I'm sure we can solve that problem, Mighty King."

Tithian smiled. "Then you'll support an edict to place me in sole control of Tyr's revenues?"

"It won't cost that much!" the mul snapped.

Tithian smirked. "Sole control. I really must insist."

The mul cursed, realizing that he had no choice except to resort to one of the king's favorite tactics: lie. Hardly able to keep from snarling, Rikus said, "I agree."

Tithian studied the mul with narrowed eyes. At last, he said, "Very well. Pass the gem to this Wrog."

"Use magic or the Way, whatever you did when you appeared in the sky at our first battle." Rikus was not anxious to trust a gem, much less a magical one, to the leader of the slave tribe.

A look of embarrassment crossed Tithian's face. "That's not possible," he said. "The individuals who helped with that aren't available. If you want me to talk to Wrog, you'll have to give him the gem."

Rikus reluctantly passed the crystal to the lask and instructed him in its use. As Wrog held the olivine out at arm's length, his eyes opened wide and he curled his lip in alarm. "King?"

The lask remained quiet while Tithian responded. After a few moments, Wrog cast a wary eye at the mul, then looked back into the crystal. He listened to the king, then closed his fist over the gem and glared at the mul.

"Your king says you are no legion of Tyr's," Wrog announced. "He says he'll pay me if you never return to Tyr."

Realizing that he had run out of options, Rikus spoke to Neeva in a calm voice, relying on the Scourge of Rkard's magic for her to hear him. "Neeva, take cover. A dozen archers have arrows trained on you right now."

Wrog curled his muzzle in confusion. "Who are you talking to?"

Before Rikus had a chance to answer, several archers cried out in alarm. "They moved!"

"Shoot!" snapped Wrog. When no bowstrings twanged, the lask repeated his command. "Shoot!"

"They don't have a clear aim," Rikus answered. He

placed himself in front of Wrog, safely out of arm's reach. "Neeva, send Laban to fetch the rest of the legion. Prepare for a fight."

"Quiet!" Wrog ordered, stepping toward the mul.

The bowstrings snapped in rapid succession. Rikus peered through the exit in the floor, glimpsing an insect-sized figure dodging down the canyon. As the arrows streaked toward the gladiator, Caelum rose from behind his cover. The dwarf lifted an arm skyward. In the next instant, a red sphere of flame appeared between the nest and the ground. The arrows sank into the fire shield and disappeared from sight, leaving the archers to gasp in awe.

"Did you stop him?" demanded Wrog, whose golden eyes remained fixed on the mul.

Rikus answered for the archers. "No," he said, meeting the slave leader's gaze. "That leaves you with the choice."

"I'll kill you all," Wrog growled.

"That would be stupid, even for a lask," Rikus said, not yielding any ground. "I'll soon have two-thousand warriors marching up the canyon."

Wrog stopped less than a step from Rikus, the sharp points of his fangs several inches above the mul's head. "You'll never live to see them arrive," the lask snarled.

Rikus glimpsed a massive claw swinging toward his head. He stepped inside and blocked the attack on the forearm, at the same time driving his elbow into the lask's stomach. Wrog hardly seemed to notice the blow, but it opened space enough for Rikus to step under the arm. As the mul passed behind his opponent, he thrust his foot at the back of Wrog's knee and pushed. The leg buckled, dropping the lask to his knees.

Before Wrog could shout any orders, Rikus leaped across the exit hole toward the Kes'trekels guarding K'kriq. He kicked the first man in the ribs, sending him crashing into the next warrior. The other two guards attacked instantly, one thrusting his spear at Rikus and the other at K'kriq.

Rikus sidestepped the attack coming at him, grabbing the spear along the shaft. He knocked the man unconscious with an elbow to the jaw, then ripped the spear away as the guard fell to the floor. At the same time, the weapon thrust at K'kriq bounced harmlessly off the thri-kreen's hard shell. The mantis-warrior rolled toward his attacker and sank his mandibles into the man's leg. As poisonous saliva mixed with blood, the man screamed in agony and dropped to the floor in a convulsing heap.

Confused shouts and angry cries filled the small chamber. The Kes'trekels drew their weapons and moved to attack. Rikus spun around and cut the cord binding one of his scout's hands, then K'kriq cried, "Beware the lask!"

Leaving his spear with the gladiator he had just freed, Rikus stepped toward the exit to meet Wrog. The lask dove across the hole, reaching out with the claws of both hands. The mul ducked and Wrog's arms slashed the air overhead. The gladiator quickly stood upright again, his shoulders catching his foe in the torso and flipping the huge lask onto his back. Wrog landed on the floor with a great crash.

Angered that he and his legion were being forced to fight fellow slaves, Rikus kicked the lask in the head. "This is stupid!" he yelled, smashing his foot into the lask's face with each word.

The blows would have smashed a human's skull, but Wrog shrugged them off and lashed out at the mul's leg. When Rikus jumped away, the lask rose to his hands and knees. "The mul is mine," he growled, eyeing several Kes'trekels attempting to sneak up behind Rikus.

The mul allowed Wrog to return to his feet, not wishing to get into a wrestling match with the huge half-man. In this battle, he knew, his advantage lay in speed and skill, not sheer strength.

As he waited, Rikus glanced at K'kriq. Six slaves were sur-

rounding the thri-kreen, hacking at his chitinous shell with
bone axes and obsidian short swords. Despite his disadvantage, the mantis-warrior was faring well against them. He
rolled to and fro, lashing out with his poisonous mandibles
and one of the two arms his attackers had inadvertently
freed. Next to him, the scout that Rikus had released earlier
was using his spear to hold several foes at bay while the next
gladiator in line worked to free their companions.

When Wrog had returned to his feet, Rikus placed himself
squarely in front of the hole. "I'm going to break you one
bone at a time," he snarled. Rikus meant every word of what
he said, though it was not the bitterness he felt toward the
lask that prompted him to speak. Wrog was a powerful fighter, but an inexperienced one. Rikus wanted to goad him into
a mistake. "When I'm through with you, my legion will
burn your nest off the side of this mountain. Your tribe will
curse your memory for refusing to let us pass."

"Not likely," the lask growled.

As the mul had hoped, Wrog started his next attack by
dashing forward. Two steps into his charge, a spark of understanding lit the lask's flaxen eyes and he slowed his pace.
"Your tricks won't work," he said.

Rikus scowled as if disappointed, though he was really far
from dissatisfied. A gladiator's tricks, especially those of a
champion, were never as simple as they seemed. He had
seen a hundred opponents stop just as Wrog had, and in the
end a hundred opponents had fallen to one of the many ma-
neuvers that could follow.

Rikus screamed and rushed forward. Wrog reached for the
mul with both clawed hands, a confident sneer on his snout.
The lask's fingers clamped down on the gladiator's shoulders long before the mul's shorter arms reached his foe's
body. Rikus grabbed Wrog's biceps and pushed with all his
strength.

The instant the lask pushed back, Rikus reversed himself

and pulled Wrog toward him. At the same time, he kicked his feet out, planting one squarely in his foe's stomach and throwing the other out in front of the knee. As the mul dropped to his back, he pulled the Wrog forward.

The lask's orange eyes opened wide as he realized he had done exactly what the gladiator had expected. Wrog tore his arms free of the mul's grip and jumped over Rikus's head, landing a full step shy of the hole in the floor.

Seeing that he had saved himself from another of the mul's tricks, Wrog cried out in triumph. "Who'll break who bone-by-bone?"

Rikus answered the question by throwing his legs over his head and springing off the floor at his enemy. As Wrog turned to face him again, the mul's feet landed square in the lask's belly. The unexpected kick sent the half-man stumbling backward. He plunged, screaming, into the hole.

Rikus dropped back to the floor, then leaped to his feet in the same instant, expecting Wrog's followers to rush him. To his surprise, no one did. The handful of Kes'trekels who were not actively fighting merely kept a watchful eye on the mul, as if defeating their leader had relieved him of the necessity for further combat.

As he studied the rest of the room, Rikus saw they were not extending the same courtesy to his followers. In the corner, three of the four Tyrian scouts lay motionless and battered in the midst of more than a dozen dead Kes'trekels. The last gladiator, streaming blood from a dozen cuts, was wearily defending himself from three attackers.

K'kriq's situation was little better. Although the thri-kreen had managed to work all four arms free and stand, the mesh remained twined around his legs. Eight Kes'trekels had him trapped in the corner. The mantis-warrior's shell was laced with deep gouges, and he oozed dark yellow blood from several wounds that had actually penetrated to his body. Nevertheless, the thri-kreen had fought well, for there were as many bodies piled at his feet as there were near the four scouts. Among them was the man with the tattooed eyes.

Though Rikus was no stranger to carnage and bloodshed, the sight sickened him. Since his days in the arena, he had not been forced to fight fellow slaves, and he found that he no longer had the stomach for it.

"Stop!" Rikus cried. "Slaves shouldn't kill slaves!"

When the battle showed no signs of subsiding, he snatched up a bloody short sword that had fallen near the hole. "Stop, or I'll have your sword arms!"

"You'll die first," said Wrog's throaty voice.

Rikus spun around and saw the lask floating back through the chamber exit. Wrog's sharp fangs were dripping saliva, and his muzzle was contorted into a mask of bloodlust. "I have a few tricks of my own," he sneered.

As the lask's upper body passed into the chamber, Rikus caught a glimpse of the golden ring that still sparkled on Wrog's finger. Apparently, its powers of levitation were more varied than the gladiator had guessed.

His anger returning at the sight of the fool who had caused all the needless bloodletting, the mul rushed to the edge of the hole and kicked at Wrog's stomach with all his might. The lask blocked with a bony forearm, sending sharp pain shooting up the gladiator's leg. Still, Rikus smiled, for his foe had exposed the hand wearing the ring. The mul brought his short sword's blade down across Wrog's fingers, slicing all three off at the knuckles.

Wrog screamed in pain. He plummeted back through the hole, leaving the finger that wore the magical ring floating before Rikus. The mul studied the gruesome digit for a moment, fascinated by the sight of it hanging in midair, unconnected to the rest of the lask's body.

As he looked, the mul realized that the ring keeping it aloft was vital to the nest's survival. No doubt, they could use ropes to haul themselves and their supplies up into the nest, but the absence of ropes or pulleys in the room suggested that they had come to rely exclusively on the ring.

The mul snatched Wrog's bloody finger and held it aloft.

"Stop!" he yelled again. "Stop, or I'll leave you trapped here!" He had no intention of abandoning K'kriq, but the threat seemed the best way to end the battle.

Those who were not heavily involved in the fight looked toward the mul with expressions of surprise, then quickly dragged their comrades away from the melee. Behind them stood K'kriq, battered and exhausted. Unfortunately, he was the only one of Rikus's warriors still standing. The last scout had fallen and lay tangled in a mass of bodies.

"You have the ring," said the old dwarf who had spoken earlier. He was spattered head-to-foot in blood. "What now?"

"I'm going to take my warriors and leave, then my legion will pass through your canyon," Rikus said.

He slipped the ring off Wrog's disembodied digit and put it on his own. To his surprise, the large band immediately shrank to the proper size for his finger.

"What do we do now?" asked the female mul. "Do we stop him or follow him?"

At first, Rikus did not understand the question. Slowly, it dawned on him that by killing Wrog, he had taken more than the lask's ring. In many slave tribes, warlords achieved their positions through personal combat. In the case of the Kes'trekels, it did not seem unlikely that the magical ring was the emblem of that authority.

"If I'm you're new leader, then you come with my legion to attack the Urikites," Rikus said.

The chamber fell deathly silent, and the mul could tell that he had made a mistake.

At last, the old dwarf shook his head. "You killed Wrog in personal combat, so we'll let your legion pass through our canyon. But you must return the ring and swear to keep the location of our nest secret."

Rikus insisted, "I won Wrog's position through—"

"You won nothing. It takes more than a gladiator's tricks to lead a slave tribe," the dwarf spat, running his eyes over the carnage in the room. "You're a fine warrior, but I see no proof that you're anything else. Do you accept our truce or not?"

SIX

Assassins

"What did I do wrong?" Rikus demanded. He bit his lip and kicked a stone with the instep of his sandaled foot. "Why couldn't I make the slave tribe join us?"

Several yards behind him, Neeva said, "This isn't their fight."

"But it should be," Rikus insisted, not turning around. "They could stop hiding from slave-takers and live in Tyr."

"Not everyone wants to live in the city," Neeva replied. There was a soft clack as she tossed a rock away from the bed she was preparing. "Not everyone wants to fight Urikites or gain revenge upon Family Lubar."

"You're right, they're cowards," Rikus said, drawing his own conclusion from Neeva's statement. "If they want to cower in their cliff-nest, who am I to lead them to freedom?"

"Exactly."

"Fools," the mul said, shaking his head and staring out over the terrain ahead.

Rikus and Neeva were preparing to spend the night apart from the rest of the legion, atop an outcropping of sienna limestone. A cool evening breeze swept out of the foothills

115

and sank into a tranquil cove of golden sand stretched out before the two gladiators. Hanging low in the sky, the ruby sun lit the dune crests with a fiery bloom and plunged the troughs into amethyst shadows. Many miles away, a delta of rusty orange stones spilled out of a twisting badland canyon, briefly encroaching on the sandy bay before being swallowed by the silent dunes.

At the tip of this delta stood a dark clump of zaal trees, their barren trunks and fanlike crowns marking the location of the oasis Rikus had been trying so desperately to reach. The long fronds of the zaal trees waved gently in the breeze, beckoning the Tyrian legion to fill their waterskins and soak their sore feet.

Unfortunately, Rikus no longer had reason to hurry to the oasis. As the legion had left the Kes'trekel canyon earlier that day, K'kriq had returned from the oasis with disappointing news. The Urikite halflings had abandoned the pool, and there was no sign that Maetan was continuing toward it. The Tyrians' prey had vanished into the sandy wastes without a trace.

At the mul's back, Neeva said, "Don't expect to sleep like we would at Agis's mansion."

Rikus glanced over his shoulder. His fighting partner had tried desperately to clear the stones from a small section of barren ground, but it was a hopeless task. No matter how many stones she moved, there were a dozen more lying on the ground.

"Don't worry about me," Rikus said, looking back to the oasis. "I won't sleep."

Neeva stepped to his side and took his arm, something she seldom did when there were others around to see. "If you're worried about spending the night outside camp, maybe we shouldn't."

Rikus squeezed her hand. "No, it'll be good to have time alone. Besides, there aren't any Urikites around here." He withdrew his arm from her grasp and pointed at the distant clump of zaal trees. "How did Maetan know to avoid that oasis?"

"Caelum says there are no other nearby oases," Neeva answered, stroking the tense muscles of the mul's back. "Even if we weren't following him, Maetan would have had to guess we'd go to that one."

"Right. But how'd he know we'd catch him there?" the mul demanded. "Someone told him."

Neeva stepped around to face Rikus. She had used part of her water to wash her body, which was now covered only by the green halter and breechcloth she had been wearing when they killed Kalak. The setting sun lit one side of her shapely form with a rosy blush, plunging the other side into alluring shadows. "Even if we had reason to believe someone had betrayed us, how could they have contacted Maetan?"

"The Way," Rikus answered. "Maetan's as strong as Agis, maybe even stronger. And don't forget Hamanu. If Maetan can't contact his spies himself, he might have something like this." Rikus pulled Tithian's olivine crystal, which he had recovered from Wrog's mangled body, from his belt pouch.

"Anything's possible," Neeva reluctantly admitted. "But who would do such a thing?"

Rikus faced the canyon from which they had just come. In the evening light, it looked like nothing more than a great shadow slicing down the side of the foothills. "The slave tribe."

"The Kes'trekels?" Neeva gasped. "What gives you that idea?"

"They've been trying to keep us from catching Maetan all along," Rikus said. "First they captured our scouts, then they tried to take us prisoner. Even after I killed Wrog, they fought with us. I should have seen it at the time—Maetan bribed them."

"Just because they didn't join Tyr's army doesn't make

them Maetan's spies." Neeva gripped the mul's arm with a warm hand and tried to guide him toward the makeshift bed.

"It fits," Rikus insisted, staying were he was. "Maetan showed no sign of knowing our plan until after we passed the Kes'trekel nest. And why else would they have insisted on fighting?"

"Because they wanted to keep their nest's location secret and they didn't trust us," Neeva said, sighing in frustration. She let go of the mul's arm and went to their makeshift bed, picking up one of the capes lying nearby for use as a blanket. "After what Tithian did, do you blame them?"

"How do we know the king really betrayed us?" the mul asked. "Wrog could have made the whole thing up."

"Maybe he did," Neeva sighed, no longer trying to hide her frustration. As she spread the cape over the space she had tried to clear of stones, she said, "You still have the gem. Ask Tithian if he lied to Wrog."

The absurdity of Neeva's suggestion jolted Rikus, and he realized he was behaving like a man obsessed. "It was the Kes'trekels," he grumbled.

Rikus pulled the Scourge of Rkard from his belt so he could sit. As his hand touched the hilt, the dusk came alive with previously undetected sounds. From overhead came the muffled beat of a flying lizard's leathery wings, and somewhere close by a snake's belly scales were softly hissing against the rough edge of a stone. Farther away, an unseen rodent scratched at the ground in a frantic effort either to hide from a predator or catch its dinner. Rikus did not pay the sounds much attention, for evening was when many creatures came out to hunt.

"Put that sword down and come here," Neeva ordered, stepping over to Rikus.

She kissed him long and hard, at the same time unbuckling his Belt of Rank. As the heavy girdle slipped from his waist, he felt the first stirrings of the savage lust only Neeva could kindle in him.

She casually tossed the belt aside, and it landed in the rocks with a loud clatter. Rikus's desire quickly faded.

"Be careful!" he objected, grabbing the belt.

"It's that worthless strip of leather or me," Neeva said, working her thumbs beneath the thin straps holding her breechcloth on her curvaceous hips.

"This is more than a 'worthless strip of leather'," Rikus said, picking up the heavy girdle and laying it neatly at the foot of their rocky bed. "It's my destiny."

Neeva popped her thumbs free of her breechcloth straps. "Destiny?" she exclaimed. "Rikus, I think you're taking that senile old dwarf too seriously."

"No, I mean it," the mul said, respectfully placing the sword next to the belt. "People make their own destinies. Mine is to lead the legions of freedom."

"Maybe you should think that over, Rikus," Neeva said. "So far, you've only got one legion, and you've nearly lost it more than once."

The mul furrowed his hairless brow. "When?"

"Kled, for one," Neeva pointed out. "If Caelum hadn't saved you from Maetan, by now your mind would be ash and the rest of us would be quarry slaves in Urik's obsidian pits."

"But Caelum *did* help me. We killed more than five-hundred Urikites—"

"And lost the *Book of the Kemalok Kings*," Neeva interrupted. "As for Wrog and the slave tribe—it's a fortunate thing the fight in the aerie didn't erupt into a full battle. One sun cleric was not going to blast that fortress off the cliff."

"He didn't have to," Rikus countered, more hurt by Neeva's criticism than he cared to admit. "Why are you doing this, Neeva? I thought—"

"I'm telling you the truth because I love you and because I love Tyr," Neeva said. She sat down in the middle of the cape and wrapped it around her shoulders, her romantic mood vanishing with the setting sun. "The way you're talking scares me. It's not like you to think this way."

"Of course not," the mul answered, sitting at her side. The sharp rocks, which had been lying exposed to the blazing sun all day, seared his naked skin wherever they touched him. "Before we killed Kalak, my purpose in life was to become a free man," Rikus said, shifting his position so that his breechcloth insulated him from the hot stones. "Now, I'm free. I have a new purpose. We all do—you, me, and Sadira, even Agis."

Neeva frowned. "Leave me out of this."

"No," Rikus insisted, laying one of his powerful hands on her knee. "Agis and Sadira safeguard Tyr from threats inside, like Tithian. It's for you and me to defend against outside threats like Maetan and the Urikites."

Allowing the cape to fall open at the neck, Neeva faced the mul and studied him for several moments. Finally, a hopeful light in her emerald eyes, she asked, "Rikus, what are you trying to say?"

The mul had seen similar expressions in his fighting partner's face before. He was no more comfortable with it now than he had been then. "I'm not sure," he answered, fearing that once again Neeva was reading more into his words that he meant to be there.

Neeva rose to her knees and faced Rikus, looking directly into his eyes. "Let me make this easy for you," she said, her voice optimistic. "Are you saying you've made a choice between me and Sadira?"

Rikus looked away, wondering how a conversation about his destiny had turned into an interrogation on his least favorite subject. Since they had killed Kalak, his fighting partner had been pressuring him to end his love affair with Sadira. Neeva insisted that now that they were free, they had to start thinking about the future and commit their hearts to each other. To Rikus, however, commitment sounded too much like captivity. Though he loved Neeva, he was not willing to yield any of his hard-won freedom—especially if it meant giving up Sadira.

When Rikus didn't answer, the eagerness drained from Neeva's face. Nevertheless, she did not look away. "Just answer yes or no."

"There's no choice to make—"

"Yes or no, Rikus."

"No, I haven't made a choice," the mul said.

Neeva stood, gathering the cloak around her broad shoulders. "I'm going back to camp," she announced. "Why don't you stay here and ponder your destiny?"

The gladiator grabbed her heavy battle-axe, then started across the mile of rocky terrain separating them from the rest of the legion. In the burgundy light and deepening shadows of dusk, it was difficult to see and Neeva began to stumble over loose stones before she had taken three steps. Despite the likelihood of spraining an ankle, she continued onward, cursing Rikus as though he had personally placed every stone between her and camp.

Rikus grabbed his Belt of Rank and buckled it on. "Wait, Neeva. If you break a leg, it'll slow down the entire army."

Her only answer was a curse.

The mul picked up his sword and started to follow, but abruptly halted. Instead of the hiss of snake scales and the beat of lizard wings that he had heard earlier, the field was ominously silent—save for a hushed chorus of contrived chirps and whistles. The noises were so soft that, had he not held the Scourge of Rkard in his hand, Rikus would never have heard them.

"Neeva, stop!" he hissed, clattering over a jumble of rocks as he rushed to catch up.

"Why?" she demanded.

"There's something out there!" the mul answered.

Neeva stopped immediately, hefting her axe into a guarding position. "This had better not be a ploy, Rikus."

"It's not," the mul assured her, stepping to her side.

He searched the ground ahead, looking for the slightest indication of movement. All he saw was an endless field of motionless rocks, flecked here and there with equally motionless boulders. Unfortunately, he could not use his dwarven vision to pick out whatever was making the sound, either. The sun, all but sunken behind the Ringing Mountains, was bathing the field with just enough fiery light to wash out all traces of ambient heat.

Rikus took Neeva's arm. "They're between us and camp," he whispered.

"What are they?" she asked, dropping the cape from her shoulders.

"I don't know," he said. "With the Scourge, I can hear them whistling and chirping—but I can't see them any more than you can."

The mysterious watchers fell silent.

Rikus cursed under his breath and brought his sword into a defensive position. "Be ready," he said, no longer bothering to whisper.

They slowly backed away, stopping when they reached the stony bed that Neeva had prepared for them. Still, the watchers did not move or attack.

"Maybe its a pack of wild thri-kreen," Neeva said.

Unlike K'kriq, most thri-kreen were not civilized. They roamed the desert day and night, hunting for prey to sate their ravenous appetites. Sometimes, if they were desperate, they would resort to eating sentient creatures.

Rikus peered all around them, searching the dusky terrain for some sign of an insect-man. The dying rays of the sun only made it more difficult to see, for they lit the tops of the rocks in muted red light. It was impossible to distinguish colors, and even shapes were soft and fuzzy, but he did not see anything large and angular enough to be a thri-kreen.

Rikus shook his head. "There's nothing big enough."

The mul had no sooner spoken than a soft chirp sounded at their backs. A small foot brushed against the rocky ground and padded toward them. Rikus spun around and glimpsed the three-foot silhouette of a bushy-haired man dropping behind a small boulder.

His stomach knotted in cold fear. "Halflings!" Rikus hissed, pressing his back against Neeva's.

"I wish you'd said thri-kreen," Neeva replied. She remained quiet for a moment, then added, "If I fall, don't let them eat me—at least not alive."

"Then don't fall," the mul answered. "If you do, I doubt I'll be in any position to stop them."

Rikus and Neeva had faced halflings before, when they had ventured into the halfling forest to recover the spear and wand that they had used to kill Kalak. The small hunters had felled them both easily, and Agis had barely been able to talk the tribe's chieftain out of eating the entire party.

They waited, back to back, for the halflings to move again. After what seemed an eternity, Rikus suggested, "Maybe they've decided against attacking us."

"You can't believe that," Neeva countered. "This isn't just any halfling hunting party. They're Urikite assassins."

As much as he didn't want to, the mul had to agree with his fighting partner. Halflings left their forest too rarely for this to be a chance encounter.

From beside them, Rikus heard the soft scrape of a foot on stone, followed quickly by the high-pitched twang of a tiny bowstring. "Down!" The mul screamed. He pushed Neeva to the ground and dropped at her side.

An instant later, a tiny arrow clattered against a rock near Rikus's side. Though the missile was hardly longer than his hand, the mul knew from his previous experiences that it would be tipped with an effective poison that knocked its victim unconscious within a few seconds. Likely as not, the unlucky victim would never wake, and if he did it would be to the sight of several halflings preparing to eat his liver.

"How are we going to get out of this?" Neeva asked. Her voice was muffled because her mouth was pressed to the ground.

Rikus lifted his head enough so that he could look around. A dozen yards to his right, he could hear a pair of halflings chittering and whistling to each other, but they remained hidden from sight. The mul could not hear or see any other man-eaters.

The gladiator dropped his head back to the ground. "Crawl," he whispered.

Neeva reluctantly left her bulky steel axe behind and they started forward. They pulled themselves along inches at a time, silently grimacing as the jagged stones scraped long gashes into their torsos. Within a few yards, warm blood coated them from their collarbones to their knees, and grating sand filled the dozens of cuts lacing their chests and stomachs.

Although Rikus was careful to keep his sword from banging against a rock, the pair could not help making more noise than the halflings. They drew heavier breaths and created soft rasps as they drew their larger bodies across the ground. Every now and then, there was a muffled clack when one of them accidentally dislodged a stone and it bumped into another. Rikus had no doubt that the halflings could track them by the sounds they were making, but he did not know what option they had except to crawl.

A pair of twangs sounded from their left, then two more darts clattered into the rocks ahead of them. Rikus cursed and used the tip of his sword to flick the arrows away. He suspected that even a scrape along the poisoned tips would be enough to knock either him or Neeva unconscious.

"Why don't they show themselves?" Neeva whispered,

looking around for the source of the arrows. When Rikus did not answer, she asked another question, "How many do you think there are?"

"Two or a dozen," the mul answered. "It's impossible to tell. Just keep crawling."

"Why?" There was an edge of fear in Neeva's question that Rikus had never heard in her voice before.

"They may be able to hear us move, but as long as we stay down they can't see us any better than we can see them. One of us should be able to reach the rest of the legion and warn it."

"The halflings are after us, not the rest of the legion," Neeva whispered. "Even I can tell that there aren't enough of them to attack two thousand men, but they don't need many warriors to assassinate a commander."

Seeing the wisdom of Neeva's words, Rikus silently cursed the Kes'trekels, suspecting the slave tribe had advised Maetan to set up this ambush.

"You're right, but let's keep moving anyway," the mul whispered. "We won't help ourselves by waiting until they come to us."

As the two gladiators crawled forward, the halflings mirrored their progress, chittering and whistling to keep track of each other and their prey. Occasionally one or two of them would fire a dart, and twice the little arrows struck within a foot of the mul's head. By the time they had crossed fifty yards of rocky ground, both gladiators were breathing hard—though Rikus suspected their weariness had more to do with nerves than muscle fatigue.

"Maybe I should yell for help," the mul whispered.

"Are you out of your mind?" Neeva hissed. "No one but the halflings will hear you!"

"It was just an idea," Rikus answered defensively.

He crawled forward again, stopping to listen every two or three yards. Most of the time, the halflings were silent, but every now and then, a chitter or a chirp let him know the assassins were closing in.

It was during one of these pauses that he heard the faint clatter of stones far past the range of the assassins' tiny bows. At first, the mul thought a halfling might have slipped, but the sound was followed by another rattle, and he knew that was not the case.

"Someone's out there behind the halflings," he whispered.

"Someone from the legion?" Neeva asked hopefully.

Rikus shook his head. "We said we didn't want to be disturbed," he said. "It has to be a Urikite."

Neeva changed directions. "Let's find him and kill him. It might be the halflings' commander."

Rikus followed. Like his fighting partner, he wanted nothing quite so bad as to find an enemy that they could fight. Of course, the halflings would never let themselves be caught in hand-to-hand combat, but with a little luck whoever was overseeing them would not be so careful.

The pair's change in direction caused a flurry of chittering and scuffling. Rikus detected at least nine different halflings relaying messages and adjusting their positions. Normally, he would not have considered nine warriors much of a threat, but the prospect of facing so many halflings sent a shiver down his spine. He did not tell Neeva the bad news.

They had traveled no more than ten yards when Rikus heard the soft tick of an arrow being nocked into a bowstring. Less than a yard away, a scrawny halfling rose from the rocks and pointed a small arrow at Neeva's back.

"Roll!" Rikus yelled.

The bowstring popped. Neeva cried out in alarm and barely managed to roll away as the arrow shot into the ground where she had been lying.

Rikus launched himself at the halfling, driving the tip of his sword into the assassin's stomach. The Scourge passed through his foe's body with surprising ease, not stopping until the tip protruded more than a foot from his back. The halfling's sallow eyes opened wide, but he did not cry out. Instead, he reached into his hip-quiver for a dart and drove himself forward onto Rikus's blade, slashing at the mul with the poisoned tip.

Rikus leaned away, then punched the halfling with his free hand. The blow crushed the assassin's skull and popped an eye from its socket. Casually, the mul kicked the body off his blade.

The twang of bowstrings sounded from directly ahead, then Rikus felt two taps as a pair of arrows sank into his belt. He dropped to the ground instantly, a panicked scream escaping his lips.

"Rikus!" cried Neeva.

Another bowstring popped and the mul heard an arrow clatter to the ground near Neeva. She rolled away, then whispered, "Are you hit?"

To Rikus's relief, he did not feel either arrow pricking his stomach. "They hit me in the belt," he said, carefully plucking the darts from the leather girdle and tossing them aside. "No harm."

He started to crawl toward his fighting partner, but the halflings fired their bows again. Several darts clattered down between him and Neeva. Rikus saw her roll away, then stop to wait for him. The mul started toward her, but again the halflings fired. This time, two of the darts nearly hit him, and two more almost struck Neeva.

"They're separating us," Neeva cried. Another bowstring twanged and she barely saved herself by rolling yet farther away from Rikus.

"Let them," Rikus answered, realizing that by trying to rejoin each other, he and Neeva would only make themselves easy targets. "Go on—we'll circle around and meet each other up ahead."

Two more bowstrings popped and Rikus rolled away. When he looked back toward Neeva, she had disappeared into the dusky shadows.

Rikus crawled away as fast as he could. Neeva could take care of herself and, even if she couldn't, he didn't see how getting killed himself would help her. As he moved farther away from the halfling he had killed, the pop of bowstrings grew less frequent and the whistled messages of the halflings sounded more urgent.

The sun sank behind the mountains completely, plunging the field into darkness. The moons had not yet risen, so there was only the faint twinkle of the stars to help the halflings see. The mul breathed a sigh of relief as his dwarven vision began to outline the glowing forms of rocks, ground, and halflings. Now he and Neeva stood a good chance of surviving, for, unlike elves and dwarves, halflings could not see in the dark. With the advantage of his dwarven vision, Rikus thought he could circle around to Neeva and escape without suffering a prick from one of the halfling arrows.

His optimism was short-lived, however. From the direction in which Neeva had gone came a halfling's astonished cry. Rikus heard the twang of a bowstring, then his fighting partner grunted in anger. There were a couple of muffled blows.

"Don't jab that thing at me," Neeva said.

There was a sharp snap, as though the big woman had broken a spear shaft, or perhaps a halfling's back, over her knee. Something soft and limp collapsed onto the rocks, then Neeva's heavy footsteps sprinted away from the altercation.

A cacophony of chirps and whistles sounded from her direction. The field near her came alive with clacking rocks and snapping bowstrings as several halflings, glowing warm red against the orange rocks of the field, rushed toward the sounds of Neeva's flight.

Rikus leaped to his feet and screamed his loudest battle cry, charging over the broken ground to help his fighting partner. Unfortunately, he could not tell how she was faring. Even with his dwarven vision, he could see no more than ten yards in the darkness.

Soon the red glow of a halfling's form appeared at the limit of Rikus's vision. The mul raised his sword, hoping to use the man-eater's inability to see in the dark to good advantage. As the mul closed in, however, the halfling suddenly stopped and cocked his head as if listening, then lifted his bow and pointed the tip of an arrow directly at Rikus's chest.

The gladiator dropped to the ground, marveling at how accurate the halfling's aim was, considering that he was doing it by sound alone. When his kneecap smashed into the jagged point of a large stone, the mul clamped his jaw shut to keep from crying out, biting his tongue in the process.

The bowstring twanged, and the halfling's arrow sailed over Rikus's head in a blue streak. The mul returned to his feet as the halfling pulled a poisoned arrow from his hip-quiver and clutched it like a dagger. As Rikus advanced, the halfling closed his eyes, relying solely on his ears to keep him informed of the mul's location.

Rikus picked up a rock and threw it at his foe's head, rushing forward behind the flying stone. The missile struck with a sharp crack and the halfling stumbled back. As the mul raised his sword for the kill, the halfling surprised him by throwing himself forward in a mad lunge.

To keep from being stabbed by the poisoned arrowhead, Rikus lunged out of the way and landed face-first in the rocks. The halfling struck the ground a few feet behind him. The mul spun around immediately, swinging his sword in a blind arc. As fast as he moved, by the time he saw his attacker the assassin was almost upon him.

Rikus knocked aside the hand holding the dart, then

brought his sword around in a quick loop and flicked the attacker's head off. The halfling's hand took one last slash at the mul, then dropped the arrow.

Behind Rikus, a loud crackle sounded from the direction Neeva had fled, then a brilliant crimson light flared. Remembering the sound he had heard just before he killed his first halfling, Rikus assumed that Neeva had stumbled into a Urikite templar.

"Neeva!" he yelled, leaping to his feet again.

A sharp pain shot through the kneecap he had smashed earlier and his leg nearly buckled. To his relief, however, the Scourge brought the sound of Neeva's voice to his ears. "Rikus is still alive," she said. "Come on!"

Not bothering to ask himself to whom she was talking, he limped forward again.

A few steps later, he stopped in his tracks. In front of him stood four halflings, all pointing arrows in his direction. Their bowstrings snapped simultaneously.

Rikus cursed bitterly and dove to the side with all the grace he could muster.

The mul felt the soft thud of four tiny darts before his feet had even left the ground. He had time enough to realize that, again, they had struck him in the Belt of Rank, then he smashed into the rocks.

In the same instant, a tremendous peal of thunder deafened Rikus and a brilliant orange light flooded the night. It washed out the mul's dwarven vision and cast strange, quavering shadows over the entire field. A searing blast of wind washed over him. Blinded by the brilliant glare and pained by the heat, Rikus covered his eyes and curled into a fetal position.

With his ears ringing and his vision clouded, Rikus realized that he was more vulnerable than ever to the halflings. He lay as still as he could, convinced that he would never know the answer to the many questions flooding his mind about what had just happened. At any moment, he expected a halfling's dagger to slip into his kidneys, or a dozen tiny arrows to prick his exposed back. Still, as much as his instincts cried out for him to stand and fight, the mul knew that moving would only draw attention to himself. Until his senses returned, he was helpless.

To his surprise, when his ears finally stopped ringing it was Neeva's voice he heard. "Rikus, are you hurt?"

The mul looked up and, through his slowly clearing vision, saw his fighting partner standing over him. She was silhouetted against a wall of flame that still burned where the four halflings had been a few moments earlier.

"Neeva, you're safe!"

"Of course," she said. "You're the one they were trying to kill."

Rikus frowned. "Me?"

"When you screamed, they all but left me alone," Neeva explained. "The question is, are you hurt?"

"I don't know, and now is no time to find out," Rikus said, rising. "Let's go—"

"Don't worry, the halflings are gone—at least for now," Neeva said, laying a hand on his shoulder. "Now, are you injured or not?"

Rikus frowned, but decided to take her at her word. If there were still halflings about, they would have struck by now. In answer to Neeva's question, the mul said, "I've been hit by half-a-dozen poison arrows, but the Belt of Rank stopped them all." He pointed at the four darts still stuck in the girdle. "Otherwise, I'd be dead by now."

"Let me have a look, just to be sure," said another familiar voice, this one at the mul's back. "Sometimes, a wounded man does not feel his injuries until much later."

Rikus peered over his shoulder and saw a dwarf's lanky form standing behind him. "Caelum?" he gasped.

"Who do you think created the wall of flame that saved

you?" Neeva asked.

Rikus ignored her and scowled at the dwarf. "What are you doing here? I told you and everyone else to leave Neeva and me alone."

The dwarf dropped his eyes. "It was a coincidence. I was performing my sundown devotions."

"I've never seen you perform any devotions," Rikus grunted. He narrowed his eyes and studied the dwarf's dark eyes. "You're lying."

"Why would he do that?" Neeva demanded.

"Maybe it wasn't the Kes'trekels who warned Maetan about our ambush," Rikus said, grabbing the dwarf by the throat. "Maybe it was Caelum!"

"That's madness!" snapped Neeva, prying the dwarf from Rikus's grasp.

"No, it's not," Rikus insisted. "He followed us out here so he could show the halflings where we were sleeping."

"No," Caelum rasped, rubbing his throat. "It was a coincidence, as I said. You've never seen my devotions because I must perform them alone."

"You don't expect me to believe that," Rikus sneered.

"It makes more sense than what you're thinking," Neeva snapped. "If Caelum's a traitor, why'd he save you from the halflings?"

Rikus scowled, unable to think of a good reason. "How do I know? He's the spy!"

"Whatever you choose to believe about my devotions, you must see that I have as much reason as you to hate Maetan. I am no spy," Caelum said, meeting the mul's gaze evenly. "Now, let me inspect your stomach. If you have been scratched, the sun's vigor will burn the poison from your blood."

When the mul did not do as the dwarf asked, Neeva reached over and unclasped the buckle. "I think we should return to the legion before sunrise," she snapped.

Caelum immediately set about inspecting the mul for wounds.

As Neeva stretched out the Belt of Rank to inspect it, Rikus saw that there were two more halfling darts in the back. Though they had probably struck him while he was crawling through the rocks, he had not even felt them through the thick leather.

"And you called it a worthless piece of leather," Rikus said, motioning at the girdle.

Neeva shook her head in amazement. "All the arrows hit you in the belt," she said. "How lucky can you get?"

"I doubt that it was luck," Caelum said. He paused his ministering to pluck a poisoned dart from the leather. "I'd say it was magic."

SEVEN

Umbra's Return

Rikus woke to a sharp jab in the ribs.

"Stop lying on ground," said K'kriq. "Find Urikites."

Opening his eyes, the mul saw that the green tendrils of first light were just shooting across the starlit sky. He rolled away from Neeva's warm body and looked up at the thri-kreen's towering form.

"Huh?" he asked groggily.

"What wrong?" demanded K'kriq, clacking his mandibles impatiently. "Why so stupid?"

"I was sleeping," Rikus yawned.

"Sleep," the thri-kreen snorted, disgusted with the mul's weakness. "Waste good time for hunt."

"It's no waste," Rikus grumbled. Taking one of the cloaks he and Neeva had been using to insulate themselves from the cold night wind, he rose to his feet and stepped away. "What about the Urikites?"

K'kriq pointed all four arms westward, toward the jagged, black wall of the Ringing Mountains. "Find many Urikites. Not far," he said.

Rikus raised a hand. "Wait."

The mul looked out over the dusty camp, where a thousand murky, inert lumps lay snoring and growling in their sleep. "Everyone up!" he yelled. "Move!"

Half the gladiators leaped to their feet with weapons in their hands, and the other half hardly stirred. "Wake your fellows," Rikus ordered, stepping to Neeva's side and nudging her with his foot. "We march in a quarter-hour."

Neeva rose, pulling her cloak over her shoulders and stifling a yawn. "What's happening?"

Rikus took her by the hand and started toward the templars' camp. "I'll explain later. Now, we've got to wake our leaders."

Within a few minutes, they had roused both Styan and Jaseela. When Rikus asked K'kriq to explain what was happening, however, Neeva objected. "What about Caelum?"

"He's probably off on morning devotions," Rikus answered sarcastically. The dwarf's unexplained appearance the night before still angered the mul. Although he had to agree with Neeva that a traitor would not have saved them from the halfling assassins, he remained convinced that Caelum had followed them to their campsite for some other purpose.

"We'd better find him," said Jaseela. She yawned, then winced in pain when her crooked jaw opened too far for its mangled socket. "If you're expecting a battle, we'll need the dwarves."

Rikus reluctantly agreed, then led the way to where the dwarves had slept. They had made their orderly camp between two spires of sandstone, on a bristly carpet of moss that reflected the faint rays of predawn light in glimmering silver and gold.

Caelum met the leaders in the center of camp, offering them each a handful of small serpent eggs. Only Styan refused the breakfast.

"K'kriq found a Urikite campsite," Rikus explained,

pointing at the distant gulch the thri-kreen had indicated earlier.

"How big?" asked Jaseela, slipping one of the leathery eggs into her misshapen mouth.

"As many as our packs," K'kriq answered, pointing one hand at each of the companies in Rikus's legion. "Many humans. Camped, waiting."

"Did you see Maetan or the *Book of Kings?*" asked Caelum.

K'kriq crossed his stubby antennae, indicating that the answer was no.

"That doesn't mean the mindbender isn't with them," Rikus said.

"And it doesn't mean he is," objected Styan. "He could be halfway back to Urik."

"We're attacking," Rikus insisted.

"Who is *we*, exactly?" Styan demanded, looking down his pointed nose at the mul. "I haven't committed my templars to anything."

"If we wait for the templars to fight, Maetan has time enough to crawl home," Rikus spat.

Styan faced the other commanders. "We must go straight to the oasis. My company finished its water last night."

"You let them finish their water? What if there were still Urikites at the oasis? Without any water your men would be unable to fight come midday," Neeva said. "Only templars would be so stupid."

"Not necessarily," said Jaseela, turning her good eye on Rikus. "We ran out yesterday afternoon."

Neeva groaned and looked to Caelum. "How about the dwarves?"

"We've been on half-rations for three days," he said proudly. "If we go to quarter rations, we'll last another day."

Styan smirked in Rikus's direction. "If you were wise enough to keep track of your gladiators' water, I think you'd find that they emptied their skins before the rest of us."

"It doesn't matter," Rikus snapped. "We did without water for three days before the fight at Kled."

"Not by choice," objected Styan. "And who's to say how long we will be without water if we attack and the battle goes badly?"

"It won't," Rikus growled.

Styan shook his head stubbornly. "If I command my men to bypass the oasis, they'll plant a dagger in my back."

"That wouldn't be such a bad thing," Neeva said. "The whole legion would be better off without you and your cowards."

Styan glared at her for a moment, then looked back to Rikus. "If you insist on this foolishness, the gladiators will attack alone."

"Not alone," said Jaseela. "Water or no water, my retainers and I are with them."

"As are the dwarves," added Caelum, stepping to Neeva's side.

Styan studied the sun-cleric for a few moments, a grim smile upon his thin lips. "Can you be sure of that?"

The dwarf's red eyes flashed in anger. "Of course!"

"Shall we see?" the templar asked. He stepped away from the small group of leaders and faced the dwarven camp. "Warriors of Kled, I feel it is my duty to speak with you for a moment."

The dwarves turned their placid gazes on Styan, prepared to hear his words.

Rikus frowned and started to grab the templar, but Jaseela quickly clutched his arm. "If you interfere, it'll look like you're afraid of what he has to say," she said. "Better to let him speak."

The mul grunted angrily, but stepped back and clenched his fists in frustration.

"The thri-kreen scout claims he has found a Urikite camp,

and the leader of the gladiators wishes to attack it," Styan said. He waved a hand at the mul, as if his audience might not know Rikus by sight. "Out of fairness to you, I must point out that there is no reason to believe that Maetan or the *Book of the Kemalok Kings* are with them."

"There's no reason to believe the book isn't!" Rikus boomed, stepping to Styan's side. "If you're too much of a coward—"

"This isn't a matter of bravery, it's a matter of honesty," Styan retorted, maintaining a reasonable tone even though he had raised his voice above Rikus's. The templar gave the mul a chastising look, then said, "If you were honest about the matter, you'd admit that K'kriq found a rear guard. Does it make sense to leave the *Book of the Kemalok Kings* with them?"

The dwarves studied both men, their steadfast expressions revealing nothing about the thoughts Styan's words had fostered.

Neeva stepped forward to support Rikus. "We don't know that it's a rear guard," she said.

"Don't we?" asked Styan, raising his eyebrows with exaggerated doubt. "Did K'kriq not say that they were 'waiting'? What are they waiting for, if not us?"

"He said they were camped," Rikus countered. "To him, sleeping is the same as waiting."

"Even if I were willing to concede that point, here is another you cannot explain away so easily," Styan said, one side of his mouth curling up in a confident grin. "As we were climbing down from the canyon yesterday, one of my men, a half-elf with eyes as sharp as those of his full-blooded brethren, saw a handful of figures struggling across the sands—away from the oasis."

"You're making this up!" Rikus shouted.

Styan ignored him and addressed the dwarves. "That is where your book has gone," he said. "And while we are fighting, Maetan will be carrying it farther away."

"Liar!"

Rikus gave Styan a violent shove, sending the gaunt man flying two yards through the air before he crashed to the dusty ground. The mul was on the templar in an instant, the Scourge of Rkard in his hand and the blade's tip pressed to the bureaucrat's wrinkled throat.

Styan's face remained serene and confident, but, above the astonished gasps and the fall of alarmed steps, Rikus could hear the templar's madly pounding heart.

"Tell them the truth!" Rikus yelled.

"But I already have," answered Styan. "Killing me will not change that."

Rikus pressed on the blade, and blood began to trickle down the papery skin of Styan's neck.

"Stop it!" said Jaseela. She grabbed the mul's arm and tried to pull it away, but the noblewoman was not nearly strong enough. "You're playing into his web."

"He said nothing to me about any half-elf seeing anyone leaving the oasis!" Rikus spat.

"Of course not," Jaseela said. "There were no figures, and there probably isn't any half-elf—but you're making it look like you're the one who's trying to hide something."

Neeva grabbed Rikus's wrist and slowly moved it aside, then nudged Styan so hard that she almost kicked him. "Get up before he kills you," she said. "Not that I'd care."

The templar showed his gray teeth in a poor imitation of a smile. "Thank you, my dear."

When Rikus turned away to sheathe his sword, he was surprised to see the dwarves falling into line and marching out of camp. "What are they doing?" he demanded, scowling at Caelum.

The tall dwarf looked away, obviously ashamed. "They're going to the oasis," he said. "Please do not blame them. It is not that they doubt your word, but they cannot understand why Styan would lie about something so important. Under such circumstances, fighting this battle would violate their focus, and they cannot do that."

"Fine," Rikus snarled. "We don't need them, either."

"Rikus, you can't mean you still intend to attack!" Styan gasped. He was careful to stay out of the mul's reach.

"I'm not going to let them get away," Rikus answered.

The templar looked to Jaseela. "Surely, under such circumstances, you'll reconsider your decision."

The noblewoman scorned the templar by turning the disfigured side of her face to him. "So far, Rikus has won every battle," she said. "I'll trust to his instincts."

* * * * *

Rikus heard the clatter of stones ahead. He drew his sword, then motioned for those behind him to ready their weapons as well.

The mul was leading Neeva and the rest of his gladiators through a deep ravine filled with pink groundstar and barbed thickets of amber tarbush. On one side of the furrow rose the stony foothills of the Ringing Mountains, and on the other the great dunes of the sand wastes. Directly ahead, the trench was blocked by a delta of stones, sand, and other debris spilling from the mouth of a dry gorge. It was in that gorge, according to K'kriq, that the Urikites had been camped last night.

Before climbing out of the trough, Rikus paused to look at the crimson sun. It hung at its zenith, a fiery orb that hovered in the exact center of the blazing white bowl of the midday sky.

"White sky," Neeva said, also studying the sun. "Jaseela should be in position." Under K'kriq's guidance, they had the sent the noblewoman and Caelum to circle around behind the enemy.

"She'd better be," the mul said, motioning toward the gorge ahead. Now that he had the Scourge of Rkard in his hand, he could hear officers barking orders to their subordinates. "It sounds like the Urikites are on the move."

The mul scrambled up the slope at the end of the trough, motioning for Neeva, Gaanon, and the rest of the gladiators to do the same. As Rikus charged over the top he saw that the enemy was marching down the canyon in an unruly jumble. The mob was a stark contrast to the disciplined legion the mul remembered from the first battle. Without exception, the Urikites' red tunics were tattered and filthy, only half carried their bone shields, and even fewer still possessed their long spears. Most were armed only with obsidian short swords, and their faces were pale and rigid with fear.

Behind them came a towering figure of absolute blackness, herding the ragged force before him like a phantom shepherd driving his flock to slaughter.

"Umbra!" gasped Neeva.

"Good," said Rikus, rushing straight toward the shadow monster.

"What's good about this?" Neeva asked, falling into step at his side.

"If Umbra's here, then Maetan probably is too."

"Good," said Gaanon, his heavy footsteps jarring the ground as he echoed the mul's words. "I'll kill them both."

Behind the trio came hundreds of screaming gladiators, spreading out to meet the mass of Urikites head-to-head. Already, Rikus could see this fight would be to his company's liking: a grand combat with no tactics and no tricks, blade against blade and warrior against warrior.

The two mobs quickly closed to within a dozen yards of each other, and the mul's concerns were quickly forgotten as battle cries filled his ears.

Rikus sprinted straight for a pair of Urikite spearmen, intending to lop the heads from their weapons and barrel past them into the throng beyond. At the last moment, however, they lifted their spears from the braced position and threw the weapons at his heart. Reacting instinctively, the mul blocked one of the spears with his sword. To his surprise, even though it struck only a glancing blow, the Scourge sliced the shaft in two.

The other spear slipped past the arcing blade but abruptly dropped and struck in the lower abdomen. Rikus cried out and staggered under the impact of the sharp point, but did not feel the deep burning of a puncture wound. He looked down and saw that the spearhead had not penetrated his Belt of Rank.

Rikus plucked the weapon from his belt and tossed it aside, grinning at the two petrified Urikites who had attacked him. The men backed away and fled into the enemy mob, screaming about magic and sorcery.

"Cowards!" Rikus yelled, rushing after them. "Running won't save you!"

He crashed into the Urikite mass, his magic blade slashing and slicing through enemy arms and bodies as easily as it had the spear shaft. Neeva followed on his right, clearing a wide swath with her axe. Gaanon came on the left, his great club launching shattered Urikite bodies in all directions.

The three gladiators tore deeper and deeper into the Urikite mass, a maelstrom of death ripping its way across enemy territory like a wind-storm whirling across the salt flats of the Ivory Plains. Now and then, Rikus raised the Scourge of Rkard to block or parry instead of attack. Each time, when his attacker's obsidian blade crashed into the ancient steel of the mul's sword, it shattered.

Soon, Rikus was aware only of what he sensed: his own voice screaming in glee, the sour smell of opened entrails, the flash of his sword, and the spray of blood hitting his bare skin. He reacted without conscious thought, his blade dancing as if it were part of his arm, his legs and his free hand lashing out of their own accord to push some enemy into the path of Neeva's axe or Gaanon's club. He loved battle as a thri-kreen loved the hunt, as an elf loved to run, as a dwarf loved to toil. It was for this that the mul had been born: to fight, to kill, to win.

As the battle progressed, Rikus was vaguely aware that, all around him, Tyrian warriors were slashing and hacking at the confused and outmatched enemy. Like him, they had spent their lives training for personal combat, and, if their talents were not quite a match for those of the mul, neither could the enemy's skill compare to theirs. Even in Rikus's own ears, the screams of dying Urikites drowned out his jubilant shouts. Out of the corner of his eyes, he glimpsed red tunics falling by the dozens. The coppery smell of blood, rising off the red-stained rocks of the battlefield, filled his nose.

It ended all too soon. Suddenly, Rikus found himself lashing out at his foes' backs, stumbling over dead bodies as he tried to keep up with the fleeing Urikites.

"Fight," boomed Umbra's voice. "Fight and die, or I will have you as my slaves!"

The shadow giant grabbed a few of the fleeing Urikites, absorbing them into his dark body as he had the first time Rikus saw him. This time, his threat had little effect. Hamanu's soldiers continued to flee, or, when they did heed Umbra's words, Tyrian gladiators cut them down as quickly as they turned to fight.

"After the cowards!" Rikus screamed, finally working his way free of the tangle of bodies littering the battlefield.

"Death to the coward Urikites!" echoed Gaanon, his voice thundering almost as loudly as Umbra's.

Now that the Urikites had stopped fighting, Rikus found that the joy was gone from the battle. Nevertheless, he set off after the fleeing enemy. Even their rout was working to the Tyrians' advantage; from the direction they were fleeing, the Urikites would soon run into Jaseela and Caelum. Although the noblewoman's company was not large enough to stop so many panicked soldiers, it would slow the mob of cowards long enough for the gladiators to finish it off.

As the mul ran, his sharp blade struck down a foe with nearly every step. Because of their heavier weapons, Gaanon and Neeva could hardly keep up with Rikus, but they loped along behind him, finishing off the soldiers that the mul had only wounded.

Suddenly, Rikus found himself staring at a huge shadow. A black hand descended on his right, grasping both a Tyrian gladiator and a fleeing Urikite. A pair of blood-curdling screams sounded above the pained cries of those suffering more mundane deaths, then the bodies of the two men melted into Umbra's darkness.

"We've got Umbra," panted Neeva, stepping to the mul's side. "Now what?"

Gaanon stepped to the mul's other side. The half-giant was speechless; it was as if the sight of a being twice as tall as he had taken his booming voice away.

Rikus looked up and found himself staring into the sapphire orbs of Umbra's eyes. The shadow giant smiled, then reached down toward Neeva. "You will pay a heavy price for your victory, Tyrian." The breath rolled from the thing's mouth on fetid wisps of dark cloud.

Neeva screamed in defiance, hefting her dripping axe and bringing it down on the black hand. The gore-covered blade passed through the shadow with no apparent effect, emerging clean and bright as it hit the rocks at Neeva's feet. The weapon shattered as if it were glass, and Umbra's dark fingers closed around her waist.

"Rikus!" she screamed, black shadow already creeping down her thighs and up toward her neck.

Uncertain of what else to do, the mul brought his sword down on the black arm. To his surprise, the magic blade bit into the shadow as if it were flesh. Umbra screamed in shock and rage. Rikus hacked at the arm again, this time wielding the sword with both hands and bringing it down with all his strength.

Umbra's hand tumbled from the end of his arm, spewing a thick black fog over the ground. Neeva toppled over backward and lay shivering as the shadow fingers slipped from her body and drained into the ground.

Bellowing in anger, Gaanon stepped forward and leveled his mighty club at the shadow thing. Like Neeva's axe, it passed through the black body without harm, snapping like a twig when it smashed into the ground. Umbra kicked at the half-giant, planting his foot squarely in the big gladiator's chest and driving him to the ground.

Screaming in agony, Gaanon tried to roll away. His efforts were to no avail, for Umbra kept him pinned securely in place as a pool of blackness slowly spread across the half-giant's torso.

Rikus struck at the shadow giant's leg. Again, the blade bit into the black form. The dark beast cursed in a series of deep-throated gurgles that no human tongue could reproduce, then slapped the mul with his good hand. The blow knocked the Scourge of Rkard from the gladiator's grasp, but the only thing Rikus felt was a terrible chill that took his breath away and made his bones ache to the marrow. Rikus tried to reach for his sword, but his cold-muted reflexes were slow to obey. The weapon clattered to the ground a few feet away.

"Vorpal steel," Umbra hissed angrily. "Where did you come by that?"

As Umbra finished his question, the sound of sizzling and sputtering echoed off the rocky walls of the gorge. A short distance away, a curtain of shimmering air shot from one wall of the canyon to the other. The fleeing Urikites, more frightened of their pursuers than the magic before them, paid the translucent barrier no attention and continued to run. As the first wave approached the strange obstacle, they suddenly cried out and turned away. Their efforts did not save them. The press of those following drove them forward. As each man came close to the curtain, he burst into flame, then disappeared in a puff of black smoke.

Umbra looked toward the commotion and again uttered a curse in his strange language. Rikus threw himself toward his sword, passing over it in a rolling fall. He grabbed the hilt and returned to his feet in the same swift motion, lashing out at Umbra in a sweeping crossbody slash.

The blade sliced through empty air, for the shadow giant had already turned away. The dark creature was striding purposefully toward the curtain of searing air, the stump of his shadowy forearm trailing black mist.

Rikus went to Neeva's side and helped her to her feet. "Are you hurt?"

"Frozen to the bone, but not hurt," she said. She rose and retrieved a pair of obsidian short swords from fallen Urikites, then looked toward the shimmering curtain up the canyon. "What's that?"

"Caelum and Jaseela, I hope," Rikus said. He looked to Gaanon. "What about you?"

The half-giant forced himself to rise. "Just c-cold," he answered, wavering on his unsteady feet. "I'm not injured." He tried to step toward Rikus, but his frozen legs hardly moved and he fell face-first to the ground.

"Wait here. The sun will warm you," Rikus said, motioning for Neeva to follow him.

"No, wait!" cried Gaanon, again rising. "I'm fine."

Once more, the half-giant's legs failed him. He collapsed to the ground, still protesting that he was ready to fight.

* * * * *

On the other side of the curtain, Jaseela pointed at the shimmering barricade and glared down at Caelum with her torpid eye. "This thing—"

"It's a sun fence," Caelum offered.

"Whatever it is, it isn't part of Rikus's plan!" she snapped.

"Rikus's plan, if he has one, is no masterwork," the dwarf replied.

Along with K'kriq, they stood atop an outcropping of granite, more or less in the center of the thin line formed by Jaseela's small company of retainers. Through the ripples of Caelum's sun fence, they could barely see the Urikites pushing one another forward and bursting into flames as they neared the scorching barricade.

"Fence burn up prey," K'kriq observed. "Leave no food for pack."

"We're not eating the Urikites," Caelum growled.

K'kriq looked down his proboscis and clacked his mandibles at the dwarf. "Pack large—need much meat," the thrikreen said. "K'kriq know what you do. Hide all for self."

Caelum looked away, disgusted.

"Take it down!" Jaseela said.

"I won't," the dwarf objected. "This is the most efficient way to stop the Urikites."

"And keep my company out of the fight," the noblewoman objected. "My retainers didn't march halfway across Athas to watch the final—"

Jaseela's mouth dropped open and she did not complete her thought, for something else had seized her attention. Approaching from the other side of the sun fence was a figure as tall as a full giant and as black as a well-bottom.

"What, by Kalak's grave, is that?" she asked.

"From Neeva's descriptions, I'd say it's Umbra," the dwarf gasped.

The shadow giant took two long strides and was standing

at the wall, looking down on the barrier with two eyes of gleaming blue. After a moment's consideration, he stooped over and a billowing cloud of black fog issued from his mouth. It settled over the sun fence like a pall, opening a gap more than a dozen yards wide before it dissipated into the ground.

Caelum's face went pale. "It cannot be!" The dwarf grabbed Jaseela's arm. "Scatter your company. Tell them to run!"

The noblewoman jerked her arm free. "I'll do no such thing. We came to fight, and fight we shall." She waved her arms at both flanks of the line, yelling, "To the center! Plug the gap!"

If was difficult to tell whether the officers could hear her all down the line, but even if they couldn't, her gestures and the situation were sufficient to make her meaning clear. As the first Urikites began to pour through the gap, Jaseela's retainers rushed to meet them. The chime of clashing blades and the screams of dying men rang off the walls of the narrow gorge, with more men from each side pouring into the battle each second.

Though the Tyrian retainers held their ground well enough, Caelum felt sick to his stomach with dread. "I beg you, my lady, sound the retreat before it is too late. Our enemy is too powerful—"

"Be still," said Jaseela. "Just because a walking shadow undoes your magic—"

"It is not my magic that he overcame," Caelum said. "It was the sun's!"

Ignoring him, the noblewoman stepped to the front edge of the outcropping. As the last of her retainers poured into battle, she shouted encouragement and commands with equal vigor. Although the Urikites outnumbered her men and were fighting with the desperate urgency of doomed soldiers, her company was holding the gap.

When Umbra stepped into the breach, however, Jaseela's pride changed to concern. The shadow giant studied the battle raging at his feet for a moment, then passed his wounded wrist over the combatants. Long wisps of black vapor trailed from the stump and hung in the air.

"What's he doing?" Jaseela demanded. "Caelum?"

The dwarf did not hear her. He stood in deep concentration, one glowing hand raised to the sun and the other stretched out over the edge of the outcropping.

As Jaseela watched, the shadow giant spread more of the black vapor from his wound in the air. The dark mist coalesced into a thin cloud and spread outward, passing over the noblewoman's head and engulfing all of her army. At the same time, Umbra grew visibly thinner, until his limbs were no thicker than those of a half-giant. The shadow giant then began to shrink to a height proportionate with those limbs.

The black cloud began to descend like a fine mist. Almost as one, the Urikites stopped fighting and, screaming in mortal terror, threw themselves on the ground.

In that moment, Jaseela realized that she had been wrong not to listen to Caelum. "Retreat!" she called. "Run!"

Her cries did no good; the Tyrian retainers were so confused by the Urikites' behavior and the black cloud that was settling over them that they were incapable of any cohesive action. Some of them turned to flee, as she had ordered. Some hacked mercilessly at the bodies of their prone enemies. Still others pulled their cloaks over their heads as if a thin layer of cloth would protect them from the dark fog descending on them.

Out of the corner of her good eye, Jaseela saw a bright, crimson light flare at the edge of the cliff. A searing heat washed over the unscarred side of her face. Thinking to protect what remained of her beauty, the noblewoman turned away and ducked, wondering what harrowing magic the dwarf was trying to work now.

"If you want to live, come here!" Caelum yelled. "You too, K'kriq."

The dwarf took Jaseela's hand and pulled her toward the edge of the outcropping. There, hovering in midair, was a hissing, crackling sphere of crimson fire. In the center of it was a man-sized opening, out of which poured a brilliant golden light that hurt the noblewoman's eyes as much as the red orb seared her skin.

"Inside!" Caelum yelled.

The dwarf pushed her off the outcropping, and before she had any idea of what she was doing, Jaseela found herself jumping into the blinding ball of light.

EIGHT

The Citadel

A sharp pop sounded a few feet away, near the granite outcropping that dominated the center of the gorge. A fleck of scarlet light appeared in midair and began to hiss and crackle. In the blink of an eye, it grew into an orb of crimson flame the size of a fist.

"Get down!" Rikus screamed.

Temporarily abandoning his pursuit of the fleeing Urikites, the mul dropped to his belly. Neeva landed at his side. All around them, gladiators cursed as they banged their elbows, knees, and even heads on rocky points and edges. The red ball grew into a roaring globe that blotted out the sun itself, its mottled surface crossed and recrossed by rivers of orange flame. A black seam appeared on the sphere's underside and slowly lengthened. At any moment, Rikus expected the joint to burst and shower his warriors with liquid fire.

Instead, the rift opened slowly, revealing a fiery yellow interior so bright that it hurt the mul's eyes to look at it. The silhouette of a woman's form appeared in this crack, then dropped out of the ball and landed on the rocky ground in a crumpled heap. Wisps of smoke rose from her blackened tabard. Her face had turned as red as the sun, and her scorched hair hung over her shoulders in stiff and brittle locks.

"Jaseela!" Rikus gasped, rising to his feet.

As the mul rushed toward the woman's scorched form, K'kriq dropped out of the sphere. The thri-kreen landed next to the noblewoman and used his body to shield her from the heat of the orb. Caelum came next, then the globe closed up and began to shrink. By the time Rikus reached the three warriors, the ball was gone.

The trio stank of singed hair and burned cloth. The heat had darkened even K'kriq's tough carapace and raised small white blisters where Jaseela's skin was exposed. Only Caelum had emerged unharmed, though his lips were swollen and cracked.

As soon as she saw Rikus, Jaseela's tongue appeared from between her lips as she tried to say something. He kneeled at her side and placed his ear to her lips. Her words were so faint that, had he not been holding the Scourge of Rkard, the mul would not have heard them.

"Why didn't you warn me about the shadow?" she gasped.

The mul glanced around the gorge. He and his gladiators had just followed the Urikites through the gap in the shimmering curtain, so he had not yet had time to inspect the area. Still, he realized, this was where Jaseela's company should have made its stand. Instead of a battlefield, he saw a barren expanse of rocks. There was not even a single body to suggest that the noblewoman's company had fought here.

"What shadow?" Rikus demanded. "Where's your company?"

When Jaseela could not find the strength to answer, Caelum did it for her. "Umbra destroyed all of them," said the dwarf. "I tried to warn her."

Rikus laid the noblewoman's head down, then summoned a pair of gladiators. "Take her to the oasis. She needs water and shade." The mul looked to Caelum and K'kriq next. "You two go with her. You need rest too."

K'kriq crossed his antennae. "Hunt not over!"

At the same time, Caelum frowned. "What are you going to do?"

"Avenge Jaseela," Rikus said, waving his warriors after the Urikites. "Finish the hunt."

"Didn't you hear me?" Caelum objected, following along. "You can't go after the Urikites. Umbra is with them!"

"And he's hurt," Rikus said. "If I'm ever going to kill him, it'll be today."

"But he breached the sun's fence!" Caelum exclaimed. When Rikus paid him no mind, he added, "If more of our warriors die, it will be on your head!"

"You're wasting your words," Neeva said. "Go on to the oasis and find out how the templars and the other dwarves are faring."

Caelum fell silent and stared at Rikus in exasperation. At last the dwarf turned his red eyes on Neeva. "If you're with him in this foolishness, then so am I."

* * * * *

A short distance from the gorge, Maetan of Urik stood before an ancient citadel, awaiting the return of his defeated legion. The fortress's builders had chiseled the structure from living rock, shaping it like a great, top-heavy argosy that sprang from the hill's limestone flanks. Four stone wheels, each twice the height of a half-giant, were carved into its foundation and decorated with concentric rings of stone flowers.

Above these unturning wheels, a square platform supported a massive edifice of tall columns and balconies with gaping, dark doors behind them. Lifelike statues of male and female humans, all armed with fanciful weapons like double-edged scythes or four-bladed battle-axes, stood scattered over these balconies.

At the top of the citadel was a deck with a single balcony that overlooked the front of the temple. On the prow of this loge stood the huge statue of a handsome man with a great mane of hair and a tightly curled beard. Unlike the figures below, he carried no weapons, and a pair of large leathery wings sprouted from his back.

"Is this edifice so interesting?" asked Umbra, gliding across the rocky canyon floor to join his master.

Maetan looked away from the citadel. Behind the shadow giant, the first wave of his defeated legion was just rounding the sharp bend that hid the rest of the gorge from view.

Looking back to Umbra, Maetan observed, "You failed." The mindbender made no comment on the dark vapor oozing from the shadow giant's wounds. He had been watching the battle through his servant's eyes and knew how he had come by them.

"What did you expect?" Umbra asked. "Your men are cowards."

"When they are led by a fool," the mindbender retorted.

"You call the Tyrian mul a fool, yet his warriors would rather die than retreat," observed Umbra.

Maetan bit back a caustic reply, for he knew how little time he had to waste arguing with Umbra. The Tyrians were following his legion up the canyon, and it would be only a minute or so before they were standing where he was now. Instead, the mindbender pointed at the ancient citadel, then said, "Perhaps my soldiers will prove braver inside a fortress."

The corners of Umbra's blue mouth turned down. "They will be trapped," he said. "At the most, they will last seven days before running out of food and water."

"That will be long enough. I need only ten days to return to my family's estate," Maetan said.

"And what will you do there? Explain to your family how you sullied its precious honor?" asked Umbra.

"No," Maetan answered. "I will redeem it." He reached down and picked up the shoulder satchel that he had prepared for himself, then slipped his hand inside and patted the cover of the *Book of the Kemalok Kings*. "Stay with the cowards until they die," he said. "Perhaps your presence will convince the dwarves that what they seek is inside the citadel."

The mindbender took a deep, steady breath, calling upon the Way to aid with his escape. He pointed a finger at the top of the cliff and imagined that all the space between himself and that location did not exist. A surge of energy rose from deep within himself, flowing outward to make what he wished temporarily so. When he opened his eyes again, where there had been only flakes of orange sandstone a moment earlier, Maetan saw a silvery tuft of ground holly growing from the crevice of a broken slab of limestone. It was, he knew, the terrain at the top of the gorge.

Maetan started to step onto the clifftop, then decided to give Umbra a last instruction. He stopped halfway there, with one foot on the sandstone in the bottom of the gorge and the other planted squarely on the limestone atop the cliff.

To Umbra, it looked as though the mindbender had divided his body in half. One part stood before him in the gorge, and the other stood far overhead, barely visible at the top of the cliff.

"One more thing," Maetan said. "Kill the mul."

Umbra raised the throbbing stump of his missing hand. "Nothing would please me more."

The mindbender nodded, then stepped all the way onto the clifftop and left the gorge altogether. Umbra took a moment to look up and watch his master climb away from the cliff edge, then turned his attention to the task of rallying Maetan's cowardly soldiers. Already, the first Tyrians had appeared at the bend and were busily hacking down the slowest Urikites from behind.

"Come with me!" called Umbra, moving toward the citadel. "You will be safe in here!"

The shadow giant's lie worked easily, for the panicked soldiers were anxious to seize any hope of salvation. There was no obvious entrance to the fortress, but Umbra could see a stairway in the deep hollow between the great wagon's stone wheels. Followed by the fastest of Maetan's cowards, he led the way to these steps and began climbing.

They passed through an opening on the lowest deck and came out on a balcony on the first level. In the middle of this loge was the lifelike statue of a fully armored woman smashing a spiked club into the floor. Beneath this club lay a shattered, sun-bleached skull, and scattered over the rest of the deck were the splintered bones of another half-dozen skeletons.

Umbra slipped over the bones silently, moving toward the door that stood at the back of the small balcony. He had time to glimpse a bright room at the end of a long hallway before a gray, insubstantial form appeared at the end of the corridor and drifted toward him.

"A wraith!" Umbra hissed.

He retreated from the corridor immediately, though not because he was frightened. No being from the Black had need to fear a wraith, for undead spirits were themselves merely shadows of the living. If it detected Umbra at all, the wraith would regard the shadow giant as a human might an oasis spirit: something dimly sensed and best left alone. Unfortunately, the same would not be true for the Urikites. The wraith would sense the life pulsing in their veins and try to drive them away.

The gray silhouette slid past Umbra and slipped over the woman's statue like a pall. The stone sculpture darkened to a dusky shade of brown, and its blank eyes suddenly glowed with a ghastly red light. As the first Urikite tried to slip past, the stony woman cried, "No!"

She swung her club, driving a dozen long spikes deep into the soldier's neck and chest. He flew off the balcony and crashed onto the heads of his fellows below. They hardly seemed to notice, for the Tyrians were closing in and a battle was already beginning to rage within a dozen yards of the citadel.

Had the choice been Umbra's, he would have abandoned Maetan's plan and gone to search out Rikus that instant. Even if he could find another way into the citadel, he doubted the Urikites would survive for very long. Unfortunately, if he did not follow Maetan's commands to the word, the mindbender would not be compelled to deliver the obsidian he traded for Umbra's services. The shadow giant could not allow that, for his wives needed the glassy rock. It was almost egging season.

Umbra stepped toward a narrow catwalk that led from this balcony to the next, pausing to address the men who had been following the dead soldier. "Fight past the statue," he ordered. "I'll find another entrance."

When the Urikites hesitated, Umbra pointed back down the gorge. "Fight past the statues or die!" he snapped. "Tyr does not take slaves, so surrender brings only death."

* * * * *

Rikus stood knee-deep in Urikite bodies, his gaze fixed on the top floor of the strange citadel. There, standing as tall as the winged statue of the bearded man, was Umbra. The shadow giant's blue eyes were studying the battlefield below, as if he were searching the bodies for a single Urikite survivor.

"What's he doing up there?" Rikus asked.

"And how did he get past all the statues?" Neeva wondered, pointing at the balconies on the citadel's lower level. Next to her stood Caelum, who was also looking at the uppermost loge, and K'kriq, who was staring at the dead with as much interest as Umbra.

Rikus studied the lower levels of the building. There was a gap in the stone railing of the first loge, and the statue that had been guarding the door behind it now lay scattered in the rocks below, broken into a dozen pieces. Despite their success in destroying the stony woman, that was as far as the Urikites had gotten.

The statue of an armored man had moved from the second loge and still patrolled the balcony, a four-bladed axe in one hand and a wide-bladed dagger in the other. Sprawled over the railing and lying beneath the balcony were more than a dozen Urikites with slashed throats, missing limbs, and smashed skulls.

As Rikus studied the rest of the citadel's lower level, he noticed that only the loge from which this statue had come was empty. On each of the other balconies stood another lifelike statue, each cradling some sort of fantastic weapon in its inert hands.

After studying the stone figures for a moment, Rikus took a deep breath, then said, "Let's go."

"Go where?" asked Neeva.

The mul pointed at Umbra, whose blue eyes now seemed to be locked onto him. "Up there."

"Rikus, I've seen you do a lot of stupid things in your

life, but this would be the worst," Neeva said. "Hasn't it occurred to you that if half a Urikite company couldn't make it past the first balcony, then neither will we?"

"No," the mul answered. He started toward the stairway concealed beneath the foundation. When he did not hear footsteps behind him, he stopped and turned around. "Aren't you coming?"

K'kriq was the first to answer. "No. T-too scared."

Rikus scowled and, not bothering with Caelum, looked to Neeva. "What about you?"

"If you can tell me how we're going to get past those statues, I'll follow you," she said.

Rikus pointed his sword toward Umbra. "The same way he did."

"How was that?"

The mul shrugged and started toward the stairs again.

Neeva did not join him until he had set a foot on the bottom step. "You're as one-sighted as a dwarf and about as smart as a baazrag," she growled.

Behind her came Caelum. Only K'kriq, who had turned his attention to picking through the Urikite bodies, did not join him.

"Even if we make it past the statues, Umbra will kill us all," said Caelum, half-hiding behind Neeva.

"No one told you to come along," the mul answered, glaring at the dwarf.

"I asked him," Neeva said. "If anyone can save us, it will be him."

Rikus grunted, then climbed the stairs. As he stepped onto the first loge, the statue moved swiftly to meet him. It was a burly man dressed in what appeared to be a full suit of plate armor. From beneath his open-faced helmet dangled long, straight hair, and his pudgy jowls were covered by a bushy beard.

"No!" the statue boomed.

He swung his four-bladed axe. The mul ducked the blow easily, but barely managed to raise the Scourge of Rkard as the statue lashed out with his other hand. There was a loud chime as the dagger met the magic sword, then the stone blade snapped in two. Rikus countered immediately, slashing at the statue's legs.

The stone man skipped out of the way, retreating to the far side of the loge. His glowing red eyes remained fixed on the Scourge of Rkard for a moment, then dropped to the Belt of Rank girding Rikus's waist. After a moment, the statue surprised the gladiator by crossing his arms in salute.

The mul stepped onto the balcony. Keeping a wary eye on the statue, he crossed to the catwalk on the other side. When it made no move to stop him, he motioned to Neeva and Caelum to follow. "Hurry, before he changes his mind."

As soon as Neeva approached the balcony, the statue cried, "No!"

He raised his weapons and leaped forward, moving with as much grace and speed as any gladiator Rikus had ever fought. Neeva barely managed to keep her head by ducking the axe and dashing halfway down the stairs. She smashed into Caelum and sent him sprawling all the way to the bottom.

"I don't think I'm welcome," Neeva called.

"Then wait here," the mul said. "I'll take care of this myself."

"It could be a trap!"

"If it is, it's the strangest one I've ever seen," Rikus answered, shaking his head at all the Urikite bodies strewn about the balcony. "You can watch me kill Umbra from below."

"Or catch your limp body when he throws it down," she answered, descending the stairs.

Rikus followed the catwalk to the next loge. Instead of Urikite bodies, it was covered with splintered, sun-bleached bones. At the back of the balcony was a door that led into the interior of the citadel, but the mul did not even bother to peer down it. He had come here to kill Umbra, not explore a ruin.

He followed the catwalk around the rest of the building, crossing a long series of loges. To one degree or another, they were all littered with bones and, occasionally, broken weapons or weathered armor. On each balcony, there also stood a statue of gray stone frozen into a lifelike pose, its weapon planted in a set of white ribs or resting atop a shattered skull.

Finally, on the thirteenth loge, Rikus found the stairway that led up to the highest balcony. Clutching his sword tightly, he rushed up the stairs.

Upon reaching the top, he found a dark doorway on one side of the deck and the huge statue of a winged man on the other. Unlike the other balconies, the statue on this one was not surrounded by bones scattered over the stone blocks around it. There was also no sign of Umbra.

"Where are you, shadow?"

There was no answer. Fearing that his prey had fled, Rikus looked over the edge of the balcony. With some difficulty, he picked out Neeva's form from the hundreds of gladiators still milling about the battlefield. "What happened to Umbra?" the mul yelled. "Did he leave?"

"No," came the reply.

"Then I'm going inside."

"Rikus, no!"

The mul faced the shadowy doorway and took a deep breath, then rushed forward. An eerie prickle ran down his spine as he stepped out of the blazing sun and into the cool darkness of a long corridor. His steps rang off the walls as he advanced down the hallway, and soon the musty smell of

mildew filled his nostrils. A soft light rose from the floor of
the room ahead, but it was much dimmer than the Athasian
day and Rikus felt half-blind.

As he stepped out of the corridor, an icy hand seized his
wrist. His whole arm went numb and painful fingers of
chilling cold shot clear into his torso.

"Rikus," Umbra hissed.

The mul ripped his arm free and dove blindly away. He
did not hit the floor. Instead, his stomach rose into his
chest and he felt himself tumbling head over heels into a
deep pit. He glimpsed dozens of soft rays spilling across a
white floor beneath him, crossing and recrossing each other from all directions. As his body turned over, he saw
above him the narrow gallery walkway from which he had
jumped.

Finally, Rikus's shoulder struck the hard floor. He
stretched out to his full length to absorb the impact along
his entire body. At the same time, he slapped at the ground
with his numb arm, trying to counter the force of his landing. If the effort did him any good, he could not tell. His
head hit the stone floor with a resounding crack, his body
exploded into bone-jarring agony, and the breath blasted
from his lungs in a pained howl.

"My master wishes you dead," Umbra hissed, his words
echoing off the stony walls of the pit. They came to Rikus
as though from a great distance. "So do I."

Acting on instinct alone, the mul tried to scramble to his
feet. Instead, he found that it was all he could do to draw
breath into his laboring lungs. Every inch of his body
stung and ached at the same time. His vision was blurred,
he felt sick to his stomach, and his head throbbed with
pain.

For what seemed an eternity, the mul lay on the floor,
trying to make sense of the wash of colors around him. Far
above he saw the brown abyss of the vaulted ceiling.

Beneath it was a beam of light that silhouetted Umbra's fuzzy black form. The shadow creature was peering down at Rikus and speaking in a deep, rumbling voice. The mul could make no sense of the words.

Rikus felt his eyes closing. For a moment he wanted to let them. Nothing seemed more inviting than to slip away from this pain-racked body. He could not tell how far he had fallen, but it seemed more than twice Gaanon's height. A tiny voice inside him seemed to say that even a mul could not fall so far and escape injury. There was no use fighting, so why not just let your eyes close and be done with the pain?

The mul would have none of that. He held his eyes open and forced himself to concentrate on the pain. As long as there was pain, he told himself, there was life.

Slowly, the mul's vision cleared. Seeing that Umbra had disappeared from the railing above, Rikus rolled onto his belly and rose to his knees. The effort sent waves of pain shooting through his back, his ribs, and especially his head. He felt dizzy. His vision blurred again, and he remained kneeling until the feeling passed.

It looked to him as though he had landed in the citadel's central room. In the middle of the chamber, near where he kneeled, a three-sided banister marked a narrow staircase that descended deeper into the fortress. Along the walls, thirteen hallways, set between high walls of dark marble, ran from the circular room like the spokes of a wheel. Each corridor ended at one of the thirteen balconies ringing the citadel's second level.

Rikus tried to stand. His knee buckled and his collarbone popped, dropping him back to the floor in a torrent of blazing agony. The mul grabbed his arm and realized immediately that the fall had dislocated his shoulder. He could not tell what was wrong with his leg, for it throbbed with a terrible ache from the hip down to the ankle.

The mul knew that if he fought Umbra now, he would surely die.

Again he tried to stand, this time placing all his weight on the side of his body that had not struck the floor. To his relief, his leg held. Using his left arm, he picked up the Scourge of Rkard and put it in its scabbard, then braced the sword against the ground like a cane. He started to limp forward, heading toward a balcony.

"It's too late to run," Umbra hissed, dropping into view from the murky underside of the gallery.

The shadow creature stood silhouetted against the creamy light that poured down the narrow hall at his back. He now stood just a little larger than Rikus, his wounds still oozing black fog and his blue eyes burning with an icy spark.

The mul turned toward a different corridor, but Umbra blocked the way before Rikus could escape. "Did I not hear you claim you would kill me?" the shadow beast chortled.

"I will," the mul answered with a confidence he did not feel.

Rikus half-hopped and half-limped toward the narrow stairway in the center of the chamber, realizing Umbra would never permit him to flee from an obvious exit. The shadow creature rushed forward, his hiss echoing off the walls like that of a viper. Rikus threw himself at the stairs, screaming in pain even before he reached the opening.

The mul plunged into a black pit, then tucked his chin to his chest and bounced head over heels down a long flight of rocky stairs. By the time he hit the bottom, agony had numbed his mind and confused his thoughts. For several long moments, he could not figure out which way was up, for he had plummeted into a pool of darkness and could not find a light.

Just when Rikus thought he had fallen unconscious, his

dwarven vision began to work. The walls and floor radiated the subdued blue tones of cold stone, and he could see that he had landed in a small foyer where three dark corridors met. Here and there, green gossamer tresses dangled from the ceiling, nearly sweeping the floor with the tips of their gauzy strands. Red, fist-sized crustaceans scuttled down the draping webs on six pinkish legs, their wicked claws held before their bodies and ready to seize any prey they touched.

Behind Rikus, Umbra's resonant voice cursed in his strange gurgling language. The mul looked toward the eerie sound and saw the shadow creature's silhouette at the top of the long stairwell, angrily glaring into the utter blackness that separated him from his quarry.

Rikus forced himself to stand. He could not help groaning in pain, but he did not think it would make any difference to the coming battle. Umbra knew that he was injured.

"If you want to fight, come down," the mul called.

He used his sword scabbard to clear a wide circle of crustacean webs.

Umbra did not respond to the challenge. Instead, the shadow creature cursed again, then stepped away from the stairwell. Rikus resisted the temptation to climb the stairs, reasoning that if his enemy was reluctant to come after him, it was best to stay where he was.

When the shadow giant did not return within a few moments, Rikus inspected his battered body. His sword arm hung limp and useless at his side, the shoulder shoved a little less than a hand's length forward of its socket. The mul thought it would be a simple thing to push it back into place, but he also knew that it would hurt. In one of the fights that had convinced Maetan's father to sell him, the mul had allowed a young half-giant to hit him with a stone club. The result had been a similar injury, and he would never forget the pain he had suffered when the healer had returned the arm to its socket.

Before running the risk that the agony would render him unconscious, as it had the last time, Rikus turned his attention to his leg. From what he could see, it was in better shape. His ankle was swollen to the size of his calf, but it seemed to be in line with his shinbone. He placed a little weight on it, and a dull ached ran up as far as his thigh. There was none of the sharp pain that he had felt on the many occasions he had suffered broken bones in the arena, so the mul breathed a sigh of relief and went on with the inspection of the rest of his leg. Although the entire thing was extremely tender, especially around the knee, there were no unusual lumps or protrusions. He had probably just bruised the bone when he landed. The last time he suffered such an injury had been shortly before he escaped from Tithian's slave pits, when he had allowed a dwarven friend to best him at cudgel practice.

Cursing himself for being such a softling, Rikus gradually placed more weight on the bruised leg. It throbbed to the bone, but did not collapse—even when the mul stood on it alone. He gritted his teeth against the pain and forced himself to keep his weight on the leg until he became accustomed to the discomfort.

Finally, Rikus was ready to attend to his injured arm. He grabbed the dislocated shoulder and shoved it toward the socket, letting out a terrible scream as it popped back into the joint.

From the top of the stairs, Umbra called, "There's no need to scream—yet."

The mul looked toward the shadow creature's voice and saw that Umbra had returned. In the palm of his good hand burned a brightly flickering flame.

At first Rikus was puzzled, though less by how Umbra could hold a burning flame in the palm of his hand than why the shadow giant would want to. The mul could not imagine that such a phantom was incapable of seeing in the dark, but that seemed the only explanation—until Rikus recalled how Maetan had summoned the creature.

A thin smile creased the mul's lips. "What's a shadow with no light?" he whispered, drawing the Scourge of Rkard.

Rikus pressed himself against the wall. The pain of resetting his shoulder had made him nauseous and dizzy. He felt like he would topple to the ground and fall unconscious at any moment. The mul clenched his teeth and fought to stay awake.

The flame in Umbra's hand cast its flickering light over the floor of the small foyer, but it seemed to take the shadow giant forever to descend the dark stairwell. At last, Rikus saw a tongue of flame glimmer from around the corner.

The mul attacked, launching himself into the stairwell and swinging his sword at Umbra's good arm. As Rikus's torso met the shadow creature's, a terrible chill rushed through him, compounding the agony already wracking his battered body. The shadow giant cursed, spewing black fog from his mouth that filled Rikus's lungs with an icy, foul stench.

The mul continued his swing, slicing through the wrist of the dark beast's good hand. As his hand and the fire it held dropped to the floor, Umbra cried out in surprise and pain. The flames continued to burn.

"I see the scorpion retains his sting," Umbra hissed. He reached for Rikus with the stumps of both arms, spraying the mul with noxious black vapors that chilled him as badly as the shadow's grasp had.

Rikus dropped to floor, throwing his body onto the fire in a desperate attempt to extinguish the light.

The mul landed on the flame squarely, screaming in pain

as it seared the skin of his bare chest. An instant later,
Umbra's cold form settled over his back and a terrible chill
sank deep into his flesh. The stairwell went dark and everything fell silent.

NINE

The Thirteenth Champion

Rikus lay in a stone box that reeked of decay. Though it was barely large enough to hold his body, the mul's captor had thoughtfully placed a jug of water on one side of the gladiator's head and a loaf of moldy bread on the other. The Belt of Rank still girded his waist, and he had even been allowed to keep the Scourge of Rkard. The long sword lay atop his burned chest, his hands neatly folded over the hilt.

Rikus had no idea where he was or how he had come to be there, but he knew he wanted to leave. The damp chill pierced him to the bone, and his joints felt as though they were lined with frost. His shoulder throbbed with a deep cold ache, and his sore leg felt like a slab of ice.

As miserable as he was, he did not think Umbra had taken him to the Black. The prison didn't seem quite horrible enough to be the shadow giant's home. The cold should have been biting, the kind that turned skin white and froze toes and fingers solid. The darkness didn't seem right, either. While it would have been difficult for the blackness to be more absolute, the mul's dwarven vision allowed him to see the cold blue tones of his stone box, the yellow-hued

169

bread, and his own reddish skin with perfect clarity. Whatever Umbra's "Black" was like, the mul did not think he would be able to see in it with any form of vision.

"It makes no sense," Rikus grumbled, more to hear the sound of his own voice than because he thought it necessary to proclaim that fact.

Speaking the words made him conscious of his dry tongue and throat. He had no idea how long he had been trapped inside the box, but it had been long enough to make him thirsty.

The lid of the mul's prison was only a few inches above his face, so there was no hope of sitting upright to drink from the water jug. He reached up and turned the vessel so that its small spout pointed toward his mouth, then tipped it slightly.

The fluid surged from the jug in a yellow-hued glob, filling the mul's mouth with the sour taste of vinegar. Rikus reflexively sat up to spit out the gummy fluid, banging his forehead into cold stone. The lid budged open enough for him to glimpse a pale flicker of yellow light, then the foul liquid in his mouth slipped down the mul's throat. He dropped back into the box and smashed his head against the bottom of his stone prison. The lid returned to its place with a sharp bang.

Where he had banged it into the stone, the mul's skull ached terribly, and the foul water he had swallowed was already making him nauseous. Nevertheless, Rikus had to restrain himself from crying out in joy. He placed a hand on the lid and shoved with all his might. The stone slab slipped off the box and crashed to the floor with a loud boom that echoed off walls not too far distant.

Returning his good hand to the hilt of his sword, the mul sat up. He found himself in a small chamber with a low ceiling. It was dimly lit in a dozen different colors, each cast by a magnificent glowing gem set into the lid of a stone sarcophagus. Carved into the top of the twelve coffins was the bas-relief figure of a sleeping warrior. On the box next to Rikus's, a huge citrine cast an eerie yellow glow over the figure of a broad-shouldered woman with close-cropped hair.

"A tomb!" Rikus gasped, a cold knot of fear forming in his chest. He did not voice the question that consumed all his thoughts: who had brought him here, and why?

The mul struggled out of his sarcophagus, his injured shoulder and leg aching terribly as he stepped over the coffin's cracked cover. The carving on it represented a bald human with features so rugged and blocky that he might have been a dwarf, if not for his round ears and long bushy beard. His eyes were sunken and wild, with a heavy brow covered by a thick line of hair. Though the dark orbs were made of stone, they seemed almost alive with ire and hatred.

In his hands, the man held a long bastard sword identical to the Scourge of Rkard. His body was covered by a full suit of plate armor, save that the visored helmet hung a little above the warrior's shaven head. In the forehead of this basinet was set an orange opal. Unlike the gems of the other sarcophagi, this one remained dark.

Though the opal was clearly worth a hundred silver coins, Rikus did not even consider prying it from its setting. With Neeva and the rest of the thirsty legion waiting outside, he had no time for grave-robbing. Besides, the tomb filled his heart with such gloom and apprehension that he had no wish to tarry in it a moment longer than necessary.

When he scanned the murky room for an exit, he found none. The walls were lined with panels of bas-relief sculpture, but there was no visible opening in any of them. The mul stepped over to the closest and inspected it more carefully, hoping to find the seam of a concealed door.

The stone carvings depicted the same bearded warrior shown on the lid of the mul's sarcophagus. The man was leading an assault on a warren of bearded dwarves resembling those pictured in the murals of the Tower of Buryn.

The visor of the warrior's helm was raised to reveal a broad, demented grin, and behind him lay the mutilated bodies of dozens of dwarves. Ahead of the armored figure fled many more, all looking over their shoulders at the gore-dripping sword that would soon cut them down.

Other sections of the panel depicted acts even more horrid. In one, the warrior had skewered the bodies of three dwarven children on his sword. In another he was drawing the blade across the abdomens of six women, leaving a trail of entrails and blood spilling from the wounds he had opened. Always, the warrior's victims were dwarves, and, always, they were depicted as frightened and dying.

Sickened by the scene and unsuccessful in finding any cracks or seams that could have been a door, Rikus moved along to inspect the rest of the panels. Like the first, the others portrayed hateful warriors leading attacks on defenseless dwarves. In one, the broad-shouldered woman depicted on the coffin with the citrine was filling a large cavern with dwarven bodies. Another showed a tall gaunt warrior attacking a group of sleeping dwarven women.

When he came to the last panel, still without finding an exit, the mul closed his eyes for a moment. He took several deep breaths, trying to fight back the despair welling in his breast. In his mind flashed images of his dry and desiccated corpse sitting in the corner of the gloomy chamber, the jug of foul liquid from his sarcophagus sitting half full at his side.

"I won't die like that," Rikus said. "If someone carried me in here, there must be a way out."

His spirits somewhat restored by the sound of his own voice, the mul opened his eyes and inspected the last panel. It portrayed a fully armored warrior leading a legion through a forest. They were slaughtering a tribe of dwarves fleeing with all their possessions on their backs.

No matter how closely he looked, Rikus found no seams anywhere in the carving.

"Let me out!" the mul yelled.

He whirled around and pushed the closest sarcophagus to the floor. The glowing amethyst embedded in its lid went skittering across the cold stones, and the coffin itself shattered into a dozen shards. A withered corpse, held intact only by the suit of steel armor it wore, tumbled out of the shattered box.

The mul stared down at the body, awed by the sight of its corroding weapons and armor. He had never before seen a suit of man-sized steel plate, not even in the armories of King Kalak.

As the mul studied the armor, a gray shadow left the glowing amethyst and slipped across the floor to the corpse. It slithered silently into the armor, then the dead man's head turned to look up at Rikus. A thin layer of gray, papery skin still covered the man's face. The corpse's leathery lips pulled back in a nasty sneer, and in the empty eye sockets twinkled eerie purple lights.

Rikus cried out in fear, then stepped back and drew his sword. Although he held the Scourge of Rkard in his hand, the tomb remained silent to his ears. The mul heard nothing but his own blood rushing through his body, his breath stirring the still crypt air, and the rapid pounding of his terrified heart.

When the corpse did not rise, Rikus dared to hope that it would leave him alone. He slowly backed away, moving as carefully and quietly as he could.

A woman's throaty voice demanded, "What are you doing? Put it back!"

Rikus stopped moving, barely finding the courage to look toward the voice. When he did, he saw the gray silhouette of a broad-shouldered woman. Although the rest of her body appeared as no more than a shadow, the woman's face remained well-defined in the form of a translucent, wavering mask with citrine-yellow eyes. If the spirit was anything to judge by, the woman had been strikingly beautiful, though there was no longer anything in her features that gave an impression of tenderness—if there ever had been.

"Put what back?" Rikus asked, trying to control his mounting fear. "The coffin?"

"That is for you to decide," the wraith answered, floating across the room to Rikus's side.

She grasped the mul's injured arm and raised it into the air. Rikus's jaw fell open, for her clammy grip seemed as substantial and solid as that of any living being who had ever touched him.

"This is what you must return."

The wraith opened her grip and Rikus's sore arm dropped like a stone. A bolt of anguish shot through his shoulder.

"My arm?" Rikus gasped, groaning in pain.

The wraith pointed at the sarcophagus from which the mul had escaped earlier. "Your body. Put it back," she insisted, pushing him toward the coffin. "The sooner your spirit departs your body, the sooner Rajaat will come."

The mul allowed himself to be herded through the dimly lit room, unsure of whether he should swing his sword at the wraith or not. So far, she had done him no harm, and the prospect of starting a fight with anything undead frightened even him.

When they reached his empty sarcophagus, the wraith patted the cold interior. "Return to the coffin."

Rikus shook his head and stepped away, ready to raise his sword if she attacked. "Let me out of this tomb."

"The time for bodies is past, Borys," she insisted, paying his demand no attention.

"Who's Borys?" the mul asked.

A distressed frown appeared on the wraith's translucent face. "The Thirteenth Champion of Rajaat, Borys of Ebe," she said, touching an ethereal palm to his chest. "Butcher of Dwarves. You."

"Me?" Rikus exclaimed. He shook his head violently. "No."

She brushed his cheek with her cool hand. In a living woman, the gesture might have been a warm one, but coming from a wraith it seemed imperious and threatening. "Have you forgotten your knights? Is that why you have been gone so long?"

"You've made a mistake," the mul insisted, stepping away from the woman's tenebrous shape. "I'm Rikus, freed man of Tyr."

"Don't say such things, Borys. There is nothing to fear," she said. "Die and join your followers, as you should have done a thousand years ago."

"How do you know Borys isn't dead?" Rikus demanded, stopping just beyond the wraith's reach. "He could have died someplace else."

"You know that cannot be," she answered confidently.

"Why not?"

The wraith pointed at the dark opal in the broken lid of Rikus's sarcophagus. "If you were dead, your spirit would have returned to light your gem."

Rikus stared at the opal, uncertain of what he should do. By convincing the wraith that he was not Borys, he might cause her to attack. On the other hand, he had nothing to gain by misleading her, since she had already made it clear that she wanted Borys dead.

After a moment's hesitation, the mul pointed at the gem, "Borys may still be alive, but I'm not him. I wouldn't know how to light that opal if I wanted to." He stepped over to the bas-relief depicting Borys slaying the dwarves. "I don't even look like your champion."

The wraith drifted after the mul and, before he could retreat, skimmed the sides of his head with her murky fingers. "It is not unusual that your appearance would change over so many years, especially if you shave your beard and crop your ears. I still know who you are."

"How can you be so sure?" the mul asked, slipping away from the wraith.

She gestured at his sword. "Is that not the Scourge of Rkard in your hand?"

Rikus's jaw fell. "That doesn't make me Borys of Ebe."

"Who else could have taken the dwarven belt?" she asked, dropping her glance to the Belt of Rank. "Only Borys."

"This was given—"

"Return the body to the coffin," the wraith snapped, suddenly growing angry. "We are anxious to summon Rajaat."

She moved toward him, reaching for his shoulders.

Rikus raised his sword. "I'm not who you think."

The wraith's translucent face contorted into an expression of anger and regret. "After all we shared, you would lift your weapon against me?"

"Yes—because I'm not Borys!" the mul yelled, his exasperation overcoming the fear he felt in the wraith's presence.

"You are!" she insisted, gliding toward the mul with an outstretched hand.

Rikus slashed at her arm with his sword, but she pulled away before the blade could strike.

"Let me touch you," she commanded. "I will undo the magic that blinds you."

"And if there is no magic?" Rikus asked, hoping that he had, at last, found a way to convince her of his identity. "Will you let me leave?"

"Only Borys can light the opal," she answered. "There is no reason to keep anyone else here."

Rikus lowered his weapon, but did not sheathe it. He was far from confident that her word could be trusted, but he was even less confident that he would win a battle with a wraith.

The wraith laid her hand on the burn in the center of the mul's chest. Though he felt the pressure of her hand, he did not experience the pain he would have expected from being touched on the wound. She closed her translucent eyes, then said, "Borys, it has been so long."

"I'm not—"

The mul stopped speaking in midsentence, for her hand suddenly turned noncorporeal. An eerie tingle spread through his body. As he looked on in horror, the hand began sinking through his bone and flesh. Rikus heard himself breathing in shallow, terrified gasps, then a distraught shudder ran down his spine as her hand crept deeper into his chest.

A ghastly pain spread through his body, then he felt a morbid prickle as her fingers closed over his heart. Rikus tried to raise his sword, but found that he was too terrified to do anything but tremble.

The wraith locked gazes with him. Her eyes were glowing red. "What is this?" she demanded in a disgusted voice. "A human-dwarf half-breed, and a knight of Kemalok's filthy kings!"

Her icy fingers squeezed the mul's heart, and Rikus felt like someone had dropped a granite pillar onto his chest. The mul backed away, but the wraith's hand remained clenched around his heart. She drifted through the air after him, her body hovering above the floor like a banner waving in the wind. Rikus's heart struggled to beat against her pitiless grip, each pulse coming more strenuously and after a longer interval. He began to grow dizzy and soon even his breath came in painful wheezes.

"What of your word?" he gasped, forcing himself to look into the thing's red eyes.

She squeezed so hard the mul thought his heart would burst. In his ears, he heard rushing wind, and the bitterness of oblivion filled his mouth.

Finding strength in the certainty of his impending death, Rikus lifted the Scourge of Rkard to swing it. The wraith clamped down on the mul's heart viciously. Rikus released the sword and, as it clanged to the floor, cried out in despair, his entire body filled with such unthinkable agony that he could no longer control his own muscles.

"Fool! While I hold your heart, I can read what is in it," hissed the wraith. "That is why I know you are telling the truth. You are not Borys."

She relaxed her grip just enough to allow the mul's heart to beat only feebly. He dropped to his knees, terrified that she would kill him.

"Before you die, tell my companions of Kemalok," the wraith demanded.

Rikus looked up and saw more wraiths rising from the glowing gems in the coffins. Like the one gripping his heart, they were gray and formless, mere silhouettes of men and women who had died long ago. Their faces were bitter and loathsome, twisted into pellucid masks resembling the visages on the sarcophagi from which they rose.

"Kemalok stands," the mul gasped, answering his captor's question.

"There is more," the wraith said. "Tell the others."

"The city's been buried for a thousand years, perhaps longer," he added, struggling to bring each word to his lips. He desperately wanted to attack the wraith, to somehow fight for his life. Unfortunately, the Scourge of Rkard lay out of reach, and, even if his bare fists could harm a wraith, he did not see how he could hope to attack when she knew his thoughts. "From what I saw, Kemalok was never sacked."

The wraiths hissed at each other in disconcerted tones. In a deep raspy voice, one asked, "And what of Borys?"

"He killed Rkard, but the king's dead body still guards his city," Rikus answered. "I don't know what happened to Borys."

"You must," objected another. Her voice was silky and smooth, but with sinister undertones that sent a chill down the mul's spine. "You carry his sword."

Rikus shook his head, for he was growing too weak to

waste his strength on simple denials.

"There is no lie in his heart," said the woman who held him. "The sword was given to him."

"Then he is of no use to us," said the raspy voice. "Kill him."

"Wait," Rikus coughed. Despite the urgency of his plea, his voice was weak and low. "The dwarves kept a history."

"The *Book of the Kemalok Kings*," said the silky-voiced wraith. "What of it?"

"It mentioned the Scourge of Rkard," Rikus said. "It might say what happened to Borys."

"Then give it to us, or we will make your death an agonizing one," ordered a wraith.

Rikus shook his head, then had to wait for his abused heart's next pulse before he had the strength to answer. "The book was stolen," he said. "I'm trying to recover it."

"And you expect us to believe you would bring it here?" hissed the woman who held his heart. She squeezed more tightly, and the mul's heart stopped beating. His vision narrowed to a small tunnel of light.

The raspy-voiced man said, "Catrion, let him speak."

Abruptly the woman relaxed her brutal grip and Rikus's heart began to pound with incredible fervor. "He's alive, Nikolos."

"Good." The wraith who had been addressed as Nikolos drifted toward Rikus, saying, "Unless we find out what happened to Borys, Rajaat will never come." He appeared before the mul, his eyes glowing amethyst purple. "You're going to help us, or you'll feel the wrath of Rajaat."

Rikus nodded. "I'll do it."

"He's lying, Nikolos," Catrion reported.

Inwardly Rikus cursed. He had come to realize that tricking the wraiths was his only hope of surviving. Unfortunately, that would prove to be difficult as long as they knew what he was thinking.

"Now he's trying to trick us," Catrion said, again closing her fist about his heart. "I'll kill him."

"No," said the soft voice of a female wraith. "We have waited for Borys long enough. It is time to find out what happened to him. We'll just have to ensure that this half-dwarf keeps his word."

"How will we do that, Tamar?" countered Catrion.

In answer, the soft-spoken wraith passed her gray hand over the huge ruby set into the lid of her sarcophagus. The stone rose from its setting and hovered beneath her hand as she drifted toward Rikus. "I'll go with him," Tamar said.

Catrion removed her arm from the mul's chest, then Tamar closed her shadowy fingers over her glowing ruby. Rays of crimson light shot from between her fingers and danced before Rikus's eyes in a mesmerizing pattern.

The mul lunged for his sword. By the time he grasped its hilt, Catrion and Nikolos stood over him, staring down at him with their eyes burning red.

"You could not destroy one of us, much less all twelve," said Catrion.

"Do as we demand, and you will live at least until the book is recovered," added Nikolos. He laid his hand on the back of the mul's neck, and Rikus felt a harrowing prickle as the wraith's fingers slipped over his spine. "Otherwise, you die here."

Rikus took his hand away from the sword's hilt and settled back onto his knees.

Tamar pressed her ghostly fist into the mul's chest. At first, Rikus experienced only the same eerie tingle that he had felt when Catrion's hand had gripped his heart. When the ruby passed into his flesh, however, it seemed that some-one had planted a burning ember in his heart.

Screaming in anguish, he lashed out at the wraith with his good arm. His fist passed through her body harmlessly, then Nikolos's hand squeezed his neck and pulled him back upright. Tamar's gem continued to sink into his breast for what seemed an anguished eternity.

At last, the pain subsided. The wraith's body flowed into the ruby in a wispy stream of shadow. Rikus looked down and saw that Tamar had lodged the stone in his left breast, with one facet exposed and peering out from beneath his skin like a blood-red eye.

I'll be with you wherever you go, she said, her silky voice echoing to him on his own heartbeats. *I'll see what you see, I'll hear what you hear, and I'll know what you're thinking. If you betray us, you'll wish I had let Catrion kill you here.*

To emphasize the threat, a searing streak of pain shot through the mul's body. Rikus gasped, then nodded slowly.

Very good, she said. *You may survive to serve our purpose.*

Rikus retrieved his weapon, then stood. "Can I leave?"

Catrion's eyes flashed brilliant yellow, then she said, "Follow me."

With that, she walked to the bas-relief depicting her slaughter of the cavern-dwelling dwarves. She stood before it for a moment, then the figures slowly came to life and backed away from the center of the panel. When they had vacated an area about as large as a man, a door-shaped area of stone darkened to jet black. Catrion stepped into the black area and disappeared.

Follow her, advised Tamar. *The portal will not remain open for long.*

Rikus reached out to touch the blackened wall and found that there was nothing there. He stepped into the portal and emerged instantly in the small foyer where he had fought Umbra. Next to him stood one of the statues from the exterior balconies of the citadel. It was the same tall, gaunt man that who had been attacking the dwarves in one of the bas-relief panels inside the tomb, and his arms were held out before him as if to carry something.

"That wasn't here when I came down," Rikus observed.

Nikolos used it to carry you down here, Tamar explained. *Outside our tomb, it is difficult for us to touch material things directly. Instead, we use our power to animate the statues.*

Rikus nodded, then went to where he had thrown himself on Umbra's flame. The shadow giant's body was nowhere in sight, but the stones where he had fallen were stained black and they felt cold to the touch. The mul smiled.

"I killed him, didn't I?" he asked.

"Who?" asked Catrion.

Rikus pointed at the stones. "Umbra. The beast I was fighting when I got hurt."

"We saw no beast," Catrion answered simply. She gestured at the stairs. "That way out."

Shrugging, Rikus climbed the stairs. If Umbra had not actually died there, then he had certainly suffered a grievous wound. Right now, the mul was satisfied with that.

After ascending the stairway into the circular chamber into which he had fallen earlier, Rikus found the hallway that led to the first loge. By the damson light flooding the corridor, he could tell that the hour outside was approaching dusk.

"I've been in here all afternoon!" the mul exclaimed, slipping between the high marble walls and walking briskly toward the outside. Never had he wanted to leave a place behind him as badly as this citadel.

When Rikus stepped onto the windy loge, he could not help gasping. The battlefield beneath the citadel was bathed in the purple shadows of dusk, but there remained enough light for him to see that it was deserted—save for hundreds of Urikite skeletons and the flock of kes'trekels that had stripped them bare.

"Neeva!" Rikus yelled, gripping the hilt of his sword so that its magic could aid him in listening for a reply.

He heard nothing but kes'trekels using their powerful beaks to crack bones, and their sharp claws to scratch for marrow.

TEN

Lirr Hunt

A beastly, deep-throated roar broke the night's cold silence. The bellow rolled across the stony barrens for several seconds, wavering from one bass note to another in an eerie song that sent a shiver down Rikus's spine. When the uncanny noise finally died away, it was answered by a similar wail far to the other side of the mul.

The cries hardly roused Rikus from his numb lethargy, and he did not even look up. Over the last few nights, the forlorn howls had become as much a part of the landscape as the stones that littered the parched ground upon which he walked.

The gladiator yawned and stumbled onward, every step a test of his determination. His good leg burned with such fatigue that he could hardly swing it forward. When he put the limb back down, the loose rocks turned beneath his foot. Inevitably, he had to catch himself on his makeshift walking staff, the headless shaft of a Urikite spear. Once his footing was secure, he dragged his injured leg, too numb and swollen to bend, over the rocks, then planted it beside the first. After bracing his crutch against his sore shoulder, he took a moment to lift the heavy lids of his eyes, then started the process all over again.

So it had gone for the last four days as he tried to catch up to his legion. During that time, he had stopped only once, to fill his waterskin at an oasis. He had taken his meals along the way, catching snakes or locusts as he walked, then devouring them raw. Rikus had not even slept, for his legion had left such an obvious trail of churned sand and overturned stones that he could follow it by the light of Athas's two moons.

Such exertion would have killed anyone else. In muls, however, the hardy constitution of the dwarven father enhanced the natural resilience of the human mother. When the need arose, such as now, they could drive themselves for days without sleep or rest. Still, as his eyelids drooped and a yawn rose to his jaws, it occurred to Rikus's fatigue-numbed mind that he was dangerously close to collapse.

The sonorous notes of another morbid beast-song rolled across the plain, reminding the mul that he did not dare fall asleep. Less than a hundred feet ahead, the dark form of a lirr scrambled up a jumble of boulders and fixed its amber eyes on Rikus. As the mul watched, the saurian creature stood upright, using its thorny tail to cling to a boulder and balance its torso over its rear feet. The thing was about the size of a dwarf, with a tubular body armored by diamond-shaped scales as rough and hard as the stones upon which it stood.

Rikus altered his course so that it would take him directly toward the beast, calling, "Come on and fight!"

Though the mul had intended to shout the challenge, nothing more than a long croak escaped his swollen throat. He had run out of water two mornings ago. Now, well into his second complete day of hard travel with nothing to drink, his tongue and lips were so distended that he could not choke even the simplest words past them.

Knowing from experience that the lirr would not let him within sword's reach, Rikus grabbed a large stone and hurled it at his would-be devourer. The mul's aim was as dismal as his arm was weary. The rock clattered to the ground well wide and far short of the beast.

The lirr flared its spiked throat-fan and snarled at Rikus, showing a mouthful of serrated teeth. The mul threw another rock. This time his aim was better, but the beast swatted the projectile away with a clawed forefoot. It remained on its rock, angrily slashing at the air, taunting the weary gladiator with hisses.

When the lirr let Rikus close to ten feet without fleeing, the gladiator began to hope it would be stupid enough to fight him. Electing not to telegraph his attack by drawing the Scourge of Rkard, the mul lashed out with his staff.

The blow struck the lirr in its scale-covered torso. Not flinching, the beast flicked its long tongue across Rikus's face. The mul's cheeks stung as though he had been slapped.

Rikus tried to yell a curse at the beast, but barely croaked instead. He swung his staff again. This time the pole sliced through the air without hitting anything, for the lirr had already jumped off the rock pile and was scampering away on all four legs.

Do not let them harass you, stupid dwarf, Tamar said, her voice echoing inside the mul's head. *They want you to waste energy.*

Be silent, Rikus ordered, resuming his weary march. *You have nothing to say that interests me in the least.*

What interests you does not matter, the wraith snapped. *Listen to me or die.*

Your threats mean nothing, the mul returned, shaking his head in an effort to keep his eyes open. *If you're going to kill me, do it—otherwise, stay quiet.*

You will do as I say! Tamar roared. *You will kill the lirrs tonight, before you collapse.*

Rikus dragged his numb leg over the sharp edge of a large rock. *I'm not going to collapse,* he responded. *We're too close to my legion.*

You have claimed the same thing every night of this trek, Tamar said.

Rikus used his staff to point at a stone that had been overturned by the passage of his warriors. The wind had not yet piled any sand around it, suggesting that it had been disturbed quite recently. *Tonight is different.*

And if you are wrong? What then?

Then I will die, and you will be trapped with my corpse—at least until a lirr swallows you, Rikus said.

When Tamar fell silent, Rikus smiled. Over the last four days, his fear of the wraith had turned to hatred. Her imperious attitude reminded him more and more of how he had been treated in his days as a slave, and the mul was determined that she would have to kill him before he let her enslave him.

Despite his hatred of the wraith, Rikus was not anxious to die, especially before he avenged himself on Maetan and recovered the *Book of the Kemalok Kings.* Therefore, as he continued to struggle over the rocky plain, he considered her advice. If he was wrong about catching his legion tonight, he would collapse from thirst shortly after the sun rose. That, he knew, was when the lirrs would move in to attack. The mul had to admit that there was a certain wisdom in the wraith's suggestion.

After dragging himself onward until he came to the base of a knoll, the mul began to stagger more than usual. Though the slope was a gentle one, the rocks covering it were much larger and the effort of lifting his leg even a little higher made his thigh muscles burn with fatigue. Just as he realized that he was more weary than he had thought, Rikus shifted the Scourge of Rkard's scabbard forward, then stumbled and nearly fell.

All around the mul, the lirrs cried out in excitement, filling the night with their gruesome songs. The beasts began to circle their weary prey in tightening rings, flicking their long tongues in his direction and flaring their large throat flaps. For the first time, Rikus was able to count their number: six beasts, not as many as he had feared, but more than he could slay easily.

The mul tripped again when his foot refused to rise high enough to clear a large, glassy rock. He plunged to the ground, barely managing to break his fall with his walking stick. Immediately, the desire to sleep flooded over him and his mouth opened in a terrific yawn.

The lirrs roared in unison, then moved in closer.

Rikus tried to spring back to his feet, but found that it was all his weary muscles could do to lift him.

If you can barely stand now, how much worse will it be the next time you fall? asked Tamar. *Lure them into striking range now—before you can neither walk nor fight.*

Seeing the wisdom of the suggestion, Rikus slipped his good hand down to his sword hilt, then lay his head on his walking staff.

Instead of rushing in to attack, the lirrs fell silent and dropped to the ground, their amber eyes watching the mul on all sides. There they remained, absolutely motionless and so quiet that, even gripping the Scourge of Rkard, Rikus heard only the soft hiss of their panting.

Close your eyes, advised Tamar. *I think the lirrs can see that they're open.*

I'll fall asleep, Rikus said. The stones beneath his body, still warm from the day's heat, were soothing the mul's sore muscles and taunting him with relaxation.

It will not matter, Tamar said. *With the Scourge in your hand, you will hear them coming.*

Anxious to draw the lirrs into battle, Rikus closed his

eyes. In his mind, he began repeating, *Stay awake, stay awake.*

With each refrain, his words seemed to grow more and more distant, and soon he could not hear them at all.

Rikus started awake to the sound of a soft clack, then felt his crutch slipping from beneath his face. As his cheek dropped onto the sharp edge of a stone, the groggy mul opened his eyes and saw a lirr backing away from him. It was using its long tongue to drag his walking staff away.

Rikus hoisted himself to his feet and stumbled after the beast, pulling his sword from its scabbard. Out of the corner of his eye, he caught the gleam of moonlight in a pair of amber eyes and heard stones clatter off to his side. By the time he turned, the second lirr had launched itself at him and was flying through the air with the claws of all four feet fully extended.

The mul raised his sword to defend himself, shaking his head violently in a vain effort to clear the fog from his mind. It was to little avail. Even under the threat of death, the reactions of his exhausted body were slow and cumbersome. The lirr struck him full in the body.

Searing pain burned through the mul's torso as the beast's foreclaws raked across the unhealed burn wound on his chest. He felt the thing's rear feet scratching at his stomach, and the gladiator knew that only his Belt of Rank had stopped the monster from disemboweling him.

Instead of fighting to retain his feet, Rikus allowed the lirr's charge to bowl him over. As he hit the rocks, he tucked his chin and used his good leg to kick off the ground, continuing the roll and throwing the beast off himself. It landed on its back two paces away. Rikus rolled over his sore shoulder, sending a dull ache shooting through his entire body, then brought the Scourge of Rkard down across its exposed throat.

The magical blade sliced through the stony scales. A geyser of dark blood shot high into the air, and the lirr howled in pain, scattering rocks to and fro as it whipped its heavy tail about.

Rikus had little time to gloat over his victory, for he heard stones clattering to both sides as two of the beast's fellows rushed to finish him off. The mul tried to leap to his feet, but his slow reflexes and battered limbs were still not up to the task. As the creatures closed in, he dropped back to his knees and spun around, swinging his sword in a wide arc.

The Scourge sliced across the first lirr's leg just below the crooked knee, then cut deep into the second's jawline. Wailing in pain, the beasts sprayed the mul with dirt and small stones as they stopped their reckless charges. Whipping his blade around, Rikus lunged at his first attacker, sinking the sword deep into its skull. The other one launched itself at its prey. The beast sank its serrated teeth into the swollen flesh of the gladiator's bruised leg. Rikus screamed, then instantly regretted his lack of restraint as the raw tissues of his parched throat burst into agonizing spasms.

The lirr whipped its head around violently and backed away, trying to drag its prey off his feet. Rikus jerked the Scourge free of the other beast's skull and brought the blade down across his attacker. The blade cut through the scales and deep into the neck on the first hack, but the saurian's jaws only clamped tighter. The mul struck again, this time lopping the head cleanly off.

The jaws remained closed. Rikus backed away with the lirr's head still attached to his leg, stumbling about in a circle to face any more beasts that might be attacking. The other three predators kept their distance, circling around the battle site, well out of the mul's reach.

"Come on!" Rikus croaked, again sending a burning wave of pain through his throat. "Let's finish this!"

Two of the lirrs stood on their hind feet and let out a series of mournful notes. The third, the one that had stolen his walking staff, angrily gnashed the wooden shaft into bits, tossing its head about and flinging the pieces far into the night.

Pathetic, observed Tamar. *There are still three of them, and you're in worse condition than before.*

Ignoring the wraith, Rikus stuck the Scourge's blade into the lirr mouth clinging to his leg, then cut the muscles holding the jaws shut. When the head fell away, blood poured from the wound so freely that he could not see how badly the thing had injured him—and he was not sure he wanted to.

The mul ripped a strip of cloth from his breechcloth. He tied it above the injury to slow his blood loss.

Cover the wound. It will heal faster.

When I get to camp, Rikus said, wincing as he started to limp forward.

You have no idea how far away your camp is!

Sure I do, Rikus said, looking toward the top of the knoll. *It's just over this hill.*

It was a statement of desperation, not fact. Nevertheless, Rikus had to believe what he said, for if he let himself think anything else he would not have the strength to continue. He knew that if he did not reach his legion soon, the combination of his fresh wounds, old injuries, thirst, and exhaustion would kill him.

Unfortunately, Rikus's warriors were not camped beyond the summit of the knoll, nor beyond the summit of the next one, nor even beyond the one after that. The mul struggled onward, always telling himself that the legion was just beyond the next ridge. The three surviving lirrs kept him company, once again giving him wide berth and sporadically bellowing their grim songs. Every now and then, they would close in and rush forward to test his reflexes, then quickly retreat when he demonstrated that he could still swing the Scourge.

As the two moons began to sink behind the Ringing Mountains, Rikus stood in the bottom of yet another rocky valley. He was looking up at the distant summit of yet another knoll, watching the soft morning breeze send tiny sand-devils skittering across the gentle slope. Already the green tendrils of first light were creeping up from the eastern horizon. The mul knew that, by the time he set foot atop the hill, the crimson sun would be shining down on him with all its fury.

Rikus dropped to his knees and laid the Scourge of Rkard across his thighs. The lirrs tightened their circle and bellowed their ghastly songs in wild glee.

Get up! Tamar ordered.

Rikus tried to rise, but found that his weary muscles would not obey. He was no longer conscious of the ache in his savaged leg. It hurt so badly from exhaustion that he could not even feel the pain of its lacerations.

You have not recovered the book. I will not allow you to quit! You can't do—

Rikus dropped his answer in midsentence, for the Scourge's magic brought a new sound to his ears. He scanned the hillside, searching its shadows for some sign of what had caused the noise. He saw nothing except motionless silhouettes, but the whisper of soft, controlled breathing was coming from behind an elongated boulder a short distance ahead. The mul struggled to his feet and limped forward. The movement drew a long series of mournful notes from the lirrs.

What is it?

Rikus did not bother to answer the wraith's question. Instead, he gripped the Scourge more tightly and limped onward. The mul had no idea what had made the sound, but he doubted that it was someone from his legion. There was still enough moonlight for sentries to recognize their commander standing in the open, and Rikus had heard no one call his name or even issue a challenge.

It hardly mattered. He had only one hope of survival: perhaps the unseen creature had a supply of water with it. The lirrs seemed to sense Rikus's change in attitude, closing the distance between them and their prey. They moved so silently that Rikus doubted he would have heard them had it not been for the Scourge of Rkard. He paid them no attention, relying on their natural caution to keep them at bay while he investigated the noise.

After Rikus had progressed less than twenty agonizing limps up the hill, whatever was hiding behind the boulder shifted position, creating a loud crackle. Fearing that their hard-won prey was about to walk into the waiting arms of some other hunter, the lirrs charged after Rikus in a mad scramble. The mul spun around to face the creatures, knowing that he was inviting attack from the rear—but having no other choice.

The lirrs leaped at him en masse, their claws slashing and their jaws snapping. Behind Rikus, stones rattled as the mysterious creature left its hiding place and came after him. Cursing his bad luck, the mul threw himself at the central lirr, leading with the tip of his sword. After impaling itself, the beast slid down the blade clawing and biting at the gladiator's head. The other two beasts, surprised by the maneuver, sailed past and met the creature that had been lurking behind the boulder.

Rikus released the sword and dropped to the ground, allowing the saurian to land on top of him. The beast feebly raked the mul's flanks and opened more than a dozen shallow scratches, then gave its death shudder and fell motionless. At the same time, from behind Rikus came several moments of scratching and roaring as the other two lirrs battled whatever had jumped at the mul from the rocks.

A thick scale shattered loudly as it was struck, then a lirr howled in pain and fell abruptly silent. Afraid that he would soon be facing whatever had killed the beast, Rikus crawled from beneath the lirr he had killed and pulled his sword free of its body.

When he looked up, he saw a cyclone of flashing arms and claws as a thri-kreen grappled with the last lirr. As Rikus watched, the hulking mantis-warrior managed to grasp the saurian with three claws, then used his fourth hand to rip a scale off the beast's throat. Finally, the insect-man bent down and inserted its mandibles into the exposed skin. The lirr howled, then began to convulse as the thri-kreen's poison paralyzed it.

"K'kriq?" Rikus croaked, only half-lowering his sword.

The thri-kreen tossed the lirr on top of the other he had downed, then used two arms to point at the one Rikus had slain. "Good kill," said the mantis-warrior. "Lirr strong."

"Why didn't you show yourself?" Rikus demanded. His parched throat ached with each word.

K'kriq's antennae curled at the question. "And ruin lirr hunt?"

* * * * *

"Give me another waterskin," Neeva ordered, tossing aside the one Rikus had just drained.

It was just past dawn, and a short time ago K'kriq had walked into the oasis camp bearing the mul's half-conscious form in his arms. Rikus now lay on a soft carpet of burgundy moss, his head and shoulders cradled in Neeva's arms. The puffy yellow crown of a chiffon tree shaded his face, and the honey-scent of its green blossoms filled his nose.

Over the mul's shoulders was a robe of soft hemp, which he had made K'kriq fetch before bringing him into camp. Tamar's ruby still peered out from his chest, and Rikus had no wish for his followers to see it. Several of those followers were gathered around him at the moment, including Styan, Caelum, Jaseela, and Gaanon. K'kriq had returned to the desert to retrieve the lirr carcasses.

Caelum handed his waterskin to Neeva, but cautioned, "He shouldn't drink too much at once—"

"He'll drink as much as he likes," Neeva snapped, opening the skin's mouth and offering it to Rikus.

The mul took the skin, but did not immediately lift it to his lips. His stomach was bloated from the first one he had emptied, and he even felt a little dizzy.

"I told you to wait for me," Rikus said, casting an accusing look at Neeva.

"We did," Caelum offered. The dwarf raised his red eyes to meet the mul's, at the same time laying his palm on Neeva's shoulder.

Rikus eyed the dwarf's hand bitterly. "That's strange. There was no one there when I came out."

"I waited five days, Rikus," Neeva said, her ivory brows raised in mixture of apology and anger.

The mul's jaw slackened. It seemed inconceivable that he had lain in Borys's coffin for five days.

"I'm to blame," Caelum said, stepping toward the mul. "I convinced Neeva you were dead."

Rikus looked up, his eyes black pits of ire. He wasn't sure why the dwarf's admission made him so angry, but there was no denying that it did. "I wouldn't get too close just yet," the mul growled.

Caelum's angular face betrayed no shock or fear. He remained standing in front of the mul.

"What did you want us to do?" Neeva demanded. "We couldn't get inside."

"They could have waited for you as long as they wished," Styan said, nodding to the mul. "Under my command, the legion has been pursuing Maetan closely—"

"And would have pursued him right to the gates of Urik—without ever attacking," growled Jaseela, sneering at the templar. She looked at Rikus straight-on, the beautiful half of her face a dizzying contrast to the disfigured side. "They thought you were dead, Rikus. What else would you have wanted them to do?"

"Nothing," the mul snapped, looking away. "Neeva will tell me what happened while I was gone."

With the exception of Caelum, the others took the hint and quickly left. The dwarf, however, acted as though it had not occurred to him that Rikus meant to dismiss him as well as the others.

"Caelum, when I said I wanted to talk to Neeva, I meant without you here," Rikus growled.

The dwarf looked up, his face a mask of perfect composure, then pointed at the wounds on the mul's savaged leg. "I will call upon the sun to mend your wounds."

"No," the mul said. After hearing the dwarf admit that he had convinced Neeva to abandon her vigil at the citadel, and seeing how he had squeezed the woman's shoulder, the thought of allowing Caelum to touch him annoyed Rikus no end. "Not now."

"It's best if I heal you immediately," the dwarf said, raising a hand toward the sun. "You're losing strength by the minute."

Rikus shoved the dwarf away. "I won't have you touching me," he shouted.

"The heat has affected your mind," Neeva said.

"Has it?" Rikus demanded. "He's the one who told you to leave me behind! Why should I want his help now?"

Without a word, Neeva pinned Rikus into her lap. "Lie down and let Caelum use his magic—the legion can't wait here long enough for you to recover on your own."

The dwarf lifted his hand to the sky again, and soon it was glowing red. Knowing that what Neeva said was true, Rikus

looked away and allowed Caelum to touch him. It felt as
though the cleric had poured molten steel into the veins.

When Rikus looked back, the flesh was fiery red. Trying
to take his mind off the pain, he asked, "What of Maetan?"

"Styan managed to keep him from returning to Urik, but
he's retreated into a village called Makla," Neeva answered.

Rikus cursed. "I know the village," he said, his teeth
clenched against the pain in his leg. "It's a supply base for
quarry gangs. It's protected by a small Urikite garrison."

As the wounds on Rikus's leg closed, Caelum removed his
hand and reached up to open the mul's robe. Rikus caught
him quickly. "No. These wounds need no attention."

Caelum scowled. "Animal scratches are the most dangerous of all," he said. "And from the ichor staining the robe,
I'd say these have already gone foul. If I don't attend to them
now, the poison could kill you."

Rikus shook his head. "I'll be fine," he said. "And I've
had about as much healing as I can stand for one day."

"Don't be a fool," Neeva snapped.

Before Rikus could stop her, she jerked his robe open. Beneath it were the scratches the lirrs had inflicted on him, a
burn in the center of his chest that had already started to
heal, and, on his left breast, a festering sore about the size of
a coin.

At its base, the inflamed sore glowed bright scarlet, but
the skin around the rupture's lip had turned an ugly dark
green. From the center of the wound oozed a steady flow of
yellow purulence that almost obscured the red face of the
ruby lodged in its center. From deep within the gem glowed
a tiny spark of crimson light that drew the eyes of both
Caelum and Neeva straight toward it.

"What's that?" Neeva demanded.

"I'm not sure," the mul lied. "After I killed Umbra, I
passed out for several days. When I woke up, it was in my
chest."

Though Rikus did not like lying, he intended to tell Neeva the truth later. With Caelum present, however, the mul thought it best not to mention the wraiths—especially since they wanted him to recover the same book that he was supposed to be returning to the dwarves of Kled.

"You woke up and it was there?" Caelum asked, incredulous.

"That's what I said!" the mul snapped, pulling his robe closed.

Caelum calmly reopened the robe, then began poking and prodding at the sore. His fingers were quickly coated with rancid-smelling yellow goo. Rikus winced in pain and pushed the dwarf's hands away. "What're you doing?" he demanded.

"I believe it to be a sort of magic vex," Caelum explained, cleaning his hands on Rikus's robe. He raised a hand toward the sun. As his fingers turned red, he said, "With the power of the sun, perhaps I can rid you of the stone."

"You'd better know what you're doing," Rikus growled. He did not know which appealed to him less: remaining at the mercy of Tamar, or being indebted to Caelum for ridding him of the wraith.

Instead of replying to the mul's threat, Caelum laid his glowing hand to the wound.

Where the dwarf touched him, Rikus felt a brief sensation of burning. An instant later, Caelum's face went pale and he let out a terrified shriek. A gray shadow crept from the mul's festering wound and moved over the dwarf's hand, darkening the glowing flesh. The blotch slowly spread up the cleric's arm, slipping onto his shoulders and up over his head until only the dwarf's red eyes shone from the shadow. Even they quickly faded from view, rolling back in their sockets as Caelum toppled over.

Rikus screamed, feeling as though someone had shot a flaming arrow into his heart. The inside of his chest erupted into a shattering agony, and tongues of searing pain ran down into his legs and out into his arms. With each passing moment, the raging anguish grew worse, until the mul feared that a fire was consuming him from the inside out. In Rikus's mind, smoky tendrils of blackness rose to cloud his thoughts, and his ears were filled with a loud, pulsing roar.

Tamar's voice came to him over the throbbing in his ears. *Your dwarven ally cannot save you,* she hissed.

The fire inside Rikus's body grew unbearable. He rolled away from Neeva's grasp, then lay on the ground thrashing in pain until, at last, his thoughts turned to smoke.

The mul did not die. Instead, Rikus saw himself inside his own mind, walking blindly through an endless bank of mordant gray fumes. As he moved onward, choking and gasping from the caustic haze, his possessions slowly disappeared: first the robe he had been wearing to hide Tamar's gem, then his sandals and the Belt of Rank, and finally even his breechcloth. He found himself completely naked and without equipment, save that the Scourge of Rkard floated at his side as if sheathed in an invisible scabbard.

The mul continued to wander through the hazy landscape of his mind for what seemed hours, but may have been days or merely minutes. Occasionally he shouted for Neeva, and even for Caelum, but there was never an answer. Rikus's stomach began to churn with anxiety, for he had seen a similar haze before.

Once, after losing a gladiatorial fight with a horrid beast his trainers had brought from the desert wastes, Rikus had hovered near death for several days. During that time, he had found himself standing atop a distant cliff, overlooking an endless curtain of gray nothingness. That ashen haze had looked exactly like the dingy fog that now enclosed him.

A shiver of dread ran down the mul's back. In retaliation

for letting Caelum try to destroy her, the wraith may have killed them both.

"Tamar! What did you do to me?" Rikus yelled. With his scream, the mul's fear gave way to anger. He set off through the gray haze at a sprint, reaching for his sword and shouting, "Come out, wraith!"

No sooner had he grasped the Scourge's hilt than the gray haze disappeared. He saw that he was standing in midair, upside down with an even surface of granite many feet below. In the next instant, he crashed to the polished floor, barely tucking his chin in time to keep from landing on his head.

A roar of raucous laughter sounded all around him. He found himself in a vast room smelling of unwashed men and lit by dozens of open-hearthed fireplaces. Around each fire whirled the lithe silhouette of a tall dancing girl, singing and shouting ribald invitations to the drunken men watching her. Serving slaves wandered the crowd, making sure that each spectator had a full cup of potent, foul-tasting broy.

At Rikus's back, a silky voice called, "See, you're not dead."

The mul scrambled to his feet and turned around, where he saw an unclothed woman with a dark complexion and long black hair. She stood before a soft bed of sleeping furs. Her dark eyes narrowed to mere slits, and a wicked smile crept across her wide, full-lipped mouth.

"Tamar?" the mul gasped.

The woman nodded, then beckoned him forward with a single long-nailed finger. "You're learning to use the Scourge," she said. "Good. You can trust it when you cannot trust anything else—even your own thoughts."

As the mul stepped toward the woman, he saw that she stood nearly as tall as he did. Her voluptuous body was sinuous and strong, but she smelled of must and decay. She opened her arms to the mul. "Come. I will teach you to use it against the mindbender."

"Why?" the mul asked, stopping short of her embrace. "You must know that after I defeat Maetan, I'll never give you the *Book of the Kemalok Kings*."

Tamar's smile turned ominous. "I think you will, when the time comes," she said, motioning for him to step into her arms. "Now, come here—if you wish to learn more about your weapon."

Rikus stood his ground, acutely aware of his own nakedness. "I've no wish to couple with you, wraith—even in my thoughts."

Tamar's eyes flashed fiery red, but her voice remained calm and silky when she spoke. "And I have no wish to lie with you, half-dwarf."

Nevertheless, she reached out as if to grasp him. Long claws sprouted from her fingertips, and glistening fangs grew from beneath her full lips.

"Stay away!" Rikus cried, slashing his sword across her stomach.

The wraith jumped away, but the blade grazed her abdomen and opened a long gash. Tamar cried out, but not in her own voice. Her hair changed from silky black to blond, her eyes from ruby red to emerald green, and her body from sinuous to powerful.

The honey-scent of chiffon blossoms came to Rikus's nose. With a sinking heart, he realized that what he saw before him was not inside his mind. He was looking at Neeva, and they were standing under the same chiffon tree beneath which K'kriq had laid him earlier that morning.

"Why?" asked Neeva.

She held her hands across the cut Rikus had opened in her stomach, blood seeping through her fingers. Her face did not show pain or anger, only shock and bewilderment.

"It wasn't you!" Rikus cried. Such a feeling of remorse

washed over him that he felt sick to his stomach. He tossed his sword aside and dropped to his knees. "Forgive me!"

The scent of mildew and rot returned, and before the mul's eyes, Neeva's hair darkened to jet black. A red spark glimmered in her eyes, then her face became Tamar's. Gray smoke rose from the ground and once again Rikus was trapped in his own mind.

The wraith stepped toward him, her ruby eyes glowing like hot coals. As before, she was naked, and there was a long gash across her stomach in the same place that Rikus had wounded Neeva.

"Fool! Never let go of the Scourge!"

She slapped the mul with an open palm. The blow rocked his jaw as though she had been holding a warhammer. Unprepared for the attack, Rikus fell over backward, his ears ringing. He closed his eyes and shook his head in an attempt to regain control of his thoughts. Finally, the sound in his ears faded, and he opened his eyes once more. Tamar still stood before him. Keeping a careful eye on her, he returned to his feet.

"What about Neeva?" the mul demanded. "Is she badly hurt?"

"Forget about Neeva!" Tamar screamed.

Again she lashed out, this time with her fist. Rikus tried to block, but the wraith was too quick. He glimpsed her hand coming toward him only an instant before he felt the blow. A terrific thump echoed through the mul's skull and his head whipped around so hard that it sent a bolt of pain through his neck. Rikus tried to counter by tackling the wraith. She changed to a translucent wisp of light and his arms passed harmlessly through her form.

Tamar rematerialized in front of the mul, this time armed with the double-edge scythe and wearing the full suit of plate armor in which she had been pictured on her sarcophagus. She kicked Rikus under his chin, rocking him over onto his back.

"Without the sword, you have no defense," she snarled, raising her scythe to strike. "You're lost."

As the wraith swung the curved blade toward his throat, Rikus visualized a huge block of stone lying in its path. He felt a queasy sensation in his stomach, then the scythe clanged against the granite slab that had appeared over him.

Tamar raised an eyebrow. "Do you think *that* will save you from a mindbender?"

The wraith threw herself at Rikus. In midair, she changed from an armored knight into a strange, man-sized horror that resembled nothing the mul had ever seen. Its underside was protected by a black carapace, save for a snapping, red-rimmed maw that stank of carrion and offal. This mouth was surrounded by six tentacles, each ending in a gnarled hand with three sharp claws. The thing had no head that the mul could see, merely a dozen eyes located at various places along the lip of the black shell guarding its body.

Desperate to escape, Rikus imagined himself turning to air. A surge of energy rose from deep within his body, and he suddenly felt very weak and tired. The beast landed over him, its tentacles holding its mouth mere inches from his body. It lowered itself until Rikus began to choke on its stinking breath, then it opened its maw for the bite of death.

Rikus felt an eerie tingle as he changed to air, then the monster's jaws snapped shut. They passed right through the mul's intangible body and clacked closed without causing him any pain or injury.

The figure over him became Tamar again, her ruby-red eyes glowing from behind her helm's visor. Rikus felt completely exhausted, and despite the terrible danger, it was all he could do to keep his eyes open.

"If you fight like this, you die," Tamar hissed, a gray fog billowing from behind her mask. "Now sleep."

"What about Neeva?" Rikus demanded. His words hissed like the wind, and even he could barely understand them.

"Forget about Neeva," the wraith growled, spewing gray mist into his eyes.

Rikus sank into oblivion. Thoughts of Neeva, the Scourge of Rkard, even Tamar, fled before the waves of exhaustion that overtook the mul.

Later, someone called his name, and Rikus felt the warm glow of the morning sun on his face. The air was rich with the honey-scent of the chiffon tree, and a cool breeze danced across his leathery skin.

"Rikus, stop waiting. Get up."

It was K'kriq's voice.

The mul opened his eyes and found himself staring up at the olive-tinged sky of early morning. The mul sat up and immediately looked about. He found nothing but his belt and sword, a dozen full waterskins, and a pile of diamond-shaped scales that K'kriq had discarded after eating the lirrs.

"Where's Neeva?" the mul demanded, rising. "Is she hurt?"

"Neeva with Caelum," the thri-kreen reported, clacking his mandibles impatiently. "Caelum with pack. Both healthy to hunt."

"And where is my pack?" Rikus asked, his eyes searching the oasis for signs of his legion. Save for himself, K'kriq, and a few winged lizards, the pond was deserted.

"Styan take pack yesterday," K'kriq explained. "Say to tell you message: 'legion cannot wait. Maetan call reinforcements to village.' Styan say you catch legion today. Fight soon."

"Styan!" Rikus yelled, snatching his belt and sword off the red moss. He hardly noticed that, save for the festering sore over his heart, all of his injuries and wounds had been healed. "Who is he to say when my legion marches?"

K'kriq slung the waterskins over his four arms. "Styan become pack leader when you die at citadel," he explained.

"I didn't die," Rikus snapped, starting northward. "The first thing I'll do when I catch up to the legion is show Styan —and everyone else—that I'm still very much alive!"

ELEVEN

Makla

"Stop where you are!" ordered the sentry.

The dwarf stood behind a low rock wall, moving his long spear back and forth between Rikus and K'kriq. Beside the stocky guard, a half-elf gladiator groaned as she heaved a small boulder atop the barrier. She gave the mul and the thri-kreen a casual glance, then turned to pick up another heavy stone.

"You know who I am," Rikus snarled, scowling at the scene before him.

In both directions, gladiators were laboring to encircle the camp with a wall of stones. Caelum's dwarves were spaced every twenty or thirty feet, their eyes dutifully peering into the lengthening shadows of dusk. In the center of camp, the templars stood in a tight circle, their attention turned inward toward the glowing light of a roaring campfire.

After waiting another moment for the dwarven sentry to move his spear away, the mul angrily slapped the shaft aside and leaped over the rock wall. He grabbed the dwarf by the throat and lifted him off the ground. "What's going on here?" he demanded.

"I have my orders," the dwarf gasped, reaching for the hand-axe on his belt. "No one is permitted to enter camp without Styan's permission."

Before the sentry could free his axe, Rikus passed the dwarf to K'kriq, saying, "If he calls out or draws that axe, kill him."

The thri-kreen accepted the sentry with three arms, clacking his mandibles in anticipation. The dwarf moved his hand away from his weapon, but did not give up on trying to stop Rikus from entering camp. "You're to wait here until Styan prepares a proper reception," he said.

Rikus ignored the dwarf and went to the half-elf gladiator laboring to build this section of the wall. Taking a heavy boulder from her hands, he asked, "What's happening, Drewet?"

The half-elf frowned in confusion. "We're building a wall," she said.

"What for?" Rikus asked. "And why are gladiators the only ones working on it?"

Drewet shrugged. "Because those are the orders Styan gave."

"Styan!" Rikus bellowed. He turned and threw the boulder he had taken from Drewet, knocking a great hole in the section of wall that she had been laboring to build. All of the gladiators nearby stopped working and looked toward the disturbance. "Why would anyone do what he says?" Rikus demanded.

The half-elf raised her peaked eyebrows. "Because he's your second-in-command, of course."

"*Second-in-command!*" Rikus thundered. "Is that what he told you?"

"He told us that after you disappeared into the citadel," she said, her brown eyes now flashing with anger. "With Neeva and Caelum staying behind to wait for you, it seemed natural."

"Natural? You thought I would put a *templar* in charge of my legion?" Rikus yelled. "So he could treat you like a bunch of slaves?"

Without waiting for a response, he faced the gladiators nearby. "The days when we build walls for templars are gone!" he roared. "Pass the word and come with me—Styan has some apologies to make!"

Leaving K'kriq to hold the dwarven sentry at the edge of camp, Rikus took Drewet and marched toward the templars. As word of Styan's deception was passed, a long series of angry shouts sounded around the perimeter of camp. By the time the mul neared Styan's company, an angry mob of gladiators was following him, and the templars had turned to face outward. When Rikus approached, they drew their short swords.

"Stand aside or die," Rikus said. He did not draw his own weapon, fearing that, as angry as he was, he would use it. "I'm in no mood for defiance."

"Styan's orders are to let only you—"

Rikus lashed out and smashed the speaker's nose with a fist. As the astonished templar fell to the ground, the mul raised his blood-covered hand and said, "Styan is not in command—I am. The next man who questions that will die."

Drewet stepped to one side of the mul, then Gaanon pushed his way forward to stand at the other. Like Rikus, they did not draw their weapons. After a moment's hesitation, the templars reluctantly opened a narrow lane through their ranks. Flanked by Gaanon and Drewet, Rikus pushed his way through the crowd, widening the path as he went.

At the center of the crowd, the mul found Styan seated on a large, square stone that someone—no doubt a gladiator—had moved into place to serve as a stool for the templar. The mul was glad to see that Jaseela, Neeva, and Caelum had not chosen to lend Styan's usurpation legitimacy by joining him at his camp.

As Rikus stepped toward the fire, Styan looked up and fixed his sunken eyes on the mul's face. "It pleases me that you have caught up to us," he said, his face washed in orange firelight. "We would have missed you at tomorrow's battle—"

"Stand up," Rikus ordered.

Styan glanced around the crowd, his brow furrowed as he tried to judge the mood of both his templars and Rikus's gladiators. Finally, he waved his wrinkled hand at a place near the foot of his rock. "Sit," he said.

Rikus grabbed the templar by his unbound gray hair and jerked him to his feet.

"You misbegotten spawn of an elven gutter wench!" Styan yelled. Several templars stepped forward to defend their leader, but the old man waved them off. Instead, he looked to Rikus and demanded, "What do you think you're doing?"

Rikus jerked Styan forward, then thrust him toward Drewet and the rest of the gladiators. "Apologize, and tell your templars to do the same."

"For what?" the templar demanded. "For keeping the waterskins of our warriors full and not wasting their lives on foolish attacks?"

"For treating my gladiators like slaves," Rikus snarled. "Tyr is a free city, and this is a free legion. One warrior does not labor while another tells jokes by the fire."

"Well said!" shouted a gladiator.

Another added, "Since you disappeared, Rikus, they've been sleeping while we work!"

"Apologize," Rikus said. He put his mouth close to the templar's ear and added, "Then I'll punish you for usurping my command, and for all the lies you've told."

Styan's face went pale and, in a trembling voice, he said,

"Never!"

Somewhere in the crowd of templars, a man's voice called, "I'll not beg forgiveness of any slave!"

"Then you'll die!" came the immediate response.

The chime of clashing weapons followed, and the unseen templar voiced his death scream. The night was filled with angry shouts and shrieks of pain as the two Tyrian companies tore into each other. Bodies began to fall one after the other—more of them templar than gladiator.

Styan spun around to face Rikus, leaving a handful of his hair in the mul's grasp. "See what you've done?" he demanded. "We should be fighting Urikites, not each other."

"From what I've seen, your men are as bad as Urikites. I won't miss them, and neither will Tyr."

"It's not that simple," spat the templar. "What of the dwarves? They follow me."

"Then they die with you," Rikus answered, reaching for his steel dagger. "It's all the same to me."

"Wait," Styan said, gently laying a hand on the mul's wrist. He stared at Rikus for a moment longer, listening to his templars cry out as they fell to the mul's angry gladiators. "You'd do it," he said. "You'd sacrifice half your legion to retain command of it."

"Only the useless half," Rikus answered, drawing his dagger.

Styan sneered at the weapon. "That won't be necessary." He turned around and raised his hands, then yelled, "I apologize, freed men of Tyr!"

When only a few of the combatants stopped fighting, Rikus bellowed, "That's enough! Stop!"

Rikus's powerful voice reached the ears of many more warriors than had Styan's, and, as they passed the mul's command on to their fellows, the melee gradually subsided. Soon, templar and gladiator alike were facing Styan, and the only sounds that could be heard in the mob were the moans of the wounded.

"I apologize," Styan said, his weary eyes on Drewet's face. "My templars apologize. We did not mean to offend you or any other freed slave."

Drewet glanced at Rikus with a questioning look in her eyes. When the mul nodded, she looked back to the templar. "I accept your apology, for myself and for my fellows."

A tense silence hung over the crowd. No one moved to help the injured. Both companies seemed to sense that, although a truce had been reached, the matter of the legion's leadership had not yet been resolved. Rikus kept his black eyes fixed on Styan, waiting for the old man to acknowledge his defeat.

Finally, Styan faced the mul and, in a weak voice, he asked, "As for usurping your command, what shall my punishment be?"

Someone in the ranks of the gladiators threw a coiled whip forward, and it landed at the templar's feet. "The lash!"

Rikus nodded, then bent down and handed the whip to Drewet. "Twenty-five strokes," he said. "And when you give them, remember all the times a templar has whipped you."

"I will," Drewet said, taking the coiled strap.

Gaanon took Styan to the boulder the templar had been using as a throne. There, the half-giant pulled the old man's cassock off, then laid him over the stone.

As Drewet took the first stroke, the crowd began to turn away. The matter had been decided and, gladiator and templar alike, they had seen enough men whipped during Kalak's reign not to enjoy the sight of flayed skin.

* * * * *

At the base of the ash-covered mountain stood Makla, a small hamlet surrounded on three sides by a high stockade of mekillot ribs. Inside this barrier lay dozens of slave pits, each enclosed by a mudbrick wall capped with jagged shards of obsidian. Scattered haphazardly among the pens were the long barracks that housed the garrison, as well as the slovenly huts of the craftsmen who kept the slave-keepers supplied with whips, ropes, and other utensils of bondage.

At the core of the village, a trio of marble mansions marked three sides of a public square. There was a great cistern of steaming water at its center. A clay duct ran from this basin toward the fourth side of the plaza, ending at the tip of a short wooden pier. The pier sat over the shallows of the Lake of Golden Dreams, a body of water whose vastness was lost in the clouds of foul-smelling steam that rose from its boiling depths.

"It seems awfully quiet," Rikus said, glancing upward. Fingers of predawn light were already shooting across the sky, casting a faint, eerie glimmer over the mountainous terrain below.

The mul's companions did not answer, for they were all staring spellbound at the sulfur-colored lake. No one in the legion had ever seen so much water in one place before, and the spectacular sight had taken their minds off the coming battle.

"By now, the outbound quarry gangs should be readying to leave," Rikus said, trying to direct his lieutenants' attention to the matter at hand.

"Maybe nobody's going out," Gaanon offered. In imitation of the robe Rikus wore to conceal Tamar's ruby, the half-giant had sewn two wool blankets together and slung them over his shoulders like a cape. "The highlands look dangerous today," he continued, pointing a huge finger east of the village.

In the direction Gaanon indicated rose a range of fire-belching mountains covered by thick layers of cinder and coarse-grained rocks. Near the summits of many peaks, lakes of molten stone cast a dome of orange light into the dark sky. In the winding canyons, fiery curtains of red incandescence hung over slow-moving rivers of burning rock. It was in that barren wilderness of cinder and lava that the quarry gangs wandered for days at a time, searching out and chipping away long ropes of glassy black obsidian.

Rikus said, "The Smoking Crown always looks dangerous, Gaanon. That wouldn't stop the quarry masters from sending out their gangs."

"What does it matter?" Neeva demanded, casting a sour look at Rikus. Though Caelum had healed the wound on her stomach, it was still marked by an ugly red scar. "You marched us up here in the dark so we could attack at dawn. Let's not lose the advantage of surprise you kept talking about."

"Fine," Rikus snapped. "Let's get on with it."

The mul stepped to the top of the ridge, then looked down the other side at his silent legion. With the exception of the dwarves, who stubbornly remained standing, the warriors all lay on their backs, their feet braced in the loose ash to keep from sliding down the steep slope. In the entire group, no one stirred or even uttered so much as a whisper.

"Get ready!" Rikus ordered, keeping his voice low enough that the morning wind would not carry it over Makla. As the warriors struggled to their feet, the mul went back down the hillside and sent his subcommanders up the slope to organize the army. Neeva started to follow, but Rikus stopped her. He had tried to talk to her last night, but, apparently angry about her injury, she had refused to speak with him.

The mul waited for the others to move out of earshot, then said, "I don't want to go into this battle with bad blood between us." He gestured at the long scar on her stomach. "You know I'd never attack you on purpose."

"I know you didn't mean to cut me," Neeva answered, meeting his eyes with a cold gaze. "That doesn't mean you wouldn't hurt me."

"I wouldn't!" Rikus snapped. "What do I have to do to prove it?"

"Explain yourself," Neeva said. "Who were you yelling at when you attacked me? It was like you were in a trance." She pointed at his left breast, where the robe hid the festering sore on his chest. "And why can't Caelum rid you of that ruby?"

The mul dropped his gaze to his feet. "I didn't tell you the truth before. The gem has nothing to do with Umbra," he said, almost mumbling.

Neeva was silent for a moment, then demanded, "Why'd you lie to me?"

"Because Caelum was there," Rikus said, meeting her gaze. "If I say how I came by this stone, you've got to promise not to tell him."

"You let Caelum try to cure you without knowing what he faced?" Neeva gasped.

Don't tell her! Tamar urged, her voice coming to Rikus on the rhythm of his own heart.

Quiet! Rikus commanded. To Neeva, he said, "Swear, or I can't tell you."

Neeva snorted in disgust, but touched her hand to the waterskin dangling from her shoulder. "I swear on my life."

If she knows, she'll tell the dwarf, warned the wraith. *I'll kill her before I allow it.*

No! Rikus objected.

And I'll do it with your hands, the wraith assured him. *That's why I made you wound her with your sword—so you'd know I could.*

"Well?" Neeva demanded.

The mul looked away. "I can't tell you."

Neeva scowled. "I swore on my life," she said. "Isn't that

good enough?"

"It is, but I was wrong to think I could tell you," Rikus said. "It doesn't matter what you swear on."

One corner of Neeva's mouth turned down in a derisive sneer. "*This* is what's wrong between us. If you don't trust me, then there's nothing more to say." She started to leave.

"Wait," Rikus said, grabbing her arm. "I do trust you—this is for your own good."

"*I* decide what's good for me," Neeva replied, jerking her arm free. "*You* had better decide whether you trust me or not—and you've got to choose between me and Sadira. You've treated me like one of your fawning wenches for long enough."

With that, she faced the top of the slope, where Jaseela and the other subcommanders were looking down on the scene with raised eyebrows. Behind them, the heads and shoulders the Tyrian legion were just showing above the crest of the ridge. "Your army awaits your command," Neeva spat, hefting an obsidian battle-axe Gaanon had given her. "Try to serve it better than you do your lovers."

"I serve them both as best I can," Rikus answered, gritting his teeth.

With that, the mul raised his sword and waved his legion toward the village. A few half-hearted battle cries sounded from ash-coated throats, but the noise seemed a pitiful squeak compared to the confident roar that usually accompanied an attack by his warriors.

The legion half-slid, half-ran down the slope, loose cinders cascading around their feet and ash billowing far above their heads. Soon it seemed the whole mountainside was avalanching down upon Makla. The ground was trembling beneath Rikus's feet, and, through the roiling cloud of gray soot, the mul could see no farther than the end of his own sword. In the absence of Tyrian battle cries, the sound of coughing filled the dark morning.

The village did not seem to be prepared for a surprise attack. A few sentries sounded the alarm, and an echoing slam announced that the main gate had been closed. Soon, Rikus heard a few officers shouting orders to their soldiers as they raced from their barracks, but the mul detected no sign of the large force he had feared was gathered at the village.

After the legion reached the base of the mountain, it did not take it long to leave the cloud of airborne ash behind. Not bothering to attack the main gate, Rikus led the way directly to the stockade. There, he began hacking at the ropes of braided giant-hair that bound the huge mekillot ribs together. Any ordinary sword, especially one with a blade of obsidian or sharpened bone, would not have cut the sturdy ropes, but the Scourge of Rkard sliced through them as though they were made of hemp.

No sooner had the mul cut away the ropes than Gaanon grabbed a rib and, groaning with effort, pulled it out of place. Without so much as a word to Rikus, Neeva slipped through the breach and disappeared into the village. A moment later, she yelled in anger, then a Urikite half-giant screamed in pain. The ground shook as he collapsed.

Rikus turned to K'kriq and pointed at the gap. "Go with Neeva," the mul said. "Be sure nothing happens to her."

"She carries eggs?" the thri-kreen asked, unable to imagine any other reason a female would deserve special protection.

"Just defend her," Rikus ordered, motioning for Gaanon to help him open more gaps. Each time they pulled down a mekillot rib, another of his lieutenants led his company or a group of gladiators into the village.

By the time the last two companies were ready to go through the wall, the sun had peeked over the jagged horizon. Barely penetrating the clouds of volcanic soot that rose from the jagged peaks of the Smoking Crown, the crimson orb lit the village with a murky, rose-colored glow. Rikus

took advantage of the dim light to look back along the stockade. Once he saw that his legion was breaking into the village without trouble, he led the last of his warriors through
the gap.

★　★　★　★　★

"It hardly seems necessary to let the slaves destroy my
village," complained Tarkla San, counting on her fingers
the number of breaches that had been opened in Makla's
stockade.

"Villages can be rebuilt," Maetan answered. "My family's
honor is another matter."

The mindbender and the imperial governor were a mile
from Makla's main gate, standing a short distance below the
jagged crest of a ridge of black basalt. In the narrow gorge on
the other side of the ridge waited Maetan's new legion, a
makeshift force of stragglers from the first battle, the village
garrison, and Family Lubar's private army.

"I cannot believe a commander of your stature fears a mob
of slaves," Tarkla said, keeping her blue eyes focused on her
village. Many years of outpost life had lined the old woman's leathery skin with deep furrows, and the cares of her
office had etched a permanent scowl into the sagging folds of
her face. "You outnumber them by almost three-to-one."

Maetan's pale lip twisted into a sneer. "Tarkla, have you
ever fought gladiators?"

The old woman shook her head. "Of course not."

"They fight like wild beasts, not soldiers. The only way to
destroy the Tyrian slaves is to corner them and starve them
into attacking us—on our terms," the mindbender said.
"Leave the battle tactics to me."

"Where my village is concerned, I leave nothing to you,"
she said. "You claimed that the enemy was so numerous we
could not possibly defend Makla. Clearly you were mis-

taken. It would have been an easy matter for us to hold them off from inside until reinforcements arrived."

"There are no reinforcements," Maetan said. He turned his body slightly away from the governor, so that she could not see his hand drifting toward the hilt of his dagger.

"But your messengers—"

"Went only to my family's estate, so the Tyrian scouts would believe I was sending for more soldiers," the mind-bender said. "Since my family army is already here, there will be no more help."

"You sacrificed my village for nothing?" Tarkla gasped. "The king shall hear of this!"

"No, he shall not," Maetan said, silently slipping his weapon from its sheath. "I have already lost one imperial legion. If I am to spare my family further humiliation, I must destroy the Tyrian slaves without risking another."

Tarkla frowned. "You would sacrifice Makla to protect your honor?" she asked, stepping away.

Before she could move out of reach, Maetan caught her and plunged his dagger into her heart. "It was unavoidable," he answered.

* * * * *

The village was remarkably quiet. A handful of Urikite half-giants and several dozen village soldiers had fallen just inside the stockade, but there was little real sign of battle. The templars and most of Rikus's gladiators were rushing toward the center of the village, anxious to take control of the water supply as fast as possible.

"Something's wrong here," Rikus said, studying the relative calm.

"It's too easy," Gaanon agreed.

The mul led his small group of gladiators toward the main gate. Along the way, he saw perhaps a dozen skirmishes between his warriors and village guardsmen, but there was little sign of the fierce battle he had expected. A few minutes later, they reached their goal without incident. There, Rikus found Caelum and his dwarves stoically standing guard just out of arrow range of the stone gatehouse.

"What's happening here?" Rikus asked. He could see frightened faces peering out of every arrow loop in the two-story building.

"When the alarm sounded, most of the garrison rushed to defend the gatehouse," Caelum answered.

"They didn't count on your sword and my strength," Gaanon surmised, glancing at the breaches he and the mul had opened together.

"Perhaps," Caelum answered, keeping his eye fixed on the gatehouse. "But it doesn't seem to me that the entire village garrison should fit inside there."

"It shouldn't," Rikus said.

"I've sent a few of my brethren to search the rest of the village," Caelum said.

"Good," Rikus replied distractedly. "Send half of your men to get some water—"

"But we're watching the gatehouse," Caelum objected.

"That's why you're only sending half of them," Rikus answered, shaking his head at the dwarf's single-mindedness. "When your scouts report back, send me word of what they found. I'll be at the cistern."

The mul turned toward the center of the village himself, but did not go directly to the square. Instead, he took his time, poking his head into barracks and opening slave pens as he went. The barracks showed every sign of being inhabited, but the soldiers' uniforms and weapons were all missing, as if the garrison had been summoned away on short notice. Most of the slave pens, too, were empty, but Rikus finally came to one where a handful of wretches with heavily bandaged hands and feet were cowering in fear.

"Come out of there," Rikus called, lowering the exit ladder to them. "You're free now."

The slaves regarded him with suspicious glances.

"We're from Tyr," Gaanon explained. "We've captured Makla, so come out!"

The haggard slaves glanced at each other, then slowly began to hobble up the ladder. When they left the pit, they kept their eyes focused on the ground, as they would in the presence of their overseers.

Rikus pointed toward the nearest barracks. "Go and take what you need from there," he said. "After that, you're free to leave the village or join our army—it's your choice."

The slaves looked up, their eyes betraying confusion and disbelief. It was hardly the jubilant sort of reaction Rikus expected from newly freed men and women, but he could understand why they might be shocked. In the pits, they had no way of knowing that the village had been invaded and their captors driven off—especially since there had been few sounds of battle to suggest what was happening.

The last slave was a young half-elf with an intelligent spark to his pale green eyes. Rikus caught him by the shoulder, then asked, "Why is the village so empty?"

The fellow shrugged. "Last night, when we returned with our quarry bags, Maetan of Family Lubar was here with a big army. During the night, he took it, along with most of the garrison, and left. They sent the quarry gangs into the hills."

"Why did they leave you behind?" demanded Gaanon, his eyes narrowed suspiciously.

In answer, the half-elf pointed to the bloody bandages on his feet. "After seven days in the Smoking Crown, it's all you can do to hobble to the water plaza."

Rikus paid little attention to the exchange, for he was too busy cursing under his breath. Maetan had again anticipated him, pulling his army out of the village just in time to keep it from being trapped against the boiling lake.

"The spy!" hissed the mul.

His thoughts leaped immediately to Styan, but he did not understand when Maetan would have had a chance to convert the templar to his cause. As much as Rikus did not want to admit it, it seemed more likely that the spy was someone who had been in contact with the mindbender. That left Caelum, his dwarves, or even K'kriq as possibilities—though the mul refused to believe it was the thri-kreen. He was tempted to blame Styan outright, but in the end Rikus decided to bide his time and keep a close watch on all the possibilities.

Once he had reached this decision, Rikus instructed his gladiators to search the pens for more abandoned slaves, then led Gaanon to the central square. There was no sign of a battle there, either. Many of his gladiators were massed around the basin, pushing and shoving at each other in an effort to get at the water. Those that had already had their fill were lounging around the edges of the plaza, dozing contentedly or joking rudely. Neeva and Jaseela were on the pier, turning the waterscrew themselves in order to keep the cistern filled.

In front of the closest marble mansion, Styan stood in the midst of a dozen casks of wine. Though Caelum had surreptitiously used his magic to heal the wounds the templar had suffered from his lashing, there were dark stains on the old man's cassock where some of the cuts had reopened and were seeping blood. Nevertheless, Styan seemed in good spirits, filling mugs of wine and giving them to his templars to pass out to eager gladiators.

Rikus found the scene as unsettling as he had the quarry slave's report on Maetan's sudden departure. There was a festival spirit hanging over the whole square that seemed out of place in the middle of what should have been a very serious battle.

"It's almost like they were inviting us to enjoy ourselves," Rikus muttered, starting toward the wine casks.

When he saw the mul coming, Styan filled two mugs and stepped toward him. "Here's Rikus!" the templar cried. "Let's drink his health!"

An immediate chorus of voices cried, "To Rikus!"

As he moved through the crowd, dozens of warriors slapped the mul's back, congratulating him on the victory at Makla. When he reached Styan, Rikus took the cup, but did not drink from it.

"Where did you find this?" the mul demanded.

The templar's face fell. "In the foyer of this house," he answered, motioning at the mansion behind him. "It was all stacked up, ready to be carried into the cellar, I suppose."

"Or ready for us to find," Rikus snapped. He had no doubt that Maetan had left the wine in plain sight on purpose, hoping that the Tyrians would be too drunk to fight when the Urikites took positions outside the town. Rikus threw his mug to the ground, exclaiming, "Isn't it obvious to you that Lord Lubar's trying to corner us?"

Styan looked at the shattered mug as though the mul had tossed it in his face. "I was only trying to make amends."

Rikus ignored the templar and turned to the crowd. "Now is no time for drinking," he yelled, running his gaze over the crowd.

Several gladiators chuckled, and someone called, "Saving it all for yourself, are you Rikus?"

No one dumped their cups. In fact, many of them quaffed down what they had and passed their mugs to the templars to be refilled.

"I mean what I say!" Rikus yelled, knocking the mug from the hand of a nearby gladiator. "Pour out the wine. We have much to do, and little time to do it!"

This time, no one laughed. "What's wrong, Rikus?" called a female human. "Have you lost your need for wine?"

"We're free men," cried a burly tarek. Like the mul, he was musclebound and hairless, with a square head and sloping brow. "We can drink what we want!"

Rikus turned to Gaanon. "Smash the casks."

A storm of protest rose from those near enough to hear, but the half-giant hefted his club and waded through the crowd to carry out his orders. Several men stepped in front of Gaanon as if to stop him, but a threatening glance from the huge gladiator was enough to clear them out of his way.

"Listen to me!" Rikus called, raising his arms for silence.

The crowd paid him no attention. Gaanon's club came down on the first cask, and rich red wine flooded the square. An angry outburst of shouting and screaming erupted around Rikus.

"We're not templars!" cried the tarek. His flat nose was flaring in anger and the lips of his domed muzzle were drawn back to reveal his sharp fangs. "You can't treat us like this!"

The gladiator stepped toward Gaanon, clearly meaning to stop him from destroying any more casks. Behind him came two human men.

Rikus lashed out at the tarek, striking his throat with stiffened fingers. The stunned gladiator collapsed immediately, choking and grasping at his damaged larynx. When even that did not stop those following him, Rikus delivered a powerful side-thrust kick to the ribs of the next man in line, simultaneously unsheathing the Scourge of Rkard. "The next man will feel my blade!"

The area fell abruptly silent.

"Good," the mul said. "Now listen carefully—we don't have much time. Maetan should have been inside this village with a fair-sized army, but he wasn't. My guess is that he's moving to attack—while we quaff down the wine he left to keep us occupied!"

The gladiators remained absolutely silent, their eyes fixed on Rikus and their mouths hanging open in astonishment. Though the reaction was more extreme than what the mul had anticipated, he counted himself lucky that they were no longer preoccupied with the wine.

"If we don't want to be trapped, we've got to sack the town and leave—fast!" Rikus continued. He gestured at a mob of about thirty gladiators. "You're our lookouts. Go to the wall and report back when you see any sign of Maetan's army. The rest of you, fill your waterskins, then find what food you can and burn everything else."

Instead of obeying, the gladiators started to back away, staring at Rikus's chest and murmuring to each other in frightened tones. Even Gaanon had fallen speechless, and, with a look of utter betrayal, simply stared at the mul.

Rikus looked down and saw that, during his scuffle with the tarek, his robe had fallen open. Now, the ulcerous wound on his breast lay fully exposed and oozing yellow ichor. Worse, a scintillating red light shone from the ruby in its center.

Rikus pulled his robe back over the wound, silently cursing the tarek who had caused him to expose the magical gem.

"What magic is that?" Gaanon asked, half-consciously taking a step away from the mul. Like many gladiators, the half-giant distrusted sorcery.

"It's nothing that will hurt you," Rikus answered, speaking loudly enough for those gathered around him to hear. "Now, do as I ordered."

As the astonished gladiators slowly began to obey, Rikus started toward the eastern end of the village, intending to open an escape route through the stockade.

The mul had taken no more than two steps when Styan caught up to him. "Where are you going?" asked the templar.

"I'll tell you when the time comes," Rikus replied, wondering if the old man had asked the question so he could pass the information on to Maetan. "Until then, stay here. Don't give anyone any orders, don't pour any more wine, and don't make me regret that your punishment last night was so merciful."

TWELVE

Crater of Bones

The Tyrian legion was making camp in a small, volcanic caldera filled with thousands upon thousands of skeletons: dwarves, tareks, even half-giants and elves. Bones lay everywhere—piled against the base of crater walls in dune-sized mounds, heaped in yellow masses over sulfur-spewing steam vents, even packed into a fire-belching fissure that ran down the center of the basin.

The Tyrians had dubbed the place the Crater of Bones, but so far no one had guessed the reason for its existence. On three sides, the basin was surrounded by sheer cliffs. On the fourth, it was blocked by a manmade wall of porous, lime-crusted blocks of stone. The gate could only be closed and locked from the outside. Beyond that, there was no hint as to the place's purpose. The skeletons seldom showed any sign of injuries, and they lay scattered at random across the caldera, so that it seemed the inhabitants had died where they stood, with no chance to flee or to fight.

After several moments of watching his warriors clear bones from small circles of ground, Rikus turned away and looked in the opposite direction. Below him, a lava flow had cut a mile-long channel straight down the ash-covered mountains of the Smoking Crown. The sheer canyon ended in a delta of jagged rock that spilled into the steaming waters of the vast Lake of Golden Dreams. On that delta waited Maetan and several thousand Urikite soldiers.

As he studied his enemy's camp, Rikus could not help sighing in regret. If he had opened his escape route at the western end of Makla's stockade instead of the eastern, the Urikites would not be camped upon the delta—and his legion would not be trapped in the Crater of Bones.

Rikus's tactics in the village had worked well. He and his army had left Makla well ahead of the Urikites, then trudged their way along the lakeshore, intending to circle around it until they found a suitable site in which to confront the enemy. Unfortunately, the terrain of the Smoking Crown had not been cooperative. After only a full day and night of marching, their way had been blocked by a river of burning rock. They had been forced to turn back, reaching the delta just ahead of the mindbender's forces.

With their warriors exhausted from what had become a thirty-hour forced march, Rikus's lieutenants had counseled him to avoid a fight and flee into the mountains. Recognizing the wisdom of their advice, the mul had led his soldiers up the narrow canyon—and straight into this dead-end crater. To leave, they would have to fight their way past the Urikites below. Normally, the prospect would not have concerned the mul, but the situation was worse than it would have been in Makla. No more than a dozen gladiators could attack from the canyon at a time, and they would be surrounded on all sides by the entire Urikite force.

A hollow clatter sounded from the other side of the wall. Rikus turned to see Neeva carefully picking her way through the tangle of bones covering the crater floor. In one hand, she carried a waterskin and in the other an obsidian short sword. Skewered on the weapon's black blade was a round cactus about the size of Rikus's head.

Neeva stopped at the base of the wall, near the rope the sentries had rigged to make scaling the barrier easier. "How about helping me up?" she called. Her eyes were drooping and puffy, the result of a sleepless night of marching.

Rikus lay on his stomach and took the waterskin and the sword so Neeva could climb the rope.

"What brings you up here?" Rikus asked, returning the sword with the cactus. The mul asked the question in his warmest tone of voice, for he hoped that Neeva's presence meant she had finally decided to forgive him.

"I came to see you," Neeva said.

As Rikus resumed his seat, Neeva glanced suspiciously at the wound on his chest. "Does that ruby relieve you of the need to sleep?"

Rikus pulled his robe over the sore. There was little point in trying to hide the gem any more, but it bothered the mul when superstitious gladiators—especially Neeva—paid too much attention to the notorious glowing stone.

"I still need to sleep," Rikus finally answered. "But right now, I have other things to do."

"Like worry about Maetan and the Urikites?" Neeva asked, sitting at his side.

"I don't know if *worry* is the right word."

"It's close enough," Neeva said, a wry smile on her lips. She pulled her dagger and began chopping the red, finger-length spines off the cactus.

"Where'd you get that?" Rikus asked.

"Drewet asked me to give it to you," Neeva answered. "She wanted you to know she isn't frightened by your glowing ruby."

"That's good news," Rikus said, relieved. "At least one gladiator still trusts me—and a pretty one at that."

"Don't get any ideas," Neeva warned, slapping Rikus on the leg with the flat of her dagger blade. A jeering grin crept across her lips, then she added, "I guess you haven't changed so much, after all."

"Me?" Rikus mocked, gesturing at Neeva. "You're the one who's been different. You'd think something happened between you and Caelum while I was gone!"

By the way Neeva's face fell, he knew he had touched upon a tender subject. She looked away and chopped the last of the spikes off the ball, leaving nothing but a stubble-covered husk with a leathery skin. "I didn't come up here to talk about Caelum—or myself."

"All right, what did you come to talk about?" Rikus demanded, holding his temper in check.

Neeva took the stripped cactus husk off her sword, then cut a small hole in the top. "I just wanted to say that you saved our lives back in Makla. Jaseela thinks so, too, and so does Caelum."

"That makes three out of a thousand," Rikus said, gesturing over his shoulders at the rest of the legion. "Everyone else thinks I led them into a trap."

"Not everyone," Neeva answered, hardly glancing up. "You have the support of the templars."

"The templars?" the mul asked, shaking his head in amazement. "You're joking."

Neeva held the opened cactus toward him. "You know how templars are. They respect strength," she said. "When you punished Styan, you proved that you were stronger than him."

"And the dwarves?" Rikus asked. He plunged his hand into the leathery husk and felt dozens of little warm bodies slithering through his fingers.

"Dwarves are dwarves," Neeva shrugged. "They're with you as long as you work toward their focus."

Rikus pulled a handful of white, scale-covered grubs out of the ball. "Nice and juicy," he said, picking out a thumb-sized wiggler and squeezing off its brown head.

Neeva sheathed her dagger, then placed the cactus husk in her lap. "It's the gladiators you have a problem with. They don't like magic they can't understand. Sooner or later, you're going to have to explain that glowing ruby in your chest. Why don't you start with me?"

Rikus avoided an answer by placing the headless grub between his teeth and sucking out the insides. It had a rich, gamey flavor a little too sweet for the mul's taste, but in the Athasian desert a hungry man ate what was available.

Neeva pulled a handful of grubs out of the thornball. As she popped the head off one, she said, "If you won't tell me about the gem, then tell me how we're going to get out of here."

"I don't know yet," the mul admitted. "That's what I was up here thinking about."

"At least you're still honest about *something* with me." Neeva made a sour face as she consumed her first wiggler, then gestured for Rikus to pass the water.

They ate in silence for several moments, tossing the empty grub skins into the lime-crusted rocks at the base of the wall. Finally Neeva suggested, "Maybe we should ask the others if they have any ideas."

Rikus shook his head. "And risk what little confidence the gladiators have left in me?" he asked. "Let me think about it for a while before I give Styan another chance to cause trouble."

Neeva remained thoughtful for a moment, then scraped her hand around inside the cactus and emerged with the last dozen grubs. She gave half to Rikus, then tossed the empty husk into the rocks. "Let's finish these and go for a walk."

"I'm all for that," he said eagerly.

No, you're not, hissed a voice from deep inside him. *There will be no matings between you and any human, half-dwarf.*

Before the mul could respond to Tamar, Neeva smacked Rikus lightly in the stomach. "I meant we should sneak down the canyon and come up with some sort of plan," she said, giving him a sad smile. "I'm not going to lie with you any more—at least not until things are better with us."

"What things?" the mul demanded, checking to make sure his robe remained over Tamar's ruby. "What do you want from me?"

"Three things that, apparently, you can't give me," Neeva answered. "Trust, devotion, and love."

Inwardly, Rikus cursed Tamar for coming between him and his fighting partner. To Neeva, he said, "I do trust you. When this is over, you'll understand."

"Perhaps that's true," Neeva allowed. "But what about love and devotion? You're not devoted to any woman, not even Sadira."

"What do you call our success as a matched pair?" Rikus demanded. "We've even stayed together since we killed Kalak. If that's not devotion, I don't know what is."

Neeva looked into the mul's eyes and smiled patiently. "Devotion is when someone else's happiness matters to you more than your own," she said. "What you're thinking of is loyalty. You and I will always have that much."

Rikus was silent for a time, then asked, "It's the dwarf, isn't it?"

Neeva dropped her gaze. "Caelum is there if I want him."

The mere idea is disgusting, Tamar hissed. *I should punish her for even considering it.*

Ignoring the wraith, Rikus said, "You don't have to feel guilty about Caelum. I understand—a heart is capable of loving more than one person at a time."

"Now you sound like Sadira," Neeva said bitterly. "She's wrong. No one can love more than one person at a time—at least not the way I want to be loved."

"So, where does that leave us?" Rikus asked.

"That's up to you," Neeva answered. "I'm still here if you want me—but be sure you know what that means."

Before Rikus could think of how to answer, Tamar said, *It's just as well. If she laid with you, I'd have to kill her. No decent woman would let anything less than a full human touch her.*

If Neeva comes to any harm, you'll never find out what happened to Borys, Rikus threatened. *I'll stop looking for the book.*

Don't toy with me, the wraith replied. *You promised the dwarves. I could kill her for no good reason and you'd still recover the book. Your pathetic dwarven blood would force you to do it.*

"Rikus, what are you doing?" Neeva asked.

To his surprise, the mul realized that he had reached under his cloak and was absent-mindedly scratching at his ulcerating sore, trying to pry the ruby from where it was lodged. He pulled his hand away and closed his robe once more. "Nothing," he answered. "The wound bothers me sometimes."

Neeva stood and took him by the arm. "Come on."

Rikus jerked away. "You mustn't touch me," he said, not wishing to test the seriousness of Tamar's threat.

Neeva frowned, showing her hurt. "Don't act like a child," she said. "It had to come to this sooner or later. Being free means you have the right to choose for yourself—it doesn't mean you can have everything you want."

Rikus returned to his feet, holding his cloak tightly closed. "This doesn't have anything to do with being free, or with whether I can love both you and Sadira," the mul said, maintaining a careful distance between himself and Neeva. "It's for your own good. You mustn't touch me."

Neeva stepped toward the rope. "If that's the way you want it," she said.

"It's not the way I want it," Rikus answered, following. "It's the way it has to be—for now."

Neeva stopped and turned toward him, an expression of

sudden understanding and relief on her face. "It's the ruby, isn't it?" she said. "It has some sort of control over you."

Deny it, the wraith ordered.

Why? Rikus objected. *What does it matter if she understands that much?*

Rikus's vision blurred for a moment. When it cleared again, he saw Tamar's dark features and narrow eyes where Neeva's face had been a moment earlier. The mul was confused for a moment, but he soon realized that the wraith was using her control over his mind to trick him into seeing her form where Neeva was standing.

"It's what I want," said Tamar, her wide lips moving as she spoke. Her control over the illusion was so complete that it seemed to Rikus that he heard her voice with his ears, not just his mind. "That's all you need to know."

Remembering how the Scourge had helped him sort through Tamar's deceptions after Caelum had tried to remove her gem, Rikus gripped the hilt of his weapon. "She frightens you, doesn't she?" the mul said to the wraith.

The figure standing before Rikus once again became Neeva. "Who am I afraid of?" she asked, nervously eyeing the mul's sword hand.

Rikus did not answer. Instead, he kept his attention focused inside his mind, where Tamar stood on a rock wall identical to the one beneath his feet, save that it seemed to continue forever across an endless lake of red, frothing fire. *If Neeva frightened me, she would be dead already,* the wraith informed him. *Tell her that the ruby has no control over you.*

"Neeva, go on," Rikus said, refusing to do as the wraith demanded. As long as Neeva understood that he had little control over what he revealed about the ruby, there was a good chance that she would eventually forgive him for his silence. "I'll see you later."

Fool! Tamar growled.

Great arcs of fire began to shoot from the red lake inside the mul's mind. Rikus dropped to his knees, crying out in agony. It felt as though his heart had changed to a flaming ball that pumped lava through his veins.

"Rikus!" Neeva cried, moving toward him.

"Go!" the mul bellowed, pointing at the rope.

Neeva eyed his hand, which continued to grip the hilt of his sword. After a quick glance at the ugly scar across her belly, she retreated slowly. "I'll get help."

Rikus shook his head. "I don't need it."

The mul turned his attention inward, imagining that the black wall upon which Tamar stood had changed into a log. It burst into flames and crumbled to ash in an instant, plunging the wraith into the fiery lake.

A malevolent cackle filled Rikus's head, then Tamar's form emerged from the lake, flaming and twice as large as before. She smiled, then stepped closer. Everything went red, and the mul's skin began to sizzle and smoke. He screamed in searing agony and pitched forward, tumbling off the wall.

As the mul fell, the lake of fire faded from his mind and he realized that he was tumbling head over heels into the Crater of Bones. He landed on his back, the thick mantle of skeletons breaking his fall with a loud clatter.

Defy me again and die, Tamar said, no longer visible inside Rikus's head. *Your corpse might be more useful to me without your insolent spirit inside it.*

Neeva, who had slid down the rope while Rikus was not paying attention, started toward him. "Rikus! Are you hurt?"

"I'm fine," he answered, struggling to his feet.

Neeva stopped a step away, visibly restraining herself from touching him. "I won't ask any questions," she said. "Just say you'll tell me what's going on—"

"When I can," Rikus finished for her. "Until then, you'll

have to trust me. Now, why don't you go back to camp? I'll take that walk alone."

The mul began picking his way through the bones and walked out the narrow gate, his mind as troubled by all the things he could not tell Neeva as by his legion's poor position. Outside, the canyon ran straight and narrow down to the Lake of Golden Dreams, a pair of sheer cliffs serving as its walls. Even at their lowest points, the crags were several hundred feet high, and there were no gullies or ravines along the way that could be used to climb out of the narrow passageway.

An idea occurred to Rikus. He stepped to the cliff and used his dagger to scrape away some of the white crust. Underneath, he found a black, porous rock resembling a loaf of dark, coarse-grained bread. He looked back to the wall, wondering what tools its builders had used to shape their blocks. If he could figure out that puzzle, he thought he could spare his legion a disastrous battle.

As the mul started forward to inspect the wall more closely, he heard the disgruntled voices of a large crowd moving toward the gate from inside the crater. Curious as to the cause of the commotion, Rikus went to meet them.

When the mul stepped through the gateway, he saw Styan leading a mob of gladiators toward him. "By the light of Ral!" he cursed.

Rikus drew the Scourge of Rkard and started forward, stumbling and staggering through the bones as he marched toward Styan. Behind the templar came half of the gladiatorial company, among them the wine-loving tarek who had tried to defy Rikus back in Makla. To a warrior, they all carried their weapons and had sour expressions on their faces.

A mutiny! hissed Tamar. *I will put an end to their defiance.*

No, Rikus returned. *Let me handle this.*

As he approached Styan, the mul grabbed the templar with one hand and pressed the tip of his sword under the old man's chin with the other. "I should have done this two nights ago."

"Please," Styan gasped, his sunken eyes opened wide in fear. "This isn't what you think."

"What is it?" Rikus demanded, not releasing the templar.

"These gladiators came to me," he said. "They asked me to talk to you."

"You're lying," Rikus said, scowling at the gladiators gathered behind the templar. "They can talk to me themselves. They know that."

"Maybe before that ruby sprouted in your chest," said the tarek. "But you're a different man now."

There are too many of them for you to discipline alone, Tamar observed. *I will summon help.*

You can do that?

Tamar cooed, *It will take my fellows but a few moments to reach us.*

Leave them! Rikus commanded, trying to imagine the disaster that would follow if Tamar's fellow wraiths appeared and threatened his gladiators. *This is my legion. I can control it.*

That remains to be seen, Tamar said.

When the wraith offered no further comment, Rikus released Styan and pushed him away. "Talk."

The templar smoothed his cassock, then glanced over his shoulder at the men behind him. "These gladiators have no wish to stay here and starve," he said, his voice gaining confidence. "They're going to fight past the Urikites."

"And you're going to lead them?" Rikus asked, a contemptuous sneer on his lips.

"They've asked me to organize them, yes," he answered.

"No," Rikus said, simply. "You can tell them no."

Styan grimaced, then looked at the ground. "They won't accept that answer."

"Do you take me for an imbecile?" Rikus yelled, stepping forward and laying the edge of his blade against the man's throat. To Rikus, this incident confirmed the templar to be Maetan's spy. "Don't think I'm blind to your purpose, traitor!"

Styan began to tremble. "What do you mean?" he gasped.

"How do you pass your messages to Maetan?" the mul demanded. "The Way?"

A comprehending light dawned in the templar's eyes. "You think I betrayed us!" he gasped.

"And you've proven it," Rikus growled.

Styan shook his head. "No," he said. "Not me. Maetan's servant came to me, but I tried to destroy her—I would not betray Tyr!"

"Do you think I'm stupid?" Rikus demanded, raising his sword.

Before the mul could strike, the tarek stepped forward, a double-bladed axe in his hands. "If you kill him, you'll have to kill me, as well."

"And me," said a broad-shouldered man hefting a huge spiked club.

"Me too," added another gladiator, then another and another.

Hardly able to believe his eyes, Rikus shoved the templar to the ground and planted a foot on his throat. "Two nights ago, this man had you stacking rocks while his templars laughed and joked around the campfire," Rikus said. "Now you're defending him?"

"He was the only one who would agree to their plan," said Neeva, appearing from around the edge of the mob. As she waded through the bones, she waved her axe at several figures following her: Jaseela, Caelum, Gaanon, and K'kriq. "None of us would listen to their foolishness."

Rikus furrowed his brow and looked at the templar. "This wasn't his idea?"

"It doesn't matter whose idea it was!" growled the tarek.

"We're free men, and we're leaving."

"We'll die in battle before we starve like cowards," added another.

"I am in command!" Rikus snapped. "You will—"

The musty smell of mildew and rot filled the mul's nostrils, and he stopped speaking in midsentence. An instant later, he noticed the gray silhouettes of eleven wraiths swimming through the bones beneath his feet. Their eyes were glowing in a variety of familiar, gemlike colors: citrine yellow, sapphire blue, topaz brown, and more.

Tamar, no!

Your warriors must learn to fear you, she responded.

As the gray shadows passed beneath the gladiators' feet, the Tyrians cried out in astonishment and alarm. The tarek cast an accusing glare at Rikus.

"What magic is this?" he demanded.

Before the mul could answer, the sun-bleached skeletons of long dead figures began to rise in the middle of the throng. Clinging to these bones like long-forgotten coverings of flesh were the gray forms of the wraiths.

In front of the tarek rose a skeleton with glowing, citrine-yellow eyes. As the abomination reached for his throat, the gladiator screamed and used his axe to lop both hands off at the forearms. The wraith adjusted its attack and thrust the jagged ends of the skeleton's arms into its foe's meaty throat.

The tarek was not the only gladiator to fall. Dozens of Tyrians lashed out at the shambling skeletons, bashing skulls, hacking off arms, shattering whole racks of ribs. Nothing helped. The wraiths ignored the damage and struck back with the jagged ends of their fleshless limbs. Within moments, fifteen warriors lay in the bones, groaning in agony or simply watching their life blood drain away.

Neeva and those with her rushed into the fray. Rikus

quickly lost sight of the others, but he saw Neeva splinter a
skeleton from head to pelvis with a downward stroke of her
mighty axe. Her effort was to little avail. The wraith simply
abandoned the shattered skeleton in favor of another one,
then rose stiffly from the piled bones to counterattack.

"Go back!" Rikus called, stepping past Styan. "If you
want to live, return to camp!"

The mul did not need to repeat himself. As he went forward, the gladiators retreated with horrified expressions,
some begging him to stay away and others cursing his name.
Rikus ignored them and stumbled toward Neeva as fast as he
could. Before he reached her, a skeleton rose at her side and
thrust a broken shard of hand into her ribs. She screamed
and spun around to hit the thing with the flat of her axe
blade, but Rikus reached it first and used the Scourge to
slice its legs from beneath it.

"Rikus, what did you do?" Neeva cried, running her gaze
over the dead and dying gladiators strewn over the bones.
"What are these monsters?"

Two more skeletons rose at her side.

"Go!" Rikus yelled, shoving her toward camp.

In the same instant, Caelum stepped out of the crowd, one
hand raised toward the sun and the other pointed at Neeva.
"Away!" he cried.

A crimson light flared from his palm, illuminating everything before it in a wash of blinding scarlet. The two wraiths
flanking Neeva hissed and shrieked in agony, then dove back
into the bones and shot away.

Inside Rikus's breast, Tamar's ruby began to sear the inflamed flesh of his wound. The mul felt as though his chest
had been pierced by a bar of newly forged iron. Screaming,
Rikus turned away to shield the wound from the dwarf's
spell. The pain eased, but did not go away entirely.

Run! Run! Hide us from the sunflame! For once, Tamar was
pleading, not ordering.

No!

The mul faced Caelum and threw his robe open to expose the ruby to the full force of the dwarf's spell. The scorching pain in his chest grew excruciating, and he heard himself howl in agony.

Stop! begged Tamar.

Leave my body! Rikus demanded. *Leave, or I'll destroy you!*

Though he feared he would burst into flames at any moment, Rikus moved forward. The pain grew more horrible with each step, and he could hardly believe that the bestial shrieks filling his ears came from his own mouth. The mul closed his mind to the sound and the pain.

The sunflame hurts, but does not destroy, the wraith said, her voice rasping with pain. *You'll destroy yourself, but I will remain.*

The smell of burning flesh came to the mul's nose as a wisp of greasy black smoke rose from his wound. Tamar's ruby gleamed bright orange, a glowing ember flickering deep inside his breast.

Who will lead your legion from this valley? the wraith pressed, every word betraying her agony. *Who will destroy Maetan, who will return the ancient book to the dwarves?*

The mul's skin began to char and blacken around the ruby, but Tamar still showed no signs of leaving.

Your warriors fear that you have become one of us. If you let yourself die, who will tell them otherwise? Tamar demanded. *Who will tell Neeva?*

Rikus looked up and saw Caelum's angry red eyes locked on his. The cleric stood with his hand thrust toward the mul's face, and in the dwarf's palm flashed a miniature crimson sun.

The mul waved a hand in the direction of the dying gladiators. "I . . . didn't . . . do . . . this!" he cried.

Caelum moved forward, his jaw set in determination and his flaming hand held out before him. A red light shot from the mul's breast, and flames began to lick across his chest. Rikus clamped a hand over Tamar's ruby, then spun and scrambled away from the sun cleric as fast as he could.

Caelum's Victory

A deep boom rumbled from beneath the crater's fiery roots, shaking the whole basin and sending an ominous shudder over the ash-covered slopes of the surrounding mountains. The night sky answered with a brilliant sheet of scarlet lightning, silhouetting hundreds of spears, glaives, and axes along the rim of the caldera. The weapons were shouldered by a long line of Tyrian warriors, anxiously awaiting Rikus as he climbed out of the deep basin below.

Ten days ago, they had gathered all their non-magical metal articles—a dozen daggers, three axeheads, some spearpoints, and an assortment of pins and buckles—and given the items to a half-elf skilled in weaponsmithing. The smith had used the fire-belching fissure in the crater to heat a makeshift forge and melt the pieces. From this small supply of metal, he had fashioned a handful of crude hammers and primitive chisels that the legion had used to carve a long series of steps into the cliffside. This stairway had allowed the legion to climb out of the Crater of Bones without descending the lava channel and being forced to

241

fight the Urikites at a disadvantage. Now the Tyrians would be able to approach their enemy from the mountainside, on a broad front.

As Rikus stepped from the last stair onto the cinder-covered mountainside, several templars uttered hushed words of praise, hailing the mul for delivering the legion from the crater's confines. The gladiators simply looked down the mountain to where, far below, the Urikites remained in camp. After ten days of drinking sulfurous water condensed from steam vents and eating whatever they could catch scurrying beneath the bones, the former slaves were anxious to begin the battle.

Caelum stepped from the crowd. After casting a wary eye at Rikus's chest, the dwarf said, "The sun will shine with favor on us today." He had to squint to protect his red eyes against the ash stirred up by the stiff wind. "The rumbling ground and the lightning are good signs."

"They also woke our enemies," Rikus growled.

He peered down the mountainside. Bathed in the flaxen light of Athas's two moons, the cinder-covered slope looked like a great pile of golden pebbles. In the shadows at the base of the hill, where the Urikites had made their camp, dozens of flickering points of light were rushing to and fro. Rikus could only hope that, in the darkness, the men carrying the torches couldn't see his legion and were responding to the tremor. Given the pale light shrouding the hillside, however, he thought it wisest to expect the worst.

"Give the order to advance," Rikus said, speaking loudly enough so that everyone in the immediate vicinity could hear.

An anxious rustle worked its way down the line as hushed voices repeated his command. A few moments later, the Tyrians began to descend, half-stepping and half-sliding down the gritty slope.

Rikus signaled for his lieutenants to join their companies,

but before they could leave, Caelum cried, "Wait!"

"Why? Is something wrong?" the mul demanded, staring at the dark cloud of ash rising behind his advancing line.

Caelum pointed down at the fissure in the caldera. The long crevice was spewing a curtain of fire and molten rock into the air. "I can call upon the sun for aid."

Gaanon peered down at Caelum. "What do you mean?"

"I can summon a river of fire from the fissure," the dwarf explained. "It will run down the valley and swallow Maetan's camp."

"Don't burn quarry!" K'kriq objected, his antennae writhing in distress.

Neeva and the others raised their brows in interest, knowing that such magic would guarantee their victory. Nevertheless, no one spoke in support of the plan.

Finally Rikus asked the question that was on all of their minds. "What of Drewet and her warriors?"

For the last ten days, the red-haired half-elf and a hundred volunteers had guarded the mouth of the canyon, keeping the Urikites from sending patrols up the narrow gulch. If Caelum filled the gorge with lava, the small company would be burned alive.

It was Styan who answered the mul's question. "Caelum offers us certain victory," said the gray-haired templar. "We would be fools not to take it."

"Then we are fools," Rikus said flatly. "The price is too high."

Jaseela glanced down into the depths of the canyon. "Perhaps we can withdraw the troops," she suggested.

"Not quickly enough," observed Neeva. "Our gladiators will join battle in minutes. It would take an hour to reach Drewet with a message and allow her to climb to safety."

"Then no burn Urikites," said K'kriq, relieved. Without waiting for further debate, the thri-kreen started down the hill after the rest of the legion.

When the others started to follow, Styan raised a hand to stop them. "Drewet and her company have already offered their lives on Tyr's behalf," he said tentatively.

Rikus stopped, puzzled by the templar's insistence. The only reason Styan still lived was his newfound popularity with the gladiators, for the mutiny had convinced Rikus that Styan was the spy. Given that, it did not make sense for the templar to press so hard for something that would devastate both Maetan's force and his popular support.

When the mul did nothing to silence Styan, the templar continued more confidently. "What difference does it make whether Drewet falls to Urikite swords or to a river of fire?"

"Not that a templar would understand, but the difference is between honor and betrayal," the mul sneered.

No. The difference is between victory and defeat, interrupted Tamar. *Give up Drewet's company. You will save more of your precious legion and guarantee Maetan's capture.*

Rikus ignored the wraith and pulled his robe over his chest. After Caelum's spell had scorched the skin around the ruby, the wound had progressed from a festering sore to a bloated, blackened ulcer that constantly oozed yellow pus and stank like dead flesh. Most of the time, the mul's left arm ached too much to use, and the fingers of his hand varied in color between putrid yellow and vile blue. Caelum had reluctantly offered to use his magic on the wound, but, after the dwarf had turned away Tamar's fellows during the mutiny, Rikus feared the wraith would use the opportunity to attack the cleric.

Another rumble sounded from inside the mountain. A geyser of orange fire shot from the crevice, spraying molten rock to both sides of the fissure. Caelum studied the beads of glowing lava for a moment, then clenched his teeth and faced Rikus.

"If my dwarves were in the canyon, I would want you to

use the fire river," he said harshly. "So would they."

"If you were with them, I might," the mul snapped, glar-ing at the dwarf. Immediately he regretted his angry words, but only because they betrayed how hurt he was by the growing relationship between Caelum and Neeva.

"A good commander would not let his personal feelings interfere with his judgment," Caelum noted, speaking in the tone of reasoned argument.

Resisting the temptation to reach for his sword, Rikus said, "Caelum, so far Styan is the only one supporting your plan." He paused and looked at his other lieutenants. "If anyone else agrees with you, you can summon your river of fire. Otherwise, we attack without it."

Caelum glanced at the other company leaders. Although they all avoided his glance, the dwarf's face betrayed his con-fidence that they would side with him.

"I'm with Rikus, whatever he decides," Gaanon said. Af-ter the incident with the wraiths, the half-giant had stopped imitating the mul's dress, but he remained one of Rikus's loyal supporters.

Caelum turned to Jaseela, his eyes still confident of victo-ry. "What do you think?"

The noblewoman shook her head. "It's a good plan," she said. "But not if it assures victory at the price of integrity. I say no."

The dwarf frowned at her. "You can't mean that."

When Jaseela nodded, Caelum looked to Neeva. She stood several yards beyond the noblewoman.

Neeva avoided the dwarf's gaze by looking down the mountainside. A great cloud of ash had risen between the leaders and their troops, obscuring their view of the ad-vance. "If we don't hurry, we'll miss the battle."

"What about Caelum's plan?" Rikus pressed. He knew what her answer would be, but if the dwarf did not hear it from her lips he would not be satisfied.

Neeva faced the mul with pleading eyes. "Don't do this, Rikus."

"You've got to answer," the mul said.

Neeva glared at him for a moment, then softened her expression and looked to Caelum. "Your river would save lives in the long run, but we just can't execute a hundred of our own warriors."

Caelum jaw's fell. "Why are you siding with Rikus?" he demanded. "My plan is good—"

"You heard her answer. That's the end of it," the mul insisted, enjoying the dwarf's disappointment. "Now join your warriors. We've got a fight to win."

With that, Rikus drew his sword and led the way toward the base of the mountain. The others followed, descending the slope in a series of great leaps. Each time they landed, their feet sank deep into the ash. They then slid a few feet before launching themselves down the hill again.

The two subcommanders that Rikus trusted most, Neeva and Jaseela, went toward the flanks. He and Gaanon charged to the center to lead the handpicked company of gladiators that would spearhead the attack, with the templars to their left and the dwarves to their right.

After more than a minute of rapid descent, Rikus and Gaanon entered the billowing gray cloud behind their warriors. The mul immediately began to cough and choke, his mouth coated with dry, bitter ash. The fine grit blocked out the weak light of the moons, and everything went black. Even Rikus's dwarven sight was of little use, for it could not penetrate the airborne soot. The only heat emanation he could see was a white glow coming from somewhere deep below the cinder-covered surface of the volcano.

Within a few steps, the mul and the half-giant cleared the worst part of the ash cloud and found themselves in the midst of the Tyrian line, which continued to descend in a steady march. Followed closely by Gaanon, Rikus passed through the tangled ranks, his superstitious gladiators scrambling to move aside before he brushed against them. Twice the mul had to stifle sharp responses as he overheard someone whisper, "Murdering sorcerer!"

When he slipped out of the crowd, Rikus saw he had almost reached the bottom of the hill. Two dozen steps away, the cinders spilled off the mountain in great fan-shaped heaps more than thirty feet high. Guthay, the larger of Athas's flaxen moons, lit the southern sides of the cinder heaps in brilliant yellow light. The northern sides, lit by smaller Ral, seemed almost dark by comparison, with a pale, milky glow washing over their gentle slopes.

Beyond the ash fans, the terrain became a jumble, with the tips of sharp, jagged boulders protruding from a shoal of black shadows. A few yards into the murkiness stood the triple-ranked silhouettes of a Urikite line, the yellow crests of Hamanu's lion gleaming brightly on most of their dark tunics, and the red double-headed Serpent of Lubar glimmering more faintly on the rest.

Though he was not surprised to find the Urikites waiting for his attack, Rikus was immediately struck by the lack of archers and slingers in the army. All three ranks were armed with long spears angled toward the approaching Tyrians, with black shields slung over their free arms and obsidian short swords dangling from their belts.

"Something's wrong," Rikus observed, stopping at the top of an ash heap. The Tyrian warriors halted behind the mul, awaiting his order in tense silence. "Maetan's not stupid. He can't think his soldiers will beat our gladiators in hand-to-hand combat."

"He's made mistakes before," said Gaanon.

"Not this obvious," Rikus answered, running his eyes along his foe's ranks.

There was no time to count, but the enemy line was nearly as long as that formed by the fifteen hundred warriors in

Rikus's legion. Considering that the Urikites stood three deep, the mul estimated that Maetan had more than four thousand troops. That number did not include any reinforcements hiding in the darkness beyond the lines.

As Rikus studied the Urikite lines, his warriors began to whisper and mutter to each other. Thanks to the Scourge, he heard every word they said.

"What's he waiting for—his skeletons?"

"He's giving them time to think about what we're going to do to them—or about what they're going to do to us."

"Look at how many there are! We'll never kill them all."

Realizing that the longer he waited, the more nervous his warriors would grow, the mul pointed his sword toward the Urikite line. "For Tyr!" he bellowed.

"For Tyr!" thundered the warriors.

His ears ringing from his legion's war cry, Rikus led the way down the ash heap. His warriors' footfalls raised a choking cloud of ash that robbed them of breath and left them with hardly enough air to keep their lungs filled.

By the time Rikus stepped onto the broken ground of the delta, his ears had stopped ringing. Despite the soot coating their throats and clogging their lungs, his men were still screaming, promising death to the Urikites and despair to their families.

Rikus paid their yells no attention, for the Scourge also brought another voice to his ears—a much more sinister voice, speaking in the hushed tones of a magical incantation. "In the mighty name of King Hamanu, I command the glass rock to rise before our enemies!"

"Magic!" Rikus shouted. "Maetan has templars."

"Isn't it enough that he outnumbers us?" Gaanon cried.

Before the mul could answer, a hissing, crackling noise sounded from the enemy line. A long spike of black glass shot from the ground, and Rikus stopped just short of impaling himself on it. Screams of pain and anguish filled the night as Tyrians were gored by the rock. Those not killed outright by the jagged shards of obsidian had their toes and feet sliced to bloody ribbons.

A loud rasp sounded beneath the mul's feet, and he jumped backward in time to avoid being sliced by a razor-sharp plate of black glass emerging from the ground. He retreated up the ash heap to gain a better vantage point and saw that the templar's barricade of obsidian had brought his legion to a halt. Most of his warriors were staring at the strange rampart in dumbfounded silence, although a few were cursing and groaning as they vainly attempted to slip between the jagged splinters. In other places, the jingle of shattering obsidian rang out as more cautious warriors tried to smash a path to their opponents.

"Call them back," Rikus ordered, pointing at the brave Tyrians who were trying to press the attack. "We're going to have to go around."

While Gaanon sent messengers to relay the order, Rikus turned his attention to his left flank. A short distance away, the enemy's barricade curled toward the mountain, forming a large pen with a steep slope at its back. From what the mul could see, Jaseela's company stood outside the pen. Fortunately the noblewoman had been wise enough to halt her advance when the rest of the legion stopped moving. Rikus sent a messenger with word to clear a passage through the curved end of the barricade.

Next, Rikus faced Neeva's end of the line. There, he saw that the barricade gradually grew lower and less menacing, disappearing entirely just beyond Caelum's dwarves. Neeva's company was lost in the shadows spilling out of the canyon, but Rikus could hear the sounds of battle tolling in the darkness.

"At least we've still got a little luck to spare," the mul sighed, relieved that the templar's magic had not been strong enough to entrap his legion. Rikus slipped down from the heap, then motioned for Gaanon to follow him toward Neeva's company. "Maetan's templars may have slowed us down, but they won't save him."

"Of course not," the half-giant agreed. "But how are we to get at him with this wall in our way?"

"Go around it, of course."

As he moved toward Neeva's brigade, the mul ordered everyone he encountered to go in the opposite direction, toward Jaseela's company. Soon, the legion was streaming toward the far end of the field, shouting dire threats over the obsidian barricade that protected the Urikites.

When Rikus reached Caelum's dwarves, they were stubbornly hacking away at the obsidian barricade and refusing to flee. The mul grabbed the first one he came to, shoving him roughly toward Jaseela's flank.

"Go!" he ordered. "You'll just get yourself killed if you try to fight the Urikites through this wall."

The dwarf picked up his warhammer and returned to the obsidian barricade. "Maetan is over there," he grunted, hardly glancing at Rikus.

Caelum hurried to the mul's side. "Why are you fleeing the battle?"

"I'm not running away. But we're not going to win anything by concentrating on breaking down the—"

The mul stopped in midsentence as the distant voice of Maetan's templar came to him. "In the name of Mighty Hamanu, the slopes of this mountain shall cascade down upon our enemies."

Rikus heard a gentle slough high above, then felt the cinder-covered mountain shudder.

"Take the dwarves and run!" Rikus shoved Gaanon toward Jaseela's company. He pointed up the slope, then yelled, "Maetan's trying to bury us alive!"

Caelum looked in the direction the mul pointed, where a great swath of cinders was twinkling in the moonlight as it slid down the slope. "Do as he says!" Caelum ordered frantically, starting to lead his men after Gaanon.

Rikus caught the dwarf by the shoulder. "You come with me."

The mul took Caelum and moved toward the base of the mountain, where they would not have to struggle against a tide of dwarves rushing southward. They had taken no more than a dozen steps when a terrible rumble rolled down from above. Rikus looked up and saw a wall of cinders crashing down the steep slope. Behind it came the whole mountainside, leaving nothing in its wake except a roiling cloud of soot.

The mul grabbed Caelum's arm and sprinted, dragging the dwarf toward the northern flank of the line, where Neeva's company would be trying to fight through to the mouth of the canyon Drewet's troops guarded. Along the rim of the lava channel ran a line of white-crusted crags; these, Rikus hoped, would act like a shield to turn aside the cinder avalanche.

They had barely reached the shelter of this ridge when the avalanche rolled into the ash heaps at the base of the mountain. A tremendous thump pulsed through the air. The piles scattered, almost as if a great explosion had forced them into the air from below. Huge plumes of powdery soot rose skyward, masking the yellow light of the flaxen moons and spreading over the rocky delta in a choking fog.

In the gray pall, Rikus lost sight of his army. On the other side of the obsidian barricade, the Urikites were alternately coughing and cheering the templar who, they believed, had vanquished their enemy with a single spell. Rikus dared to hope their optimism was misplaced, for the Scourge brought to his ears the rasping, fear-stricken voices of men and dwarves yelling guidance to each other.

Both the cries of the Urikites and the Tyrians, however, seemed but a whisper compared to the roar of the avalanche

as it continued to pour tons and tons of stone and cinder off
the mountain.

"Can you still summon that river of fire?" Rikus asked,
turning his attention from the landslide to Caelum.

The dwarf did not look away from the avalanche. "If you
had listened to me earlier—"

"Now is no time to lecture me, dwarf," Rikus snapped. "I
just want to know if you can still use your magic."

The cleric nodded. "I'll have to climb high enough to see
the flames of the crevice."

"Go ahead and climb," Rikus said, pointing toward the
mouth of Drewet's canyon. "Stay in those rocks—I don't
want you getting caught in the avalanche. And don't cast
your spell until I say the time has come."

"How will I know when that is?" the dwarf asked.

"You'll see Drewet's company leaving the canyon," Rikus
answered. "Or I'll send a messenger."

"There'll be no time for a messenger," Caelum said, pulling a smooth, round rock from his pocket and handing it to
the mul. "Throw that into the air when you're ready."

Rikus nearly dropped the stone, for it was scalding hot.
"What is it?"

"A little surprise I prepared for Maetan," Caelum answered. "It will also do as a signal."

With that, the dwarf began scaling the ridge. Rikus
slipped the hot stone into a belt pouch, then turned toward
the mouth of Drewet's canyon. Less than a dozen yards
away, the Urikites were lined up many ranks deep, pressing
the attack in an attempt to force Neeva's company back toward the avalanche. The gladiators were standing firm, but
if he was to save Drewet, Rikus needed them to do more
than hold their lines.

The mul rushed into the fray. He picked his way around
the ash-blurred forms of a dozen gladiators, then glimpsed
the tip of a spear thrusting toward him. Rikus parried, sever-

ing the shaft, then brought his sword down over the top of the Urikite's shield. The vorpal blade cleaved both shield and man, then the mul found himself standing within the first rank of the Urikite line.

"For Tyr!" he screamed, but his words were lost in the clash of blade against blade and the cries of the wounded and dying.

* * * * *

The battle went terribly. Within minutes, Rikus found himself standing where he had started, waist-deep in Urikite bodies and coated with the warm, sticky blood of his enemies. He was vaguely aware that Tyrians stood to each side of him, but there was no sign that his gladiators were even close to freeing Drewet's company. All he could see ahead of him was an endless stream of shouting Urikites, marching out of the dark night and climbing over their dead fellows to continue the attack.

"I thought I'd find you at the center of this mess," called a familiar voice. Neeva stepped to the mul's side, and K'kriq to the other. She parried a spear thrust with her short sword, then used the dagger in her other hand to slice open her attacker's chest. "What are you doing?"

"Trying to reach the mouth of Drewet's canyon," Rikus answered, his breath coming in labored gasps. He was so tired that he could hardly raise his sword, and his legs ached so badly that he could barely lift them over the bodies piled around him. "I sent Caelum up the hill. We're going to have to summon his river of fire."

"No!" Neeva cried.

"Spoil hunt," complained K'kriq.

A screaming Urikite clambered over the corpses ahead and jabbed a spearpoint at the thri-kreen's eyes. K'kriq blocked with one arm, then lashed out with the other three, simultaneously ripping his attacker's shield away and tearing out the man's throat.

"You can't do that to Drewet!" Neeva said. "She'll never escape."

"If I don't, she'll die anyway, and we'll still lose the battle," Rikus growled. "Half our legion's buried in that avalanche, and who knows what's happened to the other half. It's the only way."

"The only way to save your legion or the best way to destroy Maetan?" Neeva demanded.

"The only way to survive!" Rikus shouted. "Besides, I haven't given the order yet—"

His answer was cut short by the battle cries of a fresh rank of Urikites. As they came over the corpse pile, one soldier each attacked Neeva and K'kriq, but two thrust their spears at the mul. Rikus lopped the point off one spear and tried to sidestep the other, but stumbled when a half-dead soldier clutched at his ankle. The spear took the mul in his sore shoulder. A wave of agony shot through his body, magnified ten-fold by the tenderness of the festering wound around the wraith's gem.

Neeva's black blade flashed in front of Rikus's face, snapping the spear just above the head—and sending another surge of fire through the mul. At the same time, K'kriq grabbed the mul's attacker and sank his mandibles into him, filling the Urikite's veins with poison.

Neeva narrowly avoided being stabbed by another Urikite, parrying with her dagger. She opened the attacker's throat with a flick of the same blade that had turned the spear. "If you think we can save Drewet from here, you've taken leave of your senses," she said, allowing a broad-shouldered gladiator in a four-horned helmet to take her place. "I'll send someone to shout a warning from the rim. Maybe she can fight her own way free."

Rikus and K'kriq fought side-by-side for a few moments

longer, but the mul's wound was taking its toll. His reactions slowed to the point where he found himself lurching about in clumsy dodges, and the Scourge of Rkard felt as heavy in his hand as a half-giant's club.

"Cover my retreat, K'kriq," Rikus yelled, stumbling away from the clamor of the battleline.

The extra room only made the four-armed thri-kreen a more dangerous opponent. He tore into the approaching soldiers with renewed vigor, their speartips clattering harmlessly off his hard carapace.

Holding his sword under his arm, Rikus reached into his belt pouch and touched the stone Caelum had given him. Though it scorched the mul's flesh, he did not remove his hand. Instead, looking toward the dark canyon where Drewet's company was waiting, he let the pain build for a few seconds.

At last, he whispered, "I'm sorry. You deserve a better death."

Rikus pulled out the rock and threw it high over the heads of the Urikites. It disappeared into the night. Then a loud boom drowned out the furor of the battlefield. A ball of orange flame flared over the enemy's ranks. The mul glimpsed rank upon rank of Urikite faces staring up at the blazing globe. They were packed into the area in front of the canyon shoulder-to-shoulder, and there were still more of them marching out of the darkness.

"Hundreds and hundreds," Rikus gasped, once again taking the hilt of his sword. "We never had a chance."

The burning sphere descended and incinerated a dozen Urikites unfortunate enough to be trapped beneath it, but the loss hardly seemed noticeable in the midst of the great company.

Rikus stepped back to the battleline, ignoring the raging pain caused by the spearhead embedded in his shoulder and fighting without regard for the risks he took. Soon, Urikite corpses were heaped so high that the mul's foes began to jump down at him as if leaping from a wall. It made no difference to the gladiator. His sharp blade sliced through them at all angles, and the mound continued to grow.

Rikus was jolted back to his senses when a horrific boom sounded from the Crater of Bones. A crimson light flashed across the sky a moment before the ground began to buck. The mul's feet were swept from beneath him, and he fell to the ground, landing atop a half-dozen bleeding corpses. A pair of stunned Urikites tumbled down the body pile toward him, scattering their shields and spears behind them.

In the next instant, shrill whistles and screeching cries filled the night. Hissing streaks of flame dropped out of the sky, bringing with them the stench of sulfur. As the fiery globs crashed to the battlefield, agonized pleas for help rang from both sides of the line.

The two Urikites that had been coming at Rikus returned to their feet before the wounded mul could regain his. They threw themselves on top of him, one grabbing the shaft in his shoulder and the other pinning his sword arm to the ground.

The mul howled in pain, then smashed his forehead into the face of the Urikite pinning his arm. As the soldier rocked backward, Rikus ripped his hand free and pulled the Scourge across the bodies of both attackers.

Covered in fresh, hot blood, the mul pushed the wounded men away and rolled to his knees. The situation around him was the same in all directions, with Urikites and Tyrians wrestling on the ground while reinforcements jumped into the melee from both sides. Long streamers of fire lit the sky as burning blobs of molten rock dropped to the ground and burst into red sprays of liquid flame.

A sizzling whoosh sounded from above the mul's head, then a streak of orange light momentarily stunned him. Tiny droplets of liquid fire spattered over his body, filling his nostrils with the stench of his own burning skin. Screaming in pain and blind rage, the mul threw himself on the men he had just wounded and rolled over their bodies to suffocate the embers charring his flesh.

"Rikus hurt?"

The gladiator looked up and saw K'kriq standing over him. Although the thri-kreen's carapace was scorched and burned in a dozen places, the mantis-warrior seemed to be enduring the rain of fire with far less discomfort than the mul.

"I'll live," Rikus muttered, gritting his teeth at the pain.

"Then come."

The thri-kreen pulled Rikus to his feet with two arms. With the other two he pointed to the mouth of Drewet's canyon.

A broad river of white-hot rock was pouring out of the gorge, sweeping onto the delta in a glowing, steadily flowing river. The Urikite troops not in the front lines of the battle were caught by the lava. Panicked, they clambered over each other in an effort to flee, but to little avail. The molten stone pursued the screaming soldiers relentlessly, lapping at their heels and overtaking those who fell. As Rikus watched, hundreds of soldiers burst into columns of yellow flame, flaring for a brief instant before they vanished in a wisp of smoke and ash.

Caelum had won the battle for him, but Rikus could not help but wonder what the real price would be.

FOURTEEN

Parley

"Rikus . . . Rikus . . . Rikus . . ."

The mul straightened the sling holding his left arm, then hung the Scourge of Rkard from the scabbard hooks on the Belt of Rank. The company outside had been droning his name for two days, and now that he had recovered from his wounds enough to stand, Rikus was prepared to face them.

"Would you like me to stand with you?" asked Neeva. No one else had been brave enough to follow Rikus up into the room.

"No, I'd better do this alone," he answered.

After stepping onto a small balcony that overhung Makla's central plaza, he looked down upon the company of chanting corpses. Some were naked, with bits of singed cloth clinging to their blistered hides, and blackened stubs of bone where their hands and feet should have been. A few others had lost their legs from the waist down, and supported themselves only by clinging to huge boulders that hovered in the air before them. The largest part of the crowd had been reduced to whirlwinds of ash crowned by the vague outline of a pain-racked face. All had been part of Drewet's doomed company. At the head of the crowd, over a small circle of blackened and cracked cobblestones, burned an orange pillar of flame. The grisly undead band had appeared in Makla only hours behind the Tyrian legion, and neither Caelum's magic nor threats of violence had convinced them to move.

"Rikus . . . Rikus . . . Rikus . . ."

Their rasping chant did not change tone or inflection, and the mul could not even tell if they knew he had come to answer their call. He forced himself to stare at their gruesome forms for several moments, determined not to show the fear he felt inside.

Rikus raised his good arm for silence, but the warriors continued to chant his name. "I'm sorry you died," he called, speaking above them. "I tried to save you."

The orange flame, which the mul assumed to be Drewet, advanced a pace. The entire company followed, angrily shouting, "Hurray for Rikus!"

The mul stumbled backward, shocked by the anger in their voices. When the company came no closer, Rikus recovered his composure and returned to the edge of the balcony. This time, he gripped the stone rail to prevent himself from retreating again—and to keep his hand from trembling.

"I had to save the rest of the legion," Rikus said. Once again, he had to shout to make himself heard, for the company had resumed its chant. "You were doomed anyway."

Drewet led the company another pace closer, and again they shouted, "Hurray for Rikus!"

The mul's knuckles turned white, but he did not step from the railing. "What do you want?" he asked. Though he tried to speak in a demanding tone, there was an undertone of dread and fear in his voice.

This time, only Drewet spoke. "Tell us why," she demanded, moving closer. Tongues of flame began to lick at the underside of the stone balcony.

"I told you," Rikus answered, feeling his legs begin to quiver. "To save the legion."

The rest of the company came forward. "Hurray for Rikus!"

As they resumed their chant, it was all the mul could do to keep from turning and running. "If you want my life, then come and try to take it," he yelled.

With a trembling hand, he reached for his sword.

Don't, you fool! commanded Tamar. *Until you bring me the book, your life is not your own to throw away.* When Rikus moved his hand away from his scabbard, she continued. *Your warriors only wish to be dismissed. They are in pain.*

How do you know? the mul demanded.

Look at them, Tamar said, a bemused note in her voice. *Any fool can see they suffer the agony of their deaths. They would have abandoned their bodies long ago, had they been able.*

Rikus returned his hand to the railing. "You're free to leave." After a moment, when the company continued to chant his name, he yelled, "Go. Leave your pain behind you!"

"Tell us why!" Drewet screamed.

She rose into the air until she hovered in front of the balcony. An orange tendril lashed out and touched Rikus's sling, instantly setting the bloody cloth on fire. Screaming in alarm, the mul pulled his aching arm free, then ripped the rag from his neck and flung the flaming thing into the square.

Drewet's company moved closer and chanted his name more loudly. Thinking that he had been a fool to listen to Tamar's advice, Rikus retreated to the back of the balcony. Drewet followed, moving so close that the heat of her flaming form stung Rikus's skin. He drew his sword and held the blade in front of himself.

The Scourge won't protect you, Tamar warned.

But she won't listen!

How do you expect the warriors to accept their fate when you will not accept the onus for choosing it? Tamar asked. *If you shrink from your destiny, it will destroy you—and I have no wish to find another agent to recover the book for me.*

I am not your pawn!

Tamar let her silence be her reply.

At his back, the mul heard Neeva's voice. "I'll get Caelum!"

"No," Rikus said, accepting Tamar's advice. Though he distrusted the wraith as much as he despised her, the mul did not doubt that she was trying to save his life. As she had pointed out, she still needed him to recover the book. "I need no protection from my own warriors."

Keeping his eye fixed on the pillar of fire in front of him, Rikus slowly sheathed his sword and moved forward. Drewet backed away. When she was once again hanging over the square, the mul stopped and looked down at her company. They continued to cry his name, their voices bitter with resentment and pain. Rikus studied their tortured forms for several moments, his heart growing heavy as he accepted the full burden of what he had done.

At last, he was ready to dismiss Drewet's company. "You died so I could win the battle," he called, fixing his gaze on the flaming pillar before him. "I would do it again."

* * * * *

The chanting stopped, and Canth looked up from the mug of bitter-smelling broy that a friend had poured for him. Like the rest of his fellows, the burly gladiator and his firemates had made their camp at the western end of town—as far away from Rikus and his company of dead disciples as they could.

"I don't like the sound of that," Canth said, setting his square jaw. "What do you suppose Rikus is doing now? Has he taught Drewet and her troops a new song at last?" He suppressed a shudder.

"Who knows?" replied Lor, a brown-skinned woman with a bloody bandage on the stump of her sword arm. She held her mug out to Jotano, a quiet templar who had endeared himself to the gladiators through his uncanny knack for finding broy or wine when others had to make do with water. "I'll wager that whatever he's about, it's no good."

"A dwarf told me he's learned sorcery so he can be a king like Kalak," offered Lafus, a stooped half-elf with an unusually broad face and a bald pate. "The dwarf heard it from Caelum himself."

"I don't believe it," said Canth. "The Rikus I know doesn't care about kings or magic. I say the ruby has taken over his mind—and it's going to get us all killed."

Lafus, always as ready to argue as he was to fight, countered the generous claim. "Because you once shared a stadium pen with the mul doesn't mean you know him." He snorted. "How do you account for those monstrous things in the square?"

Jotano shook his head. "Those are unquiet spirits, longing for rest, not creatures raised by magic."

Canth nodded. "And you templars know your magic. Besides, I'll believe Rikus's word over that of a sun-sick dwarf any day," he countered. "What makes you think Fire-Eyes knows what Rikus is doing?" he demanded, using the gladiators' nickname for Caelum.

"My dwarf contact says it came to Caelum from Neeva," said Lafus, his lip turned up in a triumphant sneer. "That's why she won't lie with Rikus any more."

In a drink-slurred voice, Lor declared, "Then I'll lie with him." She raised the stump of what had been her sword arm. "Maybe his magic will grow my hand back."

She chuckled grimly, but the others looked away in uncomfortable silence.

After a moment, Canth faced Jotano. Hoping to counter the powerful case that Lafus had made by invoking Neeva's name, the square-jawed gladiator asked, "What do you hear in your company's camps, Jotano?"

The templar shrugged and refilled Lor's empty mug. "It matters little to the templars whether Rikus is learning sorcery or controlled by it," he said. "Magic is power, and it is better to have a powerful master than a weak one."

* * * * *

K'kriq burst into Rikus's room. "Come quick!" he said. "Need you."

"For what?" the mul demanded. He sat up and placed his legs over the edge of the bed. During the last three days, he had risen from it only once, when he had gone to dismiss Drewet's company. "Is Hamanu sending another army?"

"No," K'kriq said. "Just come."

Rikus forced himself to stand, gritting his teeth against the pain it caused. The spear puncture in his shoulder was already scarred over, for Caelum had used his magic to heal it long ago. Many of his other wounds, including most of the charred holes where he had been spattered by lava, were still in an awful state.

The canker on his chest, especially, had grown even more disgusting. Tamar's ruby now resembled the red pupil of an eye, looking out on the world from a black iris that oozed a constant stream of foul yellow bile. The pestilence had left his arm swollen and useless, a source of constant pain that sometimes made him gasp.

Rikus put on his robe, then followed K'kriq down the mansion hallway. Like all the other buildings in the village, this one had not escaped the ravages of the fires the legion had set during their first retreat. The whole building stank of charcoal, and the ostentatious murals on its stone walls were lost beneath deep layers of soot.

Nevertheless, the mansion was still more comfortable than anyplace the mul had slept since leaving Tyr. During the time Rikus and his legion had been trapped in the Crater of Bones, the slave-keepers of Makla had returned to reconstruct their homes and slave compounds. It was a mistake they had not long lived to regret. When the Tyrians had returned and liberated the village, the hundreds and hundreds of quarry slaves had exacted a terrible revenge on their cruel masters.

K'kriq led the mul into the mansion's great hall, a square chamber with an entrance at each corner. A fire had burned clear through the floors and ceilings of the upper stories, and now the slanting rays of the crimson sun shone directly into the room. The ruins of a massive table and other fine furniture littered the polished floor. On the walls hung charred streamers of cloth that had once been priceless tapestries.

K'kriq guided Rikus into a marble armchair begrimed with smoke. Gathered around it were Jaseela, Styan, Caelum, and Neeva, the last two standing together. In the middle of the room stood Gaanon, his head newly shaved and a crimson sun tattooed onto his forehead. In his hands, he held a larger version of the stone hammers favored by Caelum's dwarves.

Rikus was more intrigued by the thin figure with Gaanon than by the half-giant's latest attire. Standing in front of Gaanon was Maetan of Urik, dressed in a bronze breastplate and a fresh green robe boldly emblazoned with the winged Serpent of Lubar. Noting that the mindbender was dressed in clean clothes, the mul thought it unlikely that Gaanon had found the Urikite crawling around the slopes of the Smoking Crown.

Rikus looked from the prisoner to K'kriq. "Fetch my belt and sword."

Clacking his mandibles in anticipation of a good meal, the

thri-kreen left to obey.

Maetan's eyes betrayed no surprise. "I came under the water banner," he said, referring to the Athasian custom of carrying a blue flag to signal peaceful intentions. The water banner was most often used when one party wished to approach an oasis where strangers were camped, but it was occasionally adopted to arrange a parley in times of war. "I trust that even a slave will honor the courtesies of truce long enough to hear what I say."

"We might," Rikus allowed. "If you don't misbehave."

In truth, the mul didn't give a varl's eggsack about the Urikite's water banner. Such niceties were for men who regarded war as a game, and to Rikus it was a vendetta. If the mul didn't kill Maetan today, it would be because the mindbender escaped.

After glaring at the hated Lubar for a time, the mul shifted his attention to Neeva. "Call everyone back from the battlefield."

She frowned. "But many of our warriors—"

"*Now*," Rikus insisted. "Whatever he says, Maetan of Lubar isn't to be trusted. I don't want our search parties trapped if this is some sort of trick."

The dwarves and a company of two hundred warriors remained at the battlefield, searching for Tyrian survivors trapped beneath the avalanche. Although they had found twenty survivors and ten times that many corpses, the legion was still missing two hundred warriors.

As Neeva left, K'kriq returned with the Belt of Rank, the Scourge of Rkard hanging in its scabbard. Rikus put the belt on, then said to K'kriq, "Wait outside."

The thri-kreen crossed his antennae. "Maetan enemy. Stay to k-kill."

Rikus shook his head, fearing what would happen if the enemy general took control of K'kriq's mind with the Way. "Go. You're needed outside, to hunt Maetan down if he uses the Way to escape."

K'kriq's mandibles clacked together several times, but he finally obeyed. Once the thri-kreen was gone, Rikus removed the Scourge's scabbard from his belt and sat down, laying the sword over his knees.

"You needn't doubt my honor," Maetan said. "I have accepted that in coming here, I may well die."

"Then why come?" demanded Jaseela.

When the mindbender looked upon the disfigured noblewoman, he did not even do her the courtesy of hiding the repulsion that flashed across his face. "My defeat has disgraced my family," he explained freely. "By delivering a message for my king, I redeem the Lubar name—and mighty Hamanu will confiscate only half of our lands."

Rikus allowed himself a smug smile. "What is your message?"

"It is for your king," Maetan said.

Rikus reached into a pocket on his belt and withdrew the olivine crystal. "You can pass your message through me—or not at all."

Maetan nodded. "That will be acceptable."

Rikus held the olivine out at arm's length. Tithian's sharp features quickly appeared in the gem, and the king scowled in anger. "I had hoped not to hear from you again."

"I bear good news, my king," Rikus said. "We have destroyed the Urikite army that Hamanu sent to attack Tyr, and we have captured the village of Makla."

"Are you mad?" Tithian roared. "Makla's quarries are Urik's only source of trade. Hamanu will wipe you out—and raze Tyr in retaliation!"

Rikus looked away from the gem, careful not to betray Tithian's reaction since only he could hear the king's ranting. Behind Maetan, Neeva slipped back into the room.

Rikus returned his attention to Maetan. "What's your message?"

"Mighty Hamanu will suffer the pretender Tithian to sit on the throne of Tyr," the Urikite said. "In exchange, Tithian must relinquish Makla, maintain Tyr's trade in iron, and present to Hamanu all the gladiators in this legion. The mighty king of Urik will not tolerate slaves loose in the desert."

Rikus dutifully repeated the offer to the king.

"Accept it!" Tithian commanded. From the anxiety that still colored the king's face, however, it was clear that he did not believe Rikus would do as ordered.

Remembering Tithian's betrayal in the nest of the slave tribe, the mul gave the king a bitter smile, then looked up at Maetan. "Tyr refuses."

"I am the king!" Tithian screeched, his voice sounding inside the mul's ears alone. "I decide what to refuse and what to accept!"

Maetan nodded as though he had expected Rikus's response. "Hamanu thought you might be reluctant to return to your rightful station, Rikus," he said. "Therefore, he has sent his army to block all the routes to Tyr. You will not be allowed to return to your city."

Rikus raised his brow. "That must have taken many legions. The desert is a large place."

"Hamanu's army is larger," Maetan answered. "His legions have blocked every route. You have only two choices: surrender or die."

Rikus remained quiet, though not because the mindbender's words frightened him. If Maetan's claim was true, the mul had a third choice—albeit a desperate one: attack Urik itself. Even Hamanu's army was not so large that it could garrison the city and still seal all the routes between Urik and Tyr.

Taking advantage of the mul's silence, Jaseela demanded, "If Hamanu has marshaled his legions, why isn't he sending them here?"

Maetan did not even bother to look at the noblewoman. "Because that would achieve only part of his goal," said the mindbender. "He wishes to guarantee access to Tyr's iron and to use your gladiators to replenish his supply of slaves. Destroying this legion would accomplish neither, whereas a negotiated peace will achieve both."

"It doesn't matter. Hamanu's offer is refused," Rikus said.

In the gem, Tithian yelled, "You ill-begotten larva of an inbred cilops!"

Rikus silenced the king's voice by slipping the olivine back into his belt pocket. At the same time, Styan stepped to the mul, asking, "Is it wise to reject this offer? Aren't you endangering Tyr for the sake of a few warriors?"

"Would you ask that if you and your templars had to stay to work Urik's quarries?" demanded Neeva. "Stop trying to save your own life."

The templar spun on her. "I'm trying to save Tyr!" he yelled. "If that means some of us suffer, then so be it!"

"You're a fool, then," said Jaseela, speaking calmly. "Even if we could force the gladiators to surrender—which we can't —it would make no difference. Hamanu will honor his word only as long as it's convenient. I say we stay and fight as one."

"You mean stay and die," spat Styan.

"We're not going to die, and our gladiators are not going to surrender," Rikus said, leaning forward in his chair. "I have something else in mind for us."

His comment elicited puzzled expressions from his lieutenants, but only Styan questioned him. "What would that be?"

Rikus sat back. "I'll tell you when the time comes," he said. The mul had no intention of revealing his plan now, for he feared the mindbender would use the Way to communicate it to Hamanu.

Instead, Rikus turned his gaze on Maetan, who was quietly smirking at the discord. "Now that you've delivered

Hamanu's message, our truce is finished. At the moment, you are the one who has only two choices: answer my questions and die quickly, or refuse and be torn apart by the thri-kreen."

Maetan showed no emotion at the threat. "My choice depends upon your questions."

"Name the spy who has been telling you of our movements and plans," the mul demanded.

The statement elicited a rustle of surprised murmurs from his lieutenants, for Rikus had mentioned his concerns to no one except Neeva. All eyes immediately went to Styan, who, as a templar, was automatically suspect. The color drained from the old man's face.

Maetan raised his brow and barely kept a smile from crossing his lips. "My spy?"

"Answer!" Rikus yelled.

The mindbender allowed the crowd to eye Styan for several moments, then said, "Very well. It costs Urik nothing to reveal the spy's identity. Besides, his service did not prevent my family's disgrace." He pointed at Caelum. "It was the dwarf."

"What?" Neeva shrieked.

"I promised to return the *Book of the Kemalok Kings*," the Urikite explained. He held his arms up and opened his robes, showing that there was nothing hidden beneath them. He laughed cruelly, then said, "Unfortunately, I seem to have forgotten it. What a pity—Caelum will have to go to my townhouse in Urik to recover it."

Rikus stared at Caelum's frightened face with a slack jaw. He had been so convinced of Styan's guilt that Maetan had stunned him by naming the dwarf. Nevertheless, the mindbender's accusation made a certain amount of sense. Rikus had long ago voiced his own suspicions about Caelum, and he did not find it surprising that the dwarf would resort to treachery to recover the book. To the mul's mind, however, the most condemning indications of the cleric's betrayal were the times he or his dwarves had refused to do as commanded and the lengths to which he had gone to endear himself to Neeva.

"Seize Caelum," Rikus ordered.

Styan, who looked greatly relieved, moved to obey. Neeva cut him off and stepped in front of the dwarf. "Leave him alone."

Styan reached for his dagger and tried to circle around the female gladiator. Neeva disarmed him with a lightning-fast kick that sent his blade flying, then grabbed a handful of his long gray hair and jerked him into her grasp. She slipped a hand around his chin and placed the other against the back of his neck.

"Don't even flinch," she hissed. "As it is, it's been too long since I've killed a templar."

"Release him!" Rikus ordered, stepping off the marble throne. When she did not obey, he repeated his order. "Let Styan go."

"No," Neeva answered. "If you take another step, Rikus, I'll snap his neck."

"That's your choice," the mul countered, drawing the Scourge. "It won't save Caelum."

Neeva yelled in anger, then pushed Styan halfway across the room and unsheathed her own sword. "If you mean to kill him, you'll have to fight past me."

Rikus stopped. "You don't mean that," he said, his gaze fixed on her emerald eyes.

"Neeva, don't," Caelum said. He took a slow step toward Rikus.

"Be quiet and let me handle this," Neeva ordered, once again placing herself between the dwarf and Rikus. To the mul, she said, "If you believe Maetan—"

"It's not Maetan I believe, it's what has happened since the dwarves joined us," Rikus countered. "The Urikites have countered every move we've made before we made it."

"Perhaps there is a spy," Neeva allowed. "It's not Caelum, though. It doesn't make sense. He's the one who saved us from the halflings, and he fought with us at Umbra's ambush—"

"That was when we lost Jaseela's company," Styan pointed out, still lying on the floor.

"Thanks to you," Gaanon said. "If your templars would have been there, we'd have won."

"True—but the dwarves weren't there either," said Jaseela.

"How can you say that?" Neeva demanded. "Caelum was, and he saved your life!"

"Only because she was standing next to him," Rikus said. "He didn't save any of her retainers."

Caelum stepped from behind Neeva. "Rikus, I can understand why you choose to believe our enemy's word over mine," the dwarf said, his voice edged with fear and anger. "But Neeva does not deserve such an insult. Apologize to her, or I'll take measures."

Neeva scowled. "Caelum, I'm not the one in danger here. Be quiet."

Rikus shook his head, astonished by the dwarf's tone. "Take measures!" The mul shouted. "Are you threatening me?"

Caelum blanched, but he did not back down. "No, I'm warning you," he said. He stepped forward, shrugging off Neeva's hand when she tried to restrain him. "Believe that I'm the spy if you want. Go ahead and kill me. But you won't mistreat Neeva while I'm alive."

Jaseela stepped to the mul's side. "Maybe we'd better think this through," she said. "What if Maetan's lying? He has no reason to tell us the truth. He might be trying to avenge himself on Caelum for bringing that river of fire down on his army, or he might be protecting the real spy."

She glanced at Styan meaningfully, then turned back to the dwarf, who remained standing before Rikus. "Besides, I don't think Caelum's acting much like a spy."

"No, he's not," Rikus agreed. He looked from the noblewoman to the dwarf. "He's acting like a dwarf with a focus."

Caelum met Rikus's eyes evenly. "That is so," he admitted. "On the day Neeva saved my life, I swore to protect her always."

"Then it stands to reason Caelum can't be the spy," Neeva said. She gently laid a hand on the dwarf's shoulder. "Betraying the legion would be a violation of his focus."

"Unless he's lying about his focus," Rikus said, glaring at Neeva. Despite his growing anger, the mul sheathed his sword and stepped away. "I don't know whether he's the spy or not, Neeva, but he's your responsibility. If he betrays us later, you'll suffer the same as him. Nothing will save you— not even what there is, or was, between us."

Neeva's eyes softened. "You're doing the right thing." She, too, sheathed her sword, then gave him a weak smile. "Thank you."

Rikus turned away without responding. "Now leave— everyone," he ordered. "Maetan and I will talk alone."

The others frowned and began to object, but Rikus was in no mood for arguments. "Do it," he ordered. "And don't come back until I call you."

The time had come to kill the Urikite, and Rikus thought it would be safer if there was no one else in the room when he attacked. Though Maetan had made it clear that he expected to die, the mindbender had given no indication that he intended to offer up his life without a fight. With the Scourge in his hand, the mul would have some defense against the Urikite's mental attacks, but no one else had the benefit of such protection.

When everyone except Gaanon filed toward the doors, Rikus nodded to him. "You, too, my friend."

"But if he intends to attack you—"

"He'll do it whether or not you're holding him," the mul said. "A mindbender doesn't need his hands."

As Gaanon reluctantly released Maetan and moved toward the exit, Tamar demanded, *Are you preparing to kill him?*

Don't try to stop me, Rikus warned.

Why would I want to? As long as he lives, he's an obstacle to recovering the book, she answered. *But you'll need help, or he'll use the Way against you.*

Help?

Open the robe, she said. *I'll engage his mind. It will help if you can draw his attention to my ruby.*

Once Gaanon had left the room, Maetan smiled confidently. "What did you wish to discuss in private?"

"I have something that belongs to you," Rikus said, opening his robe.

The mindbender made a sour face as he eyed the wound on Rikus's chest. Tamar's gem shined so brightly that it cast a scarlet light over Maetan's face.

"What is that?" Maetan asked, gesturing at the glow.

"Umbra," Rikus answered. "And I want you to take him back. He's so foul I can't keep him locked inside any longer —he's rotting my flesh from the inside out."

A clever trick, Rikus, Tamar cooed.

A black shadow began to swim through the light coming from the ruby. Maetan overcame his revulsion and looked into the gem. "Umbra isn't foul, he's merely—"

Tamar ended his sentence by making her attack.

She filled Rikus's mind with a vast plain of frothing yellow mud, stinking of sulfur and tolling with the thick plop of bursting bubbles. From one of these bubbles emerged the rear of a gross, many-legged thing with a ruby-red carapace of square scales. When it dragged its head out of the mud, Rikus saw that it had Tamar's slitlike eyes and broad lips. In its huge mandibles it clutched Maetan's struggling form.

Instantly Rikus willed himself into the picture. He wasted no energy by assuming any form except his own, complete with the ulcerating sore on his chest. The only thing that was different, as far as he could tell, was that Tamar's gem was not embedded in the wound.

Maetan turned toward him. "You ambushed me!" he snarled. "For that, you will die."

The mindbender changed to the double-headed Serpent of Lubar. At the same time, the ground changed from boiling mud to roiling black gas, and Rikus lost sight of the snake.

"Maetan!" the mul screamed, furious that his enemy had eluded him in his moment of victory.

A brilliant blue light rose from the Scourge of Rkard, and Rikus found himself standing a short distance away from a massive arch of blue obsidian. Between him and the arch was a sandy plain. Here and there, jagged, square-edged sheets of translucent green glass protruded from the ground. There was no sign of either Maetan or Tamar.

"You said you wanted him!" the wraith's voice cried, echoing down from the clouds of the black sky. "Come and get him."

"Where are you?" the mul yelled.

The light cast by his sword suddenly narrowed to an intense beam that shone through the arch. Rikus ran toward the blue landmark. Already, he was beginning to feel tired, and he had done nothing except project himself into the combat.

A half-dozen glass sheets slipped from their places and shot toward him, their sharp edges turned horizontally so as to slice him into six different pieces from the knees to the neck. Rikus barely had time to bring his sword up, then slashed down through the plates as they approached him. They shattered into a hundred pieces, covering him with dozens of painful cuts as they struck. For many moments, the bloodied shards hung in the air, then fell upward toward the sky.

It was then that Rikus realized it took no effort at all to hold his sword with the blade pointing upward. He was standing upside down, no matter that the terrain suggested otherwise.

The mul threw his head toward the ground and his feet toward the ceiling. The icy world dropped out from beneath him, and he fell an immense, immeasurable distance. The world went black, then white again. Finally he landed in the yellow bubbling ooze, his legs buried clear to his knees. There before him, where the blue arch had been a moment ago, was the Serpent of Lubar. The fangs of one its massive mouths were sunk deeply into Tamar's scaly carapace, and the second head was darting to and fro in search of an opening.

Pulling his feet free of the muck, Rikus waded toward the battle as fast as he could. Tamar tore at the serpent with her mandibles, opening long rips that oozed foul black goo. The snake coiled its body around her and squeezed. The wraith's red scales snapped and cracked and splintered.

When he reached the battle, the mul raised his sword and brought it down on Maetan's sinuous body. The magical blade sliced through the beast's scales, sinking deep into its stringy flesh. The snake's second head hissed and turned to face the mul, then shot toward him with its venomous fangs exposed. Rikus pulled the Scourge free and swung again.

The head stopped just short of the blade's arc. The mul brought his weapon around for a thrust, but before he could strike the snake hissed at him. A blast of tepid air washed over Rikus, filling his nostrils with the sour odor of bile.

The serpent and the wraith disappeared, then Rikus found himself in the great hall of the mansion, expelled from the battle raging inside his own head. Before him stood Maetan's motionless body, his gaze locked on the glowing ruby in the mul's chest.

Sensing his opportunity to finish the battle, the mul lifted
his sword and swung it at the mindbender. Maetan disappeared before his eyes. A sharp pain shot through the mul's
ankle as the invisible Urikite kicked him, then he felt his leg
being swept from beneath him. Rikus tried to shift his
weight to the other foot, but Maetan pushed him over before
he could avoid the fall.

The mul crashed to the ash-smeared floor. As his battered
body erupted into agony, the Scourge of Rkard slipped from
his grasp and went skittering across the floor.

Cursing himself for a softling, Rikus scrambled after the
sword. As he moved, the floor changed to a plain of boiling
yellow mud, and he realized that he had been drawn back
into the battle in his mind. The Scourge's hilt disappeared
into the muck, and the blade followed an instant later.

"Fool!"

Rikus looked over his shoulder and saw the Serpent of Lubar slithering after him. The viper carried its head off the
ground, a forked tongue flickering from its mouth. It was
using the head at the far end of its body to drag Tamar along,
though she had now taken the form of a huge red bird and
pecked at the snake with a needlelike beak.

Rikus looked away and started sweeping his hands
through the mud, searching for the Scourge. An instant later, four sharp fangs punctured his abdomen. He felt the
sting of venom running into his body as the serpent lifted
him from the mud.

Realizing that he had no chance of defeating Maetan until
he recovered his sword, the mul decided to try something
desperate. Once, while being transported from Urik to Tyr
by the slave merchant who had bought him from Lord Lubar, Rikus had killed a guard during an ill-fated escape attempt. As punishment, the merchant had sent him into the
mud-flats surrounding an oasis of rancid water, telling him
the death would be forgiven if he could reach the far side.

Before Rikus had traveled fifty yards, a mouthful of sharp, barbed teeth had grabbed his leg and dragged him beneath the surface. The mul had dived in after the beast and, blinded and choked by mud, wrestled his attacker until he snapped its bullish neck. When he had pulled it from the muck, he had found himself holding a ten-foot salamander with a ring of featherlike scales around its neck and a half-dozen finlike feet along the course of its body.

Hoping that the same senses that had allowed the creature to find him in the mudflat would help him find his sword, Rikus summoned his stamina for a last stab at survival. He imagined himself as that salamander. The energy rushed up from deep inside himself, then he became a long, wriggling reptile.

He slipped from Maetan's grasp, leaving a mouthful of scales behind, and dropped into the mud below. A pair of membranes closed over his eyes, and he found himself lost in a world of slime, where there was no such thing as up or down, only forward or backward. As Rikus used his finlike feet to push and pull himself through the thick mud, Maetan's poison continued to burn through his body, clouding his mind and weakening his muscles with every passing moment. Behind him, the serpent plunged its head into the mud, blindly snapping its jaws in an effort to recapture him.

Rikus continued to swim, emitting a continuous series of high squeals. They bounced back to the feathery scales around his head, constructing something like a picture of the terrain for his mind. It took him only a moment of whipping his head back and forth before he located his lost sword, and he scrambled for it as fast his stubby legs would pull him.

When Rikus reached the Scourge, he placed a fin on its hilt, then cleared the image of the salamander from his mind. Instantly he changed back to his own form—and found himself blind and choking as he tried to breathe mud.

Ignoring the panic welling in his breast, he grabbed the sword and rose from the muck.

Behind him, the Serpent of Lubar hissed, and he knew it was striking. Rikus spun around, lashing out with his weapon. The blade slipped between the snake's fangs and passed cleanly through the back of the beast's mouth.

Lord Maetan of Family Lubar screamed.

Rikus found himself standing back in the mansion chamber just as Maetan's headless body collapsed at his feet.

The mul sank to his knees and closed his eyes, bracing himself on his sword. The serpent's venom still burned through his body, but he felt it now as profound exhaustion.

It is done, Tamar said. *Now, you must go to Urik and find the book. I must know Borys's fate!*

"I will recover the book," Rikus said. "But not for you."

The mul shook his head to clear it, but found his vision blurring. When he looked up, he saw that Neeva and K'kriq had disobeyed his orders and were rushing into the room. Behind them came Gaanon, Caelum, Jaseela, and Styan.

Rikus tried to stand, but collapsed back to his knees, too sick from the serpent's poison and too fatigued from the battle to stand.

Neeva swept the mul off his feet. "We'd better get you back to bed," she said, starting for the back of the mansion.

"And bring Caelum—a snake bit me," the mul said. He clutched at her arm. "And if he lets me die—"

"He won't," Neeva said sharply.

"Wait!" Styan called. "What about King Tithian? Shouldn't we warn him about what happened? Hamanu may send some of his legions to attack Tyr."

"The king can wait," Gaanon said.

"No, put me in the chair," Rikus gasped, smiling weakly. "Styan is right. We must tell the king."

Neeva frowned, but placed Rikus in the marble throne. The mul drew the olivine from the pocket in his belt and looked into it. When Tithian's face appeared in the crystal, the king's gaunt features were twisted in rage.

"Where have you been?" he demanded.

"Killing Hamanu's messenger."

"What?" Tithian shrieked. "You've doomed the entire city!"

"Not at all, Mighty Tithian," Rikus sneered. "Hamanu is going to be too busy defending Urik to attack Tyr."

"You wouldn't dare!" Tithian gasped. The sound reminded the mul of nothing so much as the hissing of the Serpent of Lubar.

"I have no choice—it's my gladiators' only hope of survival," Rikus said. "It's too bad you didn't hire the slave tribe. A hundred extra warriors might have made the difference between victory and defeat."

Tithian's face fell. "Wait," he said. "Don't you think you should talk this over with Agis and Sadira?"

"Give them my regards, but no," Rikus replied. Relieved to hear that his friends had returned safely to the city, he closed his fist over the gem and handed it to Neeva. "Crush this. We won't be needing it again."

Slave Gate

The tail of a whip popped over Rikus's shoulder. "Eyes down, boy!" commanded a snarling voice.

Rikus lowered his head and trudged onward, cursing the gladiator's obvious delight in berating his commander. Along with two dozen fellows, all wearing the tunics of Makla's village garrison, the imposter was driving a small force of Tyrian gladiators toward Urik's slave gate. This larger group was disguised in the tattered cloaks and bandages of quarry slaves. On their backs, they carried heavy satchels of obsidian in which their weapons were concealed.

In spite of the escort's command, Rikus kept his eyes raised enough to study the area ahead. Urik's slave gate, like the rest of the city, was square and clean. It stood at the end of a short causeway of rutted cobblestones, flanked by high walls plastered with lime and stained yellow with sulfur paints from the Lake of Golden Dreams. Bas-reliefs of a stylized lion, standing on two legs and carrying its foreclaws like hands, marched along the ramparts in long lines. On one side, the lions left the gate with spears and swords, and on the other they returned with booty plundered from distant cities. Blood-colored merlons, each carved in the shape of a lion's head, capped the walls on both sides. From between these battlements peered more than a hundred attentive archers, their squinting eyes fixed firmly on the wretched throng of quarry slaves below.

"Tell me again why we're doing this?" whispered Neeva, staring at the heavy, stone-faced gates ahead.

"First, to save the legion, and second, to recover the *Book of the Kemalok Kings*," Rikus answered.

"And how is attacking Urik going to do that?" she asked, scowling at the mul's logic.

"After we secure the gate, Jaseela leads the rest of the legion into the city. We free Urik's slaves, then lead them in revolt," Rikus answered. "Hamanu will have to recall his legions from the desert to restore order. That's when we'll take the book, our warriors, and any Urikite slaves we've freed and go back to Tyr."

"It doesn't look like most of Urik's legions are in the desert to me," Neeva objected. She cast a furtive glance at the archers along the top of the wall.

"No king would send all his soldiers out," Rikus assured her. "That's just a small garrison. After we overpower them, you take the dwarves to find Maetan's townhouse and recover the *Book of the Kemalok Kings*. The rest of us will take the slaves and sack the city."

"That might be harder than you make it sound," observed Neeva. She frowned, then asked, "With all those archers up there, it occurs to me that Hamanu may know we're coming. Has that possibility crossed your mind?"

"Not in the last few moments," Rikus said. "If he did, why would he let us march into his city?"

"Because it's easier than chasing us down," Neeva answered. "And because, once we're inside the walls, there will be no place to hide."

Rikus shook his head. "No. Hamanu would have had to

know that we would attack Urik when Maetan told us where his legions were," the mul said. "That's not possible. I didn't even give our own army enough information about our plan—or time enough to react—for a spy to give us away."

Neeva did not contradict him.

They continued on in silence, until the gladiators began to crowd into the cramped tunnel leading beneath the city wall. Someone fell victim to the jostling and shoving, stumbling over a companion's feet and falling to the ground. The orderly line became a confused jumble as those in the rear continued to press forward and those in the front did their best to avoid trampling the one who had tripped.

A few moments later, Rikus and Neeva caught up to the fallen man. To the mul's surprise, he had sun-bronzed skin and a crimson sun tattooed on his forehead.

As Neeva reached down to jerk the dwarf back to his feet, Rikus growled, "Caelum."

Once they had passed into the tunnel beneath the wall, Rikus grabbed Neeva's arm. "What's the dwarf doing here?" he demanded, nearly stumbling as they shuffled up the steeply sloped floor.

"You said he was in my charge," Neeva countered, her tone already defensive and angry.

"I also ordered him to stay with Jaseela and the rest of the legion until it attacks," Rikus said. "If he sounds the alarm—"

"Caelum is no spy," Neeva spat back. "Besides, if any of us are going to survive this crazy plan of yours, we'll need his sun-magic."

"Rikus, I would never do anything to hurt Neeva," Caelum said. "And I want the *Book of the Kemalok Kings* returned to Kled as much as you do."

The dwarf fell silent as they left the tunnel and entered the city. Looking over the heads of those in front of him, Rikus saw that they were moving toward a narrow boulevard paved with white cobblestones. To either side of the street rose yellow walls capped with spiky shards of obsidian and breached at irregular intervals by smaller gates. In the center of the avenue sat a massive, wedgelike block of granite. Located on a steep ramp in front of the slave gate, the granite block was mounted on huge wooden rollers and held in place by a hemp rope larger around than a tree trunk. Next to this rope stood one of Hamanu's templars and two half-giants armed with axes of steel. They were protected by a small contingent of gate guards wearing leather hauberks and armed with long obsidian swords.

As the group shuffled forward, Tamar appeared in Rikus's mind. Her form quickly changed from that of a silky-haired woman to a semblance of Rikus himself, save that ruby-red orbs glowed out from where the mul's black eyes should have been. A cold shiver of foreboding ran down the mul's spine, then he heard the wraith say something that, at first, made no sense to him.

Caelum, you have disobeyed my commands for the last time, the wraith said.

Rikus felt his lips move along with those of the double inside his mind, then heard his own voice repeat Tamar's words.

Still in the mul's form, Tamar clenched her fist and took a step sideways. Rikus found himself moving toward the dwarf, his fist also clenched.

Stop it, Tamar! Rikus ordered, struggling in vain to make his muscles obey his own will and not the wraith's. *You'll doom us all!*

You're sending him and his dwarves after the book, she said. *I won't allow it.*

Inside Rikus's mind, Tamar reached out. In accord with her movements, the mul found his arm rising toward Caelum.

Neeva stepped between the mul and the dwarf. "Rikus! Are you *trying* to draw attention to us?"

Tamar thrust her arm out and Rikus felt himself shove Neeva away. The satchel slipped from her shoulders and crashed to the ground, echoing off the high stone walls surrounding the entranceway. Frowning in confusion, Caelum backed away from Rikus and thrust one hand toward the sun, collecting the energy for a spell. "Have you gone mad?"

On all sides of them, astonished warriors turned toward the commotion. Seeing that Neeva had dropped her sack, they did likewise and began digging their weapons out of their satchels.

By the light of Ral! Rikus growled. Because Tamar still controlled his body, he could not look around to see how the Urikites were responding. Nevertheless, he could hear the gate guards calling for the archers to reinforce them.

Rikus willed an image of himself into his mind, directly in front of Tamar's double. He launched himself at the wraith with such fury that she stumbled away, vainly raising her arms to block the barrage of fists.

Stop! Tamar ordered. *The dwarf is ready to kill you!*

Let him, Rikus answered. He kicked the wraith in the ribs, then knocked her to the ground with a vicious overhand punch. *You're losing the battle for me—that's all that matters.*

Rikus's double suddenly faded to mist before his eyes. The mul braced himself, expecting the wraith to return in the form of some hideous monster and rip him apart. Instead, Tamar's voice echoed in the black depths of his mind. *The battle is far from lost,* she said. *Still, I will wait for a more convenient time.*

Once again, the mul found himself in control of his own body, standing in the middle of Urik's slave boulevard while war cries sounded all around him. Caelum remained in front of him, red eyes burning with anger. The dwarf held one glowing hand toward the sun, and only Neeva's firm grasp kept the other pointed at the ground instead of at the mul.

"It's over," Rikus said. "You're safe for now, Caelum."

He dropped the satchel from his back and plunged his hand into it. A shard of obsidian opened a long cut on his hand, but he paid it no attention and found the Scourge's hilt.

"Not yet," Caelum insisted. "Not until you apologize to—"

"I need no apology," Neeva snapped, pulling a pair of short swords from her own sack. "We have a fight to attend to."

After Rikus pulled the Scourge from its scabbard, he spun around to face the templar and half-giants guarding the granite wedge. Already the echoes of clashing weapons and screaming men filled the street as Rikus's gladiators attacked the gate guards, cutting them down.

At the granite wedge, the templar cried, "Plug the slave gate!" He was already fleeing toward the nearest exit from the boulevard.

The half-giants brought their axes down on the massive rope. The blades bit deep into the cord, and it snapped with a vibrant twang. There was a loud rumble as the block shot down the ramp, the logs beneath it clacking in rapid succession.

Caelum pointed his free hand at the base of the block, and a deafening boom resounded off the boulevard walls. A bolt of flame shot from the dwarf's fingertips and, arcing over the heads of the warriors in front of him, engulfed the logs beneath the huge stone. In an instant, the blaze reduced the rollers to ashes. The wedge dropped to the stone ramp and ground to a halt with a loud rumble.

The Tyrian gladiators roared a tremendous cheer, many of them calling Caelum's name, and rushed forward to finish off the gate guards. Their moment of victory was shortlived, however. A moment after the wedge ground to a halt, bowstrings hummed from atop the wall. A volley of black shafts streaked down into the street, and a dozen voices cried out in anguish as gladiators began to fall.

Rikus waved his sword at a mass of warriors near him. "You gladiators, come with me!" he cried, starting toward the nearest side gate.

The mul had taken only a couple of steps before he realized no one was following him. He stopped and faced them, "Follow me!"

A few gladiators reluctantly moved to obey, but many others pretended they had not heard and advanced down the street to fight the battle on their own terms. Such a wave of anger came over Rikus that the blood rushed to his head and he could feel the veins in his temples throbbing. He started to move toward those who had disobeyed him, but Neeva quickly intercepted him.

"Later," she said. "The middle of a battle is no time to deal out punishment." She gestured toward the wound on his chest. "Besides, you can't blame them for being reluctant. Half the legion thinks you're a necromancer, and the other half thinks you've lost your mind."

The bowstrings atop the wall snapped again. This time, it seemed to Rikus that many more voices cried out as the black shafts rained down on the crowd.

"If they don't do as their told, what they think won't matter," the mul growled, once again turning toward the side gate. "See if *you* can get some of them to follow us."

On the other side of the square portal, he found a pair of astonished Urikite guards armed with obsidian-bladed glaives. After dodging a badly timed slash and a clumsy thrust, Rikus killed them both with a single slash of his magical blade. He stepped over their bodies and went a few yards down the street.

He found himself in an austere neighborhood of neatly

kept chamberhouses. Built of fired brick, each stood three stories tall, with a single rectangular door that directly abutted the cobblestone street. Every structure and every alley appeared identical, save for a wide variety of squiggly lines painted on the chamberhouses. The place seemed eerily quiet and deserted.

"Where are we?" asked Neeva.

Rikus glanced over his shoulder to see the female gladiator coming after him. Behind her were close to fifty warriors.

"Templar quarter, I think," Rikus answered, pointing to a set of crooked lines on a doorjamb. "That looks like writing to me, and only nobles and templars are allowed to read."

"This isn't a noble borough, that's certain," Neeva agreed. "No lord would stand for having his house look like everyone else's."

"Shouldn't we go the other way, then?" asked Caelum. The dwarf was moving up from the rear of the line. "Maetan said the book was in his townhouse. Surely, that isn't in the templar quarter."

"Maybe you shouldn't come with us," Rikus said, scowling at the dwarf. "I might—uh—lose my temper again."

"I'll take my chances," the dwarf answered, stepping into line behind Neeva. "If Neeva is here, then this is where I belong."

"Have it your way," Rikus said, shrugging.

He turned down the nearest alley and started toward the wall, confident that, in the templar quarter, there would be at least one set of stairs leading to the top of the wall. The narrow lane ran between neat rows of square windows and was crossed every fifty feet or so by a larger avenue. The tidy structures lining the streets were painted identically: the two lower stories in yellow and the upper in blood red. Rikus could not imagine how the inhabitants avoided getting lost in this grid of identical buildings.

The district appeared deserted, with no sign of a templar,

slave, or any other citizen. Nevertheless, Rikus knew there were plenty of Urikites about, for he could hear their footsteps echoing down the lanes and occasionally caught the hiss of a whispered conversation.

A few yards after what seemed the hundredth cross-street, the voices suddenly became so clear that the mul swore he was standing only a few yards from them. Nevertheless, none of the templars were visible in any direction.

Rikus heard several of them call upon Hamanu's name and realized that it no longer mattered whether he could see them or not. "Magic!" he yelled.

The air itself flashed brilliant white, then claps of thunder rolled down the alleys from all directions. A tremendous blast of air struck the mul from behind, sweeping him off his feet. As he slammed to the ground, he heard warriors behind him screaming and pieces of mudbrick clattering down upon the cobblestones.

When Rikus jumped back to his feet, he was flabbergasted by what he saw. Where there had been vacant alley a moment before, a chest-high wall of thorns blocked the way. Peering over the top of this barrier were six yellow-robed templars, some empty-handed and others armed with crossbows.

"Where'd they all come from?" Neeva gasped.

Rikus hazarded a glance over his shoulder. Behind him, in the intersection where most of the templars' spells had struck, the charred corpses of twenty gladiators now lay scattered across a dozen smoking craters.

"They were invisible!" Rikus snarled.

Loud clacks sounded from all directions as the templars fired their crossbows down the alleys. Rikus spun around in time to see several dark flashes sailing at him, then felt a series of sharp thumps in his midsection as the bolts struck his Belt of Rank. When he did not fall, the mouths of the crossbowmen fell open and they frantically began to reload their weapons.

Behind Rikus, Neeva yelled, "Caelum, no!"

The mul turned his head just enough to glimpse the dwarf slipping past Neeva's larger form. In his raised hand, the dwarf held a dagger of crimson flame.

Little backstabber! Tamar exclaimed. *You were correct. He is the spy!*

Rikus lashed out with a rear stomp kick that took Caelum square in the chest. The dwarf's eyes opened like red saucers, and he sailed past Neeva, crashing to the ground more than two yards away. His hand opened and the fiery dagger fell to the ground. It slowly rolled away, changing from a weapon to a flaming ball.

The fiery globe began to pulsate, then erupted into a blazing sphere that filled the narrow alley top to bottom. It roared away down the lane, leaving nothing but ash and cinder in its path.

"You tricked me!" Rikus cried, trying to shut out the screams of his dying warriors.

The dwarf must die, Tamar replied simply. *Finish him, or there will be more accidents.*

"No!" Rikus cried.

He turned and charged away, leaving behind Caelum, Neeva, and another dozen dazed survivors. In front of him, a pair of Urikites called upon Hamanu's magic, then each hurled a glowing pebble in his direction. The stones streaked straight at the mul, trailing flames and smoke.

Rikus's stomach knotted with fear, and he let out a panicked bellow. Although the mul had worn the Belt of Rank through enough battles to know its enchantment would protect him from normal arrows, he had no idea whether it would shield him from the fiery missiles now streaking at him.

The rocks struck him square in the midsection and exploded. The impact knocked the mul off his feet, hurled him a dozen steps backward, then dropped him roughly to the street. His breath blasted from his lungs and a sharp pain shot though his back. Rikus opened his mouth to scream, then choked on the stench of sulfur as a storm of golden fire erupted less than a foot over his face.

As the yellow blaze roiled above him, the mul feared he was going to burst into flames himself. The inferno vaporized his robe and seared his bronzed skin. Rikus closed his eyes against the brilliant glare, convinced that they would never open again.

Nevertheless, the glow died away a mere instant later, and the mul was surprised to find that he remained completely conscious. His back ached from his tailbone to his neck, his body stung as though it had been scrubbed raw with a whetstone, and the inside of his lungs burned from breathing hot, sulfurous air. To Rikus, the pain hardly mattered. If the belt had not protected him from all the effects of the blast, it had at least stopped the fire rocks from penetrating his flesh and erupting inside his body.

Roaring his battle cry, the mul resumed his charge. The stunned Urikites barely managed to raise their crossbows before Rikus reached the thorn barrier. He threw himself over head-first. As he somersaulted through the air, he swung his sword at the nearest templar and separated the woman's head from her shoulders. He landed in a rolling fall and lashed at a pair of legs concealed beneath a yellow robe, then shouted in pain as his wounded shoulder rolled over the hard stones paving the street.

Rikus came up dizzy, his vision blurred and his mind numbed by agony. It did not matter, for he was now fighting on instinct and rage. Something yellow moved in front of him. He swung his sword, and it collapsed to the ground.

A foot scraped the stones at his back. The mul tucked the blade under his armpit and thrust it backward. A Urikite screamed and died.

"In the name of Haman—"

Rikus's foot drove the air from the man's lungs in midsentence, smashing several ribs over his heart. The templar fell, clutching his chest.

For a moment, the mul could not find the last templar, then he heard a frightened woman's labored breathing as she fled down a side street. Shifting the Scourge to his bad arm, Rikus pulled a dagger from the belt of the man he had just killed. Calmly, he turned and threw it.

The blade disappeared between the woman's shoulderblades, sending her sprawling face-first onto the ground.

A loud crack sounded from the other side of the thorn wall. Rikus looked over his shoulder in time to see the orange-white tail of a fiery whip lash down on the barricade. It cut a smoking swath through the hedge, then Neeva and a handful of gladiators poured through the gap.

"Rikus, are you hurt?" demanded Neeva, rushing over to him.

"I'm well enough," the mul answered, inspecting himself. Other than his reddened skin, he found no sign of fresh injury.

"What happened?" Neeva asked. "It was like you went mad!"

Though the mul did not know whether she referred to the attack on Caelum or the leap over the barricade, he nodded. "I think I did," Rikus answered. "But it's too late to worry about that now. How's the dwarf?"

"He'll survive," she replied. "He's waiting with the others. I didn't want him coming through until . . ."

When she let the sentence trail off, Rikus finished it for her. "Until you found out whether I was going to murder him."

"Yes," Neeva said. "What's wrong with you? Back in Makla, you agreed he might not be the spy, and now you're trying to kill him—even when it's clear he's a great help!"

"I told you to leave him with Jaseela," Rikus snapped. The mul turned away, then added, "Bring him through, but make sure he stays away from me."

"We won't have to worry about that," Neeva answered.

She waved the rest of the survivors past the gap. As they stepped through, each gladiator glared at the mul as though he were some sort of monster.

Caelum brought up the rear. With one hand, he clutched his chest where Rikus had kicked him. In the other, he held a coiled whip of crackling fire. The lash was made of three distinct flames, one red, one white, and one yellow, all braided together in a single tail. Its bone handle glowed red with blazing heat. From the grimace on Caelum's face and the pain in his eyes, the mul could tell that holding it caused the dwarf great pain.

"Tell him to set fire to anything he can with that thing," Rikus said, pointing at the whip. "The more the Urikites have to worry about, the better."

With that, he turned and led the way toward the wall, keeping a careful watch for another templar ambush. They soon reached a ramp leading to the top of the city walls. It ran beneath a small tower, with a portcullis of thick mekillot ribs blocking the way. A dozen arrow loops overlooked the approach to the ramp, and in each one Rikus saw a Urikite armed with a crossbow.

At the top of the walls, the archers were all firing into the cul-de-sac in front of the slave gate. Rikus could hear men and women screaming on the other side, and he knew that Jaseela had arrived with the rest of the army. If he didn't reach the top of the wall and do something about the archers, his legion would be slaughtered.

"Neeva, wait here until I breach the gate," Rikus ordered. He pointed at the arrow loops in the side of the tower. "In the meantime, see if Caelum can't do something about the

Urikites inside the tower."

"What are you doing?"

Rikus didn't wait to explain the rest of his plan, for he knew it would be obvious once he put it into action. Instead, he rushed across the short distance separating him from the portcullis. The crossbows clacked. Instinctively, the mul dodged, though he knew his belt would provide a far better defense than his reflexes. Most of the bolts missed and clattered against the stone pavement, and several more glanced off his belt or simply stuck in the heavy girdle.

Caelum's whip cracked over Rikus's head. Then the mul smelled the caustic stench of charred flesh. A man screamed, and Rikus shuddered. The searing that he had suffered earlier still caused him enough pain that he could not stop himself from thinking of the dying man's agony. The dwarf's whip cracked again.

Rikus reached the gate and began hacking at the mekillot ribs. The magical blade bit deeply each time, and within moments he had torn away the first one and was working on the second. Caelum's whip continued to pop over his head, and soon smoke was spilling out of the tower in black clouds.

Finally Rikus cut away the third rib and stepped through the portcullis, motioning for Neeva and the others to follow. As he passed beneath the tower, he paused for a moment to look up into the murderholes lining the ceiling of the arch. When the mul saw no sign of anything except flames and smoke, he continued to the other side of the tower and waited for his companions.

They caught up to him a moment later, then he led the way up the ramp at their best pace. As they neared the top, a handful of archers appeared along the wall and began firing. Neeva and the others had to stop and take shelter along the base of the wall, but Rikus continued forward. Several arrows hit him in the belt, then Caelum cracked his whip, searing one of the archers completely in half.

The mul leaped onto the wall and a pair of archers moved forward to meet him with their short swords. Rikus finished them with an effortless parry and two quick slashes, then moved on to attack the next Urikites in line. They took their bows and fled, screaming for help.

Now that the way was clear for his companions, Rikus rushed over to the wall and cut down an archer. He saw that he and his small group of gladiators had emerged at the outer end of the battlements, overlooking the front edge of the cul-de-sac before the slave gate. All down the line, archers stood every four or five yards, firing down onto the causeway below.

There, hundreds of warriors—gladiators, dwarves, quarry slaves, even templars—lay scattered upon the road, their blood spreading across the white stones in puddles. More of Rikus's legion were pouring into the cul-de-sac with each moment, only to meet a hail of dark shafts that struck them down in waves. Despite the heavy losses, a constant stream of men and women reached the gate and hurried through to the boulevard beyond.

"For Tyr!" Rikus yelled, lifting his sword.

The warriors below looked up and, when they saw the mul standing along the wall, echoed his cheer. "For Tyr!" They pressed toward the gate with renewed vigor, oblivious to the rain of arrows being showered down upon them.

Rikus rushed down the wall, screaming a battle cry at the top of his lungs. The next archer in line turned to face him, swinging his empty bow at the charging gladiator. The mul ducked the blow, then drove the Scourge of Rkard through the Urikite's heart. He kicked the man's body off his red-dripping blade and started toward his next victim.

Neeva rushed to his side and wrapped her arms around the mul's shoulders. "Wait," she said. "Caelum has a faster way."

His bloodlust already stirred, Rikus tried to break away. Neeva, however, gripped the mul's sore shoulder and stopped him. "Let him try."

Caelum stepped forward and threw his whip to the ground. It seemed to come alive, shooting down the wall like a snake. When it passed the first archer, a tongue of crimson flame lashed out and left a smoking hole in the back of the man's leg. After the snake had passed, a yellow flame spewed out of the puncture and transformed the Urikite into a pillar of flame.

When the snake slithered to the next archer and repeated the attack, the third man in line noticed what was happening and stepped away from the wall. As the fiery serpent moved toward him, he nocked an arrow and fired at it. After passing through the thing's blazing body, the shaft clattered off the stones. The blazing viper struck again.

The fourth and fifth archers fled, screaming for their companions to do likewise. Rikus sent his gladiators down the wall after the snake, instructing them not to let any of the Urikites escape alive. Caelum followed a short distance behind the gladiators, keeping the fire serpent in sight so that he could control it.

Rikus led Neeva forward until they could see the mass of Tyrian warriors gathering on the slave boulevard below. Now that the archers had been chased away, there was no sign of opposition anywhere near the gate.

"Do you still think this a trap?" Rikus asked, motioning at the clear avenue ahead of his legion.

"I don't know," Neeva said, her eyes searching the distant boroughs of the city. "My answer depends on what we find in the slave quarter."

SIXTEEN

The Crimson Legion

Rikus did not understand how he could feel so lonely. He stood atop a guardtower overlooking Hamanu's vast slave pit. Before him, standing in the lanes between long rows of shabby mudbrick pens, waited more than ten thousand men and women, all of them chanting his name. His own warriors were briskly moving along the streets, organizing the newly liberated slaves into companies.

On the far side of the squalid pits, barely visible through the thick clouds of smoke drifting in from the templar quarter, rose the high stone wall of the king's central compound. Along the crest of the imposing barrier stood dozens of soldiers and templars, all watching Rikus's preparations with great interest. In the fortress behind them lay the high bureaus of the templars, the gladiatorial arena, and the barracks of the Imperial Guard—a large company of half-giants led by experienced templars of war. From the sounds drifting over the wall, it seemed likely that the guards would soon leave the safety of their fortress.

Rikus did not think the imminent threat of a counterattack was the reason for his glum mood. So far, the battle had gone more or less as he had foreseen, despite the heavy losses. The trouble with the archers had cost him three hundred warriors, but after that the legion had encountered only minor resistance as it worked its way into the slave pens. The Tyrians now controlled both the templar district and the slave pens—nearly a quarter of the city.

Certainly Rikus had reason to be satisfied with those results, but his quick victory had been followed by a minor setback. The mul had expected Urik's slaves to rise in a spontaneous revolt as soon as they were freed, but after their captors had been killed, the slaves had meekly huddled inside their huts, as frightened of their liberators as they had been of their oppressors. Rikus had found it necessary to send his warriors into the pits to rouse the timid swarm from their hovels.

While Rikus had been compelled to waste valuable time calling the slaves to arms, Hamanu's forces had moved with astonishing rapidity to cut the Tyrians off from the rest of the city. Within minutes of the initial breakthrough, the private bodyguard of the aristocracy had block the gateways into the noble quarter. At the same time, companies from Urik's garrison had sealed off the other side of the templar quarter. Hamanu had even managed to slip several thousand soldiers around the city to block the slave gate from the outside. It had all occurred so quickly that the mul's sentries had barely sounded the alarm before the Urikite troops were in place.

"Don't look so worried, Rikus," called Neeva, climbing up the bone ladder that led into the tower. "It makes the legion nervous."

"I can't help it," the mul said, glancing down as she climbed through the trap door. "Things aren't going according to plan."

"Plan?" asked Neeva, grinning. "Did I hear *you* say you're worried about a *plan*?"

Rikus felt the color rise to his cheeks and looked away. "You heard me," he muttered. "The slaves were too slow to revolt. We're going to have to fight our way out of here on Urikite terms."

"It won't be easy, but we can do it," Neeva said, stepping to his side and looking out over the slave pens. "More than ten thousand slaves have joined us, and we have close to one thousand of our own warriors left." She paused and glanced toward the high wall protecting Hamanu's compound. "It's the sorcerer-king that worries me."

"You leave him to me," Rikus said.

"I intend to," Neeva answered. "But I'd feel a lot better if I knew how you're going to stop him."

Rikus laid a hand on the hilt of his sword. "With this," the mul said. "When the battle starts, he'll have to show himself. I'll be waiting."

Neeva frowned. "And what about his sorcery? What about the Way?"

"My sword and my belt are magic, too," the mul answered. "As for the Way, I'll have help."

Not from me, Tamar interjected. *Not until Caelum and the dwarves are dead.*

When the time comes, you will help, Rikus replied. *You need me alive to recover the book.*

Can you be so certain of that? Tamar responded.

You have no choice, Rikus said.

Neeva allowed Rikus his moment of silence, expecting him to elaborate on how he intended to counter Hamanu's mastery of the Way. When he did not, she asked, "What kind of help?"

"The kind that I can't explain—yet," Rikus answered, looking toward the gate that led to the main boulevard.

Styan's templars were guarding the gate, where their presence would not be as likely to alarm the Urikite slaves. In a broad cobblestone courtyard behind the templars stood

Caelum and the dwarves. "You'd better join your company," said Rikus. "We'll be ready for battle soon."

Neeva returned to the ladder. She hesitated there for a moment, her emerald eyes fixed on the mul. "Rikus, have you . . . ?"

Her voice cracked with emotion and she let the sentence trail off, but the mul did not need to hear the rest of it to know what Neeva had meant to ask. Rikus still did not know how to answer her, for nothing had changed since she demanded his fidelity and love at the Crater of Bones.

"Good fighting, Neeva," Rikus said, looking away.

"And you, Rikus," she answered, starting down the ladder. "Strike hard and fast—it's our only chance."

After Neeva left, Rikus summoned Gaanon, K'kriq, and Jaseela to the tower. He had no chance to discuss the coming battle with them, however. As the pair was climbing into the cramped stand, a woman's voice boomed over the slave pens.

"Captives of mighty Hamanu, listen well!"

The slaves fell immediately silent, obviously accustomed to obeying the magically amplified voice.

"Your leader has delivered you unto Hamanu, and it is by Hamanu's will alone that you shall survive!" she rumbled, stepping into view high atop the wall of the king's fortress. The woman wore the yellow cassock of a templar, and in her hand she held a golden staff of office.

"K'kriq, who's that?" asked Rikus.

"Rasia, Templar of Toil," answered the thri-kreen. "Brutal woman who herds slaves."

"Mighty Hamanu allowed you to enter Urik, he allowed you to drive his archers from the walls, he allowed you to enter his slave pens—but he will allow no more!" Rasia proclaimed. "The city is sealed and you cannot escape. You cannot resist the will of Hamanu!"

A disparaging murmur rustled through the ranks. The neatly formed columns began to break up as Urikite slaves faced the woman and angry Tyrian gladiators turned to glare at Rikus.

The mul grabbed Gaanon's arm. "Get a spear and silence her," he ordered.

The half-giant obeyed immediately, dropping off the tower in a single leap and forcing his way into the crowded slave pits.

"Captives of Hamanu, great is your despair, for on this day have you been returned to bondage—or to death!" the woman continued. "Throw down your weapons and Hamanu the compassionate will feed you as he feeds his other slaves—"

"So that we may die in his quarries!" Rikus shouted.

Though he yelled at the top of his lungs, his voice sounded meek and timid compared to the magical thunder of the woman's commands. Nevertheless, the pens were so silent that he knew his words carried even to the far side of the pit.

"Better to die years from now than to die today," the woman answered. "Throw down your weapons. Mighty Hamanu will show no mercy to those who disobey. You have no choice."

"You have every choice!" Rikus screamed.

"Heed not the mul!" the woman boomed, drowning out Rikus's voice. "His way is death!"

She began to repeat those phrases over and over again, preventing the mul's voice from being heard. Rikus gave up trying to outscream her and faced Jaseela. "Send word to the companies to prepare for battle."

The noblewoman did not immediately move to obey. Instead, she looked toward the gate, where the templars reluctantly remained on guard. "Someone warned Hamanu to expect us," she hissed. "That's why the Urikites moved so quickly to seal us off!"

"There's no time for that now!" Rikus snapped. "Do as I ordered."

Despite his command, the mul was thinking the same thing as Jaseela. The ease with which Hamanu had slipped his forces into place certainly suggested that the sorcerer-king had been expecting the attack. Not wishing to believe that his attack on Urik had been a predictable one, the mul preferred to think his enemy's foreknowledge had come from magical divination—anything except his own imprudence.

The mul looked toward the gate. Styan and his templars remained at their posts. Many were casting nervous glances at Rikus and at the woman on the wall, who was still booming her call for surrender. Behind the templars, Caelum's dwarves had already taken up their arms and stood in disciplined formation. Neeva stood with Caelum at the head of the company, her eyes fixed on the templars in front of her.

Satisfied that nothing ominous was occurring there, Rikus looked back to the slave pens. He was just in time to see a long shaft fly from the pits and sail straight toward the woman's torso. A few inches shy of its target, the spear struck an invisible barrier and came to an abrupt halt. A stunned cry rang across the enclave. As the spear fell harmlessly away, the templar threw her arms up and retreated from sight.

Taking advantage of the quiet that followed, Rikus yelled, "Warriors of Tyr, freed men of Urik. The choice is yours. You can live for a few short years toiling in Hamanu's quarries, or you can take up weapons and fight!"

A restless murmur rustled through the pens, but Rikus did not hear the resounding cheer for which he had hoped.

He raised his hand for silence and continued. "You know what to expect if you return to your pens. If you take up the fight, I can only promise that, win or lose, you will die free."

There followed a long and painful silence as each slave pondered the value of life in chains. Here and there, Rikus saw frightened men and women retreating to the shelter of their pens, but most of the Urikite slaves and all of the Tyrians remained in their companies.

At last, a haggard old man cried, "Live or die, I fight with Tyr!"

Six templars appeared at the top of the fortress wall. In the next instant, they began raining white flashes of lightning and golden balls of fire down into the slave pens. Rikus had no sooner picked out Rasia than he saw her raising a hand in his direction.

"Jump, K'kriq!" he yelled.

The thri-kreen leaped straight out of the tower. Rikus dropped through the trap door, his good hand slapping the ladder's rungs in a barely successful attempt to break his fall. He had no sooner slammed into the ground than an enormous roar shook the tower and a tongue of yellow flame shot down the ladder after him. He scrambled away just as the tower collapsed in a charred heap.

K'kriq grabbed Rikus with all four hands and dragged him behind the burning remains of the tower, where he would be out of sight to the Urikite templars. "Hurt?"

"No," Rikus answered. "I'm—"

The mul's reply was cut short by the sound of dwarves screaming from his left. He looked in the company's direction just in time to be blinded by a brilliant flash of golden light erupting in their midst. A terrific boom rolled across the cobblestones, followed in short order by a chorus of Urikite war cries. The angry shouts of dying dwarves came an instant later.

As the mul's vision cleared, he saw that a stream of Hamanu's Imperial Guard was pouring through the gate and dispatching Caelum's company with cruel efficiency. The half-giants wore full suits of inix-scale armor. In one hand they carried long wooden lances, and in the other drik-shell shields. From their belts hung huge obsidian swords.

"What happened to Styan?" demanded Rikus, searching in vain for sight of any of the templar's men.

"I think we owe Caelum an apology," said Jaseela, stepping to his side. "Styan's whole company has betrayed us."

"But slaves with us," K'kriq said, peering around the edge of the burning tower.

Rikus followed the line of the thri-kreen's gaze and noted that most of the slave companies were anxiously pressing forward to join the battle.

"Those quarry slaves will never fight through the half-giants at the gate," Jaseela said, shaking her head at the situation in the slave pens.

"Let's give Hamanu something to worry about," Rikus said. He turned around and pointed at the wall separating the slave compound from the templar quarter. "Take the slave companies and scale that wall."

"And then what?" Jaseela asked.

"Send the first ten companies into the other quarters of the city. They're to destroy everything they can—clog wells, topple buildings, burn tents, anything that causes problems. If they meet a Urikite company, they're to run, not fight. The more chaos we spread through the city, the better."

Jaseela nodded. "And with the rest?"

"Take the rest of the army and attack across the slave boulevard. Drive into the noble quarter and sack it, too. The more Hamanu has to worry about, the easier it will be for me to ambush him."

"To *what*?" Jaseela gasped, glaring at the mul from the scarred side of her face. She shook her head as if he were mad, then added, "The gladiators are right: you've either lost your mind, or it's been taken over by the thing in your chest."

Rikus was too hurt to respond immediately. Though he had been aware of the gladiators' resentment since the episode in the Crater of Bones, he had not heard anyone else put their doubts into words. "Is that what my warriors are saying?"

"Yes," Jaseela answered. "And who can blame them? It was madness to bring us into Urik—and now this!"

"I brought the legion here because it's the only way to save it," Rikus snapped. "The slave revolt will force Hamanu to recall his army—so our warriors can go home."

Jaseela shook her head. "I don't believe it. You don't have to attack Hamanu to start the revolt."

"Maybe not," Rikus admitted. "But if I kill him, Urik's slaves will be free and Tyr will be less one enemy. If he kills me, the time I buy in fighting could make the difference in starting the revolt or not for the rest of you."

The color rose to Jaseela's unmarred cheek. After a short pause, she asked, "Do you expect to come back?"

Rikus grinned. "I hope to," he said.

The noblewoman closed her eyes for a moment. "I'm sorry for what I said," she offered. "And I'm sorry that your warriors doubt your motivations. You don't deserve that."

Rikus frowned, unsure of how to accept the apology and not sure that it was necessary for Jaseela to make. "Thanks," he said awkwardly. "Now, go get your companies."

Jaseela nodded, then drew her sword and ran toward the first of the slave companies. Rikus turned toward the dwarves in time to see one of Caelum's crimson sunballs erupt in the gateway. A pair of half-giants bellowed in agony, then collapsed in a pile of charred bone and ash.

Several of Styan's templars appeared on the other side of the gateway, backing away from an enemy Rikus could not see. The mul frowned, for if they had changed sides, he could not imagine from whom they were retreating. An instant later, he heard a tremendous clatter as a handful of small boulders sailed into sight and struck the men dead.

Two of Hamanu's yellow-robed templars took the place of Styan's men, pointing their hands into the battle. Lightning bolts crackled from their fingers, shooting from dwarf to dwarf. More than a dozen of Caelum's warriors fell, filling the air with the stink of singed flesh. Finally the sizzling streaks crashed into the ground, spraying shattered cobblestones everywhere. As the shards rained back to the ground, Rikus was relieved to see Neeva and Caelum among those still alive.

Unfortunately, the rest of Caelum's company was not faring so well. Although twenty or thirty wounded half-giants lay thrashing and groaning on the ground, the cobblestones were slick with the blood and gore of dead dwarves. Rikus guessed that more than a hundred had already fallen, and it would not be long before the remainder joined them.

Fortunately, help was on the way. Most of the Tyrian warriors had been in the slave pits organizing the Urikite slaves, and now they were rushing toward the gate to join the fight. Rikus estimated that they would arrive in plenty of time to prevent the Imperial Guard from breaking through into the pits.

Seeing that there were no more orders to give, the mul reached for his sword. With some surprise, he realized that he had been so busy giving orders that he had not even considered drawing it yet.

"I'm getting to be too much of a general," he grumbled.

"Too far from hunt," K'kriq agreed. "No joy."

As Rikus's hand touched the Scourge's hilt, the horrid sounds of battle all came to him at once: death screams, clanging weapons, deafening explosions, officers shouting orders, his own breath roaring in and out of his lungs, the four-beat cadence of the thri-kreen's heart. For a moment he reeled, too stunned by the incredible din to move.

K'kriq caught Rikus by the shoulder. "Go now!"

Cringing at what sounded like a shout to him, Rikus concentrated on the sound of K'kriq's beating heart and said, "You don't have to come with me." Immediately the sounds of battle faded to mere background noise. Rikus was dimly aware of each individual sound, but was no longer overpowered by them. "You understand what I'm doing?"

K'kriq spread his antennae to indicate a positive answer. "Hunt big game," he said. "K'kriq come."

Rikus smiled, then started to move along the edge of the pit toward Hamanu's fortress. Behind him, the crack and thunder of war magic rumbled almost constantly from the gateway. The screams of the dying blurred into a single, long shriek.

The mul moved slowly along the base of the wall separating the slave compound from the boulevard outside, carefully listening for a single sound. With the Scourge's aid, he had little trouble hearing the muffled noises coming over the wall: the tramp of hob-nailed boots, war-templars shouting harsh commands to the half-giants of the Imperial Guard, the heavy breathing of messengers as they ran back and forth between the gateway and Hamanu's fortress. Often, a loud explosion or a pained scream temporarily overwhelmed the other sounds coming from the street.

After Rikus and K'kriq had progressed close to fifty yards along the wall, Gaanon caught up to them and fell into line without a word. Behind the half-giant followed a small company of warriors.

"What are you doing here?" Rikus asked.

"Jaseela told us what you're doing," answered the half-giant.

After a short pause, Rikus asked, "So?"

"We volunteered to help," answered one of the men, a square-jawed brute named Canth. "Over the past few weeks, some of us haven't understood what you're doing," he said. "But now—well, we can't let you try this alone."

Rikus smiled. "My thanks," he said. "I could use the help."

Before continuing on his way, the mul took a moment to check on the battle near the gate. The entrance yard had been reduced to a wasteland of smoking craters, littered with the charred bodies of dwarves, gladiators, and enemy half-giants. The Urikites had been turned back, and Tyrian gladiators were forcing their way out of the slave pits. Farther away, several lines of Urikite slaves were climbing ropes and disappearing over the southern wall, unruffled by the barrage of war magic being hurled at them from Hamanu's fortress.

Rikus turned back to the wall and moved forward once again. Finally, a dozen yards shy of Hamanu's fortress, the mul heard what he had been listening for.

"Mighty King, the Imperial Guard is fighting valiantly in your name," said a nervous man. "Surely you can see that?"

"The only thing I see is my guard being beaten back," responded a sharp, bitter voice.

There was a short pause before the man replied, "The Tyrians are gladiators, Mighty Hamanu. They're trained to—"

"This battle has already cost me more slaves than we stand to gain by capturing the Tyrians," spat Hamanu. "If we lose many more, the officers of the Imperial Guard will be working my obsidian quarries."

The mul needed to hear no more. "Hamanu is on the other side," he whispered. "Boost me up to have a look, Gaanon."

The half-giant laid his great hammer aside, then obediently made a stirrup for the mul's foot.

When Gaanon lifted him high enough to peer over the wall, Rikus saw the reason for Hamanu's anger. A short distance down the boulevard, dead half-giants and Urikite templars covered the street so thickly that they hid the cobblestone pavement. Tyrian gladiators were charging out of the gate leading to the slave pits, rushing forward to press the attack against the Imperial Guard.

As encouraging as the mul found the sight, however, it was another that drew his attention. A few yards away from

the gate, most of Styan's company lay scattered over the
boulevard, their lifeless bodies sprawled beneath the feet of
the Imperial Guard. Most of the men held swords or other
weapons in their hands. They had obviously died fighting.
Rikus even picked out Styan's long gray hair, crowning a
lifeless body sprawled across one of the few half-giants that
had fallen in the battle. Whatever the templar may have
been, and no matter how much trouble he had caused, the
mul now realized that he could not have been a traitor.

Rikus frowned. "If Styan isn't the traitor, then who is?"
he asked himself.

Why does there have to be a spy? Tamar countered. *You are
stupid enough to be your own traitor. Only a fool would try this.*

Rikus ignored the wraith and looked down at Gaanon.
"Lift me the rest of the way up. Send everyone else over as
fast as you can."

An instant later, Rikus found himself looking down upon
the slave boulevard from atop the narrow wall. He paused
for less than a second, only long enough to see that the
street below was crowded with half-giants, and to glimpse a
worried war-templar standing beside a tall, vigorous man
wearing a golden tunic. In his hand, the tall man held a
long staff of pure steel, with a great globe of obsidian on
the top.

Not wishing to give his victim the benefit of even a moment's warning, Rikus threw himself from the wall.
Though the figure wore no crown, the obsidian globe atop
his staff left no doubt in the mul's mind that this was Hamanu. The glassy black balls allowed those who had mas-
tered both sorcery and the Way to draw upon the life force
of men and animals for their spells. Only a sorcerer-king could
control such powerful magic.

Rikus's plan was as hasty as his fall. As the mul's shadow
fell across the king, Hamanu looked up and sneered. Then
he flicked his wrist ever so slightly.

Rikus felt the world lurch. He continued to fall, but in slow motion. As he drifted another foot downward, he had many moments to study the face of his foe. The sorcerer-king had close-cropped silver hair, dark skin stretched tight over ruthless features, and eyes as yellow and heartless as gold.

Rikus swung his sword, trying to overcome the terrible sense of dread settling over him. The blade hardly moved, leaving the mul with little to do except despair at how easily Hamanu had countered his attack.

Fool! laughed Tamar. *You let him use the Way on you.*

Help me! Rikus demanded. He could not keep the desperation from his plea.

Caelum is still alive, Tamar retorted. *I will do nothing—until I am confident you will foil the dwarf's plan and give me the book.*

I've already promised it to you, Rikus said.

And to the dwarves, as well, the wraith responded. *I require further reassurances.*

Hamanu will kill me! How will you find the book then?

If you wish my help, swear on Neeva's life, Tamar answered, ignoring his question. *Otherwise, I will allow Hamanu to slay you—and your legion perishes.*

As Rikus continued to descend, Hamanu smiled, revealing four large canines and a mouthful of needlelike incisors.

I swear, Rikus answered.

A sick feeling of guilt came over the mul, but he did not try to rationalize his duplicity. The time to choose between the two promises he had made would come later—if he lived long enough for it to come at all.

Be ready, Tamar said.

Rikus felt an ominous pang over his heart as Tamar struggled to free him. Again he tried to swing his sword, but to no more effect than the first attempt. He simply continued to sink toward Hamanu at a torpid pace. Still grinning, the sorcerer-king stepped effortlessly from beneath Rikus and moved his steel staff into a guarding position.

He's too strong! Tamar reported, her voice now alarmed and weak from exertion. *You must help. See yourself on the ground, where you should be if you fell normally.*

Rikus shifted his gaze to the cobblestones at the sorcerer-king's feet and pictured himself standing there. A surge of energy rose from deep within himself. Again he felt the eerie pang over his heart as Tamar mustered her own energies.

Suddenly the mul found himself lying on the street. He did not recall breaking free of Hamanu's mental grip, or feeling his skull crack into the stones, or even the sensation of falling as he covered the last few feet between him and the ground. In one instant, he was simply lying with his face pressed against the hot cobblestones, his vision a white blur, his body washed in agony.

Rikus rolled onto his good side and saw that he had landed between Hamanu and the nervous war-templar. More than a dozen startled half-giants stared over the two men's shoulders with shocked expressions. Several of the guards raised their spears to attack, but the sorcerer-king stopped them with a wave of his hand.

Hamanu used his staff to gesture at the war-templar. "Niscet, the slave is yours to kill."

With a pale face, the war-templar reached for the steel sword hanging from his belt.

"No, Niscet," the king said. "With your hands."

"Mighty King, the gladiator is armed. I can't kill him without a weapon!"

"No?" Hamanu replied, his handsome features animated by the glow of brutal delight. "What a pity for you."

Rikus rolled toward Niscet, slicing upward with his sword. The blade opened a long gash in the templar's abdomen, slicing through the scale armor hidden beneath his yellow robe. The templar screamed in pain and, as the mul crashed into his legs, fell face-first on top of Rikus.

The mul scrambled from beneath the dying man, then struggled to his feet. As he whirled around, he glimpsed K'kriq and several gladiators leaping from the wall. Then Rikus found himself facing a pair of half-giants who had moved forward to protect Hamanu.

"Leave this pathetic would-be regicide to me," said the sorcerer-king, stepping between the two guards. He fixed his yellow eyes on the mul, then asked, "Rikus, is it not?"

For a reply, Rikus jumped forward, swinging the Scourge at the sorcerer-king's neck. A few inches shy of its target, the blade rang out as though it had struck stone. A shimmering blue aura flared around Hamanu's body, and red and black sparks sputtered high into the air as the mul's magical sword passed through the barrier. Rikus yelled in triumph, already relishing the sight of the sorcerer-king's head flying off his neck.

The mul's cry fell abruptly silent as the Scourge reached Hamanu's flesh. The sorcerer-king glanced down at the blade, then calmly placed a finger under it and moved it aside. There was a thin line of blackish red blood where Rikus's blow had gently touched Hamanu, but otherwise the king remained uninjured.

"Answer me!" Hamanu boomed.

The sorcerer-king's voice roared over Rikus like thunder. The mul's ears, made more sensitive by the Scourge's magic, reverberated with agony. Rikus stumbled away, stunned, his head filled with terrible, sharp pain. He did not stop until he reached the center of the street, where he felt a pair of spearpoints in his back. He glanced up and saw the snarling faces of two half-giants looming over him.

Hamanu followed the mul, his fangs bared and his angry golden eyes fixed on Rikus's cringing form. "You are Rikus, are you not?" he demanded again.

The mul nodded.

Behind the sorcerer-king, Rikus's gladiators continued to pour over the wall, screaming ferocious war cries and leaping into battle with the Imperial Guard. Already the Tyrians had beaten the half-giants away from the wall and were slowly pressing the fight toward Hamanu.

For a moment, the sorcerer-king regarded Rikus with a look of bemusement. Finally he shook his head. "You are a daring fool, Tyrian. There was a time when I would have been amused by such audacity—but no longer."

That said, Hamanu muttered an incantation. Rikus felt a surge of energy being pulled from his inner being, the same as when Sadira used her cane to cast a spell. A queasy feeling of horror came over the gladiator, for he knew what the sensation meant: in preparation for using his dragon magic, the sorcerer-king was drawing power from Rikus's body. The mul's knees began to tremble, and his breath came in labored gasps. Deep within the obsidian ball that capped Hamanu's steel staff, a ghostly red light flickered to life.

A surge of anger washed over Rikus as he realized how completely in Hamanu's power he was. Determined not to stand idly by while his life drained away, the mul sprang away from the spears at his back. At the same time, he swung the Scourge at the sorcerer-king's staff, severing it before the half-giants or Hamanu realized what had happened. The obsidian globe dropped to the ground, shattering into a dozen pieces. There was a brilliant flash of red, then a glowing wisp of scarlet smoke rose from the shards and writhed about, sizzling and hissing like a mad serpent.

The two half-giants cried out in astonishment, but were not too stunned to jab their lances at the mul. Rikus parried with the Scourge of Rkard and shattered the shafts before they reached him. Hoping that a thrust would find more purchase in Hamanu's flesh than had his first slash, the mul whipped his sword around and drove the tip at his foe's heart. The sorcerer-king merely lifted his gaze from the fragmented obsidian globe and glared at the attacking Tyrian.

As the blade neared Hamanu's body, the sorcerer-king's aura again flashed blue. The Scourge drove through the magical barrier in a spray of hot sparks—then gave a loud twang as it reached its target and stopped cold. The blade flexed like an archer's supple bow.

Rikus did not even see the sorcerer-king's counterstrike. He merely felt something hit his jaw with the force of a half-giant's hammer. Everything went black, and the mul's knees came perilously close to buckling. Hamanu struck again, and this time Rikus felt each separate knuckle in the sorcerer-king's hand. The blow knocked him off his feet and sent him sailing through the air, crashing into the half-giants whose spears he had severed. Rikus dropped to the ground at their feet, as angry as he was frightened, certain that he would soon feel their huge swords hacking him to pieces.

The blows did not come. Instead, as Rikus's vision began to clear, he heard a mighty groan rumbling over the avenue. Near the wall, the battle raging between his gladiators and the half-giants came to a halt. Terrified shrieks and astonished gasps filled the air.

Rikus looked in Hamanu's direction and cried out in shock. In the sorcerer-king's place was a monstrous cross between Hamanu and a giant lion. Standing twice the height of a half-giant, the creature had a powerful body covered in golden fur, a long tail ending in a huge tuft, and the powerful rear legs of a great cat. The beast's arms resembled those of a man, though the muscles were sinuous and the hands clawed. Around his neck hung a long golden mane, and atop it sat Hamanu's head, his fang-filled mouth pushed out to form a small muzzle.

The great man-lion waved off the half-giants that were
looming over Rikus, then fixed his golden eyes on the mul
himself. "There is a difference between daring and inso-
lence," he growled. "Now I shall exact the price one pays for
confusing the two."

SEVENTEEN

Hamanu's Wrath

Hamanu stepped toward Rikus. The mul rose, swinging the Scourge in desperation. The blade struck the great manlion in the leg, bouncing off the thick hide with a muted thud. Screaming in frustration, the gladiator lifted his sword again.

Before Rikus could strike, the sorcerer-king kneeled on top of the gladiator, forcing him to the ground and pinning him in place.

Hamanu peered down at the mul's face, yellow beads of hot acid dripping from his fangs. He touched the talon of one finger, as long and as sharp as any dagger, to Rikus's throat. "Did you think I would be as easy to kill as that doddering fool who ruled Tyr?"

For the first time in his memory, Rikus felt utterly helpless. His life was completely in Hamanu's hands. Pinned as he was, the mul could not even fight back and die honorably.

"I will teach you what happens to those who resist my will," Hamanu continued.

The beast closed his hand around Rikus's throat and picked him up, at the same time jamming the mul's sword arm to his side. The king muttered an incantation, then a yellow web wrapped around Rikus so tightly that he could hardly breathe.

This time, the spell drained no life from the gladiator's body. Without the obsidian orb that Rikus had smashed earlier, the sorcerer-king could not use dragon magic to draw his energy from animals. Instead, the mul knew, Hamanu had to draw it from plants, as normal sorcerers did. Still, Rikus doubted that the lack of dragon magic would seriously hamper the ruler of Urik. The fields surrounding the city were well tended and full of crops that Hamanu could tap for his spells.

Once Rikus was completely swaddled in the sticky web, the sorcerer-king carried him to the fortress wall. There, he tied the cocoon to a merlon, leaving the mul to hang several yards above the cobblestones.

In the street below, the battle between the Imperial Guard and the gladiators Gaanon had boosted over the wall still raged. As the mul watched, Gaanon used his hammer to crack the skull of a Urikite half-giant, while K'kriq sank his poisonous mandibles into another foe.

Rikus looked farther down the street. At the side gate leading into the slave pits, the scene was not as encouraging. Hamanu's soldiers had driven the Tyrians back to the threshold and were once again threatening to break through into the pens. Luckily Jaseela had been given plenty of time to move the slave companies out of the pits and into the templar quarter. Rikus couldn't see if any plumes of smoke were yet rising from distant parts of the city, but he was encouraged by the fact that no Urikites seemed to be moving to attack the noblewoman's companies. The mul dared to hope that, even if he could not kill Hamanu, he had at least stalled the sorcerer-king long enough for the slave revolt to take hold.

"It is my wish that you know the fate of those who followed you," Hamanu said, glancing over his shoulder toward the battle. "Those that you do not see me kill will be left as a special gift for the Dragon."

"Gift?" As Rikus asked the question, the cocoon cinched down on his ribs and did not expand again.

Hamanu looked back to the mul. "Yes, in the Dragon's Nest, where you camped."

"The Crater of Bones," Rikus gasped. "You must leave many gifts for the Dragon."

"Only our proper levy," Hamanu said, a cruel smile crossing his lips.

"Levy?" the mul exclaimed. In his shock, he forgot about the cocoon—until it compressed again, and he had difficulty drawing his next breath.

The sorcerer-king trilled a laugh, his long red tongue wagging from between his fangs. "The Dragon demands a slave levy from each city, or he will extract a terrible vengeance—as the pretender Tithian will discover when he fails to pay Tyr's allotment."

From the sorcerer-king's amused expression, Rikus could tell that Hamanu enjoyed tormenting him with this news. The mul endured the abuse willingly, for the longer he detained Hamanu, the better the revolt's chances of success. "The Dragon will demand slaves from Tyr?"

Hamanu narrowed his eyes and turned to leave, saying, "You have kept me long enough."

Before the mul could ask anything more, the sorcerer-king strode toward the battle. Immediately Rikus tried to pull his sword arm free, but the web held him so firmly that he could not move so much as his little finger. The only result of his efforts was to constrict the web around him more tightly.

In the street below, Hamanu waded into the company of gladiators that had followed Rikus over the wall. Several of the Tyrians attacked with bone-tipped spears and obsidian battle-axes. The spears broke against his hide, the axe heads shattered, and the beast showed no sign that he even felt the blows. The sorcerer-king counterattacked savagely, his long claws disemboweling warriors through their armor.

A stream of scarlet fire shot from the gate leading into the slave pens. Dozens of half-giants and war-templars turned to ash in a mere instant. Once the flames were gone, Neeva and Caelum charged out into the street.

"No! Go back!" Rikus cried, his heart pounding in fear. The cocoon constricted again, filling his torso with painful cramps. "You can't stop him," he finished weakly.

With the din of clanging weapons and screaming warriors, they did not hear him. The pair turned toward the man-lion, followed closely by a handful of dwarves and a large company of weary gladiators. Rikus watched in horror as Neeva dodged past a half-giant's lance and knocked a few scales off his leg armor. As he reached for her, she found a seam between the guard's massive thigh and his lower abdomen. She plunged her sword deep into the crevice, drawing an immediate spray of blood.

A stooped half-elf stepped to Neeva's side, intercepting another half-giant who had come forward to lance her. The gladiator beat down the Urikite's shaft, then thrust his barbed lance under the shield to rip his opponent's knee to shreds. The half-giant had not even finished collapsing to the ground before Neeva ran a blade across his throat.

Rikus continued his efforts to work his arm free, but to little avail. He succeeded in moving the blade of his sword a fraction of inch and opened a small tear in the web. The yellow strands only cinched down and pinned the mul's elbow more tightly against his belly.

Rikus cursed, then silently complained, *What am I supposed to do?*

Watch your legion die, Tamar replied. *What else?*

Can't you help me? the mul pleaded. *Summon the other champions, like you did in the Crater of Bones.*

I could, but what good will that do? You would only attack Hamanu again—and destroy us both.

Near the entrance to the slave pens, the Tyrians formed a wedge with Neeva at the front. They started forward, leaving a wake of corpses, gladiator and half-giant alike, behind them.

In the midst of his revelry of death, Hamanu paused to look toward the sortie.

How touching, Tamar observed wryly. *The fools will die trying to save you.*

Not if I can help it, Rikus said. He shook his head, the only part of his body free to move, from side-to-side. "Go back!" he cried, causing himself another wave of agony as the cocoon tightened.

The wedge continued forward, oblivious to the mul's command. The sorcerer-king pointed the five claws of one hand toward the advancing Tyrians, uttering a spell. Bolts of energy streaked from his fingers, each one arcing into the center of the wedge and burning a hole into the chest of a different gladiator.

Instead of falling, the victims screamed and reached for their injuries, then broke formation and began running about in all directions. As they moved, wisps of yellow smoke poured from their wounds and spread throughout the company. Wherever the fumes passed, gladiators gave strangled cries, then collapsed clutching their throats.

Hamanu looked away from the battle and returned his attention to the gladiators he had been destroying before the wedge had formed.

Rikus closed his eyes, unable to bear the pain of watching Neeva die. He heard several more choking warriors fall, then the Scourge brought Caelum's voice to him: "To the ground!"

The mul opened his eyes in time to see Neeva and the other survivors do as the dwarf asked. Once the others were out of the way, the men who had been struck by Hamanu's spell fled the confines of the formation, not wishing to spread the deadly fumes among their fellows.

Caelum thrust an arm toward the sun, and his hand began to glow. From his fingers issued a shimmering mantle of blistering air, which spread outward and covered the gladiators like a blanket. The mantle hung over their heads, the heat rising from it and carrying away the deadly yellow fumes.

As the dwarf saved the lives of his companions, Rikus noticed that Gaanon was slipping along the wall toward him.

Another fool, Tamar commented.

He'll make it, Rikus insisted, noting that Hamanu had shown no sign of seeing the large gladiator. *I'll soon be back in the fight.*

For all the good that will do. It would be wiser to slip away unnoticed.

Abandon my legion?

It will perish with or without you.

After the smoke had cleared, Neeva returned to her feet at the head of a decimated formation, with Caelum at her back and two dozen gladiators scattered among the bodies of their fellows. Rikus guessed that three times as many half-giants remained between the Tyrians and Hamanu.

Neeva stepped forward, carrying the attack to the throng of Urikites crowding the street. The other survivors closed ranks behind her.

"What are you doing?" Rikus whispered, sadly shaking his head. "Can't you see your plan's hopeless?"

The first of Hamanu's half-giants thrust his lance at Neeva. Screaming in anger, she sidestepped it and slipped forward, driving her sword into her attacker's abdomen. As the dying Urikite stumbled away, another stepped forward and pushed his lance into Neeva's stomach.

"No!" Rikus hissed.

The stooped half-elf gladiator swung his lance at Neeva's attacker. The barbed head raked across the Urikite's face, and the Imperial Guard fell away holding his eye. A moment later, a long spear pierced the half-elf's throat. He died clutching at the shaft. Rikus saw Neeva pull the shaft from her stomach and turn to attack the half-elf's killer, then lost sight of her as the rest of the street erupted into a jumbled melee.

Rikus looked toward Gaanon. The half-giant had been forced to stop ten yards shy of the fortress wall. Hamanu had all but eliminated the gladiators fighting him, and was now unknowingly swinging his tail across Gaanon's route as he faced the last of the brave Tyrians. One of the survivors was K'kriq, who stood with his carapace against the wall, using all four hands to keep one of the sorcerer-king's claws away from his face.

All at once, the thri-kreen reversed tactics and clawed at his foe's arm, pulling it toward him. As Hamanu's massive hand closed around K'kriq's throat, the mantis-warrior stabbed at the sorcerer-king's wrist with his poisonous mandibles.

Hamanu roared in laughter. Holding his victim with one hand, he reached down and tore the thri-kreen's shell away. As his pulpy white thorax was exposed, K'kriq screeched in pain. The sorcerer-king studied the strange flesh for a moment, then began ripping it to shreds.

At the far end of the avenue, Jaseela led a company of Urikite slaves from a side gate, and more slaves were emerging from other exits. Some carried swords, spears, bone clubs, or other weapons they had scavenged from the templar quarter, but most were armed with only hammers and rock picks.

As the slaves streamed into the avenue, they ran for the nearest gate into the noble quarter. The aristocratic armies met them with a hail of arrows and bolts. Rikus cried out as

Jaseela clutched at a shaft in her throat and fell. Behind her, the rest of the slaves in the first wave also crumpled to the ground, and soon the cries of the wounded drowned out even the toll of clashing weapons.

It did not matter, for the slaves continued to charge from the templar quarter. They soon reached the other side of the street, attacking the noble armies. Unfortunately, the Urikite quarry slaves were poor substitutes for Tyrian gladiators, and they died as quickly as they reached the melee. Nevertheless, they continued to crowd the avenue, and it soon became apparent that the pressure of sheer numbers would force a breach in the nobles' defenses.

Closer to Rikus, Hamanu discarded K'kriq's shredded body and looked toward the outpouring of slaves. His tail began to swing back and forth more eagerly, smashing into the wall just a few feet away from Gaanon. The half-giant cringed and pressed himself against the yellow mudbricks, trying to remain clear of the dangerous obstacle. The sorcerer-king stepped toward the slave army, simultaneously lifting his mouth toward the sun and belching forth a puff of yellow smoke.

Gaanon slipped away from the wall. But as the half-giant took his first step, the man-lion stopped and glanced over his shoulder. A wicked grin flashed across the sorcerer-king's lips, and Rikus realized that Hamanu had been toying with Gaanon all along.

The mul started to cry a warning, but the cocoon was too tight. Nothing but a strangled gasp left his lips.

Hamanu's tail smashed Gaanon in the ribs, though not hard enough to cause serious injury. Cringing, the half-giant looked toward the sorcerer-king, futilely raising his hammer to defend himself.

Instead of attacking physically, Hamanu stared at his prey. A look of terrible pain and fear came over Gaanon, who dropped his weapon and grabbed his head, howling in agony. Blood suddenly began to gush from the half-giant's nose and ears. He fell to the ground and began rolling about, leaving long red smears on the streets.

Rikus screamed in rage. Ignoring the searing pain it sent shooting through his entire body, the mul tried again to free himself.

Don't weaken yourself, the wraith said. *Wait.*

Wait for what? Rikus demanded, fixing his eyes on Hamanu's back. His lungs were starving for air, and he could feel himself beginning to grow dizzy. *He's only going to kill me.*

Perhaps not, Tamar answered. *I have summoned help, but even wraiths cannot move so far in an instant.*

It's too late, the mul said bitterly. *What makes you think I want to live now?*

A ball of flame rolled from the tangled melee between Neeva's company and the Imperial Guard. It passed through the nearest side gate. Then, just inside the noble quarter, it erupted in a great spray of crimson fire. Dozens of Urikites voiced their dying screams, and the gateway collapsed into a heap of rubble.

In the next instant, Caelum and Neeva rushed out of the melee and through the smoldering debris, followed by the rest of their small company. Half the gladiators disappeared into the noble quarter, leaving only a dozen warriors behind to act as a rear-guard. A large band of the Imperial Guard quickly pursued, and soon the brutal clamor of battle raged from the shattered gateway.

What are they doing? demanded Tamar.

Going for the book, Rikus answered, allowing a smug note to creep into his tone.

They mustn't! Tamar snarled.

As Hamanu passed the gate Caelum had smashed, he paused long enough to spray a maroon fog over the entryway. As the mist settled over the area, warriors on both sides screamed. The battle abruptly ended as a handful of warriors stumbled back into the street, their steaming flesh dripping from their bones.

The sorcerer-king sent a company of half-giants after Neeva and the others, then took the rest of the Imperial Guard and continued toward the far end of the avenue. There, the slave army had captured two side gates and were streaming into the noble quarter at a steady rate. The rest of the entrances held firm, and the bodies were piled so high in front of the slaves that it was proving difficult for them to continue their attacks.

Rikus was just beginning to think the slave revolt might succeed when Urikite regulars began to appear at the other end of the boulevard. For a moment, the mul wondered where they had come from, then he remembered the troops that Hamanu had sent to seal the outside of the slave gate. As these fresh soldiers entered the fray, they cleared the street, driving those they did not kill toward Hamanu.

Thoughts of his helpless prisoner driven from his mind by the battle, Hamanu formed the remains of his Imperial Guard into a triple rank and began to press the slaves from his end of the street. As he marched down the boulevard, the sorcerer-king gestured at the two gateways that had been breached. A shimmering wall of force appeared in each, hardly visible save for occasional glints of yellow light flashing off the transparent barriers.

Rikus watched the destruction in disheartened silence, knowing that the slave revolt had been a failure, that the sorcerer-king regarded him as so slight a threat that he had been left unguarded. Hamanu's response had covered every possibility, and the mul had done little except play into the sorcerer-king's traps. He had no doubt that a few of his warriors would survive and escape, but only enough to return to Tyr and tell of the great disaster that had befallen them in Urik.

The blame for his legion's defeat, the mul knew, did not lie with the soldiers themselves. Quarry slave, gladiator, dwarf, or even templar, they had all fought as bravely as any warrior could. They were still dying bravely—if foolishly—as Hamanu set about constructing simple but efficient death traps.

Each time Maetan had anticipated his schemes or pressed him into a corner during the long trek from Tyr, the mul had believed the misfortune to be the work of a spy, someone who had betrayed the legion to the mind-bender. Now it was clear to Rikus that he was the one who had betrayed the warriors. Styan had died fighting, as had all the templars. Caelum was struggling against terrible odds to recover the *Book of the Kemalok Kings* and to protect Neeva. There was only one person left for Rikus to blame, and that was himself.

In vain, the mul tried to close the screams of the dying from his mind, but he could not do even that. The web kept his fingers closed firmly around the Scourge of Rkard, and as each voice cried out for the last time, it rang in his ears with the clarion knell of a wealthy lord's death bell.

I wish I could take it all back.

There is no such magic, Tamar said. *But you can still recover the book.*

In the street below, Rikus saw several gray forms rise from the cobblestones. One of them glided to Gaanon's still form, then slipped over the body. The half-giant's corpse slowly rose, then lumbered to the fortress wall and climbed up the surface with a grace that it could never have managed in life.

Just kill me and be done with it, Rikus said. *I'll never give you the book.*

You will keep your promise, Tamar responded confidently. *It is the one thing left to you.*

Gaanon's corpse reached the top of the fortress wall, then

removed the cocoon cord from its merlon and slowly lowered Rikus to the ground. Once the mul lay face-first on the ground, the wraith abandoned the half-giant's body atop the wall and slipped back down to the street on its own.

Another wraith limped up in a body so mangled that Rikus could not even recognize the gladiator to whom it had belonged. This one rolled Rikus onto his back, then used an obsidian dagger to laboriously cut the cocoon away from the Scourge of Rkard. When the sword was free, the wraith used the magical sword to slice away the rest of the web.

After he was free, Rikus remained on the ground, refusing to rise. The gladiator's corpse grabbed him by the shoulder and hoisted him to his feet, then thrust the Scourge of Rkard at him. Rikus made no move to accept the sword.

You swore on Neeva's life, Tamar reminded him. *It is your choice whether we leave Urik with the dwarves' book or with her corpse.*

Rikus took the sword and screamed.

EIGHTEEN

The Book of Kings

"Caelum, give me the book," Rikus demanded, keeping a tight grip on the Scourge of Rkard.

The dwarf clutched the leatherbound volume closer to his chest. "I'll carry it back to Kled myself."

They stood on opposite sides of the Lubar townhouse's central courtyard. It was a large enclosure full of earthenware pots brimming with dazzling, crescent-shaped blossoms. From a net on the ceiling dangled long strands of sweet-smelling moss, and several small trees sprouted from circles of ground left uncovered by the flagstone floor.

Rikus had sometimes been kept here as a young gladiator, so it had been an easy matter for him to make his way through the battle-torn streets of the noble quarter and find the townhouse. He had hoped to beat Caelum and Neeva to the mansion and recover the *Book of the Kemalok Kings* before they did, but he had not been so fortunate. By the time the mul had arrived, they had already fought their way inside, leaving the front door smoking and hanging off its hinges, the bodies of household guards and Tyrian warriors scattered over the foyer beyond.

Rikus lifted his sword and started across the compound, his black eyes fixed on Caelum.

Behind the dwarf, Neeva stepped from a doorway leading deeper into the house. A blood-soaked bandage covered the wound on her stomach, and she looked as though she were ready to collapse at any moment. She was using a slave rope to lead a skinny old man with bound hands. The fellow had a wispy white beard, sad gray eyes, and wore a fine robe of green hemp. On his forehead was tattooed the Serpent of Lubar, identifying him as a special slave to be killed upon sight if found outside the family compound. If the old man was interested in the strangers in the courtyard, his eyes showed no sign of it.

When Neeva saw Rikus, her eyes lit with surprise and joy. "Rikus! How did you escape?"

The mul ignored her and continued to advance on Caelum. "I'll have that book, dwarf," he said. "I need it to protect Neeva."

"Protect her from what?" Caelum demanded. He narrowed his eyes suspiciously and fixed them on the gem in Rikus's chest. "From the wickedness lodged in your breast?"

The dwarf shoved the book into Neeva's hands, then thrust a hand skyward in preparation for casting a spell. "I have another way to protect her," he snarled. "A more permanent way."

Stop him! Tamar commanded. *If he destroys me, Neeva's life is forfeit—Catrion and the others will see to it.*

Rikus was already rushing across the courtyard. He crashed through a pair of flower jars, then reached Caelum just as the cleric's hand turned crimson with the sun's energy. The mul pressed the tip of his sword against Caelum's throat, and the dwarf pointed his glowing hand at the gladiator's chest.

"Cast your spell," Rikus snarled. "Before I die, I'll kill you."

Caelum did not activate his spell, but neither did he withdraw his hand.

"What's this all about, Rikus?" Neeva demanded. She stepped from behind the dwarf, being careful to keep her body between the mul and the book. "You promised to return the book to Kemalok!"

"I can't keep that promise," the mul explained. As he admitted his failure, a deep sense of shame came over him—though he remained determined to do what he must to save Neeva. "Give me the book."

"No." Neeva dropped the slave rope and slipped the tome under her arm, drawing her sword with her free hand. "And if you kill Caelum, you'll have to kill me, too."

"Neeva, take the *Book of Kemalok Kings* and leave," said Caelum, his red eyes still fixed on Rikus's face.

"So you two can kill each other in private?" Neeva scoffed. "No."

We are anxious to have the book, Tamar informed Rikus. *Neeva will not be harmed—unless the dwarf tries to stop us.*

No sooner had the wraith spoken than the old slave backed toward the doorway, crying, "Phantoms!"

A dozen gray silhouettes, their eyes glowing with the hues of various gems, rose from the cracks of the floor and encircled Neeva. She cried out in alarm and swung her weapon at the nearest one. The black blade passed through the shadowy form without harming it.

Caelum started to move his hand toward the wraiths, but Rikus pressed the tip of his sword against the dwarf's throat. "Don't," he warned. "You'll get her killed."

The dwarf stopped moving, his red eyes flaring in anger. "If she comes to harm—"

"She won't," Rikus interrupted. "Unless you cause it."

Neeva swung her sword through the wraiths twice more,

then one with glowing yellow eyes held out its hands.

"Give the book to the wraith," Rikus said.

Neeva hesitated. "I won't!" She clutched the *Book of the Kemalok Kings* under her arm.

The wraiths tightened their circle, and the one with yellow eyes slipped forward until its gray hands were almost touching Neeva.

"Give them the book!" Rikus yelled, afraid that his fighting partner would insist on dying before she gave up. "You can't stop them from taking it—and if you try, you'll only get killed." He looked to Caelum. "Tell her!"

The dwarf scowled at Rikus, then nodded. "Let them have it," he said. "Rikus's betrayal leaves us no other choice."

Neeva stared at the yellow-eyed phantom, then reluctantly held out the *Book of the Kemalok Kings*. As she lowered it into the wraith's waiting hands, the black tome slowly turned gray and insubstantial. Soon, the book was no more than a shadow.

The wraiths sank back into the flagstones, save for a single, blue-eyed phantom that slipped into the narrow space separating Rikus and Caelum. The mul lowered his sword and backed away. *What now?* he asked. *You have the book.*

The wraith did not respond. Instead, it slipped its nebulous hand into the festering wound on the mul's chest. A fiery pain filled the gladiator's breast. Rikus cried out in agony, then collapsed to his knees as Tamar's ruby was pulled from his body. The phantom closed its fingers over the gemstone, then sank between the flagstones and disappeared. Rikus remained on the floor, gasping for breath.

"Get up, traitor!" Caelum spat, his hand still glowing with the fury of the sun. "Let us finish what we started!"

Rikus lifted his head and looked into the dwarf's red eyes. Letting the Scourge of Rkard drop from his hands, he said, "You finish it. I have no reason to fight."

"I have no compunction against killing one who surrenders to me!" Caelum warned. "At the least, my village deserves your death."

"Then be done with it!" Rikus yelled.

Caelum took a step backward and leveled his hand at Rikus. Before he could utter the word that would cast the spell, the flat of Neeva's sword blade slapped his forearm and knocked it down.

"I won't let you kill him, Caelum," she said, keeping her weapon ready.

"He betrayed his word. My father—"

"I don't care," she said, sheathing her sword. "I loved Rikus once, and I won't—"

"Let him," Rikus said. He did not know which hurt him more: that Neeva felt he needed protection, or that she no longer loved him. "I've lost everything—my legion, my honor, even you," he said. "I don't want to live."

Neeva whirled around and grabbed the mul by the chin. "Did you survive twenty years as a gladiator to throw your life away here?" she demanded, pulling him to his feet. "Maybe it would have been better for you to die in the arena —but don't you dare do it here, not now."

She reached down and picked up the Scourge of Rkard. "You may not be much of a general, but you're still the finest gladiator I've ever seen," she said, holding the sword's hilt toward him. "Caelum and I could use your help getting Er'Stali back to Kled. Maybe we can still salvage something from this disaster."

Rikus stared at the sword, feeling almost as ashamed of his despair as he did of betraying the dwarves and losing his legion. Finally he sighed and took the sword from Neeva's hand. "Who's Er'Stali?"

"Er'Stali was translating the *Book of the Kemalok Kings* for Maetan," Caelum explained, raising his glowing hand and allowing the fiery color to drain from it. "His knowledge may help repay the loss you have caused."

Rikus frowned. "Translate?" he asked, thinking of the decades Caelum's father had spent trying to decipher the language of the ancient kings. "How can he do that?"

"Sorcery," Neeva answered, looking toward the door into which the old man had disappeared. There was no longer any sign of the sorcerer. She cursed, then started toward the townhouse. "He must have run off. I'll go after him—"

Rikus caught her by the shoulder. "Don't you think it's his decision whether or not to come with us?"

"Er'Stali has read the book. That makes him a part of dwarven history," Caelum said, starting toward the door. "Kled will treat him like an *uhrnomus*. He'll want for nothing."

"Except his freedom," Neeva sighed. "It's his choice. Taking him against his will would make us no different than any other slave-taker."

Caelum cursed in the guttural tongue of his people, then looked at the ground and shook his head angrily. "I cannot deny you, Neeva," he said. "But can I at least find him and ask what he wishes?"

"There's no need for that," said the old man. He stepped from the doorway, holding his hands out to be unbound. "I choose freedom—with you."

Rikus cut the old sorcerer free, then Er'Stali led the small party into the labyrinthine streets of the noble quarter. As they made their way toward the city walls, the mul saw that Hamanu's well-planned counterattacks had not entirely crushed the slave revolt.

The few hundred quarry slaves that had crossed into the noble quarter were taking angry vengeance on their masters. A thick pall of smoke filled the streets, at times reducing visibility to a dozen steps. Even domestic slaves roamed the streets in angry gangs, killing nobles and destroying all they could. Several times the small party had to hide in a looted mansion while a company of the Imperial Guard rushed past, pursuing a mob of rampaging slaves.

Once, the group barely escaped death when they rounded a corner and ran headlong into a noble company. Rikus killed the officer with a quick thrust, then Er'Stali surprised the combatants of both sides by blocking the alley with a magical wall of ice that allowed the companions to make a hasty retreat.

At last, the four reached the outer wall. Here, Rikus was relieved to see that some of Urik's slaves were fleeing the city. Hundreds were gathered in cheering throngs, waiting their turn to climb the black slave ropes that had been strung over the wall as makeshift ladders. A company of doomed noble retainers battled at the edges of the crowd, having made the mistake of trying to stop the escape. In one spot, several of Hamanu's half-giants had even fallen, though not without taking dozens of slaves with them.

"At least some slaves will see freedom," Neeva observed.

"Yes, but at a terrible price," Rikus said. He started toward one of the throngs waiting to climb out of the city.

"We have no time to wait in line," Er'Stali said, leading them away from the crowd. "Come with me."

The sorcerer guided them to a space along the wall where there were no ropes, then took a piece of twine from his pocket. He pointed one palm downward. The air beneath his hand began to shimmer, then a barely perceptible surge of energy rose from the ground and into his body.

Once the sorcerer had collected the energy for his spell, he muttered a quiet incantation. The twine in his hand rose skyward, growing thicker the higher it went. By the time it reached the top of the wall, it was the size of a sturdy rope. Er'Stali grabbed the line and scrambled to the top of the wall as spryly as a man a quarter his age.

Neeva sent Caelum up next, then followed herself. Unlike the old man and the dwarf, she moved slowly and with great effort—a sure sign that her wound was troubling her. By the time she had reached the top, a crowd was gathering at the bottom of Er'Stali's rope, anxious to put this new escape route to good use.

When Rikus's turn came, he moved even more slowly, for his left arm still hurt too much to use. He had to pull himself up a short distance with his good arm, then wrap his legs around the rope and hold himself in place while he reached higher. Nevertheless, his progress was steady and he soon found himself atop the wall.

Once the mul had joined the others, Er'Stali took another strand of twine from his pocket and started toward the other side of the wall. Rikus did not follow. Much of Urik was visible from this vantage point, and the mul could see greasy columns of smoke rising from all parts of the city. With the Scourge of Rkard's aid, he could even hear the shouts of rioting slaves as they destroyed what they had so reluctantly created and the dying screams of the indolent masters for whom it had been built.

That much he had expected, but what sickened the mul was the sight in the main boulevard. Near the slave gate, the bodies were heaped in piles taller than a half-giant. As Rikus's gaze followed the street toward the king's gate, the corpse piles gradually grew smaller. A few yards shy of Hamanu's slave pens, Rikus could even see the bloodstained cobblestones through the tangle of dead flesh. Already the kes'trekels had descended on the feast and were ripping at the bodies with their hooked beaks and three-fingered hands.

When Rikus looked toward the templar quarter, he saw the reason the Urikites were not putting more effort into stopping the outflow of slaves from the noble quarter. Gathered along the top of the city wall, a half-mile or more from where the mul stood, were several thousand quarry slaves. From what Rikus could see at that great distance, they were attempting to flee the city by sliding down ropes, climbing the rough mudbrick surface, or even jumping.

Pressing them from both sides were large companies of Urikite regulars. Hamanu himself wandered behind the wall, plucking slaves off and passing them down to guardsmen waiting below.

Rikus looked back to the carnage on the slave boulevard. "I did this," he said. "I promised them they would die free, and all they did was die."

"Don't be too hard on yourself," Er'Stali said, stepping to the mul's side and trying to guide him to the far side of the wall. Neeva and Caelum had already descended without Rikus noticing. "Perhaps it's not so unreasonable to have believed you could destroy Hamanu. After all, I am told that you destroyed Kalak."

"No," Rikus said. "I was one of a handful who destroyed Kalak. All I did was throw the first spear. Without Agis, Sadira, and Neeva, I would have failed at that, too."

"One cannot accomplish great things without risking great failures," the old man said.

"This wasn't even a great failure," Rikus answered. He pointed toward the sorcerer-king, who was still plucking slaves off the wall on the other side of the slave gate. "Hamanu must know that I've escaped, but he's more concerned about losing quarry slaves than he is about recapturing me."

"We can thank the moons for small favors, can we not?" Er'Stali said. Again, he tried to guide Rikus toward the far side of the wall.

As the mul started to turn away, a great uproar of panicked cries and pained shouts erupted from the crowds inside the city wall. Rikus ran over to the magical rope Er'Stali had raised earlier. There he saw that more than a dozen companies of Imperial Guards were pouring out of the smoke-filled streets of the noble quarter. While the mul looked helplessly on, the half-giants rushed toward the escape ropes, using their lances like clubs to knock slaves out of their paths.

Below Rikus, a gaunt, gray-haired man wearing the hemp robe of a domestic slave clutched the rope. He began to climb, casting frantic glances over his shoulder as the half-giants drew closer. The mul grabbed the line from the top and tried to pull the old man up, but he was of little help. With his left arm still weakened by the wound in his chest, he could not grip the rope with both hands.

The first guardsman reached the wall when the man was about half-way up. "Come down, boy," the guard ordered, brandishing his lance.

The old man stopped climbing and looked up at Rikus, his rid-rimmed eyes silently pleading for help. The mul tried again to pull the rope, but he barely succeeded in raising it a foot.

The half-giant touched the tip of his lance to the slave's back. "Come down or die," the guard growled.

The old man stared at the brute for a moment, then repeated a saying that Rikus had often heard in his days in the Lubar pits: "My death will free me."

With that, the slave looked toward the sky and started climbing, though he knew he would never reach the top of the wall.

*   *   *   *   *

"Thus the book begins:

"*Born of liquid fire and seasoned in bleak darkness, we dwarves are the sturdy people, the people of the rock. It is into our bones that the mountains sink their roots, it is from our hearts that the clear waters pour, it is out of our mouths that the cool winds blow. We were made to buttress the world, to support—*"

Er'Stali pinched his eyes closed, trying to remember what word came next.

Along with Caelum, Neeva, and all the dwarves of Kled, Rikus held his breath, not daring to exhale for fear of disturbing the sorcerer's concentration.

For the first time in a thousand years, dwarves had gathered in the Tower of Buryn to hear the history of their race. One hundred magical torches, each kindled by Er'Stali and set into its sconce by Lyanius himself, lit the great hall's ancient murals in all their vibrant glory. On every pillar hung a gleaming axe or sword, especially polished and shined to remind the audience of the incredible wealth of its heritage. Even the dwarves themselves were adorned for the occasion, wearing beautiful cassocks of linen, dyed red in honor of the crimson sun. It was a gathering of which Rikus felt sure the old kings would approve.

At last Er'Stali opened his eyes and shook his head. "I am sorry, I cannot remember the story from there. Perhaps I will do better with the story of how King Rkard drove Borys of Ebe from the gates of Kemalok."

An approving murmur rustled through the hall. Lyanius lifted his hand for quiet, and the room once again fell as silent as it had been for the last thousand years.

"*It was in the fifty-second year of Rkard's reign that Borys returned. Of our knights, only the king and Sa'ram and Jo'orsh remained, with five hundred dwarves to each. Borys of Ebe brought with him a host of ten thousand, with mighty siege engines and his own foul magic.*

"*Kemalok was the last dwarven city, and with it would die the last of the dwarves. That, Rkard swore, would not happen. The great king ordered Sa'ram and Jo'orsh to flee through the ancient tunnels, taking half the citizens of Kemalok with them. The others stayed behind to conceal the passages when the city fell, to die so that Borys would not guess that others had escaped to carry on our stalwart race.*

"Not long after the knights left, Borys used his magic to drive twelve great holes into the city walls. It was at the last of these breaches that Rkard and Borys clashed in fierce combat. Before many strokes passed, Rkard felt the bite of his foe's terrible sword, but our king's sparkling axe also cleaved a mighty gash in Borys's armor. The two commanders fell, each on their own side of the wall. Borys's host carried their wicked leader back to his tent and summoned their healers. We loyal followers of Rkard returned with our king, the enemy's blade still buried in his chest, to the Tower of Buryn. Then we sealed the gates and prepared for the final battle.

"Our great king soon died of his wounds, and with sad hearts we waited for Borys to renew his assault. On the tenth day of the siege, the enemy broke camp and we knew that Rkard had not struck his last blow in vain. Borys, too, had finally died of his wounds—"

"That is not what happened," boomed a deep voice.

All eyes looked up and saw a short figure standing in the gallery that overlooked the great hall. He wore a battered suit of black plate mail, trimmed at every joint in silver and gold. A jewel-studded crown of gleaming white metal capped his helm, and two yellow eyes burned from the depths behind his visor.

"Rkard!" gasped Rikus.

"The last king speaks!" cried a dwarf.

The hall was suddenly filled with astonished voices, all crying out in excitement.

Rkard's thunderous voice again quieted the dwarves. "That is what the keeper of the book believed, but that is not what occurred."

The room remained expectantly silent, but the ancient king simply stared down on the gathering with his yellow eyes and said no more. Finally Er'Stali asked, "Will you tell us the truth, great Rkard?"

The long-dead king fixed his eyes on the sorcerer. "I do

not know why the host left that day—perhaps Borys's wound was too severe, perhaps Rajaat had summoned the Thirteenth Champion's army, or perhaps it was another reason entirely—but Borys did not die on that field. I know this because he returned many years later, to accomplish alone and in less than an hour what his hosts had failed to do in ten days. He drained the life from all the city's dwarves, leaving only ghosts to remember that Kemalok had been visited by the Dragon."

"The Dragon!" Rikus hissed. All around him, others also gasped or uttered astonished cries.

"It is good that you have returned to your home, my people," Rkard said, his voice booming over the commotion in the great hall. "But be watchful of Borys—he would not wish to see Kemalok restored to its former glory."

Rkard stepped back, disappearing into the murky depths at the rear of the gallery. The dwarves, stunned by the ancient king's warning, remained in their seats.

Rikus rose immediately, disturbed by Rkard's dark words. Hamanu's remark about what would happen when Tithian failed to deliver the city's slave levy to the Dragon was fresh in the mul's mind, and now that he'd heard how the Dragon had destroyed the city of Kemalok, he worried that Tyr itself might be in grave danger.

Removing the Belt of Rank and Scourge of Rkard from his waist, the mul stepped past Er'Stali to Lyanius. "I was going to return these later, but it's time for me to go back to Tyr," he said, offering the artifacts to the old dwarf. "I'm sorry I didn't prove worthy of them."

Lyanius regarded Rikus for several moments, then his gaze dropped to the mul's breast. The festering wound there had finally healed, leaving an ugly scar over Rikus's heart. "Caelum told me what you did," he said.

The mul forced himself to keep his eyes fixed on Lyanius's face. "I can't undo those shameful deeds," he said. "I can only return these."

The old dwarf nodded, taking the belt and scabbard from Rikus's arms. "The book's loss is a great one, but I cannot blame you for the decision you made," Lyanius said, detaching the Scourge of Rkard from the Belt of Rank. "At least you brought us Er'Stali, and what he remembers of the book is more than I learned in all the years I studied it."

After looking at the two items in his hands, Lyanius laid the Belt of Rank over his arm. "We will take the belt back," he said. "Perhaps, in time, there will come a dwarf who can wear it better than you did."

"I hope so," Rikus replied.

"This, I want you to keep," Lyanius said, returning the Scourge of Rkard to Rikus. "From what Caelum says, in all of Athas, there is no warrior more worthy of it."

The mul looked toward Caelum.

"Many harsh words have passed between us," the dwarf said. "But I can't argue with what you did to protect Neeva."

"Given how badly I failed you," Rikus said, "the Scourge of Rkard is a magnificent gift." The mul was so overcome by the dwarf's generosity that his words were barely more than a whisper.

"It is a gift of which you are quite worthy," said Lyanius. "Never doubt that. No one should fault you for trying what few others would even dare to dream."

"My thanks." Rikus closed his eyes and inclined his head to the dwarf, wondering if he would have been as charitable in Lyanius's place.

After a respectful pause, the mul turned to Neeva. "Will you come with me? I promise to be more giving, to at least try to offer you the things you need from me."

Neeva's emerald eyes filled with tears, and she gave the mul a weak smile. "I know you'd try, but I've already made a promise of my own," she said, moving to Caelum's side.

"Kled, and one day Kemalok, will be my home."

Rikus nodded. "I wish you happiness." He sighed deeply. "Losing you is like the guilt I feel for the destruction of the legion—it's the price of my failure."

The mul turned to go, but Neeva caught his arm. "Don't feel too badly. You may be less one lover and finally free of the notion you're a brilliant military mind, but that's only because you've accepted the responsibilities that go with your destiny."

The mul frowned. "What do you mean?"

"You told me that it was our destiny to protect Tyr from external dangers," she said. "I didn't choose that fate, but you did. Because of that decision, you mustn't think you 'lost' me or the legion—no one took us from you. You sacrificed us for the sake of Tyr."

"She speaks the truth," Caelum said sincerely. "You led thousands who died for Tyr, but they followed you willingly, knowing they might be killed. Few men would have had the courage to let them die." The dwarf bowed to Rikus. "With you as its guardian, the dream of freedom will live in the city of Tyr forever."

*Follow the road to epic struggles
in the DARK SUN™ World!*

Road to Urik

Road to Urik

A great army is sent from Tyr, across the burning
wastelands of Athas, to conquer the nearby city-
state of Urik, setting the course of future history.
This new DARK SUN adventure module is
presented in two spiral-bound flip books and
includes the exclusive short story, **Loyalties** by
M. C. Sumner.

On sale April 1992.

FORGOTTEN REALMS

Fantasy Adventure

THE LONG-AWAITED SEQUEL TO THE MOONSHAE TRILOGY

Druidhome Trilogy

Douglas Niles

Prophet of Moonshae   Book One

Evil threatens the islands of Moonshae, where the people have forsaken their goddess, the Earthmother. Only the faith and courage of the daughter of the High King brings hope to the endangered land. Available March 1992.

The Coral Kingdom   Book Two

King Kendrick is held prisoner in the undersea city of the sahuagin. His daughter must secure help from the elves of Evermeet to save him during a confrontation in the dark depths of the Sea of Moonshae. Available October 1992.

The Druid Queen   Book Three

In this exciting conclusion, the forces of the Earthmother are finally united but face the greatest challenge for survival ever. Available Spring 1993.